I0612191

UNMAPPED

The Completionist Chronicles Book Thirteen

DAKOTA KROUT

MOUNTAINDALE
PRESS

ACKNOWLEDGMENTS

To my wife, for being the constant support that makes it possible to write.
To my kids, who want to hear me read them my stories at bedtime.
To the fans, for loving my novels and giving me a reason to make the next book faster.

Thank you all.

PROLOGUE

"Ahh! The sky's on fire!"

"Forget the sky, put me out! *Put me out!*"

"I've got you, brother!"

"How? No... why is the Jötunn covered *Inflame?*"

Thousands of people made up the raid group, yet only the first thousand were actual members of the Stormbinder's Tower from Vanaheim. The remainder were support staff of humans or Dwarves hired on Jotunheim to help them search the massive planet for the World Boss, carry provisions and weaponry, or harvest the lesser monsters they were forced to hunt on their expedition.

Whether they were from a higher world or not, Grandmaster Fari—who had descended to take direct control of the mission—knew that, if they didn't escape in the next few seconds... every last one of them was going to die.

As she opened her mouth to give the order to retreat, the cliff face they were standing on cracked apart; hundreds of tons of stone and dirt fell away into a valley filled with slowly solidifying lava. Fari choked on her words as a cloud of dust and smoke as thick as steel wool blasted into her face, singeing her nostrils and burning her throat as she tried, yet again, to sound the retreat. As she spat out a wad of phlegm, scorched skin, and soot, she couldn't help but wonder how things could have gotten this bad, so quickly.

The entire hunt had been a study in failure and flagrantly false information, to the extent that she had to wonder if they were being intentionally sabotaged. First, what had been meant to be a difficult trek along a frozen tundra had instead become a thousands of people sweating through their clothing, having donned gear which was *far* too heavy for the first changing of the seasons ever recorded on Jotunheim.

Spring had officially sprung across the entirety of the world, changing the surface of the planet from a uniform journey across hundreds of meters of snow and glaciers to rushing rivers larger than small oceans on other planets, valleys that felt as though they reached the core of the world, and *impossibly* high mountains that touched the edge of the atmosphere.

Second, and far worse, was the 'intelligence' that had been gathered on the World Boss they were there to hunt. The entity was *meant* to be a titan of stone and frost, exuding an aura colder than the depths of space. Instead, Fari found herself staring at an abyssal creature the size of a mountain range coated in raging flames—its details impossible to make out behind what could only be described as an endless volcanic eruption on the move.

She tried anyway, but even with all of her Characteristics and perception-enhancing skills, the Grandmaster was forced to make decisions based on the silhouette. There was only flame and light, alongside constant thunder as the atmosphere of the planet was set ablaze, making her unable to properly gauge even the distance to the entity due to the heat-ravaged, buckling air.

"Careful, another section is falling!" Fari was pulled back as a Dwarven voice shouted in her ear, yanked out of the way barely ahead of the ridge collapsing further. In a heartbeat, the ground was gone, leaving only hardened, igneous rock extruding into the air like a twisted, broken crown. "What in the *abyss* is going on here? I was told we were hunting a World Boss of *ice-*"

"Is it possible we just found another one?" Fari finally found her voice, only to realize it sounded desperate and pleading instead of the calm, confident tone a leader should be presenting themselves with.

"Not unless the other towers broke their oaths and used a Hidden World Boss Mythic Core while we were distracted," came the grim reply from the stout defender, his jaw muscles creaking as he ground his teeth at the unfortunately-not-unrealistic thought. "No, this is something else. Whatever changed here has set us too much off balance. We need to leave—but at least we have new information."

"We have *nothing*!" Fari snarled, her tongue lolling out of her mouth as she swiped her claws over her thick coat of fur. The Grandmaster Wolfman glanced down at the Dwarf, who met her furious stare with a resigned one of his own. "I can't get so much as a *read* on the World Boss. We've spent thousands of talismans attacking it, only to not know if they are dealing even the *barest* amount of damage. What am I supposed to tell-"

"I've already been able to extrapolate its size," the Dwarf offered in a soothing tone. "You would have been able to do the same if your head was in the game. Look... we just about fell into its footprint; I've got its approximate height, length, and weight."

Fari followed his gesture unwillingly, blinking as she realized he was talking about the valley that seemed to be a bottomless pit, an impossibly wide chasm filled with cooling lava and glassy obsidian. "You mean to tell me... that's just a *footprint?*"

"Grandmaster!" the Dwarf snapped bluntly, like the edge of a tool long since worn down from overuse. "We've got its attention, and while we had intended for that *previously*... from a strategic standpoint, the titan focusing on us is only a bad thing now that we know what we're facing. We need your orders."

Though still reeling from the rapid shifts in their situation, Fari's thoughts cleared swiftly at the idea of running *now*, after a full year of searching Jotunheim and finally, *finally* tracking down their quarry. At the speed this thing moved—incredibly fast with each step, yet deceptively slow due to its sheer size—by the time they managed to retrace their path, it could have migrated to practically anywhere on the planet. "No! We won't leave. Not... not without at least making a full-effort attempt. I'm ordering all squads to deploy offensive talismans."

Hundreds of members of the Stormbinder's Tower pulled out thick packets of paper, the lowest-ranking among them being at the peak of the Expert rank. Hundreds of Masters lined up their talismans, and as the titan seemingly slowly spun in place to face them—spawning a hurricane and dozens of tornados—the Grandmaster barked out an order. "*Unseal!*"

At her word, the strips of paper, each inscribed with thousands of shimmering words and diagrams, exploded into confetti as they unleashed the power that had been contained within them. Many erupted into bursts of flame of all colorations; others *crackled* with unleashed electrical energy, hypnotic glimpses of void energy, or shards of deepstone condensed into crystalline structures.

With such a large target, not a single one of the attacks missed. For the span of a sigh, the hunks of armor—glistening with amalgamations of icy stone plating the size of skyscrapers —were visible to those among the raid group with the highest Perception. Massive runewords appeared in the air, blasting the outer shell of the World Boss and doing their best to sear deeply enough to breach its burning hide.

The forces unleashed would have reduced a city to rubble... but the carapace of this entity merely splintered, sending shards the size of cathedrals tumbling down its mountainous shin. Finally witnessing their attacks landing true, the raid group's morale shot upward, their cheers ringing out like bells ringing at a festival.

Sadly, their delight only lasted until the broken fragments hit the ground around them.

The ice the damaged section was composed of would have

been a prime crafting material: harder than diamonds, practically immune to melting while still being fully composed of ice. Even Fari allowed herself a heartbeat of eyeing it covetously.., allowing her to witness the exact moment the section that had been hidden from the open air *rippled*. A nimbus of unutterable cold wafted outward, flash-freezing the nearest unfortunate Dwarves they had hired to guide them.

"Well, *there's* the cold we had been expecting." The Grandmaster *tisked* in annoyance when she saw how many among her group rushed to re-equip their freeze-effect-negating gear. Then she flinched away as the jagged surface of the ice was covered in a carpet of what appeared to be *moss*, of all things. The foliage had grown across the entire surface between breaths and was joined by hundreds of tiny yellow and orange petals as they bloomed across the frigid surface...

...then violently exploded into flames.

The air around the fragment warped into thunder as the extreme temperatures worked to consume each other. In moments, the building-sized chunk of armor had lost a third of its mass, pouring down on them as a molten slag as the temperature violently vacillated between one extreme and another.

"Abyss!" her Dwarven advisor growled in frustration as another handful of members of the raid party who had just re-equipped anti-cold gear burst into flame. "Four out of five of those attacks were meant to impact against a cold or solid surface and were consumed by the flames. We're operating at twenty percent of our potential damage output. We need to change out our kit and try another time, Fari!"

"I'm not having us lose a year of our efforts and *handing* the Defenders Tower the advantage!" She snapped back at the Dwarf, reaching into her personal talisman binder to begin joining in on the assault. "We are going to make this count and go home with a Mythic Core in—*celestials!*"

Her Dexterity allowed her to swap the talisman she was beginning to pull with a different, far more precious version: a Grandmaster seven-layered defensive talisman. She ripped it in half in the same motion, allowing a web of glowing script to write itself onto the world around the most dense cluster of her raid party, only a few score left outside of the dome as it firmly anchored to reality itself.

The titan's attack landed just then, an endless gale of cold pouring from the creature's unseen mouth as it released a continental expanse of air from the deepest part of its lungs, a gale which may have been trapped there for a thousand years. The breath met the barrier, and the dome held, even as the world around them went still.

Smoke pouring off lava turned crystalline and fell toward the now-solid ground far below. Color fled from the earth and sky as all turned dead and frozen... only to return as an all-consuming tsunami of greenery coated every surface not sheltered by Fari's protection. Even as yellow and orange petals began to bloom atop the growth, the Grandmaster held up a second talisman with shaky hands, a deep, resentful surge of unwillingness filling her as she tore it in half.

There was a flash, the briefest flicker of time, before the world turned white-hot, and hundreds of miles of land was melted into an oceanic-scale glass sculpture.

Miles above the tiny blister of stone remaining on the otherwise-smooth surface, the titan peered down through the smoke and watched as the protected area popped and revealed a scorched and jagged surface incongruous with the rest of the smooth area.

"They chose to live? To *flee*? After all that bluster?" The Jötunn let out a long, low laugh reminiscent of glaciers forming across a tectonic plate. It glanced down at its body, covered in enormous plumes of fire that clung to every surface... yet couldn't penetrate any deeper. Each plant only bloomed faster under his *Aura of the Boomerang Nebula*, growing, flowering, and reproducing hundreds of times per minute.

"While I admit I was annoyed at first, I now find these flames... amusing."

CHAPTER ONE

Joe sat in the lotus position at the exact center of the celestial observatory, chin down and fists clenched—utterly unaware of the stars, planetary bodies, and meteors slowly drifting along the three-hundred-and-sixty degree panorama surrounding him. He wasn't meditating.

There was no serenity to be found in what he was doing.

"Another failure." Grandmaster Snow spoke in a neutral tone as she witnessed the thread of mana manipulation Joe was looping through his body curve out of his control, looping back onto itself and *fizzling* inside his body until he finally, forcibly reabsorbed the power. "Don't let it get to you. Healing damage this extensive is the work of decades, and you've already come so far."

Taking a ragged breath, the Ritualist slowly opened his eyes, annoyed beyond compare at the dampness of his robes, the steam rising in a slow haze above his head, the general feel of even the *slightest* filth coating his skin. "I just want my Neutrality Aura working again. You're sure this is the pattern I have to complete if I want that up and running?"

"There are certain, hmm, *waypoints* if you will, scattered

throughout your body where that skill has been activated time after time. It has left its mark on you, and I can clearly see where the skill once flowed. Although your pathways have been erased, leaving your energy body entirely *unmapped*... you may yet find a way to fix that. Just be glad it was only at the Expert rank, or it would be unlikely you would be able to use that spell again until your Mana Channels had been fully reconstituted."

The Dwarven Grandmaster of Mana Manipulation heaved a gentle sigh of annoyance, knowing exactly what he was going to follow his first question up with.

Yet, he managed to surprise her. After almost a year of ending their sessions in the same way, he instead asked a variant of the same question he'd blurted out the moment he'd first stumbled his way back onto Jotunheim. "I've been able to read through the mana weave manual you gave me... but I think I've reached a hard plateau. It's just not working for me anymore. Grandmaster, what am I doing *wrong*?"

"It is working... just very, *very* slowly." Snow offered her hand to the bald, slightly overcooked Ritualist. "You're a vastly different person in all ways from the man you were when I gave you that manual. When the core identity of your Characteristics has shifted so far, why would you ever think what once was tailored exactly to your previous form would fit? That would be like gaining a hundred pounds of pure muscle and expecting to fit into the suit you used to wear. It'd be all wrong for your form, so why would you expect this to be any different?"

He considered her words for a long few moments, inclining his chin ever so slightly as he finally accepted something he had been in denial about for far too long. "This method won't ever work for me, correct? The harder I work, the slower it seems to go. It's not *just* about diminishing returns."

"Haaa..." The Dwarf let out a long sigh, running her fingers through her mustache in consideration. "I want to be able to tell you it *will* work. But I have seen you working on rebuilding your mana pathways then creating the spell forms associated with those main meridians. Your mana used to fully suffuse your flesh, but even *that* had structure; though you weren't perceptive enough to see it. That base-level building block which took in and passed on mana has been terribly damaged by the cascade of divine energy that washed through you. To answer your question, I am fully uncertain if the incredibly advanced weave we have been working to implement can act as a surrogate for the foundation that has been destroyed."

"Thirty percent restored." Joe let loose a long sigh. Though it was clear he wasn't happy about what Snow was saying, there was a minute relaxation in the tension he held in his shoulders now that the truth had been spoken. "Backup plan it is. I'm just glad I didn't wait until now to get started on the design-"

"I don't think you should give up entirely. Look, you've almost got your aura back." Though she tried to remain positive, Snow's commendation carried the weight of loss instead of triumph as she spun her hand along Joe's torso. "A bit more work, and you'll be able to weave an Expert-rank spell out of sheer mana manipulation, all without the help of the system. That is *no* small feat. Although the difficulty can be compared to swimming up a waterfall-"

"Yeah... I understand it's *technically* possible." Joe grimaced as he cut her off then stared down at his digits, forcing his palms open and allowing blood to flow through his previously clenched fingers once more. "Still, you'd think it would be easier to manipulate my mana in my arms and hands than it was in my shins and feet, you know? I get it-"

"It's because you didn't make a mana *path* through your arms; you made the equivalent of a super highway." Snow's lips twitched, and she sniffed with professional disdain as she eyed the thick rope of power that surged from the palms of Joe's hands down to his core. "I legitimately have no idea what gave you that idea. You'll be able to dump mana into your rituals, but once your core is empty? What then?"

"That's why I created the telescoping iris sections along the path. I should be able to regulate the exact flow of power I need. Or, I can force as much mana as needed for activation. That was my greatest weakness when fighting against Artifact-ranked aspects... I simply couldn't overpower them with the throughput I had. I had to make sure that'd never be an issue again."

Joe's breath hitched as he got to his feet with careful motions, pain *zinging* through his chest. He offered a small, respectful dip of his head to his long-term instructor. "Thank you for all you have done, but I think both of us know asking for more tutelage is simply wasting both of our time. I'm going to get out there and figure something else out. Perhaps find a treasure that can accelerate this process or earn a reward grand enough to seek divine intervention once more."

"You'd... trust that?" Snow bristled as she took issue with his words. "After your own deity lost control of his emotions in some ill-thought-out attempt at revenge against some distant enemy? It would have literally been better for you if he had accidentally killed you with a flash of potency rather than slowly roasting you from the inside out and destroying everything in his path."

Joe offered a thin smile, eyes hooded as he looked at the stars in the distance. "I'll be *far* more careful going forward; you can trust me on that."

"Humph." Snow started walking toward the door, not bothering to argue with him any longer. Just before she exited the building, which was the signal for those waiting outside to come back in and study the heavens around them, she turned back and offered a small parting gift to Joe. "Thirty-*one* percent restored, Joe. Your last push didn't fizzle out entirely. If you look closely, you'll see that you managed to reach another one percent threshold. Well. Our business is concluded, and I consider all of my *personal* debt to you repaid."

"As do I." Joe blinked as a golden light connecting them suddenly appeared in his vision, rapidly turning dull and fizzing away like fireflies spreading out into the night. As the last bit of the karmic bond that had connected them vanished, dozens of

Dwarven Ritualists piled into the building, rushing to their favorite spots to get the best view of the stars they were studying.

Feeling deeply contemplative, the Ritualist stepped out onto the carpet of lush green grass that had sprung up across what used to be a barren, frozen tundra. "I know she meant well there, that there was still hope in this method. But, nearly three months just to get an additional one percent with a final push? That, alongside diminishing returns, definitely seals my decision for me."

Picking up the pace, Joe was soon running at full speed, only to *jump* onto a building then continue the motion and recapture his momentum by throwing himself to the top of the wall surrounding Novusheim. The guards on patrol barely spared him a glance, long used to the bouncy Ritualist and his disregard for protocol. Destination now in sight, he ran along the walls, jumping only when absolutely necessary—a large departure from what his brain still told him was feasible with Omnivault. Yet, trying to empower that skill would almost certainly cause him to fall to the ground caught in an agonizing spasm, offering a free meal to the random monsters who were even now meandering through the killing field between walls.

Leaping over the final crenelation in a clean arc, Joe allowed himself to tumble twice before shoving off the wall halfway to the ground and launching himself out and away. He didn't even need to tuck and roll, simply absorbing the landing with his immense Characteristics and sprinting to the east in a straight line. The Sect territory, which had been visible from his previous vantage point, was now hidden. Still, the Ritualist had crossed this distance twice a day for nearly a full year, and the path he had worn into the grass made the route home extremely obvious.

Forty-five miles due east of Novusheim, the Wanderer's Sect had created its second ever Hamlet, which had immediately shifted into the special type of settlements only Sects had access to: Sect Territory. Unlike the clearly delineated tiers standard settlements had, from Town to City and such, 'Territory' was exactly what it sounded like: a cross between settlement and claimed land. Lastly, as there were no kingdoms to partition off sections of the planet, Jotunheim seemed to have far more lax rules for expansion:

If you can protect the land, it's yours.

Joe had nearly half an hour of running ahead of him, and as he sprinted down the path fast enough to leave a billowing cloud of dust behind him, his mind wandered back to the conversation he'd had after returning to this planet.

Aten had caught up with him, congratulating him profusely on his success on Midgard, only to realize Joe was in pretty bad shape. Thankfully, the Sect leader had allowed Joe to keep the topics light, and they had delved deeply into what would happen next.

"I don't want to say that what happened to you is a good thing…" Aten had lifted his hands in apology as Joe raised an eyebrow, absolutely uncertain where the conversation was going. "But, at the same time, I like the idea of not having ritual towers here to protect the city. No, I mean it! I think people need to get involved in building up our defenses and city with their own hands."

"Seriously? You're going to tell me you wouldn't rather have a defensive wall, towers, and shelter in a day… instead of taking months to build something *half* as good?" Joe had barked out a humorless laugh and flicked his hand, trying to brush off the words that had landed as an insult, no matter what the Sect Leader may have intended. "Look, this isn't really going to impact my ability to make rituals. Luckily, that's all stored in my head and isn't an actively casted spell or effect. I can make it happen; just might take a little bit longer."

"No, I don't *want* that." Aten's voice had been firm, though Joe detected a note of relief hidden behind the steely tone— likely because his First Elder hadn't turned *totally* useless. "Let me explain. Why is it, do you think, that no one from the higher worlds went back to Midgard? I'm sure you'd have all appreciated a bit more help from the stronger members of the Guild, right? Er, Sect. Whatever. Sure, some of it was because they couldn't physically get there in time, but the reality is that no one felt the need to do so *because* they hadn't put any roots down."

The Sect leader had leaned forward, trying to convince the decidedly unpersuaded Ritualist. "Think about it. You built practically the entire town originally, and yeah... they turned it into something way worse, but why wouldn't they? No one lost anything, not even the *effort* they put into the town. Here? We're not just building a fortress to keep ourselves safe, we're building a home for the guild. Having to lift it up together, having to protect it as a group means we'll build trust, and the experience will allow us to bond in a way that just going out on quests together doesn't."

"Trauma bonding. Fun," Joe had snarked, still unused to the constant pain and extremely agitated by his fresh wounds. "So what should *I* do?"

Aten had sat back, a quiet smile growing on his face. Tossing his arms akimbo, the man had gestured around the area. "Take as much land as you need as your own space and do whatever you want."

For almost an entire year, the Ritualist had done exactly that.

Thoughts returning to the present as he passed through the boundary between unclaimed land and the main headquarters of the guild, Joe slowed down and shifted his direction slightly. The settlement was coming along well, and between all of the members working for large chunks of each day and hundreds of Dwarves from Novusheim who were hired to help build the structures and defenses of their neighboring ally, the area had grown quickly.

No two buildings on the outskirts looked exactly the same, as those commissioning the structures were given free rein to choose their designs. Plenty of the large buildings had court-yards of their own, some flat and stony, clearly designed for practicing combat forms. Others had personal gardens growing along terraces all the way up to the front door. Yet, the vast majority were full of enormous carcasses from monsters that had been hunted and dragged back—those buildings all needed to have some form of magic either preserving the bodies or eliminating the smell.

Closer to the center of the sprawling Sect area, the buildings turned far more similar, though extremely ornate. At a distance, they appeared nearly identical; yet up close, the artistry and intentionality stood out. From the carved walls to the river stones placed along walking paths, every extra detail showed the owner's personality. But, Joe wasn't heading for the central area.

Swinging slightly to the northeast, he followed his worn path toward the enormous chunk of land he had claimed for his own, idly wondering if the grass and flora would quickly retake his route now that he wouldn't be commuting each day. When he had first told Aten exactly how much land he wanted for himself, the Sect leader had originally been hesitant out of sheer shock at the ask: a full square mile just off the main drag of the Sect's territory.

Joe had been forced to make a few concessions. The first was promising to protect the area without needing the guards of the Sect to patrol the vast swath. Second, he'd also guaranteed to open the area as a final fallback point, should they come under attack from an enemy intent on destroying their settlement.

"Kinda telling, now that I think about it. He doesn't want the sect protected too much by my rituals, but at the same time, he knows everyone will rush here as soon as it all starts to go south. Whew... this gets harder every day."

The ground under his feet rose in a gentle incline, a phenomenon Joe had noticed shortly after they claimed the area. Apparently, the Sect Territory of any Sect needed to be placed on a mountain, and if it wasn't... one would grow underneath them. If Joe's guess was correct, in the not-distant future, the land he had claimed for himself would become its own mountain peak, as he *was* the First Elder. Though he sometimes felt uneasy about grabbing so much for himself, he smoothed his nerves with his oft-repeated phrase, "If *I* haven't earned the space and freedom, no one in the guild has."

The automatic terraforming was one of the reasons they needed to set up so far away from Novusheim: depending on how powerful they became, they might form a full-blown mountain range and accidentally knock over the other city.

When it came to how to use his space, Joe had originally started small. For over a month, there had been a residence and workshop combo with a spacious courtyard where he could relax.

That had quickly blossomed into a full-blown manufacturing and skill training-focused district. His house sat at the northernmost point of a four-acre circle of grass and trees, with a path extending out in each of the cardinal directions. Within an easy walking distance stood extremely large structures with wide doors, high ceilings, and fantastic ventilation, which would only get better as the area slowly transformed into high elevation.

An Expert-ranked forge filled with ingots and alloys was directly adjacent when moving clockwise along the circle, and he had the profession increase to prove that he'd gone there likely too often over the last few months to work through his frustrations.

Ritualistic Metalworker. (16/20).

*+25% → **30**% success rate on all attempts to create ritual-specific metalwork items.*

+25% → 30% speed of production for all ritual-specific metalwork items.

*-50% → **-40**% success rate on all attempts to create non-ritual-specific metalwork.*

You now have a random chance of intuiting the design for any forged item created for the purpose of usage in a ritual and will automatically gain a blueprint should you do so!

Then, clockwise around the circle to the next stop would bring him to an alchemy hall, then glass blowing station, an Evergrowth Greenhouse to take care of the area's vegetable and herbal needs, a Rare-rank general workshop he was using for Enchanting, an open plot of land for various summoning needs, and yet another space marked as the future home of the Celestial Observatory—now that he didn't need an area to work in when he was visiting Grandmaster Snow.

This accounted for only *half* of the circle, and counter-clockwise from his house was a massive field covered in scorch marks and churned earth, where even now dozens of Ritualists were battling against each other. Pausing for a moment to observe, Joe watched as two rows of Novices faced off against each other, various rituals being activated and impacting the other side even as their targets frantically hurried to counter or release their own attacks.

It was a wonder to behold and represented Joe's eventual ticket to Grandmastery, but as he looked on at the fumbling Ritualists who were trembling from the shock and surprise of their rituals breaking down or channeling more mana in a single go than they were used to using, he could only shake his head.

"They've got a *long* way to go before they're ready to go out and hunt even the smallest Penguin." Joe reached up and rubbed at his chin consideringly. "Maybe *this* is what Mirascible feels like? No wonder he's always spoiling for a fight and willing to train people up just to get a chance to throw down with them."

Whump.

Joe could feel the shockwave in his chest and turned his attention to a different group of Ritualists, these ones *far* more exciting to watch. Each of them were already Journeyman in at least one of the main class skills, and going by how easily *one* confident-looking man amongst them was dismantling his opponent, there were even a few nearly ready to break into the Expert ranks. The ritual he was controlling had wrapped thick strands of grass around his opponent, and it was easy to see that they were *squeezing*.

The other man was gasping for air, struggling against the cocoon of vegetation wrapping him up, but no one was worried in the slightest, and for good reason.

Before the ritual could do any permanent damage, *Joe's* ritual came into effect. Out of nowhere, the grass suddenly lost its desire to crush the man it was gripping, falling off and scattering as the fallen combatant gasped for air.

"Master Ritualist on the field! Wanderers, salute your First Elder!" The voice, pitched to carry, came from the most advanced trainee Joe had personally taught; a Dwarf he'd trained up for months before handing over most of his duties. In a flash, the trainer was at his side.

"Any issues, Devoe?" Joe murmured quietly, even as he nodded encouragingly at the Ritualists.

"Not since you worked out how to modify that ritual. The badges work perfectly." The Dwarf spoke softly, which meant he was only loud enough for anyone within a *hundred* feet to hear him, instead of all the way to town. "Anytime they drop below half health, whatever is affecting them just… refuses to work."

"No more incidents with monsters getting the same treatment, though, right? Pretty sure I worked out all the issues there, but modifying the Ritual of the Refusal of Three wasn't quite an exact science. That was a *seriously* ancient spell circle." Joe's question received only a firm nod in response, though the Dwarf still had a strange expression on his face. "What's the matter?"

"There's some people waiting for you over on the jumping grounds." There was a note of something dark in Devoe's voice, and Joe wasn't sure what to make of it. Typically, the Dwarf was extremely good spirited. "Now, I say people, but… *Elves.*"

"Elves? Here?" Joe reared back in surprise, his previous interest now tainted with concern. "At least they had the good sense not to try and find me over in Novusheim, but who's watching them to make sure they-?"

"Gage."

"Ugh… of course it's *Gage*. Probably invited them in the first place."

"Mmm… no…" To his credit, Devoe pushed through his dissatisfaction with the annoyingly proficient physically minded trainee to give a proper explanation. "These ones came down from Vanaheim, and they walked into town already looking for you."

CHAPTER TWO

Joe didn't move right away, instead watching as the more advanced Ritualists fought back and forth, dancing out of the way of incoming effects where possible and tossing out shielding rituals or various counters at the last moment when dodging was unlikely. His own Expert-rank ritual came into effect by the end of each match, powering down the various debuffs, interrupting elemental effects, and even removing damage over time such as someone having been lit on fire.

All in all, his training center was thriving. Enormous mana stabilizers were jutting out of the ground, ensuring the smooth and easy practice of even the weakest of rituals. His mind wandered to his collection of natural aspect jars, each of them full to the brim and wasting their potential by not being able to generate additional aspects each hour. "We've got land, we've got people. They're fed and becoming more powerful. Resources aren't scarce here, and even with as expensive as it is to be a Ritualist, no one shows even the slightest *hint* of being uncomfortable with tossing out their most extravagant designs."

Finally unable to hold off any longer, Joe turned his quizzical gaze on Devoe, trying not to show how his stomach was sinking. "Elves from Vanaheim... what could they possibly want?"

The Dwarf shrugged nonchalantly. "Abyss, after you laid it all out like that, maybe they wanna get trained."

"Hardy-har." The Ritualist sarcastically bit back his first thought, deciding in a snap that he would take the meeting instead of sending them away. "I swear, if I walk over there, and even *one* of them starts making demands, I'm just going to go ahead and attack. On that note, hand me one of those badges, would ya?"

Displaying the silvery Wanderer's Guild crest proudly on his chest as though it were simple ornamentation instead of a method to dampen any long-term or channeled attacks these unknown people might direct at him, Joe made his way over to 'the jumping grounds'. As he didn't have only Ritualist skills, and apparently could make use of Mastery Merits from any skills to advance his other ones, he'd set up an elaborate course which made use of real obstacles and intricate illusions. Soon enough, the merits would be rolling in, and he'd start his push into the Grandmaster ranks.

At the very end of the course was a recreation of the exact challenge he had overcome in order to gain the inspiration to achieve Mastery with Omnivault: the end of the G.O.A.T. path where he'd learned to jump off of any water at all—even clouds.

As of yet, no one had managed to replicate his feat. But, as much as Gage frustrated him to no end, he was getting close. The man had immense Dexterity and drive—it was quite likely he'd become the first Master of some variant of Jumping under Joe's tutelage. "If only he wasn't always trying to skip steps... but, I guess... that tracks with what he's learning? Jumping past all obstacles?"

The Ritualist came to a halt at the edge of the jumping ground, where a slight shimmer in the air was the only impediment to his view of the people waiting on the other side. To anyone else, this was a thin curtain of hazy mist completely blocking the view of anyone not on the whitelist for the area. There were certain skills he was able to teach that he didn't want unknown people gaining access to, so the privacy curtains —as he'd dubbed them—had become a necessary inconvenience between each of the different workshops and training areas.

They served the secondary purpose of muffling noise and dampening smells, allowing him to—for instance—shape metal while belting out a mantra at full volume *without* gathering a crowd of flabbergasted students from a separate discipline. In general, Joe was extremely pleased with how well his tiny empire was coming along, especially having been able to stick around for long enough to find the things that annoyed him, then *solve* those issues with elegant solutions. Not to mention, there was always the extra benefit they provided: unexpected bonuses, such as allowing him to get a good look at who was waiting for him before they had a chance to size him up in turn.

A half-dozen people were arranged loosely around a table, some awkwardly hunched, as they were far too tall for the accommodations. No surprise to Joe, Gage was sitting at the table as well, perfectly comfortable with the arrangement as he sipped a cup of tea in one hand while holding a thin wafer of a cookie in the other and told some story to the guests. The man burst out laughing, while all the others merely exchanged glances or offered polite smiles.

As a tall Elf shifted abruptly, Joe leaned forward, a ritual pointed directly at the androgynous face suddenly appearing mere inches from his braggadocious star pupil. When the Elf merely asked a few questions, then blurred back to his own seat with a slightly disgruntled expression, the Ritualist relaxed. Slightly.

After a few more moments of careful assessment, Joe allowed himself to glance away from the pointy-eared threat… and his jaw dropped slightly in shock as he saw the person who must be in charge of the group.

The others, humans, Dwarves, and Elves had only been

surprising to see in that they were all together without some form of infighting. Each of them was clearly a Master in their field, easily distinguishable by the tidy way their mana interacted with the ambient energy fields around them. Yet it was the final... guest... who now had all of his attention: a Grandmaster. A *Wolfman* Grandmaster.

She was practically sitting on the ground to be able to eat from the table at all, and at first he'd mistaken her for part of the huge pavilion of a tent they were sitting under to get out of the sun. Schooling his features, Joe stepped through the illusion and calmly walked toward the table, his bald head brightly reflecting the sun—though he noted with relief that no one seemed to need to squint at him. Technically, the reflection was only supposed to impact the vision of people who meant him harm, but he couldn't rely on that entirely. Some people were just more sensitive to light than others.

"Welcome to the Wanderer's Sect." Joe's arrival had the entire group on their feet in the same instant, though to his surprise, each of them inclined their heads at him in a show of respect. Inwardly pleased that the interaction was already going better than he'd expected, the Ritualist casually waved back at the table. "Please, don't allow me to interrupt your respite. I'm Joe, the First Elder of the Sect, and I hear you've been looking for me?"

"If it's all the same to you, I'd rather not get all scrunched up again." The Wolfman he'd marked as a Grandmaster stepped around the others, walking toward him with a polite, dignified gait. For the briefest of instances, Joe could have sworn he saw something else in her eyes—desperation, perhaps—but it was gone so quickly he could only put the idle thought to the side.

Standing tall and thrusting his chin into the air as a sign of trust and welcoming, Joe had to fight to keep a smile off his face at the shock the Grandmaster showed. "Not a problem at all, Grandmaster. To what do we owe the pleasure of your visit?"

"I see you've had dealings with The People before; I can

only hope they were pleasant." Her words caused Joe to press his lips together, holding back his true thoughts on the matter. "I am Grandmaster Fari of the Stormbinder's Tower. We've had... some *trouble* on Jotunheim, and I was told you were the one to see about solving impossible problems?"

"Hoo~oo, *boy*." Joe let out a blast of air through puffed-up lips. "Look, every time someone's started a conversation with me like that, I've gotten wrapped up in real nasty situations. Still haven't recovered from a few of them, so I'm going to pause you there and let you know that I won't make any promises or deals by the end of this meeting. So long as you don't start the conversation with the expectation of agreement, I'll hear you out."

There was a slight narrowing of her eyes, but the Grandmaster didn't press him for details, instead moving to the side and motioning at the table. Joe stepped under the pavilion, sent Gage a *look* with an arched brow, and unclipped his Ebonsteel mug from his belt. "I see you're having tea. Now, I've never really developed a taste for soggy leaves. I've got coffee, and if anyone wants to upgrade their drink of choice, just let me know."

The Dwarf and human took him up on the offer immediately, though the Elf appeared absolutely *scandalized* at the blunt statement. Then Mate appeared, derailing the talks before they truly started. He cheerfully washed over the table and filled the outstretched mugs of the others, who watched on with great interest as the elemental returned to the cup, winked at Joe, and vanished from the plane with a tiny, *All better! Drinky-drink!*

"Interesting mug you have there..." The Dwarf stared at the dark metal of the mug, which had clear cracks running through it that had been repaired with some amalgam of gold and another metal. "How in the *abyss* did you manage to break *Ebonsteel*, but only a little without shattering it?"

"Long story, but something tells me we're not here to talk about me and my lengthy chronicles of bad decisions I've completed." Joe took a sip, enjoying the way the solid gold rim felt against his lips. "No, I think we're here to talk about some bad decisions I *might* make? But there's no diplomacy without caffeine, so I'm glad we got that settled. Now, you took the bifrost to Jotunheim, managed to get out of Novusheim—without *too* many issues, by the look of you—ignored everything else, and came to find me? Did I miss anything?"

"Ha! You think *highly* of yourself-" it was the Elf who snorted at the casual recounting, but a glance from Fari quieted the man before he could reply too derisively.

"We were sent on a hunting expedition and recently returned to Novusheim after I... abjectly failed in my mission." The Grandmaster took a deep breath as the other members of her party suddenly found the bottom of their cups very interesting. "We've been hunting the World Boss, and six months ago found traces of its movements. It still took nearly half a year to find it, and when we did, it only took twenty minutes for us to be forced to flee. Now, here I stand, without any hope of being able to find and defeat the World Boss before my competition does."

"At least," meeting his eyes directly, she lifted her chin slightly in supplication, "not without the help of a wild card. I've failed my expedition, and the only positive note is that I was able to escape with the vast majority of our team. We were not expecting... what we found."

Joe gently placed his coffee cup on the table, then motioned for her to continue. "I'm sorry, I'm just not seeing what I have to do with any of this? As I'm sure you can tell, I'm merely a Master in my highest skills. I can barely fight an *Artifact*-rank monster on equal terms, let alone create anything that would allow you to hunt a World Boss effectively."

"I'll speak as plainly as I am able, but there is context you must be aware of." Fari's lips twitched as she forced herself to speak. "Historical records speak of the World Boss as a mountain range of ice and snow, slow-moving yet incredibly difficult to damage. Instead, what we found was a titan wreathed in flames so intense that even I could not peer through them."

The Ritualist forcibly held his face still as he realized that their trouble may be in part his fault—he had, after all, scattered the seeds of the fiery flowers that had brought spring to this world of endless winter. He wouldn't be surprised in the slightest to find what remained of them futilely attempting to burn down the World Boss. Still, there was no need to inform the Grandmaster of that fact, not when it might weaken his negotiating position.

"We were prepared to counter frost and cold, suppressing or redirecting the attacks that came at us. Instead, we were met with boiling ground and a sky on fire. Now… what I need from you is not combat-oriented, but merely a way to find the monster and get to it, so that we can collect its core."

"You want me to be your… GPS and transport service?" Joe drummed his fingers on the table. "Seems a little *Reductionist*."

"Then, if my informants are correct, perhaps I *have* come to the right man?" Fari didn't even try to hide the hope in her voice. "If we don't collect the Mythic Core and allow our tower to advance first, the path to higher worlds in our universe may be blocked for decades or centuries to come. Asgard and Hel, forever barred to Vanaheim. Is it within your capabilities? If so… I will ensure it's worth your time to do so."

"I have decades of work to do on my own," Joe began with a slight shake of his head. "Grandmasters and even a *Sage* have promised me training and instruction directly under them. I can get access to almost any resources I need all on my own. You say you'll 'make it worth my time', but I'm still not even certain exactly what it is you're asking for."

Fari held up one massive paw, lifting a finger. "I need a way to reliably find the World Boss each time I set out to hunt it down."

"More than once?" Joe managed only one blink of confusion before the Grandmaster's next raised finger signaled the resumption of her words.

"I need to be able to get in range of it faster than my competitors, so not only finding it but getting as close to it as possible." A third finger joined the others. "Lastly, I need it ready to go at any time, as it's hard to say when the Mythic Core we collect will be used, and the World Boss will respawn. So... some way to alert us to when that happens? As I'm sure you know, communication between worlds is... spotty. If you plan to leave, having a system in place is paramount."

"You're making a *whole* lot of assumptions about what I can realistically do." He was halfway through a silent 'no' long before the request was complete, his motions small but certain. "The entire planet is unmapped, and trust me when I say I know a thing or two about that right now. The mana is so turbulent that it may as well be malicious in terms of tearing apart waypoints and mana signatures. Not to mention the scope of the project? Have you not noticed how absolutely massive Jotunheim is? Finding anything, even a mountain range, especially when it can move? This isn't a skill issue, the scope of the problem is just... too much."

"I don't have an *expectation* that you will succeed. Just the ambition that you might do so." The Grandmaster scooched away slightly, her enormous form no longer looming over Joe quite so obviously. "My ambition is that you can do this; my expectation is that you will be able to do *something* that will make it easier for us. Before you say anything, allow me to make an offer I hope you will be unable to refuse."

Despite himself, Joe was intrigued, though a tiny, regularly ignored part of him was quietly screaming that he'd already made enough commitments and didn't *need* another one. "No harm in knowing what the job pays, right?"

"Indeed." As Fari spoke, the system *chimed* gently in Joe's ear, making his eyes go wide as he realized he was being offered a genuine quest—something that couldn't be falsified, especially when it came to the rewards. He'd seen firsthand what happened when someone tried to back out of paying up, and it hadn't ended well for anyone even *associated* with them. "If you can do what I have described, I will give you the Mythic Core the first time we get it."

"Huh." Remembering one of the dangerous parts of holding onto a Mythic Core, Joe decided to clarify. "You'll make sure *I* hang onto it? You won't hand it over, then kill me on the spot, knowing it will drop upon death even if it's stored away in a spatial storage device?"

"I only require that the core be used within forty-eight hours of us handing it to you. We will do everything in our power to ensure it remains yours to do with as you wish, so long as you don't bring it to anyone on Vanaheim." Fari's words were followed by a slight *chime* as the quest itself was updated. "Once we kill the World Boss, I have a strong suspicion it won't keep its flaming aura. Once it has been taken down, we'll know *exactly* what's required to repeat the hunt, and we have everything we need to make that happen."

"Heh, yeah, those flames will probably vanish." Joe fought off a blush as he realized the others were looking at him questioningly, and quickly changed the subject. "Again, this comes back to: why me?"

"Our divinations fail. Our tracking skills give us chaotic results. It is well known that rituals are constantly recasting themselves, and we believe they will give us the most accurate results, as it's our *channeled* skills that are breaking down as they interact with this world." Fari's nose twitched in distaste. "In an effort at being fully transparent, I have lost faith in my ability to lead this expedition without outside help. I don't want to spend years hunting this creature, only to find upon my return that my competitors have already returned with its core, and the way forward has been sealed long ago."

"Farming Mythic Cores… fascinating." Joe shook his head in bemusement while getting to his feet. "Thank you for coming to me with this opportunity. As I told you at the start, I won't agree to anything right now, but I'll admit I'm quite intrigued. How long will I have to complete the quest if I do take it?"

"I only care that we succeed before someone else does." Fari's group stood and offered polite bows to Joe, everyone fully aware of plenty of spells and skills that could harm others with a simple touch—handshakes weren't a part of their society. "There is no punishment for failure. My only hope is that you will succeed where I have failed. If you would like to make an attempt, just let me know within a day if you want the quest. Either way, I'll be moving to the next option and making the same offer. Whoever succeeds first…"

She trailed off, leaving the rest unspoken.

"I'll let you know." Joe didn't bother to see them out of the Sect Territory, simply walking away and passing through the nearest privacy curtain without a backward glance.

CHAPTER THREE

"Well, don't just stand there and *let* it hit you!" Devoe's exasperated voice rang across the field, causing Joe to perk up out of the introspective spiral he'd begun to sink into. "I've read some of your history; by chance, are you the descendant of one of the Englishmen that would stand in a line and take turns firing at the other side? Because that's what you look like! Do it again, and I'm gonna make you wear a red coat for the next week!"

"What am I *supposed* to do?" Joe's eyes went wide as the Ritualist being instructed snarled back at the teacher. "He's already targeted me; it's going to hit me no matter what I do!"

The Dwarf flashed across the space, hand snapping out to land a blow across the trainee's face. Yet, at the last moment, a shield sprang into place, blocking the open hand and putting a grim smile on the Dwarf's face, even as the disgruntled human stared at him in shock. "Oh, look! A *shield*. Looks like a standard directional defense, perfect for blocking big bursts of damage flying toward you from a ritual that stays in *one place* after activation! Why not toss one of these right in front of the Elemental

Burst, making it useless? Why just stand here and let it bash against you while your opponent is setting up yet another strike?"

"It's just *practice*; how many rituals do you want me to burn through-" Before the argument could spiral out of control any more than it already was, Joe made his presence known by zipping across the area and appearing next to his designated instructor.

Before the Dwarf could call everyone else to attention, the Reductionist waved him down and looked over the suddenly *very* silent Journeyman. "Everyone, listen up! First, please remember you're all here voluntarily, but that does not mean you get to treat your instructor poorly when you're upset. This is a frustrating path, and it is expensive. It's *understandable* that you don't want to use all of your resources, but you need to practice as though this is life or death. Second, perhaps it would be best if we gave you an example of what you should be trying to achieve."

Turning his back on the belligerent human, Joe raised an eyebrow and shot a half-grin at Devoe. "Up for a quick spar? Would be good for working out some of my frustration, and I think you're the only one who can keep up."

"My pleasure." The Dwarf's angry glare at the man he'd been instructing shifted over to Joe, turning calculating as he prepared to use his superior Constitution to brute force his way past whatever the First Elder of the Wanderer's Sect was going to throw at him. All around the field, red-faced trainees came running to watch the show. Most were breathing hard, many had unhealed wounds covering them, but to a man they were intrigued by getting a chance to see the highest-level ritual combatants on the planet throw magic at each other.

Letting his hand drift to his side, Joe quietly *clicked* his Ebonsteel mug into place on his belt, the carabiner sounding like a gunshot in the sudden, mounting tension of the impending fight. "What's got you so worked up, Devoe? Normally you'd just blast someone across the field and into one of the walls for insubordination. Not like we don't have a dedicated healing ritual setup over there."

The Dwarf practically *growled* as he began moving in a half circle around the calm, bald Reductionist. "They're fighting like *Mages*, not Ritualists. Send out a blast of power, rely on your team to hold the enemy at bay while you prepare your next attack. It's like they think they're meant to be ping-ponging spells back and forth instead of *fighting* with rituals."

Adjusting his voice so that he was addressing the crowd instead of only his opponent, Joe half turned away from the Dwarf, though he made sure to keep an eye on him at all times —he was well aware that combat had already begun. "What are the two greatest advantages to being a Ritualist instead of a Mage, since instructor Devoe has been so kind as to point out the major flaw in how we've been fighting?"

As he was attempting to reach each of them, Joe made sure to choose his words carefully, acting as though he were one of the people making mistakes and subtly attempting to enforce a feeling of community and solidarity. "When *I* first started learning rituals, I didn't have the benefit of training with people who knew what they were doing. Luckily, after years of trial and error, and being forced to get better at all of this and work on my flaws, I've figured them out. The first advantage is that our rituals will reactivate endlessly until they run out of power or material-"

The Dwarf chose that moment to *move*. Dirt exploded into the air as he dug his toes into the ground, sprinting at Joe in a full-blown bull rush. Joe leapt to the left, the space he'd vacated exploding as a geyser of dirt and stone a moment later as the Dwarf punched the ground, his hand having suddenly gained a set of knuckledusters tipped with glimmering gemstones.

Joe hadn't jumped high, simply sailing through the air a couple inches above the ground. As his opponent stepped out of the dust cloud, fists raised and shifting back and forth like a professional boxer, the Reductionist found himself grinning like an idiot. "I'm amending my previous statement to *four* advantages. The second is that we are able to pursue other forms of combat while activating other rituals and leaving them to do their job, as instructor Devoe has so clearly exhibited for us. Everyone clap at him-"

Before he could finish his jab at the Dwarf, Joe was forced to bound into the air, tucking in and somersaulting in position as the Dwarf went under him. This time, instead of punching the ground to arrest his momentum, Devoe simply jammed his fingers into the surface and yanked himself backward, nearly catching the human as he landed–

–only to be bounced off a shield that appeared in front of Joe, getting tossed backward as the force of his attack rebounded on himself. The bald man landed with practiced ease, his words flowing on without skipping a beat. "The third, and I'd classify this one as the most important advantage we have over Mages, is our ability to remain mobile and scatter both attack and defense rituals across our chosen battlefield as needed. Before we talk about the final advantage... anyone want to guess what our main *disadvantage* compared to Mages is?"

Lifting a hand, Joe sketched a circle in the air, rapidly drawing out a set of triangles and leaving a shimmering pattern behind. Several half-hearted answers were mumbled by the assembled group, but Joe focused in on the man who'd been arguing with Devoe. "That's right! While we can have a contingency ready for any situation, we need to plan it out well in advance, and it's *expensive*. Resources, study, and time investment are all things we need to think about."

As the Dwarf rushed him once again, Joe's eyes went wide as he saw nearly two dozen fireballs outlining the stocky combatant. If he jumped away or tried to go up, he'd be pelted by an unknown amount of fire damage. *"Really?"*

"Oh yeah," came the half-snarl as Devoe tossed out a tile, a wave of disrupting energy pounding the air in front of him in a cone. Joe felt the distinctive tingle of a counteractive force striking his barrier, which attempted to rebuild itself, only to

fizzle out again as the counteracting ritual pulsed in time with it. At the last moment, the human leaped backward, but not fast enough to fully avoid the punch to his gut, which tripled the amount of speed with which he went flying backward.

Letting out a grunt, Joe dismissed the notification of damage taken, doing a half barrel roll and getting his feet out and behind him so he could land on the ground instead of impact it, digging a shallow trench as his momentum bled off. *"That's* why we need to maintain our first advantage! I just stood there and took a hit for absolutely no reason."

"Pretty hard to dodge when you're just standing around lecturing people." Devoe's smile was wild now, and it was clear he was flying high from having drawn first blood.

"Too true! In that case, let's take a look at what ritual combat specifically should look like." Joe pulled a thick stack of rituals out of his storage ring, even as he reached up to wipe a small dribble of blood away from the corner of his mouth. "Why don't we try that again?"

For the next few moments, the open field turned into explosions of dust and dirt as the Dwarf charged Joe, only for the bald man to calmly evade and reposition. The trainees watched all of it with rapt fascination, each of them having the Characteristics required to watch the entirety of combat, though it would've looked like nothing more than flashes of light interspersed with detonations to a base human.

Finally, Joe appeared in front of the group, seemingly ignoring his opponent as he stood there with his arms stretched out wide as if to invite them to notice how his hands were now empty.

"What I just did was activate a large set of rituals, what I'm calling a 'ritual cluster'."

Devoe appeared just then, still halfway across the field. His eyes narrowed as he took in the sight of Joe casually standing in place, not having any visible defenses around him. The Dwarf took a deep breath, his legs bulging as he positioned himself, then threw himself forward.

"Specifically, I call this set of carefully chosen rituals, which are coordinated to have maximum effect, the 'despair cluster'." Joe turned to observe the oncoming Dwarf, his impromptu lecture not faltering in the slightest. "After a couple months of research, I decided to start this cluster off with a simple Ritual of Redirection, which is the base portion of the one-way barrier each of you has demonstrated competency with."

Devoe stumbled over an ankle-high barrier at that moment, while Joe's voice remained steady and unhurried, "As you all know, the ritual creates a plane of force which rebounds the force of an attack back on the attacker. Yet, when it's stripped of specific purpose and instead directly applied to a target, it instead works to counter each directional movement they take. In this case, it acts as a powerful slowing effect, pulling against every push they make and pushing against every pull."

The Dwarf's speed had been drastically reduced, and by the time he was three-fourths of the way across the distance to the Reductionist, his momentum had dropped by easily ninety percent. His face was pulled in a snarl as he pushed himself to break through the containing force, but found himself all but immobile.

"That has to be at least an Expert-rank ritual," one of the students called out in an apathetic tone, "you want us to blow something that hard to make in *practice*?"

"Nope. That's Apprentice rank." Joe turned back to them, winking at the surprised Ritualist. "To be fair, knowing how strong Devoe is, I stacked eight of those on him, but this should still demonstrate how you can have an eye for resources while taking down your opponent. Which of the advantages does this correlate with?"

"First one. The rituals will reactivate endlessly," someone called out, though another voice neatly overlapped in the next moment.

"The third! You were able to apply all of those while remaining mobile yourself." The speaker pointed out ritual tiles scattered over several hundred square feet of space. "You also made it hard to target the source of them, as they aren't set up next to each other."

"Correct, bonus points to both of you! Truth is, he's breaking through at least three of them each second, but they're getting reapplied as the others work to hold him still. Otherwise, he'd be back to moving at full speed every other second or so." Joe moved on to the points of the second person, "Since I have lots of focus on mobility in my standard combat, being a peak Master of *Jumping*, I take as much time as I need for both avoiding attacks and setting up my cluster."

"Doesn't that mean you're... what, basically a glorified trapper?" came an ever-so-slightly condescending call. "Doesn't that mean people who started as Rogues or the like would have better luck with this class?"

"Nope, I'm definitely a Ritualist. Take a look. Slowing him down is just the first stage in the cluster. That's followed by a set of rituals meant to cause damage over time; specifically, these ones directly impact his resources. Stamina, mana, health, all of it is drained." As Joe spoke the words, various tiles around the space lit up, flashing green, blue, and red in order as he called them out. At the same time, gentle glows appeared on Devoe's body in different spaces, and his expression turned haggard and desperate. "Now, as all of you know, I haven't been feeling my best for the last, heh, *year...*"

After trailing off, Joe shook his head and spoke up for the crowd who had been waiting patiently. "To make it easier on myself, I kept all of my rituals to the Apprentice rank or below. Now, I could try to let these rituals drain him until he either gives up or is defeated, but as we know, low-rank rituals have built-in time limits. Combat rituals especially won't last more than a handful of minutes below the Expert rank. In the moments we have remaining, let's go over what I've done so far."

Though he was pointing at Devoe, he kept his attention on the enthusiastic onlookers. "First is slowing the target, though it'd be far better if I could hold him in place perfectly. Because I *can't*, the next set of rituals is less effective, hitting him in places like his arm or leg instead of the chest or throat, where it would have the greatest impact."

Many interested eyes turned to look at the Dwarf, noting with excitement the wince the Dwarf had on his face each time one of the three lights managed to strike the aforementioned areas.

Joe pressed on, another set of tiles beginning to glow as he did so. "Still, the cluster wouldn't be complete without direct damage. This is the order I've found most effective in sustained combat. Slow your target. Begin to drain them. Finally, hit them with direct damage to shave large chunks off their health while the resources dwindle in the background. For today's demonstration, I'm passing the drained resources into a secondary set of rituals, which return them as specific types of damage."

Energy rushed into the tiles, and the amorphous clouds of green, blue, and red were sucked into them, then returned as beams which hit the Dwarf like strobe lights at different angles. "Stamina tossed back as a wither effect, which increases Stamina loss by other rituals. Mana turned into concussive blasts that work well against flesh and easily penetrate armor. Health corrupted and returned as *pain*."

The Dwarf cried out as he stumbled, reaching into his pockets and tossing out his own tiles. Barriers appeared around him, catching the strobing lights and redirecting them into the air or down to impact the ground.

Joe raised an eyebrow in approval. "Rituals don't need to be explosive. They don't need to defeat your opponent outright. They just need to take hold, to *linger*, but most importantly, they need to interact. If you do it right, you'll never even have to bother learning your enemy's attack pattern. At the same time, they *can* be explosive."

The ritual he'd drawn in midair at the start of combat suddenly flared to life, only a few feet from where the Dwarf had collapsed to the ground... and well within the bounds of the barriers he had tossed up around himself. The slight shimmer had been ignored by everyone else until now, but as it detonated and rebounded off the interior of the barriers Devoe had put up, the field they were in suddenly flared with golden light, and all of Joe's active rituals were destroyed in a single moment.

"Now, this brings us to our final, and fourth advantage-"

The Reductionist glowed with a soft green light, showing he had won the match, and the spectators burst into applause. No longer held in place, the Dwarf got to his feet and walked over somewhat unsteadily, one eye swollen shut while the other remained locked on the victor of the spar. "That can't be *it*, right? Explosive isn't an advantage; almost every class has some skill that explodes."

"Hold on, I'll get to it, Mister Concussion." Joe grinned as he reached out and clasped Devoe's hand, shaking it to show his appreciation for the short fight. "Our fourth advantage is that everything we do is *fun*. Doesn't matter if you want to focus on crafting, combat, or utility—our class has something for everyone."

As the groups spread out once more, split up by their various tiers, they spoke animatedly about what they'd seen and how they could use their previous skill sets more effectively. Only Devoe kept his eyes locked on Joe, who was doing his best to hide the grimace on his face. As the Master Ritualist resumed his journey toward his house, the Dwarf fell into step beside him.

"Keeping it at the Apprentice rank for *their* benefit, huh?" The Dwarf tugged at his beard knowingly. "Didn't get the best news from Grandmaster Snow?"

"I've plateaued," Joe admitted without a hint of shame or hesitancy. "We knew it was coming, but I was hoping I'd be able to push through in at least a *few* areas before needing to rely on my backup plan. Not to mention... seriously, *eight* movement inhibitors, just to slow you down that much? How high are your Strength and Constitution?"

"Dexterity is actually why I was able to keep moving, just as a heads up. As to how high my Characteristics are getting? The majority of them are pushing the seventh tier. I've almost, er... never mind, you'll find out." Even as the next words formed on Joe's lips, Devoe held up a hand and shook his head. "No, I physically cannot give you any more hints on how to break through into the sixth tier. Just like how you found out about the link between skills and lore, telling you how to push your Characteristics past that bottleneck would limit your final potential. If I could even figure out *how* to let you know."

"Tier seven..." Joe let out a low whistle. "You're almost at five hundred with at least a couple of them. How'd I even keep up with you-"

"Let's be honest here, you *didn't* keep up with me. I let you show the trainees what they needed to learn." Devoe gently clapped Joe on the shoulder. "I could've broken out of that anytime I wanted, but then how would they have learned what you were trying to teach them?"

"Mmm... yeah. If your stats are that high, my rituals wouldn't have been 'sticky' enough. The seventh threshold for Characteristics means you're essentially a Master-tier body, so I'd need, at minimum, Expert-ranked rituals to truly keep you contained."

"At least," the Dwarf easily agreed. They walked in silence for a few more moments, as Joe contemplated the fight and felt his ego deflate rather rapidly. "Still, it was quite impressive. 'Ritual clusters', huh?"

"I've got a few sets at different tiers, if you're interested." Joe patted at his robes then manifested a small notebook from his ring. "Consider it a training manual. Once you get the hang of it, I'll come around and let you try them out on me."

"Thanks. Also..." Devoe hesitated slightly as Joe opened the door to his residence and stepped in, needing to look back at the Dwarf over his shoulder. "I'm looking forward to having a serious match with you once you're back to full power."

"It's a deal. Hey, don't look so *concerned*, buddy. Now that I know this is my best shot at it..." Joe flashed a dark smile at his friend, then turned to look at the absolute mess of sticky notes on walls, half-formed diagrams scattered across tables, and at the center of all of it: the inhibitor gear he'd been wearing on Midgard.

"...that day's gonna come sooner than you think."

CHAPTER FOUR

Instead of going straight to work, Joe took a deep breath and slowly sank into a plush chair, resting his head in his open palm. "I wanted a better answer than... no, who am I kidding? I knew the system wasn't going to let me fix this easily. Still, only thirty-one percent? At least I know that, with a few more weeks of practice, I *might* get my Neutrality Aura up and going again."

He hadn't had *any* success with his Exquisite Shell, Joe's body still feeling like he was dipping it in acid if he attempted to activate the divine-granted spellform. Grandmaster Snow had told him that was likely only a psychological block, a persistent reminder that Tatum had essentially chewed him up and spit him out, all while failing to save more than a *single* person from the cauldron.

"Poor Ed." The Reductionist shook his head at the memory of the confused man who had been pulled out, having lost most of his skill levels and class. The last time he saw the guy, he'd been on his way to take a farming job and stay far, far away from combat. Joe thought about all the other Sect members who had been taken by Gameover and felt his heart pounding as fury coursed through him. "Someday, I'll pull that smug *pot* out of the bowls of Tatum's temple and find a way to destroy it *permanently*."

Taking a deep breath, then another since the first hadn't done much, the Reductionist decided to stop dwelling on that particular problem—one he had no control over at this point. It was only a small consolation that he'd done his best to help; though, of course, he was still paying the price a year later. Pulling open his character sheet, he glared at the myriad of *other* problems which had been plaguing him.

Name: Joe 'Monarch of Mana' Class: Reductionist
Profession I: Arcanologist (Max)
*Profession II: Ritualistic Alchemist (9 → **14**/20)*
Profession III: Grandmaster's Apprentice (15/25)
*Profession IV: Ritualistic Metalworker (7 → **16**/20)*
*Profession V: Ritualistic Numerologist (**10**/20)*
Profession VI: Arcane Enchanting Theorist (5/5) This can now be used as a prerequisite for __any__ enchanting-based profession!

*Character Level: **30** Exp: 465,000 Exp to next level: 31,000 (Locked.)*
Rituarchitect Level: 14 Exp: 92,250 Exp to next level: 12,750
Reductionist Level: 12 Exp: 84,065 Exp to next level: 6,935

Hit Points: 4,064/4,546
Mana: 2,994/3,901
Mana regen: 39.86/sec
Stamina: 2,983/3,229
Stamina regen: 7.39/sec

Characteristic: Capped Score (Raw score)

Strength (bound): 289 → 299
Dexterity (bound): 288 → 299
Stoic Constitution (bound): 291 → 299
Light Intelligence (bound): 293 → 299
Ritualistic Wisdom (bound): 280 → 299

Dark Charisma: 239 → 299
Karmic Perception: 292 → 299
Luck: 241 → 299
Karmic Luck: 4

Body and Mind Skills increases:
Artisan Body (Journeyman 0 → Journeyman VI)
Battle Meditation (Expert 0 → Expert VIII)
Coalescence (Journeyman VIII → Expert 0)
Combat Ritual Orbs (Journeyman VIII → Expert V)
Mana Manipulation (Journeyman VIII → Expert 0)
Mental Manipulation Resistance (Beginner V → Student I)
Teaching (Journeyman VI → Expert IX)

Crafting and Gathering Skill increases:
Alchemical Rituals (Journeyman 0 → Expert IV)
Enchanted Ritual Circles (Journeyman 0 → Expert VII)
Magical Matrices (Journeyman VI→ Expert VIII)
Ritual Circles (Master II → Master III)
Ritual Duplication (Apprentice II → Student V)
Ritual Magic (Master VII → Master VIII)
Ritualistic Forging (Expert III → Expert VI)
Somatic Ritual Casting (Journeyman VII → Expert IV)

While all of his professions had seen an overall increase, Ritualistic Numerologist Novitiate had evolved twice to become Ritualistic Numerologist Generalist then Ritualistic Numerologist. From there, the profession had rapidly gained complexity and been extremely difficult to increase. Joe could only assume it was because of the profession finally reaching the 'standard' type he'd been used to acquiring.

Ritualistic Numerologist Generalist. (10/10). The generalist no longer passively observes equations. A new dimension is added to mathematics, and they are able to peer through this as an interpretive lens to recognize trends and outliers.

They still C.A.N.T., but now they can simulate the doing.

The first evolution had reduced the 'ninety-nine percent speed of alteration to ritual-specific matrices down to only twenty-five percent. Even so, the main benefit of the first evolution had been a profession trait called 'mathematical residue recognition', which allowed him to passively detect rituals up to ten minutes per profession level after they'd been cast and give him a chance to reverse engineer the remnants of them.

This, combined with his Ritualistic Wisdom, had given him access to dozens of rituals pulled from confluences of power in the natural world as well as giving him a fantastic ability to rapidly understand what rituals were being used against him when he was training other people.

But that hadn't been the end of the benefits. When the profession evolved once more, the exponential increase in complexity had come with another gift, one he was certain he wouldn't have gained if he had started with this version of the profession from the get-go.

Ritualistic Numerologist. (10/20). The Ritualistic Numerologist no longer relies on theory. They are now able to read, interpret, and restructure ritual matrices in real time.

By sacrificing the ability to make things easier for themselves, you've gained +100% skill increase speed when increasing the Lore skill 'Calculus and Number Theory'. This profession has narrowed its focus and can now only gain profession experience by challenging more and more difficult ritual-specific Magical Matrices. [Level 5 bottleneck: Journeyman-Rank Ritual Matrices no longer give experience. Level 10 bottleneck: Expert-Rank Ritual Circle redesign only grants 50% class experience.]

Evolution trait(s): Mathematical Residue Recognition. Revisionist Cipher.

Revisionist Cipher: The mathematical matrices of all ritual circles, regardless of tier, are treated as a half tier lower when being read or analyzed.

Now you only C.A.N.T. when you want to not.

As always, there was a reason Joe had started with the thing he'd gained the most with: he needed to see his wins before he glanced at the major impediments. First, while almost all of his other professions had increased substantially, Havoc had been out on some hush-hush mission and had been unable to offer him skill increases or help, leaving his Grandmaster's Apprentice profession to languish. Even worse, though he had many discussions with Dwarven Enchanters, there hadn't been anything truly unique they could offer that he felt was worthy of his Arcane Enchanting Theorist 'Prerequisite' certification.

If he'd wanted some standard form of Enchanting profession, he wouldn't have jumped through the complex hoops to get something that would allow him to gain absolutely *any* Enchanting profession. Joe was absolutely *positive* there had to be something out there that was near impossible to attain without this, and he was going to hold out hope as long as possible in order to get his greedy little mitts on it.

"Then there's you..." Joe glared at his Characteristics, each of which was locked at the bleeding edge of the sixth threshold. "What is it that's holding me up from crossing you? It can't be a lack of training, I've been pushing myself this entire time, as shown by my skills making such massive progress."

As he read over them again, the fact that Strength and Dexterity hadn't gained a prefix, though all the others had, stood out to him with glaring obviousness. "That's got to be it, right? But how do I get a Characteristic shift on those? All of the other ones were gained either in desperate situations or entirely by accident... huh. When's the last time I went out and actually fought something for real? Gathered my own resources? Had a desperate situation? Was it really back when Gameover had his last laugh, and I shattered my Mass Resurrection skill?"

It was a strange feeling to realize that, although he'd been pushing himself, he hadn't been doing so with the same lack of fear he used to have. "Maybe taking damage that actually stuck around has messed with me more than I've let myself believe? Okay... I guess, now that I no longer have to spend a chunk of my day training under Snow, I'll fill that time with getting out there and fighting monsters with my fists and orbs. Anything to get those last two Characteristics where they need to be. And if that doesn't do it, I'll *shake* someone until they finally give me the answer—loss of potential or not!"

Wisdom +1! (Deferred)

Joe glared suspiciously at the system message, wavering between deciding whether the system was agreeing with his plan, telling him to go and shake the answer out of someone, or just messing with him. "I'd have to bet it's... probably just messing with me."

Finally, he looked at his skills, happy that at least the *passive* skills he'd earned and been imbued with hadn't been impacted by his damaged mana channels. While not a single one of his active combat skills had increased, his constant training with Grandmaster Snow had finally pushed him into the Expert ranks for his Mana Manipulation and Coalescence, which had been the catalyst for pushing everything else up so far over the last few months.

As for his crafting skills, although they could be rather mana intensive, as soon as he'd recreated the channels through his arms and to his hands, they'd functioned perfectly well. Crafting required him to expel mana and manipulate it outside of his body, typically within the items he was working with. It didn't care that his internal structure had a blender applied to it, only that he could suffuse metal, imbue potions, or carefully drip power into an inscription tool and carve glowing lines with a steady hand.

Lastly, his Lore skills... Joe couldn't bear to look at them. Each of them had gained exactly two ranks over the course of his recovery, all of them except 'Knowledge'. His singular attempt to reaccess *that* particular spell pathway had resulted in him slipping into a week-long coma. Even then, he had only woken up after he'd been found face-first in the mud, and he'd spent a week having the swelling in his brain tended to by a Master healer.

For obvious reasons, he hadn't tried twice.

"Good..." Joe let out a deep breath, allowing his frustration to seep out of him now that he'd finished what he called an 'accusation audit'. "I've seen all of the positives and negatives, and now that I've acknowledged them, hopefully I'll be able to focus on what I need to do to keep the good things going and fix what's gone wrong."

With that thought in mind, he turned his gaze to the focus of his studies: the inhibitor gear he'd needed to wear on Midgard. This was the only item he knew of that cleanly incorporated each of the core class skills of a Ritualist. Now, as his first option had failed, Joe only saw one path forward: relying on his own skillset to fix himself.

Instead of going out of the seat, he leaned forward and grabbed the table, dragging the multi-hundred-pound piece of furniture across the stone floor with a casual pull. "Ritualistic Forging, Alchemy, Enchanting, Matrices, and Ritual Circles. Five different disciplines I need to perfect so I can fix this mess."

Joe had been working on this project long enough that he fully understood that fixing his situation would require some combination of either a massive amount of time, resources, or skill. "I'm fine trying to get good at what I do and dumping everything I earn into solving the problem, but the idea of taking the next decade to slowly piece my channels together is absolutely going out the window."

Pulling open his notebook to the bookmark he'd left in place, he looked down at the incredibly detailed sketch of himself he had designed. Flipping the page, he looked over the energetic overlay he'd drawn out in a half-fugue state while holding onto a Ritual Orb imbued with Essence Cycle. Making a note, he murmured softly, "Gonna have to update this a little bit now that I've bumped up my percentage of recovery by a point."

Holding his orb, Joe sought out the minor imperfections in the diagram, sketching with his main hand as perfectly as possible. He had to work in short spurts, as he only had a third of the mana he should have, and recovery was slow. Just as he finished up, a neat stack of his notes rustled in the air as they were scattered off the table and drifted across the floor in a chaotic pattern. "Hey! What...?"

His eyes zeroed in on the small creature sitting on his table, uncaring that she had displaced his project. The cat casually licked its paw, studying the markings Joe had been making while extending her claws, then retracting them twice, before finally deigning to look over to meet his eyes with a bored expression.

Joe raised an eyebrow then flicked his notebook into his storage ring without breaking eye contact. Taking a deep breath, he burst into motion, throwing himself out of his chair, scrabbling across the table, and sucking all of the sensitive documents and prototypes he'd been making into his ring before this tiny agent of chaos could casually destroy them.

Finally the room was practically spotless, and the Ritualist turned back and inclined his head at the fluffy kitty watching him with a bemused expression. "Queen Cleocatra. It's been a while. If I'd been expecting you, I wouldn't have left breakable things out."

"I found it surprisingly difficult to find someone to carry me off of Alfenheim willingly," the Nyanderthal spoke in a breezy, yet slightly accusatory tone. "Eventually, I found myself forced to stow away in a pack like a rat on a ship. Not an analogy I use lightly, mind you. It's almost as though the people who *knew* I was on the planet and being *incredibly helpful* simply abandoned me there."

Joe grimaced at her words, but he truly had decent reasoning for not having gone looking for the diminutive queen of the hidden race. "Understandable, as that world is all but barred to me for the next... well, until I'm far stronger than I currently am."

The cat dropped her gaze to Joe's left hand, which had a light tremor running through it at the moment. "Yes, I can see you've been not only busy but completely without proper direction. This is what happens when you allow the untrained to be led by fools. I suppose it's a good lesson for you, and I didn't even have to teach it myself. Only two classes of entity can leave permanent wounds that follow you through respawn, at least in the worlds to which you have access. Deities and *my* kind, though those who would use our powers in that way have long since been banished."

Just before he was going to ask why she could damage people on the same level as a deity, the Ritualist paused and looked at her consideringly. His lips pressed together, and he leaned forward with great interest. "If you can inflict this kind of damage on someone... is it possible you know how to fix it as well?"

"Doesn't work like that, Joe. You should know that by now." The cat shifted back and forth, kneading the top of the table as though the worked wood was a plush pillow. "*True Damage* doesn't *heal*. It has to be mended by the one maimed. Still, there are hints I can give you and false paths you might be searching down that I can... redirect you away from. Beyond that, I can give you a bit of hope."

"Honestly? I could really use some hope right now." The Ritualist straightened his posture, having not even realized he'd been slumping. "Maybe start with that?"

"Certainly," the cat replied primly. "First, when you *do* repair what has been inflicted upon you, your channels will become hardened. The type of damage you recover from will no longer impact you as much going forward. Since it seems to have been some form of divine energy attack, and it was so *very* thorough, recovering from it should give you a *massive* resistance on par with near-immunity. Second... you have all the tools you need to make the repairs, you just don't have the skill. Yet."

"You read my notes?" Joe perked up excitedly as curiosity overrode his composure. "What did you-"

Cleocatra raised a paw to cut him off. "Not right meow. You're missing a key component. Something fundamental that you simply haven't been *looking for*. There is the physical component: you've been mapping out the overlay of your energy pathways, but so long as that debt remains... it will be nearly impossible for you to purge yourself of the foreign power that still lingers like impurities in molten metal."

"Debt? Who do I owe?" His words were met with a subtle shake of her head, the cat face somehow perfectly conveying disappointment.

"It's not *you* who owes the debt. This imbalance has been growing for a long, long time. There have been periods where the scales have gotten closer to becoming even, but... when one party continuously benefits from another and even still asks for more, offering rewards laced with selfish desires, the burden can *only* become heavier." She crouched forward, then leaped at Joe faster than he could react, for the first time showcasing a portion of her true power by blurring through the air and leaving afterimages as she closed in on his face.

Bap. The tiny paw smacked the bald man between his eyes, right where his nose blended with his forehead.

"Look, and see for yourself."

Glancing around with oddly watery eyes, Joe found that his vision had shifted ever so slightly. Fine filaments of light extended from his body, reaching out in all directions. There was even a strand of cheerfully golden motes reaching from the Nyanderthal queen to himself—somehow, he knew with a glance that *she* still owed *him* a debt somehow. Following the other lines, he could see very few going *from* him to another; almost all of them were flowing into the subtle sheath of golden energy clinging to his body like a second skin.

"I don't know what you're talking about, still. Also, why does it look like you still owe me a debt? I haven't done anything for you in literal years at this point, and-"

"Shh... this is what I was talking about earlier; the untrained being led by fools." Cleo blinked once, slowly, as if waiting for something. "Right. The reason I still owe you is that I've taken on the responsibility of the subjects of mine that you saved. A life debt is no easy thing to repay, nor should it be. Still, as I have more freedom of movement than they, I can more easily work to achieve balance. Focus, Joe. Simply look toward Asgard."

Following the gesture of her paw, the Ritualist looked upward, but found himself confused as he stared at what looked like a filled in halo hovering directly above him. "A circle? It's a golden circle, right?"

"No." The cat practically hissed in anger, though somehow Joe knew it wasn't directed at *him*. "For reference, even the life debt I have taken responsibility for shows as a casual thread waving through the air between us. This? You are just seeing the bottom of a *pillar* of Karmic debt. From my perspective, it is a beacon extending across worlds in a straight line, no bends or curves, no question about to whom you are connected. I could pinpoint your position on this planet from the bifrost as I rode along it. For those sensitive to this energy, there is no way for you to hide."

"It can't be all bad, though, right? Having a deity owe you so much seems like a good place to be." Joe's attempt at levity failed as the queen actually reluctantly bobbed her head.

"His desperate *need* to give you inflated rewards in an attempt to bring you into alignment is not a terrible thing for you." Her lips twitched as she prepared her next statement. "But the fact that the world will keep pushing you into situations where you can *earn* those rewards may not be something you are too excited about. Tell me, have you ever had an encounter where it seems the difficulty has suddenly ratcheted up to near impossible? A casual stroll turned into a desperate battle against monsters that shouldn't even be in that area? A ritual failing spectacularly, only to be offered a single chance at saving it from melting down and taking hundreds of lives with it?"

"That's just... how it is here, isn't it?" Joe was sweating now, even more than when Devoe was swinging his ham-sized fists at his face. "Constant battles, an endless push for Mastery in your skills?"

"Only for people who have constantly had an outsized debt owed to them by an entity far above their power level, with no true repayment ever happening," Cleocatra succinctly summarized for him. "Tell me, Joe... knowing what you know now, when was it that a deity first came to owe you enough that the world would begin pushing you into terrible situations?"

"Uuhh..." Joe shrugged helplessly, shoulders dropping to his sides as though gravity had suddenly doubled. "Tatum didn't have any followers, so he asked me to be his first so that he wouldn't fade away entirely. That was, um, during class selection?"

"You're saying... a deity all but owes you a life debt and has since you arrived in Eternium?" The Nyanderthal sat back suddenly, blinking rapidly as she processed Joe's words. "I think you should go ahead and show me the ritual you were planning on using on yourself. Knowing this, there's... there's *going* to be issues that need addressing."

CHAPTER FIVE

As Joe laid out his notes in precise order, he pressed Cleocatra for clarification. "You're saying that putting out so many shrines, giving him leadership in a pantheon, multiple places of power, a Legendary temple attached to the Pathfinder's Hall, the entire population of the Dwarves following him, and a high priestess means he owes me... um? Actually... you know, when I lay it out like that..."

"There must have been signs he was getting desperate to repay you," Cleo murmured as she went from document to document, even circling around the inhibitor gear disdainfully as she spoke, batting it angrily before moving on. "Access to skills you shouldn't have had? Rapid advancement in others, all while he desperately tried to hide what he was doing from those who could hold him to account? Small attempts at repayment, perhaps a skill directly connected to him which would activate without your input? Doing anything he could to trick the system into letting him give you more without you technically earning it in the system's eyes? You know, trying to pay you off just 'cause, without *just cause*?"

"Hmm." Even if they were having a frank discussion, the

Ritualist knew better than to state aloud the details of what Tatum had done for him. "I see your point, though I *can't* think of *anything* that might be-"

"Sure, sure." She chuckled knowingly. "Tell you what, why don't we change the subject? Tell me about this attempt at infusing yourself with power and how *this* version will be able to fix the problems caused by you... being infused by said power."

The abrupt shift caused Joe to frown, but then he noticed that the queen was staring at a corner of the ceiling where there was nothing. No decorations, nothing to follow with her eyes as she currently was—at least, nothing *he* could see. He slowly moved over to the starting point of his research, reaching out and tapping the document.

"Even the short explanation isn't simple, but I can break it down fairly easily. All of this starts with Ritualistic Alchemy." He traced the carefully written words he'd been considering for months. "The plan is to generate a potent substrate I can use to essentially tattoo the entirety of my body, from the marrow inside my bones, all the way out to the skin. If I can create permanent etched pathways, I can carve out new conduits as needed."

"Of course, the actual application requires tools that can reach every part of my interior, so I need to forge equipment that can move the alchemy the way it's supposed to be moved." Joe lifted a page, showing her a pod that appeared quite similar to the mechanism that had originally brought him into Eternium, crossed with a sewing machine. "I figure all of it should be applied at once, or as quickly as possible. That means injection from all angles all at once."

"Simple in theory, rather horrific in practice, if you step outside of the conversation and think about it." The Nyan-derthal queen spoke without inflection, forcing him to draw his own conclusions. "There's still a few problems with your plan, no?"

"The main issue is permanence," Joe admitted without hesitation, carefully placing the page with the others in the same note set. "If I get killed and go to respawn, I'd have to get back in the pod and reapply the substrate. I've no doubt the challenges will only get harder from here on, so I'm trying to see if I can compensate for that with Ritualistic Enchanting. If I can take those tattoos and have them follow me through lives, that should fix all of the problems I'm finding."

"Only two things can follow you through death... memories and True Damage," Cleo told him in a warning tone. "What you're talking about so casually is little more than applying ritualistic scarring to your soul. The worst part is that it might even *work*. But how would you possibly account for growth? If you were to complete this scarification, new pathways-"

"That's where the Magical Matrices come in." Here he pulled out a thick binder filled with mathematical formulae, more than half of which was crossed out. "My goal is to create an open formula, which allows for new input and output based on the parameters I give it. Essentially, I need to make it so that the enchantments and alchemy work in tandem, accepting new input as variables instead of immutable objects."

Before she could object again, however casually or brutally she might, Joe revealed the final piece of his work: a ritual design he'd been crafting by himself. Cleo winced away as she looked at it, the Master-rank concepts she was unfamiliar with shining through and causing her mental anguish. "Last, a ritual circle that can keep all of it working together, guiding, implementing, and synergizing the effects."

"Put it away." Cleo gathered her thoughts for a few moments as Joe shuffled around the room with a tangible air of excitement about him. "Yes... I do think it can work. Not the way you designed it, but yes. Before you ask, it is clear you are doing all of this to the best of your ability. Unfortunately, to put it bluntly, that isn't enough."

Walking to his alchemy plans, she reached out and smacked it off the table, where it fell to the ground with a *thwap*. "Do you really think the work of an *Expert* is going to be enough to repair damage done at the Sage rank or greater? The basis is sound, but no matter what you do, whatever it is you put in place, it is putting a bandage on a fatal wound. Instead, I can tell you what you need to *actually* fix this."

"Finally! All I want is a straight answer." Joe lifted one hand in silent invitation, "Please. It's been an entire year without knowing what I should do."

"While simple, it is not easy." Cleo rubbed against the inhibitor gear, winding between the gear that looked like a cross between a torture device and an abstract art piece. "Once you cross the seventh threshold of Characteristics, any damage you've accumulated in the past will be restored. Not only will your body and mind fundamentally transform, but they will take on an entirely new form where even structural damage such as this will only be to your benefit."

"Sure, so I just need to get more than five hundred Characteristic points in every stat," Joe agreed with feigned brightness powered by sarcasm. "I might've been trapped at two hundred and ninety-nine with no guarantee of being able to breach that anytime soon, and training each individual Characteristic has a baseline of almost three hours *if* I can find training tools that work at that rank in the first place. Let's say I can. I'd still be looking at suffering through at least another year like this, if all I did every day was work to boost them."

"Oh, *no*, in fact. Specific training doesn't work the same way once you reach the sixth threshold. It becomes *much* harder."

He stared at the cat, giving her a flat look reserved for people who confused ambiguous words for helpfulness. "Then your advice is…?"

"*Absolutely* make the bandage." Cleo locked her intense eyes on Joe and began prowling toward him. "But I've seen what you've been doing out there. If I'm being frank, I think this forced loss of momentum has been good for you. *Finally*, you are starting to rely on others, to delegate tasks, to be okay not burdening yourself with someone else's load. The rate at which you have been accruing Karma has slowed from all sources but *one*. Even then, the others can simply be severed and turned into Mastery Merits once they have matured properly."

"Is that where those come from?" Joe murmured with academic interest, though he was fully ignored by the shin-height queen.

"*But*," here, her voice became imperious. "The bandage you slap on your soul needs to be of the highest possible quality. Each component must be at least the Master rank. In order to have them all function correctly, the guiding ritual must originally be at least one tier higher. You're looking at creating a Grandmaster ritual using *yourself* as the entirely-contained output of the working. Anything less than this will guarantee your inability to breach the seventh threshold."

"I..." Joe's eyes frantically flickered to his skill sheet, where his most potent usable ritual skill, Ritual Circles, had long-since languished at Master rank three—even then only having gained a rank thanks to the completion of one of his quests. "I don't think I *can* make a Grandmaster-rank ritual."

"Not. By. Yourself." Cleo slowly nodded her head. "Or, just maybe, not *here*. You are exactly correct. I think, if it were me, I would decide it was time to start calling due some of the debt you are owed. Now... you have a visitor, so I'm going to go explore Jotunheim a bit. It's been a few hundred years since I was able to hunt down mice the size of a boulder, and nothing else has really come close to filling me up."

The Ritualist glanced to the door, wondering who could possibly be visiting him, "How do you know-?"

By the time he looked back, the question died on his lips. Cleo was gone, and nearly half of his research notes, meticulously created over the last several months, were gently floating to the ground as little more than confetti. Joe dashed forward, frantically grabbing at the ruined papers, near-involuntarily bellowing all his frustrations as a single word.

"*Cat!*"

As he began cleaning up his study, which took up the vast majority of the space in his house, Joe intermittently looked at his quests as he waited for this 'visitor' the cat had mentioned. It'd been a long time since he'd made any progress on his combat quests, but now that he was planning on heading into the wilderness once more, he felt that he was due for a refresher.

As he hadn't been able to do much, his most recently completed quests still remained showing in his quest log, so he skimmed those as he moved to look over the fresh ones.

Quest complete: Student Reductionist III. Reward: A blueprint or template useful to your class based on the discipline used to complete this quest. Access to Student Reductionist IV.

Blueprint gained: Matrix Expander.

The Matrix Expander is a mathematical calculation device which allows you to take blueprints, templates, or ritual designs and break them into their constituent parts. The original design will be destroyed in the process. The time required for the production of the blueprints of the constituent parts is based on the tier of the provided design.

Quest complete: Expert Ritualist. Reward: +10 to skill: Teaching. +1 to all Ritualist core class skills. Access to Expert Ritualist II.

Quest gained: Mastering Ritual Combat III. This is the second of five Ritualist-Tower generated chain quests consisting of increasing difficulty, which will help you determine your final specialization for combat-based rituals.

Now that you have an understanding of your personal combat prowess, you should have a good understanding of where your passion for the craft lies. Now it is time to begin honing your skills as you begin seeking out your first specialization.

1) Use 500 Apprentice ritual combat circles in live combat. (101/500)

2) Use 300 two-discipline Apprentice ritual combat circles in live combat. (54/300)

Reward: 1) Choose a combat ritual in your possession, and any synergistic rituals in your possession will be highlighted based on the disciplines you use to complete this quest.

2) Gain a three-circle flourish along the cuffs of your Ritual Tower robes, denoting you as an Apprentice combatant. The circles will be embroi-

dered in silver thread and will shimmer faintly in direct light. Though almost entirely ornamental in design, your portion of the spoils increases by 3% from successful combat challenges on behalf of the Ritualist Tower.

Progress toward the next quests in this quest line, such as using higher-ranked rituals, will be tracked but locked until the current quest is completed. Additional rewards and profession opportunities may be unlocked based on your performance.

Expert Ritualist II. You have created a successful coven that has raised a Journeyman student Ritualist. As you have embarked on the path of a Class Sage by raising all your personal Core Class skills to Expert with no sign of slowing down, prove you are worthy of being called a Master by raising five distinct Experts, each with at least one distinct Core Class skills achieving the Expert rank.

Expert Ritualist promoted: 4/5. Reward: 1) +1 to all Ritualist Core Skills. 2) Access to Master Ritualist class quest.

Each of these were exactly as Joe had expected, but even as he mentally reached to close the page, a new notification slunk onto the page, quietly awaiting his approval. As soon as he read over the prompt, Joe frowned, knowing without a doubt that this new quest had been offered to him by the Nyanderthal queen.

Quest offered: Dulling the Sword of Damocles. Your deeds have not only written your own legend but are closely tied to and therefore empower the hidden deity Occultatum. Though you have worked hand in hand, there is no doubt that he has benefited far more from your actions than you have. Every act you complete sharpens the blade, and if this tie were to be severed or the debt called in, you would be unable to survive the infusion of power.

You must find a way to lighten the burden and slow the increasing debt. There are three conditions to completing this quest.

1) Let go, even if just for now. Remove the title 'Tatum's Chosen Legend', formally placing your granular bond on hold. (0/1)

2) Take three steps into the light. It has become easy for you to complete projects using the gifts given to you by your faction leader. You must complete at least three major workings under your own recognizance which would be easier to complete by using the resources on hand. Do not invoke or empower him. (0/3)

3) Convert at least one of the divinely granted skills you have been gifted into an arcane version which works entirely off your own understanding. (0/1)

A reward will be granted for each condition you complete, but take heed. Once you have completed any condition, you will be unable to undo the effects until this quest is fully complete.

Accept?

"Bah... I guess if I had to start separating out from him, I might as well get rewarded for it along the way." Joe begrudgingly accepted the quest, letting out a soft sigh as he glanced at his most potent title.

Tatum's Chosen Legend. You are the Legendary Chosen of a deity and have earned his respect.

+20% speed of learning any water or darkness related abilities.

-10% learning speed of any fire or light based abilities.

+20% favor gained (retroactive).

+30% damage against opponents who have a higher level than you.

-15% Damage against opponents who have a lower level than you.

Reputation gained at 2.5x normal rate, and lost at .25 the normal rate.

Capturing places of power now proceeds 25% faster.

Caution! You will be worth 50% more experience and favor gain to Champions of other gods who manage to kill you.

With a tap, Joe unequipped the title and stored it in his necklace, the Pearls of Wisdom. Immediately, he felt a strange sense of loss and knew without having to guess that Tatum had just looked at him through the bond they'd formed over the years. "Yeah, gonna miss that thirty percent damage bonus against higher-level opponents. Sorry, buddy, but we need to start figuring this out."

Let go, even if just for now. Remove the title 'Tatum's Chosen Legend', formally placing your granular bond on hold. (1/1). Reward gained!

Karmic Shroud Collar. This silver-black collar looks like it belongs on a small, domesticated animal instead of around your surprisingly beefy neck. The small bell in the center of the collar chimes with an odd noise, producing immense echoes and rendering all attempts at stealth as failures.

Silencing the bell will activate a shroud that hides all of the karmic bonds of the wearer for a full 24 hours from all entities... even the system itself.

The collar contains three charges and fully recharges after being worn for a single day after the final active usage expires. Current charges: 3/3.

This is a Mythical item. It becomes soulbound to the first person who wears it.

"It only has a single effect, yet it's a *Mythical* item?" Joe turned the thin scrap of material over in his hands, and the tiny bell let out a bright, silvery and cheerful chime that echoed through his house half a dozen times before even *starting* to fade. "This is basically the key to walking around on Alfenheim, isn't it? Not even trying to be subtle with how annoyed you are that I left you there, are you, Cleo? Now... can I bind this to myself without having to wear it all the time?"

In reply, a prompt popped up, asking him if he wanted to silence the bell. Joe accepted and felt a slight tug at... *something* deeply connected to himself. "*Hurk.* Abyss, did I just feel my *soul?*"

He swung the collar back and forth, but no further sounds were produced. Rolling his shoulders, he tried to store it in his storage ring, only to get a warning that doing so would deactivate its shroud functionality. "Ah, there's the trick. Let's try this-"

Dropping the Mythical item on the floor, Joe took a step away, only for the black and silver device to vanish and appear clasped around his neck, bell bouncing merrily yet silently over his hyoid bone.

Before he could run any further tests, the door to his house suddenly blew apart, the shrapnel turning into splinters, then dust before traveling three inches.

"Who *dares* kill my trainee in his own home?"

Joe was tossed back against the far wall, pinned in place by the simmering aura of power rolling off someone he'd never expected to see on Jotunheim.

"I'm fine... for like five seconds, unless you don't let me go," the Ritualist gasped out as his blood was forced out of the pores in his skin along the back of his body by the immense pressure. After only a moment of hesitation, the aura cut out, and Joe dropped to the floor, gasping for air as his vision swam. "Do you have *any* idea how long it takes to get blood out of these white robes when I don't have access to my best skills anymore, Mirascible?"

"Invest in *bleach*, you whiner!" Mir barked at him, eyes narrow as he scanned Joe from top to bottom. "What happened to you? Why'd your beacon vanish? Lastly… what in the *world* are you wearing on your neck? Got bored of merely sparkling, and now you want to add *noise* to the sensory overload you already push everyone into?"

Getting back to his feet, Joe took a deep breath and offered a smile to the Class Sage. "Hey there, Mir. How'd you manage to get through the blockade to Jotunheim?"

"What do you *think* happened? I walked up to the bifrost and got on it. Who's going to stop *me*?"

CHAPTER SIX

"Since you're not dead, show me why you're acting like you are." Mir turned around and stalked out of the destroyed doorway, not bothering to look back and see if Joe was following him. To be fair, the Ritualist had no choice in the matter, as he found himself floating on a small pillar of air that dragged him along in the Class Sage's wake.

"There's sunshine on this planet, but you're even paler than the last time I saw you. Have you really been down here thinking about joining the Blood Rites Tower? You'll need to figure out how to get some hair, but otherwise you'd fit right in."

Joe tried to speak up and defend himself, but the Elementalist was having none of it. Only a few moments after their initial meeting, he found himself roughly deposited on the ground of the sparring field he'd recently vacated. Mir finally turned to face him with a hopeful glint in his eye. "You've had an entire year to practice, get better, and put my advice into play. Let's see what you've come up with!"

"That's the thing, Mir, I had a skill get-" Yelping, Joe threw himself out of the path of a fireball that looked more like a will-o'-the-wisp. The flames were an ethereal white, and as they zipped past him, the dirt underneath melted and resolidified instantly, creating a path of igneous rock that extended from the Sage's outstretched hand to where Joe had been standing. Then the ball simply winked out of existence, perfectly controlled even at a distance.

"Not the most graceful escape, but it seems you've been working on using more of your physicality in a fight. Good! Most of your people take decades to learn that lesson." Mir lifted his left pinky as though he were about to take a sip of tea from a delicate cup. "But I want you to *defend* yourself."

The air around Joe shattered with a thunderclap, and he was hit from five angles simultaneously, actually causing him to be unable to move more than an inch in any direction as the competing forces applied equal pressure from all sides. The Ritualist desperately activated an Apprentice-rank shield, a small bubble of force appearing around him and expanding out ever so slightly. This gave him just enough room to catch his breath, though a small part of his brain latched onto the oddly beautiful pattern the attack had created.

A cone of compressed air had manifested at five points around him, then practically acted as an immense gravity field, making a perfect star-shaped pattern with him at the exact center. Even now, the design was digging deeper into the ground, not tossing any dirt or dust into the air, but simply filling the space with air that was hundreds of times denser and therefore heavier than the actual atmosphere. A soft whine came from his ritual tile, and Joe noted with concern that the shield around him was rapidly distorting.

"I had a skill get shattered by a deity!" the bald man bellowed at his erstwhile mentor. "My mana channels got all messed up, and I can barely activate even this rank of ritual! Back off for just a *minute*, would you?"

Mir blinked at him as though Joe's words weren't registering, and as the shield began cracking ominously, he finally responded exactly as Joe had feared he would. "Did I say I was here to listen to your sob story or to assess your combat capability? I'd recommend dodging if you-"

The bubble burst at that moment, and Joe barely managed to jump away at an angle, passing through the space where two of the cone-shaped spells intersected. Though he was buffeted back and forth as he passed through the boundary—taking a few hundred points of damage for his trouble—he wasn't in the center of the space where the air collapsed once more. The ground instantly flattened, converted to sedimentary rock under the pressure, only for *that* to shatter and begin integrating with the next layer of topsoil.

"-don't want to die." Mir finished with a casual twist of his thumb, extending a hair-thin, focused thread of water across the space between them. It let out a soft *hiss* as it cut through the ritual tile Joe had just pulled out, and the Ritualist barely managed to pull his hand out of the way before he lost a finger. "If you can't use magic, figure something else out. I'm sure you haven't simply cloistered yourself away for the last year, even if your pallid skin seems to suggest that."

"Ahem... well, actually-" Six Ritual Orbs shot away from Joe in that moment, spiraling out and around in an attempt to harry the Sage from different angles. Mir's hard-pressed lips shifted slightly as the Ritualist exploded into motion, practically flying across the ground as he leapt forward with all his might.

Just before he came in range of a quick strike from Mir, Joe slammed his hand down and flung himself sideways, sliding across the ground and leaving churned earth in his wake as three of his Ritual Orbs finished their arc. The first and the fastest was, of course, the Ritual Orb of Intelligence, shaped like an icicle and spinning like a drill. It dove in, all while two of the others curved to box in the Sage from alternate angles.

The instant the spike was about to drive itself into his head, the Sage didn't so much dodge as just *flicker*. As far as Joe could tell, the man didn't move from his spot, yet the orb sailed clean through its target without impacting flesh. Having expected something like this, the Ritualist didn't bother getting upset or lose himself in hesitation. Turning his momentum into a cartwheel, he pushed off the ground and caught himself midair on the Ritual Orb of Strength, which was shaped like a small dumbbell.

Tightening his core, he pulled up and flipped, completing a double jump whilst completely altering his trajectory. As he started his descent, Joe reached to the side and plucked his orbs out of the air as though pulling an apple from a tree. Twisting to the side, he whipped the orb downward, catching another of his orbs mid-spin as he mentally pulled it into range, completing his movement by throwing another then two more before bracing for impact.

Each of the spheres slammed into the ground, digging several feet into the soft surface as Mir sidestepped so smoothly that it looked like Joe had missed him on purpose. Knowing his mentor hadn't told him to stop, Joe simply relinquished control of the buried orbs, pulling others off his belt and throwing them in sweeping, snapping, or curving strikes. One aimed for the Sage's knee, another spun up and drilled down, while a third looked to be rolling across the ground before bouncing off a rock and zipping at his head.

A pivot, a lean, and a tilt of the head had each of the failed attacks sailing away from the Sage uselessly. Joe was inches from the Sage at this point, fist coming up in a brutal uppercut, having used the orbs entirely as a distraction-

-only for Mir to poke him in the stomach like the Pillsbury Doughboy and send him rocketing away, bent so far over from the sheer force of the strike that his fingertips and toes were touching. When he finally hit the ground, Joe felt his tailbone crack. The landscape was destroyed until friction finally asserted itself and pulled him to a stop.

"I've seen enough." Mir's words brought a swift sense of relief to Joe, though as he painfully pulled himself to his feet, he grimaced at the thick sludge of mud that had mingled with the blood staining his robes. "Minor improvement in your physicality, but a major reduction in your magical capabilities. Nothing worth rewarding, and therefore I'm going to hold onto what I brought with me. Now, that aside, why don't you find me some tea and get me caught up on what happened to you? Guess I'm ready for that sob story."

Joe started limping along, planning to return to the stone table behind the privacy curtain where he'd enjoyed a conversation with a Grandmaster Wolfman only a few hours previously. By the third step, he was instead reaching into his spatial codpiece and pulling out two chairs he had taken to carrying around ever since he'd found himself wanting to match the comfort of Poppy's couch back on Midgard during conversations.

"Coffee okay?" At Mir's reluctant nod, a spare Ebonsteel mug appeared in Joe's hand, which Mate gladly filled for the Sage. The Ritualist began speaking, telling the tale of the immense difficulties he'd been struggling through since their last meeting.

The entire time he was speaking with the Sage, the Ritualists who'd been training on the field continued their drills and fights, far past the time where they should've finished and moved on to other things. Joe didn't blame them for surreptitiously sneaking glances and murmuring to each other, wondering who the stranger was who could show up, slap their Class Trainer around, only to end the visit with casual conversation and drinks. After the first ten minutes, it got a *tish* unnecessary, as a few of them pretended to stretch, going so far as to do lunges across the field to get close enough to hear the conversation.

"-and that about sums it up." Joe finished his tale of woes with a grimace. "Went down to Midgard to do some training, got caught up in the excitement of finally being way stronger than the enemies around me, only to stroll face-first into a massive conspiracy against me. Got a few benefits, upgraded my Guild into a Sect, then got my insides shredded by Tatum. I've been here ever since, trying to fix that."

"Should've just pressed on and gotten to the seventh Characteristic threshold," Mir immediately replied, shaking his head at the Ritualist. "Wouldn't have done you any harm to train like a Warrior for a while. Sitting in a bunch of rooms and meditating is such a... *Mage* response to a setback like this."

"A year of no one telling me that would've fixed this, then I hear it twice in one day." Joe shook his head in frustration at the Elementalist, who raised an eyebrow in interest. "I suppose *perhaps* other people were trying to get at that as well, but they just kept asking me if I'd managed to breach the *sixth* threshold yet. It would've been nice if they'd have explained themselves more clearly."

"Interesting," Mir stated consideringly as he leaned back on the chair and contemplated the last dregs of coffee in his mug. "Now you're looking to head out and fight in the wild again, which would've been my suggestion anyway. Any other short-term plans? I'd ask about how you're thinking of attaining a Mythic Core for Pete, but clearly that's on hold for at least the... medium term?"

"Actually, I might have a lead on that." Joe shook his head to stave off the inevitable follow-up question, his voice lowering in expectation. "Before that, I was thinking of heading back down to Midgard and trying to figure out how to have a Characteristic shift. Only Strength, Dexterity, and Luck haven't gained a modifier yet, and I feel like that might hold the key to breaching the sixth threshold."

As he spoke, he carefully studied the Sage's face, but it may as well have been carved from stone for all of the reaction he got for that piece of information. Mir merely mirrored his murmur. "How *exciting* for you. Still, I can't imagine that punching down at weak monsters would be enough to earn you anything very impressive."

"Maybe, maybe not." Joe slumped ever so slightly at the casual confirmation that no one was going to help him solve this particular problem. "I have an ongoing quest back there that's actually at my level, and I've already completed half of it."

"A level thirty quest on *Midgard*?" Mirascible's expression turned thunderous. "What quagmire have you found yourself floundering through back on such a weak world that it would give you a quest beyond the bounds of the Mortal Limit?"

"In fact, I've had this quest for a *very* long time." Joe settled into position with a bit more confidence, pleased that he'd finally brought something up which had sharpened the Sage's focus on him. "It all started when I captured a place of power, just after I destroyed a cult and fought off an endlessly respawning monster. No big deal. A Tuesday, really. Well, the system seemed to like that, so it gave me a quest called 'The Other Three'. All I have to do is find the other places of power and clear them out. Since there's only two to go, I figured I could use those as a whetstone for pushing my Characteristics where I need them to go."

"That's..." The word hung in the air for a long moment, and the Ritualist prepared himself for a nod of approval, or perhaps some advice on how he should tackle the issue. "Are you just a *glutton* for exile, or what? Is there *nothing* on Midgard you want to see for the next few years that you're fine with just-"

"Whoa, hey, hold on," Joe sputtered as the Sage grasped the arms of his chair and began standing up, shaking his head the entire time. "What're you even talking about? Why would finishing the quest get me exiled?"

"Isn't it obvious? Even if you managed to somehow find and cleanse the other locations, how would you propose dealing with the World Boss without the vast majority of your combat capabilities?"

The Ritualist frowned at the Sage. "The first part of that made sense, but then the second half completely went off the rails. What's a World Boss have to do with any of this?"

"Midgard is far too weak to have a *standard* World Boss roaming around it." Mir spoke with carefully chosen words, calming slightly as he studied Joe's face and saw only blank incomprehension. "No one could handle a rampaging Mythic monster down there, not without plenty of preparation and warning. You'd have to figure out how to get around the world's restrictions on potent spells and abilities, else you'd be forced to rely on the rulers of Ardania to step in and put down the threat themselves. You'd leave the entire planet twisted and warped and have absolutely nothing to show for it. Wouldn't you agree that would perhaps leave them somewhat sour toward you?"

"You're saying that has something to do with my quest?" Before Mir was forced to explain, Joe put the pieces together himself, smacking himself in the forehead as it clicked. "Abyss... if it couldn't be a *roaming* World Boss, that would mean there'd have to be some sort of conditional release if we wanted to get access to it. Something like proving we could handle high level, deadly dangerous monsters and threats. Let me guess, it'll only get summoned if one person or group has control of all of the locations at the same time?"

"That should be-"

Any other words Mir might've been saying were drowned out by a calamitous alert from the system as Joe's quest updated, sparkles and phenomena covering his vision as the sound of horns and drums filled his ears.

Quest updated: The Other Three → Germinate the Cutting.

Germinate the Cutting (Difficulty: Raid). You have captured two Places of Power in the Forest of Chlorophyll Chaos. Only two remain. Capturing any of them can give interesting benefits, and binding all four will germinate a force which has slumbered for centuries. One that may have been lost to time for a reason. Places of power captured: 2/4.

Reward: 1) Variable, depending on location. 2) Immediate access to The Cutting. (Major Raid). Recommended group level: 30+.

Failure: None.

"Hold on, I just got a quest update and the difficulty suddenly ramped up." Joe focused on the prompt, sharing it across to the Class Sage. "The recommended level just jumped to thirty *plus*, but that doesn't even make sense, as we're going to have to wear limiter gear anyway."

"It's a major raid," Mir scoffed at Joe, a sour expression on his face. "You're going to need multiple Guilds, or—I suppose—

your entire Sect, if you're thinking about actually going about and completing this quest. If among all of you there's not a single method of allowing you to bring outsized strength to bear, don't—wait, let me say this more clearly… do. *Not*. Finish. This quest."

"I have a few other things I was thinking about doing, but that was definitely going to be my priority." The Ritualist grumbled as he shifted the quest out of his line of vision. "Well… I guess it's a good thing you came around when you did. That was pretty-"

Congratulations! You have had a fortuitous change in the way you interact with the world, and the Characteristic 'Luck' has become 'Red Luck'. People have come and gone in your life, but each of them has played a small part in bringing you closer to those who would categorically shift the balance of power in the world or your personal fortunes.

Your Luck has become more closely aligned with external entities. When you are actively pursuing the completion of a quest, you may find yourself presented with a red line tying you to people important to the outcome of your pursuit… if you're lucky enough to have the means to view it.

Stay alert, as not every entity you find yourself tied to may have your best interest in mind.

Even before he could explain why he'd zoned out of their conversation once again, Joe felt a slight tingle in his eyes, the telltale mark of his Karmic Perception at play, and felt his jaw go slack as a bright red line suddenly extended from Mir, only to vanish halfway to himself as the end tying them together vanished when it came within range of his Karmic Shroud.

"Abyss!" Mir swatted at the line, his hand passing through it harmlessly. But the thread was already fading, blowing apart like dust caught in a strong breeze now that the Sage had passed on his wisdom about the quest and would apparently no longer have an effect on it. "What was that? What did you just do?"

"I… had a Characteristic shift." Joe chuckled in disbelief, even as Mir subtly edged toward him.

"You could *see* that thread, then? Thought it was a worm for a moment. Looked like a nasty little parasite from, uh… hold on. In other words, you already have at *least* two Characteristics aligned toward Karma? You're going to be a dangerous individual someday, Joe." The battle maniac's eyes practically sparkled as he flicked a tongue out to moisten his lips. "I can't *wait*. Quick! Tell me what else you're trying to do, so I can get you stronger."

CHAPTER SEVEN

"-Then they asked me to figure out how to track down the World Boss and get them there." Joe finished his explanation somewhat lamely, unable to ignore how Mir's eyes had glazed over. "It seems like something I could figure out, I just don't know if I should."

A long moment of silence stretched, and the Sage finally blinked, clarity returning to his eyes as he refocused on the Ritualist. "Abyss. *That's* the sort of thing you agonize over? Large-scale... crafting? Here I thought you were... never mind. Look, there's a pretty simple solution to all of this. Do you want the quest, or do you want someone else to have it and maybe get the reward? Lots of use to be had out of a Mythic Core."

"Right, but what would that do to the balance of power on Vanaheim?" Joe bit his lip, frustrated that he knew so little about the internal struggles on the next world. "Am I going to cause major problems by helping this group out, maybe even accidentally aligning myself or the Ritualist Tower to the wrong group? Will setting this up and allowing this group to have free access to the World Boss make it harder for me to get them in the future if I need them?"

"Oh, for-!" Mir was abruptly on his feet and looked to be holding himself back from simply walking away, even if only just barely. "Who *cares*? *That's* the real question. Why would you care about the balance of political power among a world you don't know anything about? They've been stagnant for centuries. Anything that breaks the deadlock one way or another can only be *good*. At least they'll be forced to make a choice, blast them!"

"Well, why don't you step in and push the issue?" Joe responded defensively, though he fully understood that he was speaking to a man who only wanted a good fight, not a battle of wits among bureaucrats. "Pretty sure a Class Sage taking a stand or intervening would move things along pretty quick."

"Look, I've been reading up on how you Travelers have been doing warfare before you came in here, so I will speak in terms you might understand a little better." Mir lifted a palm above his head, and a brilliant glow of intense fire appeared on his hand. In the next instant, it elongated and widened out into a stream of fire, and the air began swirling intensely as it transformed into a massive cyclone of flames.

Dark clouds began crawling across the sky as loose dirt and stone was swept upward, adding to the mix and quickly shifting the composition of the creation. Then, just as suddenly as he had created the devastating display of his elemental powers, Mir made it all vanish with a simple clenching of his fist.

When he spoke again, the Sage's words were surprisingly bitter. "You don't drop a nuke on people who are trying to solve things with diplomacy and negotiation. If I were to go in and start making demands, every other Class Sage on the planet would suddenly start making an appearance. All of a sudden, we'd have the same problem the current group is facing, except now all of my peers would be forced to sit in on the meetings and debate our own points. It's the same reason I can't just start running around this planet and collect the Mythic Core for Pete on my own—too many competing interests at work to make that a valid option."

"Not to mention it would cheapen the experience of actually getting one, right?" Joe offered in a placating tone, shifting in place with intense discomfort now that his robes had suddenly been dried by the intense heat wave. They weren't fitting correctly, being too stiff and crunchy with dried blood and mud to hang loosely across his body.

"Yeah, I don't care about that." Mir spat to the side derisively. "But if I go out there hunting World Bosses, the others would do the same, only to most likely toss the cores they collect in a vault somewhere. Just like that, no more people reach the Sage rank, which means the only people who can give me a good fight are already at my level. Nothing new to improve myself on, no powers I haven't already bested."

The powerful man swept his gaze over Joe one last time, the expression turning dismissive. "I'm going to head over to the other side of the planet and find something that can take a punch. Last thing I'm going to say is: don't worry about not getting more of the Mythic Cores if you need 'em in the future. It's not like they're growing on the side of the road and you can just reach over and pluck 'em whenever you need a little refresher. You're going to need a massive number of people, a level of power you don't even have access to currently, or figure out a way to barter for something that's absolutely priceless. A quest like this? I'd say go ahead and figure out if the terms they offered you are the best you can get. Now, unless you want to fight me for real, I'm going to go do some exploring."

There was a soft *thwoom*, and the Sage vanished without waiting for a response.

Joe remained where he was for a few moments, turning over the man's words. "Hmm... loopholes and bartering... you know, why *should* I get paid only once when I'm providing them a service they can use forever? Yeah... they also didn't ever say anything about me going out and hunting the World Boss on my own after I figure out a way to reliably find it. Maybe this is just work I would've eventually done anyway, but if that's the case, why not get paid for it?"

A sudden swell of noise caught his attention, pulling him out of his reverie—it was for the best, as he hadn't realized he was grinning like a maniac and rubbing his hands together and chuckling. Joe looked over to a group of Journeyman Ritualists who'd been sparring with each other, a frown twisting his lips as he noted with immense displeasure that a duo was on the ground beating on each other as they screamed furious words.

One of them was glowing a soft red and the other a soft green. The red-glowing man was straddling the other, fists coming down like pistons as he rained blows on his opponent.

Crack!

The man went tumbling across the ground as Joe appeared next to him, a clean slap to the chest sending the infuriated fighter off of the bleeding man. "What's wrong with you? Combat was decided; that means you *stop*! You want to fight to the death, get off my training field and go hunt Penguins."

"He didn't beat me with rituals! He's *never* been able to beat me!" Already the red glow was fading from the trainee Joe had slapped away, but he was on his feet and defiantly glaring as he raged. "Now, all of a sudden, just before he's about to lose *again*, an arrow comes out of nowhere, and I lose after not having taken a single hit the whole match!"

"We're... *supposed* to integrate our combat styles into the fight," came a groaning reply as the apparent victor of the match began peeling himself off the ground. "I shot that arrow at the start of our fight, practically straight up. Losing was your own blasted fault for not moving from that spot the entire time. Of course it feels like it came out of nowhere; you *never* look up!"

"Did you not see me face-tanking Devoe's fists earlier?" Joe chimed in on the side of the Archer-turned-Ritualist. "What do you think the whole point of that was? Mobility is key. Feces, half of our combat manual is designated to taking mobility *away* from our opponents."

"Some of us didn't come here from combat classes," the poor loser stated stiffly, chin thrust out as he looked between the two people trying to argue with him. "What am I supposed to do, crochet him a shirt with no arm holes and force him to wear it mid-fight? The only fighting skills I have come from being a Ritualist, and that's what we're supposed to be training as!"

"*I'm* a pure Ritualist," Joe countered with a single hand up-raised, as if to remind them that he did indeed exist. "Everything I can do comes from practice and usage of my class. Make no mistake, my *base* class is Ritualist. I couldn't even make a shirt, so you'd already have the advantage over me if I were training with you. Why don't you figure out how to use that? Weave a net or something and wrap people up, for all I care, just be creative. Both of you are getting a time out. You-"

Pointing at the suddenly unsure Ritualist, Joe shifted his hand and pointed into the distance. "Get over to the Ritual of Forced Pacifism until you cool down. I don't know what came over you, but to me it looked like you gained some kind of Berserker skill. If you find you can't control it, we'll do it for you."

"Hey... come on, that's-" Now somewhat despondent, the man lifted his hands and took a step away from Joe, "I don't need to do that; I heard you already!"

"You need to get a handle on that new skill if it really is what I think it is." Joe stared the man down until he saw the fight go out of him. "There can't be any hostile actions from within or outside that designated area. Every action taken will be evaluated by intent, and if your mind is clouded by rage, at least your poor choices under a haze of rage will be quashed."

"Yeah... but the effect lingers for *hours* after you step out of it-"

Joe shook his head stiffly and responded in a cool tone. "Shouldn't be an issue; I think your training has come to an end for a while. As for *you*..."

As the major offender turned and walked away with a heavy tread, Joe nodded with appreciation at the Ritualist-Archer. "Great work. You got new information and adjusted almost instantly. That's going to be essential to your class as you progress further."

"I'm always ready to go in another direction. Probably why Dexterity is my highest stat." An arrow appeared in his hand, and he twirled it around his fingers, spinning it behind his back to his other hand before letting go of it and having it sink into a hidden quiver strapped to his back.

"Fun." Joe gestured in the other direction. "I think you earned a reward; why don't you go over to my house and use the sauna? I've got a Ritual of S-tea-mina going in there. Spend an hour in there, and you'll have half a day of boosted Stamina regeneration. It's not much, but it should let you push a little harder, if you want."

"Ehh…"

Joe frowned as his offer was met with hesitancy and a strange spark of discomfort in the man's expression. Looking around, he saw a handful of people waving to catch the Archer's attention and shaking their heads. "Don't suppose I could take a rain check or maybe a pass to let someone else in to take my place?"

"What's all that about?" Crossing his arms, Joe patiently waited for an answer, not giving the highly dextrous individual a chance to dodge his question. "It's a good buff! Lasts a long time, and it follows you around."

"Yeah, it's just that… it works by dousing you in hot tea constantly. Everyone that's come out of there has been damp and slightly burnt-"

Joe threw his arms up, "It's a good buff! What else are you going to use that stuff for? *Drinking*? Beyond the Stamina boost, think of the other health benefits! Plus, the one thing I'll give to tea is that it smells pretty good. Practically *nothing* smells good on this planet."

"Finally we know the real reason he made that ritual. He's trying to infuse us all with herbal scents." Though he whipped around immediately, Joe wasn't able to see who it was who'd spoken.

Rolling his eyes, he decided he'd done everything he was required to and started marching away, muttering darkly about his desperate need to figure out how to recast Neutrality Aura. "Stinky people. Why are they all perfectly content wearing filthy clothes and not bothering to wipe the dirt off themselves after they've been rolling around on the ground for hours at a time? Yet, suddenly *I'm* the strange one for trying to help them out?"

"*You!*" Joe spun around, pointing at the nearest person, who froze like a deer in the headlights. "Go find the expedition group from Vanaheim and let them know I'm going to take them up on their quest, but we need to discuss the specific terms first. Get them to my house within the hour, and I'll sit down with you for an hour or two and help you with any problems you're having in your Core Skills."

"Really?" Immediately the man's countenance shifted, and he spun on his heel and sprinted away.

"Hey! Why can't I have *that* reward instead of the tea steam…" the Archer Ritualist trailed off and coughed into his fist as Joe outright ignored him and stomped toward his house in the distance.

As he got closer, the Reductionist was reminded of the fact that his door had been obliterated, thanks to watching the wind carrying grass clippings and the like through the open hole in the side of his house. Trying to ignore the sad sight for the moment, he entered the space and glanced around.

After taking one look at the detritus all over the floors, such as his notes that had been turned into confetti, cheerfully chirping bugs that had invaded his property, and all manner of things blown in by the wind, he grabbed his table and hauled it outside, setting up a seating area in the shade.

He'd barely finished setting out parchment and quills for a large group when Grandmaster Fari prowled up to him, her anxious hope only noticeable due to the way her head dipped ever so slightly downward. Jaxon's teachings about Wolfman mannerisms came into play unexpectedly, worlds away from where he had first learned them. "You sent a runner for me; that was unexpectedly swift deliberations on your part. Hopefully you have not mistaken my desire to succeed for abject desperation and hope to take advantage of that fact? Many have died for less."

Responding with a smile that was only slightly forced, Joe gestured at a large, stone bench. "Please make yourself comfortable. I don't have any chairs for someone of your height, and something tells me you'd prefer unyielding stone, either way."

"It wasn't my imagination, then. You *have* had interactions with The People, more than testing your might against theirs. Not many know of our unwavering commitment to training our bodies at all times." Fari perched on the edge of the bench, in what Joe could only think of as the most uncomfortable possible position. "Go on then."

"First, I'd like to see what you're offering, so I can have a better understanding of what your needs are and what needs to change." Joe parried the opening round of negotiation, wanting her to set an anchor point. "The official offer, as it were."

"Hmph." Though she obviously understood his intentions were more self-serving than he let on, Fari narrowed her eyes at the human, and a moment later, a notification appeared.

Quest offered: World (Boss) Sa-Fari. The Stormbinder's Tower of Vanaheim is seeking a method of reliably tracking the untrackable, finding a pebble in a mountain range. It is said that the Jötunn moves with glacial speed, altering the world as a whole by his very presence. Yet, finding and getting within striking distance of the World Boss has proven to hold a difficulty beyond unreasonable. To that end, you have been asked by Grandmaster Fari to create a reliable method of locating and tracking the entity.

Main objective: Create a permanent method of pinpointing the location of the Jötunn. Reward: 1) You will be given the first Mythic Core to be harvested from the World Boss if this method is used to find the Jötunn. 2) Additional rewards based on the reliability of the method as well as its level of permanence.

Secondary objective (Optional): Offer transport to the location of the

World Boss once it has been found and each time it respawns. Reward: Variable, based on distance travelled.

"I suppose that's something *other* people might accept right away," Joe muttered as his eyes scanned the radiant lettering, which he just now realized was common across both of his quests involving a World Boss.

"Why only other people?" The Grandmaster replied with a literal growl, her hackles raising as she drank in Joe's dismissive stance. "A Mythic Core is appropriate for the scale of this task."

Joe began listing off the problems he could see at a glance. "While the Mythic Core is certainly greed-inducing, you're asking for a tracking method with perpetual, potentially unlimited usage, with only a single payment. Who knows how much upkeep that'd require over the years? At what point am I stuck here maintaining it when I should, by all rights, be conquering Asgard or something? Next, each of the other rewards is completely arbitrary. 'Additional rewards' *as* the reward? Variable rewards based on distance traveled?"

Giving the Grandmaster a frank look, Joe firmly shook his head. "Just thinking for *your* benefit at this point. What would stop me from routing you around the planet ten times just to drop you off fifty miles away from here? Then I could claim entirely outsized rewards? Is that appropriate? Then there's no mention of bringing you back. Does that count toward the travel distance as well, or should I plan to leave you stranded with no easy way to return?"

"You've made your point, now respond with an offer." Fari tapped on the table, completely ignoring the quill and parchment Joe had set out for her to take notes on.

"The way I see it is: you're looking for someone to build world-spanning infrastructure. That means immense materials, upkeep, calibration, and all sorts of other fuzzy logistical issues which elude me at this time. Beyond the sheer size of the planet, figuring out a way to traverse oceans to different continents is going to be a massive hassle on its own." Joe let his words linger for just a heartbeat, knowing she was likely already frustrated with how slow he was speaking and moving, what with the massive difference in Characteristics they were sure to have between them.

"The Mythic Core is a great start, and I absolutely want the first one harvested. After that, I want every *tenth* core harvested-"

"This has been a fun conversation, but I have plans to meet with people who don't want to waste my time."

"Hold on, I'm not done." Joe moved on to his next point, refusing to allow his momentum to be broken. "I'm also certain that, if I figure out how to *find* the World Boss, I'll be able to drop you right next to it. For that service, I don't want my reward to be an afterthought, 'additional', or 'variable'. I want a *percentage*. A twentieth of all Mythic material harvested. On the plus side, I only care about total weight. I don't care if it's skin, tongue, or toenail, so long as it's Mythic, I'm fine with that being my cut."

"Too high. All of it is too high. The expedition logistics alone, payroll for the combatants, danger pay, not to mention the materials invested in the actual attack on the World Boss— which has no guarantee of success in the first place!" She remained in a half-standing position. "What you are demanding would bankrupt not just my expedition, but my tower as a whole."

"I'm not *demanding* anything," Joe reminded her bluntly, letting his annoyance at her lack of negotiation skill shine through for a heartbeat before reigning himself in. "From where I stand, I'm just planning to make a massive, planetary-spanning, constantly searching and updating system so *you* can go on a hunt. You just have to show up and kill it. My job sounds a whole lot harder than yours, so all I'm asking for is fair compensation if you use my services."

Fari studied him for a dangerous moment, then barked, "One one-*hundreth* of the harvested Mythic material, as well as increasing percentages for each lower-rarity tier. Every *fiftieth* Mythic Core to you, and all of this *only* if we are using your service and not someone else's."

"If you use any part of my transportation, it gets considered as using my service, and I get rewarded as such," Joe firmly countered, unwilling to budge on this point. "If you want me to tell you where it is, then let you spend months getting there instead of arriving within the hour, I suppose that's your prerogative. But getting you near it necessitates knowing where it is and triangulating the location to get you there."

"Fine-"

"Hold on, I'm not done negotiating. I want one-fiftieth of the Mythic material and every twenty-fifth Mythic Core harvested, not including the first one." Joe wrote his thoughts out on his own parchment, leaving the page glistening with wet ink. "Furthermore, if I manage to do this, I'll guarantee the method is available exclusively to only you and me. After I get the first core, I will further ensure that it remains viable for you. After you get the second Mythic Core, to do with as you wish, either of us will be able to back out of this deal at any time."

"I suppose that makes sense, as neither of us wants to... how did you put it? Be trapped on this world working when we could be conquering the gods?" the Grandmaster all but sneered as she inclined her head in agreement, "These terms are acceptable, so long as any Mythic Core we hand you is used within forty-eight hours of us handing it over to you. Also, you must agree to not give the core to anyone from Vanaheim. Our goal is to raise Sages within our own faction, so we cannot have you hoarding them and making it impossible for the World Boss to come back and be hunted once more."

"Only the *first* Mythic Core you give me, and we have a deal." When she didn't respond, Joe raised an eyebrow in delicate annoyance. "By the time I get a second one, you'll have used twenty-four of them. If I can't help out my own tower with my own profits by then, what's the point of me getting more of them?"

"I suppose." Slowly, she extended her massive paw of a hand. "Besides, who knows how long all of this will take? You're probably looking at one core for yourself every seven to ten years, so why wouldn't I agree?"

"As long as your team gets out there and fights every time I find it, I think we can do a little better than that." Joe's broad grin almost convinced the Grandmaster to try her hand at renegotiating, but instead she swallowed her doubts and shook his hand—all while the Ritualist accepted the final version of the quest that popped up in his vision.

Quest offered: World (Boss) Sa-Fari. The Stormbinder's Tower of Vanaheim is seeking a method of reliably tracking the untrackable, finding a pebble in a mountain range. It is said that the Jötunn moves with glacial speed, altering the world as a whole by his very presence. Yet, finding and getting within striking distance of the World Boss has proven to hold a difficulty beyond unreasonable. To that end, you have been asked by Grandmaster Fari to create a reliable method of locating and tracking the entity.

Main objective: Create a permanent method of pinpointing the location of the Jötunn. Reward: 1) You will be given the first Mythic Core to be harvested from the World Boss if this method is used to find the Jötunn. 2) You will receive each 25th Mythic Core successfully harvested from the World Boss if and only if your tracking or transportation method are used.

Secondary objective (Optional): Offer transport to the location of the World Boss once it has been found and each time it respawns. Reward: 1/50th of all Mythic-grade materials (by weight) harvested from the World Boss if your transportation system is used.

Clause 1) If the first Mythic Core has been delivered successfully, the tracking and transport system must be maintained and operational until a second Mythic Core is successfully harvested by Fari or her subordinate. Upon successful harvesting, either party can terminate the quest upon final delivery of rewards with no further obligations.

Clause 2) The first Mythic Core delivered to Joe must be used within 48 hours of delivery and cannot be given, traded, or sold to any individual or organization with political power on Vanaheim.

Clause 3) The tracking and transportation method, when used to find and get close to the World Boss will be exclusive to Fari of the Storm-

binder's Tower and the raid group she leads, with the only exception being Joe and a group he leads.

Failure: *No penalties apply to either side if a viable method is unable to be established.*

Quest accepted.

CHAPTER EIGHT

"Jake, I know you're in there!" Joe reached out and pounded on the door of the Pyramid of Panacea, his fists barely making the softest of sounds as he put his full strength behind each strike. "Was three months not enough time to do whatever you wanted in there? I've got to get moving on some projects, and I need your help!"

Still there was only silence, except for the soft clinking of the massive chains extending from the obelisks surrounding the inverted pyramid—so large, and with so much weight pulling on them that Joe would've thought they'd be as stable as Ebonsteel bars instead of able to sway with the unnatural wind that had sprung up. "Come on, door! I built you. Be a pal and let me in?"

Joe felt a tingle run along his spine as the weight of the structure's burgeoning intelligence regarded him for a few long moments, then a frown tugged at his lips as he was just as easily dismissed. There was no magical seal springing up in front of him, nothing blocking him from attempting to enter, yet there was still no acknowledgment of his presence, and no doorknob had appeared to let him try his luck. "Look... I don't want to have to do this, but if I need to pull out the fact that I'm still owed training based on quests completed, and escalate this through the *system-*"

The long, marble walkway he stood on began to emit a soft **hum**, only audible thanks to the immense amount of power suddenly running through it, combined with his Magical Synesthesia. So, when frost began creeping along the soles of his shoes and up toward his ankles, he wasn't caught unaware, though the defensive reaction still surprised him.

"Enough of that." The monotone voice in front of him was pitched just above a whisper, yet Joe froze in place under the disgruntled scrutiny of the Alchemist who'd suddenly appeared in the doorway. It took a few moments before the Ritualist even realized he had no idea where the door had gone. At the Alchemist's command, the frost impacting Joe vanished as if it had never been there, then Jake's eyes flicked up to regard his somewhat-hostile guest.

"You should know better than most that there's no reason to get the system involved in our dealings. I don't take kindly to threats, and it's not my fault you are interrupting me at a time when I am *decidedly* busy." Jake stood in front of Joe, his arms folded, black and purple robes glittering under a light dusting of powder. His dark eyes inspected his erstwhile apprentice, yet he betrayed no hint of his thoughts on the entirely too youthful, perfectly still and neutral face.

The soft breeze brought the pungent aroma of powerful herbs, carefully harvested monster remains, and oddly metallic fumes into Joe's nose, causing him to sneeze harshly. "Always a pleasure to see you! Not sure how I'm supposed to know if you're busy or not-"

"Hundreds of people are employed as messengers and couriers; just because we are on a new world does not mean the standard decorum for visiting people has been left behind." One of Jake's eyebrows twitched at Joe's stricken expression. "Have you really *never* thought about sending advance notice before you go somewhere? That's basic job security for a large number of people doing fetch quests, Joe. Also, polite. Especially when interrupting a… *Master* who might be working with extremely volatile compounds."

"Master. *Sure.* You're at *least* a peak Grandmaster, and we both know it." The sheer disbelief rolling through him pulled Joe from abashed discomfort, though Jake didn't respond with anything other than a slight tightening of his lips. "Listen, I have a secondary reason for coming here other than training, and… I'm not sure how to make this happen, but I need your help on a very personal project."

"Can we speak inside? I wasn't being facetious when I mentioned volatile compounds, and I'd rather be able to monitor the Ichor I'm working on in person." Jake stepped into the building, needing to reach out and physically grasp the door as it tried to shut automatically. "Stop that, he's a welcome guest. Just because he's only working on a single path of alchemy does not mean we should exclude him… entirely."

Joe quickly stepped into the building, rather impressed with the establishment's ability to think for itself, though it was still rather young by the standards of Enchanted objects. "The pyramid is becoming ever more impressive, Jake. I assume you've some hand in how it's been developing more quickly? I'd love to learn more about that, if you're willing to share."

"Simply a matter of giving a young mind plenty of things to learn and all the resources it needs in order to grow well." Jake breezed past the question with a non-answer, turning on his heel and quickly making his way deeper into the building. Joe did his best to stand directly to the side of the Alchemist but found himself almost troubled by the immense amount of change he saw within the pyramid itself.

While the mana outside had been mostly pacified by his rituals, the dense layer of power inside its walls was frigid, searing, and oppressive in turn. In short, the fluctuating energy was wildly unstable. Though this was already concerning enough, it was actually the *visuals* of the pyramid that had captured all of the Ritualist's attention: the walls no longer gleamed with the molten luster of flowing magma, as they had back on Alfen-heim. Instead, they'd shifted to become faceted, crystalline with frost-like patterns growing over the obsidian the initial influx of molten stone had formed as it cooled.

"Is this area... larger than it used to be?" Joe muttered as he realized what was throwing him off the most. "I haven't seen spatially expanded areas in a while-"

"Exposure to Jotunheim has been having a fantastic effect on the pyramid. It's adapting, as was always the intention." The barest hint of warmth colored Jake's voice as he swiftly marched through hallways that seemed to stretch just a *bit* longer than they should. "The sheer amount of power feeding into the framework, the seemingly endless variety of materials and components flowing in and being worked upon each day? All of it is viewed by the pyramid, giving it a greater understanding of what it is capable of."

The floor *crackled* underfoot, and Joe flinched away as whorls of condensed, eucalyptus-scented mist wafted into the air. Before he could ask if that was meant to be a dangerous effect to those who were uninvited, Jake began speaking on more of the changes. "As you've seen, the outer surface of the pyramid has remained almost untouched, giving passersby the calming sensation that nothing is changing and allowing them to maintain their routines without overmuch concern. If I'm correct, the marble pentagon platforms, the obsidian obelisks, and the crystalline outer surface will remain the same until the very end of the pyramid's molting process."

"Molting?" An image of a snake shedding its skin slithered through Joe's mind, followed quickly by a swift moment of concern for his missing friend, Jaxon, before returning to the subject at hand.

"Simply the best descriptor I have at the moment." Jake smoothly moved on to the next topic. "As you saw, the suspended walkway brings you to the main entrance, and currently we are moving through the 'visiting Alchemist' work rooms. I thought it would be appropriate to separate out different areas, seeing as I am certain you will consider all of your... Sect... as people who deserve entry. The antechamber area can be used for visitors, as I mentioned, or you could cordon it off for outer Sect members or hopefuls who are intending on joining you but need to prove themselves."

Jake walked into a wall of flowing steam, which was pouring from the top of the wall like a waterfall and pooling up to knee height. Joe followed right on his heels, yet when he stepped through the disorienting condensation, the Alchemist was a dozen paces ahead. "Simple defensive measures such as this will ensure that only inner Sect members or invited guests can come through to where the more important, valuable, or dangerous goods are stored. Obviously, this area is far smaller than the previous one, but... how many people deserve to be here in the first place?"

"I'm glad everything has been shifting to your liking, but are you at all concerned that the pyramid is picking up some of your bad habits and general dislike for people?" Then Joe blinked rapidly as another realization struck him. "Does this mean you're willing to allow Alchemists from the Guild—sorry, *Sect*—to come and work here?"

"Most certainly, most certainly." Jake's head bobbed in deliberate agreement. "I'm even willing to give them pointers-"

"Why would you need Mastery Merits?" Joe interjected with all the subtlety of bringing a sledgehammer down on an egg. "Again, it's clear that you're far more powerful than you let on."

"*Hahhh...*" The Alchemist let out a long sigh, pinching the bridge of his nose as his stride slowed for the first time since the start of their stroll through the structure. "Let's pretend I'm as amazing as you think I am. Even in that case, am I only allowed to achieve Mastery with my core class skills? Even you are helping others learn a physical skill. Jumping, if I have heard tell of your training grounds correctly. Do you have any idea of the absolute *plethora* of supporting skills involved in the subtle minis- trations of alchemy? Anything from selecting the herb and rare earth minerals based on compatibility, to temperature control, and even techniques for properly bottling and sealing the vials at the end of the project?"

Jake turned to lock eyes with Joe in a measured and deliberate motion. "Certainly it is true that you can only become a Sage in one particular arena, but the only thing stopping you from being a wildly accomplished *Grandmaster* in all others is lack of effort."

"Huh." This conversation ran directly counter to what he'd been learning from Mirascible, but certain facts about his Class Sage mentor started to fall into place. "Let's say someone used only their five core class skills and focused on those to the exclusion of all else. Combat-oriented type. I don't suppose you think they'd have multiple other skills-"

"Do you have any combat skills, Joe?" Jake smoothly redirected as he picked up the pace once more. "I'm certain you do. Now, are you satisfied with the base damage they deal and the malleability of them as they are, or would you want to inflate those numbers and guide them toward new and interesting variations by applying as many passive skills to them as possible? Yes, I saw Mirasable arrive. From a great distance. In case you were wondering, I will be remaining *inside* with the doors locked until that battle maniac leaves this world. Now, to answer the question you still haven't quite asked; yes, I am more than certain he has *scores* of passive skills supporting all of his core ones. For the most part, he just ignores that they exist."

"You know Mir on sight? Even being on a first-name basis and knowing his habits?" The Alchemist ignored Joe's question, though the bald man was able to put another mark in the 'Jake is way too powerful for this world and is more than he pretends to be' scoreboard he'd been keeping in his head. "Very interesting."

"I believe there was some talk about you needing a favor?" The Alchemist shifted the conversation abruptly once more, clearly unwilling to discuss his personal history. "Now, when you say that, are you asking to call in the true, *major* favor I owe you?"

Immediately, Joe was all business, his inquisitiveness buried deep within him as he remembered that he was here to fix his broken astral self. "I guess I don't know? It depends on what that really means and if I could just pay you for your service instead."

"Why don't you just explain the issue to begin with, and I will give you some options that best suit your needs?" Just like that, the Alchemist seemed to be nothing more than the calm, placid shopkeep Joe had met so long ago in Ardania. The Ritualist took a deep breath and quickly explained what he'd been working on, as Jake was well aware of the damage he had accrued the last time he'd worked with Tatum.

"-And so, since each section of the imbuement to my... *self*... needs to be at least at the Master rank, the controlling ritual by necessity has to be at the Grandmaster rank. I'm hoping I can get you to help me design and create the *Ichor* I need to make that part of all this work. Ya know, since I'd rather get this right the first time and not cause more damage." By the time he'd finished his explanation, Jake had led him into the primary chamber of the Alchemy Hall. "Is this what you used Brisingr for? 'Cause... those look *suspiciously* like veins coated in quartz."

The walls of this central area weren't marble, nor obsidian, instead being entirely composed of thin, crystalline pipes with different semi-liquids flowing through each of them. There was dark, sludge-like material Joe could only assume was leftover impurities from alchemical reactions, mana of varying purities contained and condensed within one section, but mostly dozens and dozens filled with fluids coming out of enormous distilling vats placed around the room. He took all of this in at a glance, for the most part keeping his questions to himself as he waited for Jake to absorb his story fully.

"Let me see what you've come up with so far." The Alchemist finally spoke, holding out a hand. Without hesitation, Joe dropped a small notebook into the outstretched palm, and Jake began leafing through it, his eyes widening then narrowing in what could only be termed as *disgust*. "This is hot garbage. If you injected this into yourself, it would be years of effort to clean it out. Look at this... the threading you want to do here requires a thicker ink, so it can be stretched *over* the space instead of sloshing *through* your capillaries like spilled wine. You want to make a lattice for long-term mana adhesion here, not a circle—not everything is *supposed* to be a ritual circle, even if it is created with rituals in mind."

After reaching the end of Joe's proposed diagrams, Jake directly handed the notebook back to him. "I see what you're trying to do, but you only have the baseline idea correct; the execution is entirely flawed. The redesign by *itself* will cost you your major favor. No. Stop. Before you complain, understand that you aren't just asking for an Ichor, you're asking for one that will be able to interact correctly with Artifacts from separate and distinct professions, while allowing itself to be controlled by yet *another* one. And I do mean 'allow'-"

"Because anything at that rank has at least a *little* bit of its own intelligence, I get it." Joe sighed softly as he thought of the half-dozen sets of enchanted clothing he'd burned through over the last few years. "I'm good with that. Really, I don't even know where to start if my first attempt was that bad."

"It would have worked perfectly as a method for fully removing someone's access to their own mana long-term, if you ever wanted that option on hand." Suddenly, Jake's eyes were practically glittering with excitement. "Come to think of it, there's no reason to throw that notebook away. You have enemies... I know you have enemies. Some of them come back after you if you put them down, so perhaps making an example out of a few of them would be truly beneficial. Have to crack a few eggs to make an omelet, and all that."

"Seems like the kind of thing that gets you real cursed, real fast." Joe lifted a hand to wave away the thought, but Jake leaned in and prodded him directly below his sternocleido-mastoid.

As the Ritualist choked, letting out a startled cough as his muscles reverberated, the Alchemist's lips twisted upward slightly. "You should know better than anyone at this point that curses are just incredibly *specific* blessings. They might not seem like it to you, but the fact is that they are enhancing something beyond belief. If you were to think of the issue you are having right now not as immense damage to your magical capabilities, but instead as horrendously difficult training to be completed, you might even come to realize the true benefit it is affording you. What do you think happens when you are able to use a spell you've lost without the help of the system...? Think on that, perhaps. Now, get out. I have work to do, and I am fully ready to not have a favor of this magnitude hanging over my head."

"Whoa, hold on." Joe grinned as he started pulling aspect jars out of his storage ring and setting them on a low table nearby. "I told you I was here to get help *and* do some training. I feel like I'm getting close to breaking into Mastery for Ritualistic Alchemy, and if you're only going to be designing this instead of making it for me, I need to get ready to do it myself."

Clang.

"What... monstrosity is that?" Jake stared at the bizarre metal contraption Joe had just dropped on the ground. "Who did you manage to convince to make exercise equipment look like abstract art in that way?"

"Naw, this is my alchemy cauldron! It's just upgraded since the last time you saw me." Joe leaned down and scooched the device closer to Jake, releasing a horrendous *screeching* as it dug thin furrows into the crystalline ground it was resting on. "Take a peek!"

His Infernal-touched ritual cauldron had shifted after meeting the upgrade requirements, and now the cauldron portion looked like a rose caught mid-detonation. The 'petals' were actually the nested gyroscopic rings, and though they looked like twisted slag metal, the entire contraption worked perfectly well. The coloration had shifted, taking on a violet-black luster with the majority of the color focused on the 'flower' then slowly fading until the back half of the grip bars were a black darker than night.

Abyssal Bloom Ritual Cauldron (Unique. Upgradable.)

Primary effect: allows three-dimensional reagent placement within the sealed compartment.

Secondary effect: Infernal reinforcement has bloomed into an Infernal funnel, reducing risk of pill explosion by 19% and allowing the user to convert up to 30% of the raw material cost of failed alchemical products back to their base material.

Tertiary effect: Infernal purification. By paying 1% of the total mana and material cost of the previously created alchemical item, you may instantly purge all contaminants, residue, and imperfections from the interior of the cauldron. Using the tertiary effect will engulf the cauldron in flames, rendering it unusable for 5 minutes while it uses the heat to self-repair and reset to optimal condition.

Quaternary effect: Infernal roots. Much like how deep growth plants can be lost in a fire yet regrow, provided they have time and resources, the Abyssal Bloom ritual cauldron is able to remember how to reconstitute the last three successfully completed alchemical sequences. Memory can be activated to guide mana shaping, placement, and temperature flow, decreasing the difficulty of recreation by up to 50%.

Upgrade conditions: successfully create 1,000 Expert-rank alchemical products using this cauldron. After doing so, paying 100 times the material and mana of the cauldron's most recent upgrade cost, as well as sacrificing one Master-rank core, will allow you to bring it up to the Artifact rank.

721/1,000 products made. 0% material and mana cost imbued. 0/1 Master-rank core sacrificed.

"That's quite... something." Jake poked it a few times, looking it over back and forth, even flipping it several times before setting it down and sharply nodding. "Got it. I perfectly understand how to use this now. You want training? Good... I hope you're prepared to put in some serious work, as you've truly irritated me slightly today. First lesson of the day-"

He tossed a small bag to Joe, who caught it without thinking, only for the sachet to pop like a water balloon and scatter powder across his hands. A flare of burning, itching heat raced up his arms, far beyond where the powder had actually landed.

"-Never catch something you can't identify at a glance. Good, now, lesson two: focusing under duress and completing your Brew even when your skin is starting to flake off. You're barely an Expert if you can't manage even *this* much, and certainly nowhere near being a Master."

CHAPTER NINE

"If I see another drop of sweat land on your cauldron, I'm going to consider this Brew a failure, no matter what the system says about it." Jake didn't *quite* hiss the words, but his threat was more than enough for Joe to subconsciously try to actively control and close pores in his skin to hold his sweat in—to no effect, as that would be a ridiculous ability to have.

The Ritualist instead grunted unintelligibly as his muscles shook from the strain of holding the multi-hundred-pound trap bar cauldron setup in the air for yet *another* hour, making this the… fifteenth hour in a row? The Abyssal Bloom was glowing with an angry red light, the gyroscopic rings having been spinning so long that the scent of heated metal was starting to overpower the potent miasma of odors filling the room.

He had passed out a couple of times, falling into a deep dreamless sleep until Jake figured he'd rested enough and had awakened him with a sprinkle of dust that had practically sent him into shock each time it was absorbed into his flesh.

"Do you even understand what alchemical silver would shift into if you contaminated it with your disgusting excretions? I know you are sweat-soaked, but are you a self-saboteur as well?

Right now, it'll allow you to have a higher mana conversion when you are pouring power into a ritual circle, but if it gets a taste for *you*, don't be surprised when your health is ripped out of your meat-sack instead!"

"You're so calm most of the time; why do you get like this when you watch me work?" Joe ground out through clenched teeth as he did his best to gently lower the cauldron contraption onto a set of tables he'd positioned around himself. He was breathing in slow, controlled gasps, and as he stepped away from the heat, a thick mist rose off of him as the near-freezing temperature of the room interacted with his overheating body. "Look, now it's not sweat, it's just *effort* rolling off of me!"

"I'd call you out for not understanding how sublimation and precipitation work, but you wouldn't have gotten this far if that were true." Jake's head shifted slightly to the side, and he once again regarded Joe's contraption with a disdainful *sniff*. "You won't get better at alchemy by overcompensating with your less than impressive physique. You could use a standard cauldron at any time; there's no reason to burden yourself like this. Besides... that thing won't serve you very well once you reach the Master rank. *If* you reach the Master rank."

"Oh, I think I'm going to get there sooner than you might think." Joe glanced slightly to the side, a swell of pride filling his chest as he saw the notification he'd gotten from the system not ten minutes prior.

Alchemical Rituals (Expert VIII → Expert IX). Congratulations! You have become a peak Expert in Alchemical Rituals! To become a Master, all you must do is attain inspiration with this skill.

*Your profession has reached a new threshold! Ritualistic Alchemist (15/20). +25% → **30**% chance to create ritual-specific alchemical items. +25% → **30**% speed of production to ritual-specific alchemical items. -50% → -**40**% to all attempts to make non-ritual-specific alchemical items. All ritual-specific reagents you create will have their elemental affinity listed and can be sacrificed to a ritual to add or negate a specific elemental effect without the remaining effects of the reagent impacting the* *ritual. You may now use* **complex elements (poison, faith, etc.)** *to enhance, balance, or negate!*

"Achieving Mastery is a bottleneck for a reason. I can tell you of hundreds of Alchemists I have trained over the years, doing my best to bring them across that boundary, only for them to find themselves needing to get comfortable at that rank for the rest of their lives." Jake's lips were pressed into a firm line as he shook his head gently.

"Please let go of my face." Joe muttered as he pushed the Alchemist's hands away from where they'd been squishing his cheeks as the man twisted it back and forth. "You were the one saying how disgusting my sweat was, then you go and dip your hands in it?"

"Foul human," Jake acknowledged in a low tone as he looked down at his own hands, clearly trying to decide if he should run off and wash them. "Bottle your Brew, then it's time for you to go. I have nothing left to teach you in the short term and an interesting project to try my hand at."

"You have *nothing* to teach me in the short term?"

"Fine! Your stirring rhythm was off, as you weren't able to maintain a steady stance, which could have been completely negated by using a standard cauldron. You overused your mana in at least three different locations, nearly causing the Brew to fail, and you lost three percent efficiency by allowing your personal cooling system to drip onto the cauldron and cause an uneven heating distribution." Jake tucked his elbows in, keeping his hands from touching anywhere on his body. "There's plenty to teach you, but these incredibly minor details won't grant you *Inspiration*. Believe me, I've tried to simply force people past this point by having them do the work perfectly every time. But being a perfect Expert is not enough to be a *Master*, and there's just no way for me to explain that *well*."

"Thanks, Jake. This has been… really beneficial." Joe slowly twisted the Abyssal Bloom, and the thick, liquid silver poured in a brilliantly shining laminar stream into the awaiting vial. Joe carefully corked the container and stored it away, then activated his favorite function on his cauldron.

It exploded in a ball of flame, Infernal fire erupting from the center of the flower, only to strike some invisible barrier and be absorbed back in, twisting and wailing as it consumed every last impurity and remnant of the potion that hadn't been taken out. "I'll be out of here in about five minutes, once this is cool enough to store."

"I'll caution you again... that tool won't be useful to you very much longer. I understand it is upgradable, but you can't trust Infernal-touched equipment like that." Jake watched the flames as they twisted and curled, their eerie purple and green light reflecting in his unblinking black eyes. "It's trying to get its hooks into you. So far, it has only shown you benefits, being easy to clean, and while somewhat difficult to manage, it leaves you with a feeling of satisfaction and a rush of endorphins from using it. My guess is that, once you've upgraded it another time, it will have severe detriments waiting for you... and you won't even care, because you've used it for so long and given it so much that your sunken cost fallacy won't allow you to abandon it, no matter how bad it becomes to use."

"I can always make a different one, I suppose." Joe glanced at his cauldron, which was now glowing white hot with heat but rapidly cooling in the frigid environment. "Still want to see what it can eventually become, though, you know?"

"That's how it gets you," Jake cautioned one last time. "I saw the upgrade prompt. I'll remind you that it didn't tell you it required an Artifact-ranked core, it told you it required the *sacrifice* of one."

"I mean, what's the difference?" Suddenly, the already sinister appearance of the cauldron had a veneer of *more* that made Joe frown.

"No idea, since I don't *use* Infernal or Abyssal equipment." Jake's irreverent answer nearly caused Joe to stumble as he stepped closer to his cauldron to store it away. "Now, like I said, go away and seek out some grand realization, and come back as a proper Master. Feel your brain explode with understanding, a cosmic slap in the mouth! *Inspiration*! Then I can explain in a way you'll *understand* how you won't be able to make any further progress until you fix the issue of not having enough mana to create even the most basic Ichor."

The Alchemist paused then, a slow smile spreading across his face. "As a matter of fact, yes… that would work quite well for me. I'm sure that, after I create the design you need for the Ichor you plan to desecrate your body with, you'll want someone who can actually make it. How wonderful would it be for our situation to be reversed, me paying off a major favor, and you owing me one almost immediately afterward? I can think of many things I could request for my assistance."

"No need to be mysterious, Jake," Joe admonished him with an aggrieved sigh. "Can you just tell me what you want most off that list now, so I can start searching for it?"

"I want you to upgrade the pyramid to a true Legendary status, instead of the pseudo-Legendary state it finds itself in currently," Jake replied without hesitation, obviously having planned this exact request in advance. "Truly, you wouldn't even need to do much to make it happen-"

"You want me to repay a Master-rank creation with a *Grandmaster*-rank one?" Joe calmed down immediately as he settled into the comfortable realization of needing to barter for what he wanted. "That seems like a good way for you to find yourself in debt to me once again. How strange, Jake! I thought you were excited about not owing me favors anymore. But, if that's what you really want…"

Jake sniffed delicately, turning to look at the softly pulsing veins frozen to the walls. "It's not *quite* the same, though, is it? My work will require effort, and yours a simple agreement. All you need to do is allow me to permanently apply the Mythic Core already in this pyramid, allowing it to be absorbed fully instead of treated as an accessory. Then the pyramid will be able to slowly upgrade itself over the course of a few months.

The sheer abundance of energy in a Mythic Core will compensate for any resources it is lacking."

Pausing for a moment, the Ritualist surprised himself by actually considering the request. The fact of the matter was, he had gained the Mythic Core entirely by accident, a loophole of the system killing the Alfenheim World Boss on a technicality. He hadn't really done any work to get it in the first place, beyond being there to catch the core when the system practically dropped it in his pocket. *"Maybe. If I don't have another use for it, then... I will think about this, but come up with a couple other payment plans in case this one doesn't work out."*

"Every other option will require *far* more effort on your part," Jake practically whispered, turning the simple statement into a dark threat. "*If* I accept the commission in the first place. I've told you what I want and what will guarantee me producing this for you. Yes... think on it. That's a *good* plan."

As Joe made his way out of the Pyramid of Panacea—this time without an escort, which allowed the building to freeze his shoes to the floor every few steps without getting reprimanded—he found himself decidedly out of sorts. Something about the interaction was niggling at him, causing his lips to twist into a frown at regular intervals. "Even as a Master, I won't be able to make whatever he thinks is necessary, huh?"

"It's not even just that I can't do it *yet*. If what he said was correct, I'll need a lot more mana to make it, but I need it done so that I can fix my mana in the first place." Joe straightened his back and took a deep breath, not even flinching as the door to the pyramid slammed closed behind him with more force than a stone dropping off a cliff. "Yeah... I suppose that tracks. If I didn't have double the mana capacity of other people, it would've taken a little more than half of my total mana pool to make that last Brew. As it was, it took everything I had in me, which is thirty-one percent of my normal total, or sixty percent of what anyone else would've had. I just *hate* it when other people are right."

His pace slowed as he rapidly thought through the situation, feeling better by the time he was stepping off the final marble step. "Then again... I don't cook. I don't tend to the grass that's growing all the time these days. I can't even wash my own clothes anymore by just wearing them. Maybe the way that I stay in control while I'm working through this is... choosing what I give up, instead of pretending I don't have limits. Yeah. This is me delegating. Not surrendering."

An uneasy peace filled him at that moment, while at the same time, the system let off a soft chime in a tone he hadn't heard before. "Was that enough to adjust my Dexterity or something? Because I had a *flexible* mindset?"

It turned out that, no, the system wasn't altering his Characteristics—but the actual message was *almost* as good.

Congratulations! One of the Experts you have been training in the way of 'Jumping' has received Inspiration and broken through the Expert bottleneck. As your insights and training directly contributed to opening their path, you have earned your first Mastery Merit.

As this is the first time you have earned a Mastery Merit, additional information will be provided. You may earn additional Mastery Merits by guiding others along the same path; however, no more than 100 Merits may be earned from any single skill source. Whether you choose to bring one hundred people down this path of Mastery, 10 people from Master-rank zero to Master nine, or some combination of those—after the 100th Merit is earned, this skill as a source will be closed to you forever.

Current Merits earned from skill source: Omnivault. (1/100)

Note: Gaining 100 merits does not mean you cannot train other people but only that the system will no longer directly reward your efforts.

Why are Merits important? While Mastering a skill can be done entirely on your own, a Grandmaster is literally defined by the system as a 'Master of Masters'. To qualify to increase a skill to the Grandmaster rank, you must have:

1) Three skills Mastered for each that becomes Grandmastered. Yes, this does mean that there will be a soft cap for some of your skills.

2) 100 Mastery Merits gathered from any source per skill you wish to push into the Grandmaster rank.

3) Achieve a moment of Enlightenment which creates the foundation for the skill advancing. This can be done before reaching the peak of Mastery in the skill.

Blinking away the message, Joe considered the strange tangle of excitement and resigned acceptance running through his mind. "Always good to see my efforts rewarded, but only a hundred possible merits per skill? I guess I wasn't the first person who wanted to set up a bunch of schools to create an infinite feedback loop. Then again, it's kind of nice to know that there's actual incentive for people who've been teaching others their skills to hand it off to the next set of instructors-"

He stopped short as he realized the opposing perspective of that situation: everywhere he'd gone, Joe had seen people attempting to learn from Grandmasters and the like. Having so many Experts trying to bypass the people who were willing to teach them, specifically to learn from people who wouldn't gain merits from teaching them? "Were all of them thinking they could learn faster than the people who were *already* Masters and get closer to becoming the next Sage without needing to help the competition? I suppose, if you were brought up in this sort of hierarchy, that only makes good sense... only six *possible* Sages per class."

Lifting his mug, he winked at Mate, who filled his cup and vanished in the same instant. "Thanks buddy. *Slu~urp*. Glad I don't have to worry about that with Omnivault; all of my Mastery Merits are definitely going directly into my Ritualist core skills."

Feeling good about how much effort he'd put in over the last few days, Joe began leisurely strolling out of Novusheim and back toward the Sect territory. "This is nice."

He followed his usual path, deviating only to avoid a pack of Verglas Leaping Leopards hunting a lone, heat-exhausted Penguin.

Squueeee!

Rrr-raa-raaw!

As the cacophony of combat faded away, Joe took another slow sip of his coffee. "Mmm... the sounds of nature."

Only a few minutes later, another noise caused Joe's ears to perk up: the rapid staccato beat of feet pushing off the ground as someone hurtled along at breakneck speeds. Stepping off the path, the Ritualist watched to see who was in such a rush, only for his heart to sink into his stomach as he saw Devoe sprint past.

The Dwarf saw him as well, and Joe could only grit his teeth as the stocky Ritualist slammed his feet down and screeched to a halt, turning around and quickly approaching the bald man. "We've got a problem, Master Joe."

"Uh. Great. It must be serious if you're getting all formal with me like that. What's going on?"

"It's your jumping grounds… one of the trainees just reached the Master rank and is trying to get people to split off with him. Thought you should know."

"Splitting off? After everything I built to let them train up to the-" Joe's eyes narrowed in suspicion. "It's not Gage *again*, is it?"

"Absolutely it is."

"Abyssal brat… when *isn't* Gage the issue?"

CHAPTER TEN

Even as he chased after Devoe, quickly entering Sect Territory, and only slowing to a professional pace as he approached his own little slice of civilization, Joe's mind was on how nice it had been just to walk through the wilds on his own for a little while. No impending quests ticking down, no backstabbing new Masters trying to take over his school. Really nothing to worry about except the massive monsters wanting to rip him to shreds for sustenance.

"Why's the idea of just being attacked by something trying to eat me more pleasant than the idea of coming back and having another meeting or one-on-one session?" Joe slowly exhaled as he looked at the jumping grounds he'd set up so long ago. "Maybe it's because I just prefer the... *concept* of all of this, instead of running it all? I'm geared more toward seeing a problem that needs to be solved, fixing it, then moving on. Perhaps I'm just not cut out for all of the social maintenance that comes with long-term habitation in a single area."

The jumping grounds didn't take up anywhere *near* as much space as the ritual training field, but that was only due to how it had been designed with an eye more toward vertical challenges than needing large, open spaces for people to blast each other with magic. Then again, if it weren't for the various illusions his rituals were creating, the training area would look like a cross between a skyscraper in the scaffolding phase and an intense obstacle course. Each section of the jumping grounds were connected by only a single small pass-through, which could only be accessed by *Jumping* to it in one way or another.

In the Novice area, a basic version of the Ritual of Feather Fall reduced people's weight, causing each jump to send them tumbling in an uncomfortable manner as an effort to create the reflexes necessary for the skill Aerial Acrobatics. Simple wooden poles stuck into the ground allowed them to move back and forth, and the goal was to reach the far side of the area without touching the ground a single time. This was by far the most frequented area, as even people who had long since moved past the Novice rank enjoyed the weightless sensation and being able to turn a single jump into what amounted to a long glide.

Once the trainee moved to the next section, the difficulty ramped up quickly. Instead of relaxed gliding, they were meant to jump from platform to platform. Most new students didn't understand that it was far less dangerous than it seemed, as the illusions he had set up made it appear that missing your target would send you tumbling off a cliff. It was always fun to hear a first-timer let loose a shrill scream, only to find themselves passing through the bottom of the illusion and landing with what usually ended up being a gentle bump.

Only one... or *maybe* two people had the worst possible instincts and landed directly on their face when panicking, but typically such a short fall wasn't enough to damage someone who'd managed to ascend to Jotunheim.

In total, Joe had designed six different areas, which should've been enough to bring someone from the Novice all the way to the peak of the Expert rank. It had been a pain doing everything until he'd carved the large Mana Channels through his arms, but he had put a massive amount of effort into simplifying the designs of his rituals so that he could manage.

While he hadn't gained any levels in his Magical Matrices for such work, his related profession had certainly seen a bump —but he ground his teeth as he remembered that reaching level ten as a Ritualistic Numerologist had only come with further restrictions, instead of benefits.

"No, focus on the positives in the situation! People are gaining levels, and I'm helping them get there. Gotta love that." Until possibly today, no one had completed the final challenge in the Expert-rank area, a recreation of Joe's successful jump across the G.O.A.T. path, which led to fundamentally altering his skill. Since that had been a major moment of Inspiration for him, he'd hoped that allowing other people to experience it would bring them closer to success.

"Maybe it *did*, now that I think about it," Joe murmured excitedly, caught between a readiness to go and verbally beat down Gage, or pull him into a room and excitedly question every aspect of what had allowed him to finally achieve Mastery. But, as he and Devoe got closer, and the Ritualist spotted the newly manufactured Master standing with a puffed-up chest as he spoke to a crowd of Experts, the urge to congratulate the man vanished without a trace.

"-In a massive world like Jotunheim, where getting to the next town over could take a month of travel, and the terrain is brutal, maintaining *mobility* is key. You know, even more than just for getting around." Gage's voice carried far and wide, and even from a distance, Joe could see his words resonating with the others. "Maybe we should all be more comfortable with not chaining ourselves to an *anchor* just because it's familiar. All of us are explorers, aren't we? I'm pretty sure that you, like me, are excited to get out there and make your mark on this planet! Let's be real… a broken anchor can only weigh you down. It isn't going anywhere, in life *or* in-"

Joe didn't increase his pace, nor did he shout to interrupt the impromptu meeting. Still, when Gage turned his head and met his eyes, the lecture came to a faltering halt and the smug expression on his face shifted to one of fear—for just an instant —before snapping back into place alongside a haughty chin thrust. Though he wouldn't admit it, the moment of recognition made the Ritualist feel far more powerful and in control then he had any right to be, just barely allowing him to keep his temper in check instead of coming in swinging.

"Congratulations on achieving the Master rank, Gage." Joe considered the fact that he managed to keep his tone conversational a personal victory. "Please, don't let *me* interrupt your sharing of insights with the group. I'm just here to hang out and listen. You know... since I'm not going anywhere."

Gage's lips twitched, clearly forcing his gut-punched facial expression to turn into a smile that was all polite teeth. "Yeah, I've got a lot of thoughts on all of this, and I certainly don't mind sharing a few of them. There's a lot of good people here, Joe. Talented people. People who finally have options."

"Op-tions." Joe spoke the word slowly, as though tasting and savoring it as he let it flow across his tongue. "That's an interesting way to describe your immediate attempt to scoop up as many Experts as you could and run for it the *instant* you achieved Mastery. Really shows the respect you have for how you got here."

"Look, thanks for the tips along the way, but you don't own the Jumping skill." Gage settled into a defensive position with his arms crossing over his chest. "I can be here, giving people direct training all of the time, instead of just setting up a jungle gym and popping in once a week to give pointers. Now that I'm a Master, I can help *all* of these people *way* more than you can."

The crowd began shifting uncomfortably, glancing between the two of them with conflicted expressions. Joe didn't mind, as he was perfectly happy to *jump* headfirst into uncomfortable situations. "You can be... *here*, training them? You do realize the training grounds are mine? The rituals that help you get the supporting skills? The illusions that allow you to gain skill quickly, since it simulates truly dangerous situations? Recreations of how I achieved my personal Inspiration to break through the bottleneck into Mastery? Not to mention that I am second in command of the Wanderer's Sect itself?"

"More like *third* in command," Gage interjected, as though that were enough to sweep away the rest of what Joe had already covered.

Not allowing himself to be derailed, Joe simply nodded agreeably. "Right, Mike is probably the Vice Sect Leader or something. Sure. Tell me, man. Does creating the entirety of the infrastructure that allows you to rapidly gain and progress these skills not count as being helpful, even without constant direct tutelage? The Mastery Merit I gained when you ranked up certainly seems to *indicate* I had some part in your success."

The silence which followed his calm listing of his help had Gage rapidly glancing at anyone who would meet his eyes, though that wasn't many people, once they'd been reminded of what they would be giving up should they acknowledge a different trainer. Just before the tension came to a head, Joe decided to extend an olive branch. He knew he'd made far too many enemies in the past, and he had no desire to make more over a short-term issue such as this. "I own all of the tools, the land we train on, and have reached the peak of the Master rank in my own variation of jumping. *But…*"

He let the word stretch for a moment, just until Gage unconsciously leaned in, showing that he was open to something *other* than snatching a group of Experts and running into the wilderness. "You are correct in that it would be nice to have someone around here who can pick up the slack when I'm gone. A dedicated Master who can help people, a Master who still has plenty to learn from me? Well… that sounds like someone who can take over the *entire school* once I've gotten the paltry hundred merits I can earn here."

Gage's jaw dropped, but Joe wasn't concerned with *his* reaction. No, it was the sudden spark of hope and understanding in

Devoe's eyes, the way the crowd of Experts on the cusp of reaching Mastery in their own skills suddenly started paying serious attention. Joe knew Gage was talented, and kicking him out over wanting to be beneficial to others, even if it was self-serving, would be no better than throwing out a helpful, specialized tool.

And, if there was one thing Joe could truthfully say about Gage, it was that the man was a tool.

"Even better..." the Ritualist pretended to make a realization as he sweetened the pot. "Depending on what your skill actually is now, I might even help you set up a training area focused on what you can do, at some point. No reason *not* to have as many options for people as possible, since the best among you will *inevitably* leave to start your own schools. I suppose what you decide to do next is going to set a serious precedent, Gage. I'm not going to *force* you to stay, but if you keep trying to undermine what I've built... I'm not going to *let* you."

Gage's expression darkened, curdling like milk left in the sun too long. His obvious humiliation warred against the surprisingly generous offer Joe had made, which the new Master clearly hadn't expected after what he'd just tried to pull. "You know, maybe I don't need all this equipment. My skill works perfectly well on flat ground, no need for fancy tricks and illusions."

"That's wonderful! Now that you mentioned it, you never did tell me exactly what your skill morphed into. Unless... you didn't get a perfect upgrade from Expert jumping to Master jumping, did you?" Frankly, Joe hoped he hadn't, as that would actually make Gage even more qualified to teach the actual skill than himself.

"I got a high-rarity evolution!" Gage declared proudly, some of his confidence reappearing in his voice as he spoke. "No longer am I constrained to merely jumping up and down, I generated an entire movement skill! Witness with your own eyes... *The Bounding Step of the Unburdened*!"

Turning, Gage began running forward, then he gently pushed off with his right foot and absolutely *launched* himself forward with far more power and speed than Joe's estimation of his Characteristics should allow. He came down once, pushing off the ground with the lightest touch of his left foot. Arcing up at a shallow angle, Gage just barely managed to clear the edge of the roof of one of Joe's buildings, reaching the opposite boundary of the building by practically floating there in the next instant, then pushing off with more strength to sail across the open space and hop along the next.

In under half a minute, he'd fully circled the area Joe had developed, coming to a graceful landing in front of the Ritualist with a swirl that dispersed his remaining momentum. The crowd began cheering and clapping wildly, and Joe didn't hold back as he joined in, a brilliant smile on his face as he stepped forward to shake Gage's hand.

"That was wonderful! Your pace increased with almost every step, and by the time you were moving at full speed, you were practically a blur!"

"Like I said, I don't need all of this fancy equipment to teach what I have to offer–" Gage's words were cut short as the grip on his captured hand turned iron-hard.

"Unfortunately…" Joe allowed his statement to dangle, dancing out into the open air just as the excitement had fully died down, and therefore reaching every ear present, "As you previously stated, that's clearly a movement skill, not a jumping skill. It's very pretty. I bet it gives you a, what, three-times speed multiplier compared to normal running, right? Unfortunately, while you can cover horizontal ground even faster than a Verglas Leopard, your verticals aren't anything close to the terrain-conquering leaps we're trying to teach. It seems your skill evolved *away* from jumping. As I had once predicted, you've become a Master… at *skipping*."

There was a heartbeat of silence, then a few of the Experts had to stifle laughs as Gage scowled deeply, still unable to remove his hand from Joe's grip without causing a scene. The

Ritualist kept speaking, finally letting go and stepping away from his new contemporary only when it became obvious the man wasn't going to try and rush off in a huff.

"Don't get me wrong, that looks like a fantastic travel skill, and I certainly wouldn't mind learning it from you after you've gotten some practice teaching others. The ability to chew up flat ground would be only helpful for all sorts of reasons. But Jotunheim has hills taller than skyscrapers, mountains ten times higher than Everest, and valleys so deep that it's impossible to see the sun at the bottom. *That's* the kind of terrain I'm trying to train people to navigate." Joe waited, but he wasn't interrupted again, which he appreciated.

"I'll make you a deal. Stick around, help me bring either a hundred people up to snuff in the skill I'm actually trying to teach, or however many it takes for me to get my merits, and I'll personally help you build and design a school tailored to your skill path." Turning to face the crowd, the Ritualist met each of their eyes with a steady gaze. "That goes for all of you! I *want* the Sect to have the best options available, so when you're ready to have your own schools, and you've been fostering a good relationship with me, I'll help you make it happen. I have the tools, the resources, and—even though I'm only *third* in command—the sway within the Sect to make that happen!"

Turning back to Gage, he spoke in a softer tone, which was still pitched to carry. "I kid you not... the idea of constantly being around one area and having to be the person in charge of every little thing holds basically *zero* interest to me. The best thing I can possibly do for the Sect is make myself as unnecessary as possible for anything except the most major events, as quickly as I can."

Joe held out a hand, and the last bit of resistance Gage had in him cracked, a rueful grin appearing on his face. They shook and stepped apart, and while the crowd didn't exactly erupt into cheers, they were certainly in higher spirits now that the two Masters among them had settled their issues and were seemingly on good terms.

The two of them started walking around the area, with Joe calling out to anyone who hadn't yet heard the news, praising the new Master and the hard work he'd done to achieve his new status. By the time they'd finished the loop, both of them had gotten what they truly wanted. On Joe's part, there'd been no mass exodus, no break in the continuity of the training hierarchy which might impact his Mastery Merit gain. As for Gage, he had gained the beginnings of his own reputation, with dozens of people looking at him with excitement and interest.

Feeling they had reached a comfortable point, Joe stepped away. "Congratulations again. Now, if you'll excuse me, I'm going to go find some semblance of free time."

"Sure thing. I suppose... you've earned that, haven't you?" For the first time in a long time, Gage's words didn't sound like a veiled jab or some form of backhanded compliment. "I hope you figure out how to fix whatever your deity broke."

"Faction leader," Joe corrected as a matter of course. "No matter what the logic of this world is, they *aren't* gods. Just ancient and powerful people who've proven themselves fallible time and time again. That's one of the big reasons I don't have a bunch of anger toward Tatum, if I'm being honest with myself. He made a mistake, but I never *expected* him to be perfect."

"Yeah, that's cool." Gage shifted away from Joe and waved at him over his shoulder. "I'm going to go to the tavern and see if I can find any ladies who want to get carried around in my arms like I'm a superhero."

"That's... one way to react to becoming a Master." Joe blinked rapidly as Gage took off, blurring into the distance in only a few moments. "I don't really have anything to say about that. Huh. I guess I'll... go back to-"

Thinking that *perhaps* he had time to go and work on his personal projects, he turned toward his house. Joe took a single step before he realized that the crowd in that area was in fact a *line*. Not just one or two people. No, there were at least a dozen clustered in loose knots, all clearly waiting for *him*, as shown by the intense glances they shot his way. Some had notebooks. One at the very back of the line was setting out a bedroll and had a small pack of camping equipment, as he was clearly expecting a long wait.

In theory, this was great. People wanted his help, and they recognized that Joe could provide an immense value to their life. But, in practice, exhaustion crashed down on Joe as the realization that he'd spent almost the entire past year constantly in other people's business washed over him. Meetings, training sessions, apprenticeship oversight... obligations layered on obligations. His own projects, everything from making the most of his skills, world-hopping opportunities, mana channel recovery—all of it had been crammed into the margins.

Now, looking at the impatient faces queuing up at his house, he finally understood why Grandmasters on the lower worlds had become half-mythical figures only seen once in a decade, making people book appointments months or even years out. They weren't arrogant, as he'd once thought.

They were preserving themselves.

Without even realizing it, Joe had taken a step backward. Another. Before he consciously made the decision, he was sliding through one of the massive shifting curtains of mist he had installed to section off his area.

Emerging on the other side, he definitely didn't break into a run—just a professional jog with his eyes on the horizon. To anyone looking on, it appeared as though Joe were making haste to fix some problem, and the truth was they would even be *mostly* correct.

After so long cooped up in one area, working with so many other people, his social batteries had finally sputtered out entirely. He rubbed his spatial ring, then grabbed at his codpiece to check on his storage devices before hastily snatching his hand away as he realized what this would've looked like to an outside observer.

"I'm not going to worry about grinding my skills, fixing my broken mana, or... *any* of it. I've got everything I need to spend a few weeks in the wild." For the first time in a long time, a *calm* smile appeared on his face.

Then, he was at the edge of the Sect Territory and running. Then *sprinting*, leaving a trail of dust lazily drifting to the ground behind him.

CHAPTER ELEVEN

"Is it bad that I'm running away from my responsibilities like this?" Even as he contemplated out loud to himself, Joe didn't stop running. It'd been far too long since he'd been able to get some true alone time without someone trailing along behind him with questions, criticisms, commentary, or an ill-timed backstory or Quest needing to be completed.

Eventually, he could only nod his head in chagrined acceptance. "Yes, probably not the best thing for me to do. Not exactly a long-term solution, but maybe it'll give people the chance to realize they can help themselves every once in a while, instead of knocking at my door at three in the morning because the illusions have 'started showing spooky faces'."

Joe had flinched when he spoke back to himself, only then realizing exactly how silent the area was. Sure, the wildlands of Jotunheim could never truly be considered quiet, not with the sheer volume of wind that had to flow across the seemingly endless surface, or the actual sound of plants rapidly growing, since they were so massive that every bit of their explosive growth sounded like a carcass being torn asunder. "Pretty wild what happens when a planet that had been locked in eternal winter gets its first chance at spring."

Eventually, he slowed to a halt as he found a clearing, probably only a dozen miles wide, but still the flat space mostly taken up only by bare stone and dirt, instead of grass larger than trees on Midgard or local trees as large as skyscrapers. "This looks like a good place to set up camp and test out some theories."

Snapping his fingers for dramatic effect, the Ritualist unloaded dozens and dozens of ritualistically forged metal structures. Each of the various shapes had been happily hammered into their current form under the influence of the Mantra of Metal and a repetitive refrain. Squares, triangles, cubes, pyramids, then finally star-shaped metals and long rods. Even with them having only been dumped into piles, the air and light around each set shimmered or actively distorted.

These weren't his usual stabilizers, which would allow him to ensure a safer activation of rituals, spells, and the like. Instead, these were ritual *destabilizers*. Where the standard version anchored mana and smoothed it out, these were designed to twist it. The nodes were deliberately imperfect, edges formed fractions of degrees off angle, mathematical equations etched with missing clauses and incorrect variables. Instead of calming the turbulence, these would *increase* the jaggedness until moving through the area was akin to subjecting the astral self to the equivalent of dozens of serrated blades.

Every mistake was a choice, each error a feature, and every carefully separated pile was designed to work with each of the lesser variants to maximize the disharmony.

"Perfect... even with the density and chaotic nature of Jotunheim's ambient mana, it still doesn't reach the threshold of what happened back on Midgard when I was casting Master-rank spells and rituals." Joe began laying out the enormous array of metal pieces into a carefully designed oval. Lifting one of the triangular nodes, he grinned at his distorted reflection, where he'd allowed drips of slag to pop up like pimples on a pizza delivery boy.

"If I can just replicate that correctly, then I should be able to figure out what I need to do to work *against* it. Stabilizing through the distortions and allowing me to use my full arsenal when I hunt down whatever the World Boss will be down on Midgard." He carefully placed the triangle, and the air around where his fingers still touched the bronze colored sheet of metal flexed and twisted as though he were looking through a heat mirage. "Jake says I can't make Ichor without fixing my Mana Channels, which likely means Master-rank stabilizers are out as well. That means I have to figure out a workaround. *Doesn't* it, little cube-y cube?"

Joe tossed the cube into position, dozens of feet away from the warped pyramid he hurled the opposite direction. Both had corners bent, melted, or sheared at carefully chaotic angles. As the fifth oval went up, the Journeyman portion, the world finally reacted. For just a moment—so short that he would've discounted it entirely were it not for his immense Perception—his vision doubled, as though he were looking through a set of binoculars not quite properly aligned.

He began pushing the metal bar stabilizers through the star-shaped ones, and a warning tingle of energy raced up his spine, the hairs on his arms standing up as power accumulated within the bounds of his ovals. Unfortunately, when the full placement had been completed, although even the light passing through the space seemed thicker and waving his hand through the space distorted his view of his fingers, all he'd managed to do was concentrate the already chaotic nature of the world within the space.

"Hmmm, not quite there yet?" Joe pulled a set of glass bottles out of his ring next. "That's two of my core skills at the Expert rank working together already, between the forging and the Magical Matrices I built into 'em. Let's see if three is enough, or if I'll need to add in enchantment, or even some active controlling with a ritual circle."

Following along the ovals, Joe carefully placed a dash of each of the bottles onto their corresponding destabilizer, in exactly the same pattern at which he'd placed them originally. The Novice Elixir was gone in a flash, the Beginner Draught barely lasting any longer. The Apprentice Vial had two additional drops remaining, which Joe stored away for safe disposal at another time. The Student-ranked Philter needed to be scooped out with the assistance of a tiny spoon, too thick and viscous to easily pour in controlled measurements.

Once again, it was the Journeyman version that tipped the scales. As Joe applied the final droplet of the Tonic, the world showed an immediate reaction, the distortion ramping up but not *quite* passing the threshold he needed. "All right, Expert Brew, it's all up to you."

The pitch-viscous, indigo-colored Alchemy product stayed *exactly* where he smeared it on the slightly off-kilter rods. In fact, Joe had to firmly press on it after application to shift it around even fractionally, as it hardened into place like amber solidifying around an insect it had trapped. As he dabbed the last smidgen into place, he finally achieved what he'd been attempting: the world within the large open space shifted and swirled as though reality itself had become malleable.

"Hah, maybe Van Gogh was looking through turbulent mana when he created that Starry Night painting. That rock formation looks like it has a whirlpool forming—it's gone. This is so *neat!*"

Back when he'd been temporarily wrecking Midgard, he'd been far too concerned with survival and the panicked messages of the system to take in the strange beauty of the oddities that were created by the crackling, warping, turbulent energy flowing through the area. For a few moments, Joe simply admired his handiwork, amazed that simple placement of—admittedly *magical*—items could create such an impactful change in the world.

Then he reached into his pocket, pulling out a single ritual Enchantment token. "I've got the effect I'm looking for, now I just need to expand it out a bit."

Stepping directly into the oval where the active effect was

occurring, Joe felt his Mana Channels spark and become irritated, as though he were squirting lemon juice directly into an open wound. Glancing at his hands, he found that a thin layer of power was collecting around him, exactly the effect he could perfectly recall from activating a magical effect a single time outside of the bounds of what was allowed on the lower world. "I think I've got it."

Wading through the warping effect, Joe felt a minuscule, yet ever-present lingering weight pushing against him. Simply focusing allowed him to push the intrusive feeling aside, and he marched toward the exact center of the oval he'd created. Reaching down, he carefully scooped out some dirt three inches off-center then dropped the token in position at a two-degree incline *away* from perfect horizontal placement. "Just a single token of area of effect expansion, when a *minimum* of three are required to stabilize an enchantment. Then-"

Joe channeled mana directly down the enormous pipeline he'd created in his arm, absolutely *dumping* power into the enchantment and bringing it up to the minimum threshold for activation. The token began to glow, softly at first, then rapidly brightening as the myriad lines inscribed on its surface and throughout the entirety of the tiny disk came to life.

A bubble of energy, a thin film of power, pushed out then *exploded* into being. The Ritualist stumbled away, quickly exiting the outer ring of the oval formed by the destabilizers. He cracked a crooked smile when he realized the immense turbulence was no longer contained only to the space directly within that boundary. He quickly began jogging away, and it was only after he'd reached three-quarters of a mile from the space that he crossed a previously invisible delimitation.

He inhaled sharply as everything became slightly easier, quickly whipping around and examining the enormous bubble of turbulence that had been generated by what he could only hope his friend Socar would at least begrudgingly call a *Formation*. "Technically not a ritual, even if it has all the hallmarks of a ritual. No active effect, that means not technically a ritual. Therefore, formation! Where's my new skill, system?"

Putting his jokes aside and stepping back into the distorted space, Joe began drawing out a Novice-rank ritual in midair— only for it to pop like a soap bubble the *instant* he channeled power into it. The detonation of mana was quickly absorbed by the chaotic landscape, exactly as the Ritualist had hoped. "Good... at least my Mana Manipulation skills work the way they're supposed to. Abyss... if those broke along with the rest of me, I don't know what I would do to fix all this."

Briefly frowning as he thought back to the dozens of times he'd needed to explain the details of his current ailment, how it was specifically his *active* skills and *interior* Mana Channels that were broken-

"That's right, just because the power is out in a neighborhood doesn't mean the generator has melted down. I've got a few neighborhoods where the lights are on, and... uhh, that metaphor is breaking down." Joe shook off the annoyance then eased his mind by allowing power to pump down his arm and into his inscription tool. The sharpened tip of the aspect-generated implement began glowing brightly, and he let out a long sigh of relief.

"No one was ever able to explain to me why my passive skills were all fine, but my active ones have all suffered? Placement in the astral body? Perhaps passive skills are closer to the core of my being, like my lore skills are *technically* just knowledge at the end of the day? Was-" Joe's eyes snapped to the distance as a strange sound interrupted his thought process.

Squeeeark?

A massive black and white blubber tank with a serrated beak—which could only *generously* still be considered a penguin —was bouncing across the ground within the distorted space the Ritualist had created. Joe prepared a few of his Ritual Orbs, only to realize that he hadn't yet been noticed; the massive creature had other problems.

It was trying to bounce along the ground as it normally

would, only to launch itself upward, lean forward, and belly flop to the ground to thrash around like an upside down turtle placed perfectly on its shell. The cries it was releasing became more frantic as it finally flipped back to its feet, hopping forward before launching upward once again, only to strike the ground in the exact same manner. Another came into view, running forward with its wings flaring to the side as it tried to balance, only for the gentle breeze to catch the bird and send it rolling and squawking indignantly across the stony surface.

Soon, a half dozen were within visual range, then *dozens* as a flock of them were drawn to the sounds of distress. The chorus of shrieking only got louder as the agitation of the polar-bear-sized birds continued rushing into the turbulent zone.

Verglas Leopards soon followed them into the area, perfectly happy to hunt the off-balance and unprotected penguins. Their bounding strides brought them into the clearing quickly, trailing ice bridges with every leap. But, as the first of them crossed into the bubble, the sparkling bridge hanging in the air behind it like a glass highway formed and immediately shattered into shards.

The Leopard dropped out of the air as though it had been smacked down, managing to land only awkwardly as it impaled itself on the ice of its own making. Dozens of small wounds showed spots of blood as the great cat hissed in anger, pain, and fury.

A few more were directly behind their leader, not getting the memo as they jumped into the area, only for their own frost trails to shatter and fall like glittering knives. Just like the first, they tried to compensate, but their enormous size and relatively low altitude meant that they landed on their sides, shoulders, or even tumbled across the ground instead of managing to get their feet under them.

Joe sucked in a sharp breath as he finally realized what he was seeing. "Turbulence has an impact on natural skills and spells as well?"

The wildlife was rapidly adapting, but now they were having

to run or waddle around awkwardly, impacting their mobility significantly. "They're still monsters; not being able to use their skills as easily only makes them a little less deadly. It's an irritation... but what would this do to trained casters? Actually, I guess I already know the answer to that, seeing how useless the Mage Corps became during the fight against Gameover."

A frustrated leopard lunged at a penguin, front paws extended, back legs pushing, only to generate a wall of ice in front of itself and smack into the solid barrier hard enough to force the cat to walk away, shaking its head and trying to regain its bearings. The penguin shrieked at its attempted attacker, retaliating by rushing at the cat and rearing back, slamming its head and beak forward like a mining pick. Blood sprayed into the air, and the predator and prey groups began throwing themselves at each other.

Less interested in how nature was reacting than the ambient mana, Joe instead turned his thoughts to the destabilized region. "How high can I boost this, I wonder? Especially after I can make Master-rank versions? I can just drop a pocket of turbulence wherever I need, then use my non-mana skills to crush whatever's in there. Doesn't look like there's going to be any permanent effects, so why not? This is basically an anti-magic formation-"

Skraww!

A shriek of triumph echoed across the clearing, yanking Joe's attention back to the now-finished battle. One of the penguins, now freely bleeding from dozens of wounds, stood above the bodies of at least three different leopards. Its wings flapped furiously, and the distortion around its form noticeably increased. At that moment, Joe stumbled forward, drawn toward the bird by a tidal wave of power as the thickened ambient mana rushed into the penguin, suffusing its form and completely hiding the creature from sight.

The overlay of energy shifted and grew, the silhouette growing larger and larger before bursting away from the bird as motes of light that flared and twisted into nothingness like fireworks having spent their load. Joe looked up at the penguin, and up… and up. A dense scent of brine and blood washed over the area as the penguin flapped its thirty-foot wingspan, sending dust pluming as its lesser brethren tumbled away.

Zone alert! A Field Boss has spawned.

A Goliath penguin (Tyrant class) has been formed in the wilds on the outskirts of the territory of The Wanderer's Sect. This monster will rapidly gain Strength and Intelligence, forming an army based on its original form.

It is recommended that this becomes a priority kill for any raid group in the area, before the Tyrant has gained an army large enough to fortify its position and wage war against its neighbors.

Even before Joe had finished reading the notification, he was at the center of the enormous distortion, pulling apart the destabilizers and carefully yet rapidly packing them away. "Yeah, I should probably move my campsite before anyone comes to investigate, if I'm going to stay out here for any length of time."

As he reached for the Enchanted token, it sparked and popped, burning his hand. Joe quickly drew his fingers back, putting the burned spot in his mouth and gently blowing on it to try and cool down the small wound. "Yeah, can't leave you active. Who knows what would happen if one of those birds swallowed you and somehow managed to get a massive area-of-effect skill based on that. Everyone would know it was my fault, so…"

Power rushed out of Joe's hands as the immense amount of concentrated ambient mana began flowing out, the area rapidly equalizing to its standard chaotic baseline. A cage of light formed around the active token as he formed an Ascendant Matrix, drawing on his Mana Manipulation to form the spell outside of his body. With a twist of intent, the token the enchantment had been imbued on was absorbed, leaving the structured power to explode outward.

Joe jumped back at the last moment, just as the token began to crack, rolling to his feet and sprinting as hard as he could as the Goliath penguin in the distance roared—clearly bent on investigating whatever had wreaked such destruction within its newfound territory. Gaining a bit of distance, he slid to a stop, slamming his foot down and cratering the ground. Yanking a ritual tile out of his codpiece, he activated and dropped it into the new hole before covering it with a swipe of loose dirt.

A voice crackled out of the hole, "Hello? This is an emergency frequency only, whoever is on the other side, swap to standard communication if this is not-"

"First Elder of the Sect, Joe the Ritualist." As soon as he confirmed his identity, the person on the other side went silent. "I'm leaving this communication device next to the spawning point of the Tyrant penguin that just appeared. We are three hours northwest of the Sect Territory, at a hard pace for someone below the sixth threshold. Get a strike force together and kill this thing before it can become a Master-level threat and make an entire flockin' army."

"We're zeroing in on your location as we speak, First Elder." The person on the other end responded professionally. "Are you offering this as an official Sect quest?"

"Sure, it's threatening our territory, so I can justify that, right?" Joe murmured mostly to himself, realizing he wouldn't need to pay for this kill quest out of his own pocket, as the bird was threatening the Sect directly. "Contribution based on speed of kill and rank of threat. Bonuses paid out of my personal account for rapid extermination and for bringing the corpse back for me to study. It's a Tyrant class, we haven't run into any of those yet."

"Understood, First Elder. Kill squad being dispatched as we speak. Going radio silent to ensure we can follow the beacon."

As Joe sped off into the towering grass surrounding the clearing, he felt a massive surge of giddiness at the accidental prank he'd just pulled. "Making a mess and leaving it for someone else to clean up... did I just find the *real* benefit of being in charge of stuff?"

CHAPTER TWELVE

Fwoosh!

Joe hit the ground as a black and white missile shot over his head at race car speeds, just one more penguin among the thousands rushing toward the area. His robes rustled in the wind of the birds passing, and he grit his teeth as yet another one landed almost on top of him, spraying him with dirt and shocking his system slightly.

"Abyss, that took an unexpected turn." He took a sharp breath and pushed upward, abandoning his original plan of going deeper into the wilds to avoid this mess. Since the penguins were coming from where he was trying to go, the Ritualist figured he could probably rush back to Sect Territory. "Celestial feces, did I just unleash a Beast Wave on them from the opposite side?"

The kill squad should be on the way, but he hadn't expected them to be outpaced by this sheer quantity of creatures. When he turned around and started going with the flow of bodies, Joe found himself moving far more easily through the terrain, which had been practically flattened smooth by the migrating birds. He ran alongside them, his Ritual Orbs cast into the air above him to give him advance warning if a massive body was flopping down at him from an angle he was unable to see. Even then, it was only his immense stats that allowed him to feel the disruption and dance or dive out of the way of the crushing weight.

Soon the birds were landing on each other, squawking indignantly at those above them, but then the black and white tide of flesh started crashing together, weaving, and bouncing ever higher. If Joe hadn't been here to see it for himself, someone would've needed to work very hard to convince him that these flightless birds were getting so immensely airborne by bouncing off each other. The oddest part was that they weren't only rebounding on the ground, but also *midair*, ricocheting around enough that those at the very top of the pile were starting to gain serious altitude.

"What *is* this?" He glared at the enormous creatures swimming through the open air, some of them approaching the lowest-hanging heavy clouds that still covered the entire sky. "I guess physics are just a *suggestion* now?"

The only silver lining was that they seemed completely unconcerned about his presence in their midst, the creatures using the airborne bounce pads to get ever closer to their new Tyrant, no matter if they smashed their brethren out of the sky and into the ground far below. Those were the most dangerous moments for the Ritualist, as individual penguins got separated from the others above and below, then spiraled down to the ground beak-first to splatter across the surface.

"Feces!" Joe shouted as he narrowly avoided a penguin-shaped dart that cratered the ground as it landed, blood soaking into the dirt before being greedily sucked up by the ever-thirsty plant life. "What's black and white and red all over? The surface of Jotunheim! *Yikes!* Fine, you know what? If I can't beat 'em, I'm joining!"

Pushing himself to sprint even faster, Joe threw himself forward, doing a flip and smashing his feet down onto a penguin as though he were an Italian plumber navigating an ice world. To his great surprise, the blubbery creature's body compressed sharply then flung outward. The Ritualist found himself dozens of feet off the ground, tumbling helplessly— purely from sheer shock—before coming to his senses and aligning himself as he began his descent. Getting his feet under him, he hit another penguin, launching himself upward at a new, absurd trajectory, now that he was ready for the effect.

For a moment, another penguin was rising through the air right next to him, stubby wings flaring as it stared at him with a cross between confusion and hunger in its eyes. It thrashed toward him, but its sheer mass dragged it out of range just before the razor-sharp beak could sink into his thigh. Joe kept his eyes on the creature, and, unlike the rest of its kind, this one remained entirely focused on him as well. "You *eyeballing* me? When I have the high ground?"

With a mental nudge, the Ritual Orb of Intelligence swung into position and began spinning, going from a lazy twist to a whirling menace in under half a second. A quick calculation later, the drill bit-shaped orb punched straight down through the air, hitting the thick skull and being halted only for a breath before auguring directly through.

Damage dealt: 378 Piercing.

"How? How did damage notifications get turned back on?" Joe dismissed the intrusive flashing lights with a sharp flick of his fingers, once again putting his messages to 'critical only'. For its part, the penguin fell out of the sky, pretzeling away from the pain in its head yet somehow still functional with a hole directly through its brain. The Ritualist pushed off another feathery platform and watched as the aggressive monster tried to regain its bearings... and failed spectacularly. The terrain damage finished the job, the bird slamming directly into the hard surface of the ground *far* below...

...calling Joe's attention to the fact that he was easily a tenth of a mile in the air.

"The sheer amount of lift these things generate is absolutely ridiculous." Not for the first time acutely missing the mana-empowered functionality of Omnivault, the Ritualist took a few minutes to enjoy the luxury of rocketing through the air with only regular jumps. Only as he reached the cloud level—far lower here than on other worlds—did he reluctantly make the choice to return to the ground. "Good to know for the future, though. If I can find a swarm of penguins, I can get back up here pretty easily, then travel through the clouds using Omni-vault... haah. When it's fixed, at least."

Ffft.

The sharp sound passing by his ear reminded Joe of an arrow missing him by centimeters. He flinched away, tucking and rolling as a penguin corkscrewed down through the cloud. It was moving far faster than gravity accounted for, and immediately an ominous feeling crept up his spine as Joe tucked in and nose-dived alongside it. After gaining some distance, he leveled out and looked upward, easily able to ignore the pressure of the wind trying to force his eyes shut.

It became clear what had happened only an instant later, as dozens, then hundreds of penguins rained down through the obscuring vapor, having entirely lost their bearings in the thick cloud bank. Another bounced up from below, striking a falling monster. The bird that had just exited the cloud shot back up into it, squawking happily, while the other that had struck its exposed belly was slapped out of the sky, shooting down at least thrice as fast as it had ascended.

"Stay in the open where I have a clear line of sight. Noted." Glancing back at the ground, Joe sucked in a sharp breath as he realized exactly how far he'd traveled in a short amount of time. Far below him, there was a massive rookery of the beasts circling around the Tyrant, creating a black and white whirlpool effect that stretched farther and farther as additional penguins joined in.

Where they passed, the ground was smoothed; all traces of vegetation were completely pulped, gravel and dirt compressed, and frost spread outward. When the creatures were on the newly created frozen terrain, they moved faster, far faster than they possibly could on a surface less suited to them.

This meant that the closer they were to the Tyrant, the faster they circled—creating a practically hypnotic display.

A sharp tingle dragged Joe's attention from the display, and he immediately scolded himself—it was a rookie mistake to be daydreaming in an active combat zone. His core braced, muscles twisting to the limit as his Ritual Orbs erupted outward like chaff countermeasures. His left hand shot out, seizing the Orb of Strength. One brutal yank corrected his trajectory, in the next heartbeat sending the weapon spinning toward a penguin that had folded its wings, neck speared forward like a living dart aimed straight for his chest.

The weapon rang off its beak, brutally shoving its head to the side, though the bird swung back to glare and snap at him, furious at having been denied a meal during its descent.

From then on, Joe was constantly on the move, passing over the epicenter of the Tyrant event still unfolding—and therefore in the thick of it as thousands of creatures moved through the air or along the ground, creating a dense weave of whirlpooling bounce pads. Now not only did he need to evade the birds dropping from the clouds above, but even those below him, especially as the awareness of his presence slowly proliferated through the colony. His Ritual Orbs endlessly lashed out, striking with no intent to kill—only precision meant to alter the paths the birds took or open a way for him to slip through.

One round orb would clip a joint in an outstretched wing, causing the penguin to flinch and pull its limb in, just in time for Joe to *whoosh* around it. Another would bounce off an eye staring at him a bit too intently, giving him a much-needed break from its line of sight. Never did he allow his orbs to sink into mouths or pierce into bodies; any of the weapons not bound to his stats would be permanently lost if he did. Though he had extras, Expert-ranked items weren't something he was willing to casually throw away.

After a few minutes of carving a bloody path through the

sky—orbs bouncing off birds like the jackpot round of a pinball machine just to keep his personal space clear—Joe got through the worst of it and managed to take a breath and assess the situation. Once again, he had traveled much farther than anticipated, and the Tyrant's whirlpool was now far behind him. Then, Joe unexpectedly impacted another penguin, being sent back flipping toward the center once more due to the sheer size and momentum the surprised monster was able to bring to bear.

Righting himself with an outstretched palm shoved against a snow-white belly, Joe grasped a long feather and swung up and over, landing on the bird's back gently enough that he wasn't sent flying. He was breathing heavily, partly from exertion, partly from exhilaration, but mostly because of the strangely dense energy collecting around his legs. "This is... Omnivault, kinda? It feels like it, but there's no way for me to activate-"

Slamming a foot down, he bounced straight up half a dozen feet, twisting into a plank position as a penguin shot through the air like a fighter jet just where he'd been lounging. "Whew, close one!"

Somehow, that jump using the resources at hand was a tipping point, and the energy collecting around his body began to pour *into* it instead. There was no time to examine it, to contemplate or meditate on what was happening. Yet, as it turned out, that was exactly what was needed.

Omnivault was a purely physical skill for the very first jump. It only required an influx of mana and stamina on *subsequent* reactivations. While it was entirely possible that other skills would, this one didn't care about dignity in the slightest. The Master-rank skill cared about momentum, unique adaptation, and interesting improvisation when being used. Even more than that, the skill had mostly come about from his desire to move freely and have fun while doing it.

Even though he was literally surrounded by monsters in all directions, a sphere of death just waiting to dig its beak into him, Joe forgot about the danger as he began to fall. For a moment that seemed to stretch on and on, he wasn't just falling with style.

He'd managed to jump so well, and so many times in a row, that he was *flying*.

His thoughts harmonized with the odd ambient energy, and it synergized with him, coalescing into a moment of perfect clarity: *Enlightenment*.

Congratulations! Omnivault has formed a firm foundation and is ready to evolve and grow into the Grandmaster rank. Two of the three require-ments have been fulfilled, and by supplying Mastery Merits, you will imme-diately be able to bring Omnivault to the next tier!

Enlightenment gained: True.

At least three other skills at the Master rank per skill attempting to become Grandmaster rank: True.

100 Mastery Merits applied: False.

"Are you serious right now? I'm trying to save my Mastery Merits for my Ritualist skills, and you show me that I might be able to upgrade my jumping skill into something that might directly give me the ability to *fly*?" Joe scoffed in disbelief, barely holding himself back from calculating how long it'd take to save up all the merits he'd need and looking over his skill list to see what sort of effort he wouldn't need to put in.

Mainly because he was actively falling out of the sky.

Joe glanced back down at the three-dimensional whirlpool of penguins creating a frozen fortress around the tyrant, and... perhaps it was the moment of Enlightenment he'd just had, or the fact that he was simply open to more than survival, it suddenly dawned on him that thousands of large animals scraping along a surface should be heating it up, not cooling it down. "Wait, this is magic."

His eyes flared wide, and his Ritualistic Wisdom overlaid his vision with connections of power between the world, the minions, and the Tyrant. "So many creatures trying to do the same actions in a confined space, bouncing, moving, adjusting on the fly. This is a chain reaction, no... it's a layered interaction. One lands on another, bounces up, pushes its fellow into the sky; it does the same for the others."

Looking into the distance, to the outskirts of what was now clearly a natural ritual forming, Joe saw dozens of birds unable to participate in this strange dance, pushed off at incorrect angles, falling out of the sky and dying as they hit the ground. "Even *that's* a necessary component of this! The birds are a sacrifice being made to power this whole thing up!"

Taking a few moments to land on passing birds, Joe pushed himself up and out of the most dense area of the swarm once more before glancing back at the natural ritual as his mind spun with ideas as quickly as the birds themselves slid around their Tyrant. "Is that the key to pushing my Master ritual circles to the Grandmaster rank? Other people keep telling me they are supposed to feed into each other, to play nicely. This part works with that one, *this* component goes just here, no deviation allowed."

Unbeknownst to him, golden light was now collecting around his head, as impossibly, a *second* Enlightenment began forming as he methodically thought through the situation.

"Maybe… is this why the Tower of Ritualists on Vanaheim has never had any luck in getting their other Grandmasters up to the Sage rank? Maybe alchemy can be brute forced, and that's why Pete is so close, but the rest of them need each other… just not in the way every other profession does. What if, instead of laying everything out and having it flow from point A to point B, I layered them in a way that caused them to bounce off each other like these penguins are?"

"Would that amplify them? Creating resonance across the whole thing… or is discord itself the actual goal? Creating an entirely new effect not able to be assumed by the parts that have gone into it?" It made sense to him, *too* much sense at the moment. "After all, water should be immensely explosive. Oxygen explodes. Hydrogen explodes. Together, they form water and get rid of fire-?"

Joe blinked slowly, realizing that, for some odd reason, his vision had been replaced with a massive green screen. "Wait, did I just break the world or something?"

Then he hit the leaf while falling at terminal velocity.

He slammed into it like a cannonball, and the house-sized frond flexed and bent, stealing much of his momentum without returning *too* much as terrain damage. Then the vein-covered surface ripped in half with a sound like a set designer's nightmare of a theater curtain being torn down the middle. Joe punched through, shredded greenery and a deluge of sappy fluid flowing along with him.

His greatly-slowed speed began ramping up again as he plunged toward the ground, somehow avoiding the colossal branches as he crashed through layer after layer of foliage. He reached for a vine, only to realize that the only reason it looked like he could fit his hand around it was because it was nearly a mile away.

By the time he reached the final layer of leaves, only to begin speeding up again, he was *woozy*. The ground rushed up to meet him, and enormous blades of grass caught him and transitioned his freefall into a painful, bouncy slide along a rough surface. The Reductionist bounced off an aphid the size of a motorcycle then spun almost to the edge of the piece of grass before finally striking the ground.

As Joe lay on the loamy surface, staring up at a literal labyrinth of greenery, he could only let out a sigh of relief that he'd survived at all, even as he spat out a mouthful of blood from where he had split his lip and... loosened at least three teeth?

"Ha! I lived! I can do *anything*!" He half-lifted his arms into the air, waving them back and forth drunkenly as his vision doubled. Noticing a blinking notification, he laughed out loud as he realized he even had a new natural ritual design waiting for him to collect from the system.

While he was celebrating, the golden energy of enlightenment that had been collecting around his head quietly dissipated.

CHAPTER THIRTEEN

Arms spread wide, Joe stared up at the verdant, sky-filling plant life above him. Breathing deeply, he hacked out the last bit of blood-flecked phlegm, physically feeling the loss of his healing spells and aura.

Finally, as his vision settled and his head stopped spinning so badly, he sat up and groaned. "Well, now I know that amplifying turbulent mana as a multi-mile blender of power is effective, but pretty bad for my health. I wonder what exactly it was that sparked the transformation of the penguin into a Tyrant?"

The Ritualist froze in place for a moment as he realized exactly how lucky he'd been that the penguin had come out on top and had ascended to a field-boss Tyrant, instead of one of the Verglas Leopards. "Ugh... Mate?"

Coffee time? the tiny, ever-excited voice came from the depths of the mug clipped to his belt. Soon the elemental itself made an appearance, swirling up out of the cup and flowing over the edges without draining away.

"Yes, please. Anything to help this headache." To Joe's delight, the entity swirled out of the cup, leaving behind a full mug, while remaining summoned as it looked around the new area they were visiting. "Wondering where we are? I'm out exploring Jotunheim and got a *little* bit beat up. Still, I managed to test and prove one of my experiments. Well... the first part of it, I suppose. I was able to disrupt the environment to a significant degree, but never did get a chance to calm it down. Going to have to work on that again. Perhaps have that in place *before* expanding the turbulence out? Yeah, that... that probably would've been a better idea."

Seeing that the Ritualist was speaking to himself, Mate didn't have any qualms about reaching out a hot tendril of coffee and wrapping it around some of the plant pulp on the ground. As the bald man muttered to himself a bit more, the elemental wrapped the pulp entirely, swirling it around before pouring a green-tinted shot of liquid into Joe's mug.

The man went silent, staring at the suddenly extremely aromatic brew, then took a cautious sip. "That's pretty good, Mate. Hints of vanilla, and I want to say orange? How did you manage that with *grass*?"

Yay! The elemental cheered at Joe's praise, swirling around his arms and shoulders before unsummoning itself by diving into the refilled mug.

Staring at the cup, Joe could only shake his head in bemusement and take another sip. "Note to self, summon Mate every time I'm in a vastly different environment. Maybe by the time I get to another world or two, he'll be able to rival an entire coffee shop on his own."

Since he didn't want to move just yet, and had something to occupy his hands, Joe finally pulled up the notification that had been blinking unobtrusively in the corner of his vision.

Natural ritual conflux viewed and understood! You have gained a new ritual, thanks to your Ritualistic Wisdom Characteristic.

Ritual gained: Sutra of Fragmented Oneness (Broken). This Master-rank ritual is designed to intentionally break other rituals used as inputs into fragments, which are then assembled into a new, final effect as an output.

"Broken?" Joe considered the word, which oddly enough, had a slightly different flavor to it than what he might see on a piece of equipment that had broken during use. "This is more like a broken *title*, isn't it? Perhaps because it can be combined with other things? That makes sense. But other rituals can already use rituals as inputs, can't they? Why's this one special enough that it specifically had to be called out?"

Pulling out a specially prepared ritual design sheet, Joe accepted his reward and watched as the Master-rank ritual was written out in real time right before his eyes. Though his Ritual Lore skill was only in the Expert rank, he was a Master of Ritual Circles and was easily able to discern where sections of the design given to him were fragmented. "How odd... it looks like it was intentionally sheared off here, not like it's missing a piece. But the shape? The Master circle is perfect, but it's clear there are modular break points along it, while the lesser sections *actively* have chunks missing."

The answer was obvious, at least to him. "This is designed to work with chunks of rituals ripped from Expert and below ranked circles, but can potentially work with Master rituals as well... if I'm willing to risk myself by breaking the ritual during activation to pull in effects from other Master-rank designs. Sounds like setting off a bomb in my hands and hoping I'll be quick enough to place limiters on it before it explodes. Gonna have to have a *lot* of practice before I try something like that—even then, only in an unpopulated area."

As he set the document down, a crimson line extended from his hand to the broken ritual. Frowning slightly, he reached for the sutra once more, only for the line to vanish as soon as he touched the design once more. "Hand pulled back, red line appears. That's—*oh*! That's my Red Luck! That means this is a potential solution to one of my quests? Or at least a major component? Uhh... which one do I have set as active right now? Most recently gained, so that means-"

A wide smile appeared on his face, so intense that, for an instant, Joe could've been mistaken for the twin brother of Jaxon. His grip shook slightly on the ritual diagram as he stared at it with hungry eyes, "That means this is possibly the key to figuring out how to make a map or travel system to hunt down and get to the World Boss? Or… fixing my body?"

The tip of his tongue slowly moved along his upper lip as he sank into his thoughts, wondering how exactly this would function to help him complete either quest. "Giant circle of penguins swirling around a Tyrant, creating an icy landscape around it. More penguins moving in at all times, bouncing off each other, rendering a three-dimensional map of moving parts in the sky, all while others were sacrificed by moving out of alignment and falling to the ground. I bet if I went back, I wouldn't be able to find a single body; all of them were likely absorbed by the natural ritual as sacrificial materials and components."

Joe shot to his feet, clipping his mug on his belt as he looked up to the leaves of the tree, miles above his head. "What was the final result of all of that? Do I need to, no, wait. The zone warning said it was making defenses, which will probably end up being some kind of frozen fortress. One part of that was preparing the surface, then the air and space around it, but there was a third component: the call that went out. That means some kind of beacon effect or area emplacement to get more birds migrating."

Absolutely thrilled with his new toy, Joe found a space to set up a very bare-bones camp, then he sat down to study the intense design.

The further he went, the more he studied, the more Joe realized that the sutra's function was simple to describe, but as far as he could see, it was practically impossible to control with its current built-in functionality. "Feed in multiple rituals, a total of up to seven inputs on the Master circle itself, and it breaks them and collides the largest fractured chunk from each that it grabs. What if the chunks don't work well together? This is basically begging to create disjointed rituals that have randomized effects. Wait, could it be that this is some kind of ritual randomizer? A natural gatcha game?"

Stymied by his inability to actually practice the ritual—as

even a single activation would require an Artifact-rank core—the Ritualist wasn't about to waste his most potent cores on *testing* this magic before doing everything he could to diagram, theorize, and narrow down the potential output. Progress was frustratingly slow, as he could only *hypothesize*, but progress did happen, thanks to the sheer breadth of his relevant lore skills, which were doing the majority of the heavy lifting.

Ritual Lore and Magical Syntax Lore allowed him to assess the foundational grammar of the circles, their clauses, how they *should* interact with whatever was given to them. Calculus and Number Theory, alongside Magical Matrices, allowed him to make information-based predictions on where the break points of rituals given to the input would be, alongside where they'd be placed in conjunction with the other largest chunks. Even so, he was having trouble determining the final position of the outer, Master-rank circle until he glanced upward, a breeze flowing over him and forcing his eyes away from the page.

He caught a glimpse of the stars at that moment, as the grass swayed, and the leaves far above shifted in the wind. "Ah! I'll need to add in Celestial-Arcane interaction, there's no way I'm going to forget to take the constellations into effect for something this powerful. It's going to need all the help it can get, so I suppose I can put that piece off until I get back to the observatory."

The realization that he could offload some of the design until later allowed Joe to put placeholders down in his notes and skip large sections of the work that he was otherwise trying to brute-force. Still, working on his diagram as pure theory felt like speaking in four different languages and trying to combine them into a fifth on the fly.

"If ritual input A is split along *this* axis, colliding with B, it'll be expressed as AB fragments, right? But that's assuming it takes *entire* clauses at a time and cuts them off at neat junctures instead of just wherever it wants. It could well be that it's absorbing the active effect of the ritual and nullifying the rest of it, generating an entirely new magic circle that it inserts here.

How could I shift this to the intersection point here? I need some kind of a... a weighting mechanism or something. A way to bias the output toward my desired goal instead of randomizing. But how can I focus the effects of the ritual at this point, instead of across the entirety of-"

Glancing down, Joe realized he was fiddling with a ritual token, rolling it across his fingers as he was lost in thought. "Eureka! Heh, always wanted to say that. I need a *magical focus*. I already know how to do that; it's the basis of almost every Enchanted weapon, and there's an entire section on magical foci in my Ritual Orb templates."

Papers began to pile up around him, held down by large rocks in some cases, a reaction to the immense downbursts of wind on this planet. Just as he was hastily finishing his thoughts on yet *another* loose leaf paper and sending it next to the ring he was making around himself, a terrific shockwave rolled over him, nearly flattening the grass he was using to shield the small alcove he'd been camping in. Still, the noise was thunderous, and fully broke Joe out of his deep dive into ritual theory.

Without missing a beat, the Ritualist jumped atop the bent blade of grass, managing to get in position just before it sprang back to its normal height, projectiling him into the air as though he'd launched himself from a ballista which had *itself* been tossed into the air by an oversized trebuchet. Thanks to the majority of the flora closer to the epicenter of the blast still laying flat, Joe was then able to see the rampant destruction on the horizon.

As the view opened up, it revealed miles of terrain warped from some enormous skills or spells that had gone off, flattening the Tyrant penguin's burgeoning rookery-fortress. Hundreds of massive penguins were slowly arcing toward the ground, making no move to catch themselves as they fell head-first. Even the refrozen ground had transformed under a wash of blistering heat.

Small flashes of light in the cloud of rising smoke and dust signaled that the kill squad had arrived, and the battle was ongoing. As Joe slowly returned to being under gravity's hold, he breathed out a slow sigh of relief—perhaps mixed in with a *tiny* pinch of envy at not being able to generate such massive effects on his own at the moment. If he were being honest with himself, the Ritualist would have to admit that he liked to be the solution to the problems he created, not a bystander biting his nails and hoping someone else would clean up his mess.

"No, it's *fine*. The Sect can handle this one, and I'm even going to be paying them to do it." As he allowed his Ritual Orb of Strength to lift off his belt, grabbing it for an instant to spin up into the air and slowing his downward descent significantly, Joe tried to force himself to let go of his frustration. "Delegation is normal. That's a source of income for them, job security, and gives them purpose. I can't keep doing everything for them, even when I'm the one…"

He landed on the springy grass, sliding down with his arms crossed petulantly as he waged an internal war with himself. Finally, he kicked off at the last moment, landing on the ground and rolling once, coming to a stop in his original position surrounded by notes. "I need a change of pace. What was I doing? Right! Magical focus!"

Pulling out a blank token, Joe hesitated for only a moment, looking around at the thin layer of defenses he'd put in place throughout the area. "I should be fine to sink into an enchantment trance, but just in case…"

He placed dozens more rituals around his camp, concentric ring after ring, going out nearly three hundred paces in total before he felt fully confident that he'd be able to handle any of Jotunheim's threats at a moment's notice. Then he returned to his central area, arranging his stabilizers around himself until he was sitting in a ring of shining metal capturing the ambient power of the area and only allowing it to reach him after it was a soft, soothing touch to his painfully sensitive arcane senses.

"Okay, system. I'm not trying to make a mana focus for some random weapon, this is specifically going to be for my rituals, to artificially stunt inputs in one area and overemphasize them in another, based on where I place it. I can't show my intent more clearly than this." Glancing around and hoping for some sign of acknowledgement, only to receive none, Joe pressed his lips into a firm line and could only hope the token wouldn't detonate in his unshielded hands. *Any* enchantment he tried to make that wasn't specifically for rituals would automatically fail, and he'd probably lose a finger or two at the minimum. Without access to his healing spells, he was far less willing to take that risk.

He stared at the palm-sized disk of silvery alloy, took a deep breath, and focused on his Tokenization Mindset while allocating a small part of his mind to aligning the enchantment he was trying to create with the constellations which governed this particular magical item.

The world faded around him, and in an instant, Joe was no longer at the base of the grassy forest. For a long heartbeat, he was in a space of absolute darkness, then stars appeared above him, galaxies swirling out impossibly fast and settling in place as his intent to make a magical focus enchantment was infused into the token.

Lifting his hands, Joe had only a heartbeat of time to manifest an inscription tool in each of them before an immense lattice appeared in front of him. His balance shifted suddenly, and the Ritualist glanced down in surprise, only to find that he was standing on a slice of darkness shaped like a surfboard leaving a soft wake of glittering stardust in the void behind him —and he was beginning to move faster.

The combination of the two minigames caught him completely off guard, as the interaction of Celestial Surfing and Tokenization Mindset hadn't been something he thought was possible. "Still, this is pretty... *pretty*."

His hands smoothly moved to his sides, the tips of his inscription tools lighting up as they came in contact with the dull lines he needed to trace. From that point on, he was constantly in motion, mana and aspects pouring out of him. They were held in place and applied precisely only thanks to his

Mana Manipulation skills and the fact that he was working with his power *outside* of his body.

Thanks to the surfing, he also needed to focus somewhat on his balance and position, shifting his core to the side to dodge asteroids big and small, representations of imperfections in the blank token itself that he needed to work around and compensate for as he inscribed. Sometimes it was impossible to fully escape the hit *and* trace the lines perfectly, more due to his lacking ability than anything else. The minor defects in the enchantment were possible to compensate for and were even somewhat expected. But if too many of them accrued, the token would fracture, and the enchantment would fail.

His feet shifted back and forth across his surfboard, a far more forgiving device than an actual one would ever be. It moved with him, always underfoot, so long as he maintained his focus on reaching the first of his many destinations. Joe ducked under a massive block of ice-coated iron crossing his path, noticing almost too late that there was a sigil he needed to trace along its underside. He barely got the inscription tool in place, hands deftly flicking along the lines, before he was out and moving along a clear path once more.

Joe's route took him between a binary moon, the two celestial objects orbiting each other. For a long few minutes, he spun around them as well, drawing out a long ouroboros of power that pulled together and settled around the moons. The line began pulling them together and forming a singular node—a representation of the first major enchantment nexus he'd created in the token.

Hours passed as his speed increased endlessly, flashing past planets, around stars, endlessly avoiding obstacles wherever he could. At last, the final stretch appeared, a descent into a blank space he couldn't see anything on the other side of. There was no sensation, no pull of gravity, yet as the surfboard approached the edge, it slowed, then Joe tilted forward, his direction changing by a full ninety degrees as his speed increased more and more.

The lines around him suddenly shifted; instead of long stripes, which were symbols of sympathetic energy connections, or sigils that needed to be sketched out in passing, these became a chaotic blur, a funnel that needed power placed along nearly every inch of it.

Joe leapt upward, leaving his surfboard to vanish into the depths as he spun in place, his mind nearly splitting under the strain as he spun and infused power into his inscription tools for fractions of a second and minutes at a time. Mana and aspects streaming and bursting from him all in one as he became a whirlwind. As he drew closer to the bottom, he spun ever faster, somehow not getting dizzy or sick at the motion.

Finally, the last dashes were above him, and he drew his hands together in a sun-salutation pose, sealing the lattice from the bottom.

He gasped, back in his own mind once more, surrounded by grass, people, and metal instead of void and celestial artifacts; it took another heartbeat before the ozone tang of starlight faded from his tastebuds. In his hand was a shining ritual token, enchanted as well as he possibly could at his level, especially after having been caught off guard by the two minigames working together.

"Well, the system let me make it, which means it should be able to function with the World Boss finder-" Joe stared at the token blankly, blinking a few times as his mind caught up to his current situation. "Err... wait. Surrounded by grass, metal, and... people?"

"Now, why would someone, all on their own, who isn't even a Grandmaster, have *succeeded* in forming a way to find the World Boss?"

"Tiny castle that talks?" Even as Joe felt the words leave his mouth, he shook off the last dregs of his confusion and fully snapped back to reality, eyes searching the massive set of armor placed in front of him,

"You *damaged*, human? I see dried blood on your face, so I'll assume *yes* and let the short joke go. Once." A glowering face appeared in the wall of metal, and it took the Ritualist a moment to understand that he was actually looking at a Dwarf who'd just lifted the visor of his massive platemail armor.

The interloper slammed his kite shield into the ground point-first, leaving it in place as he extended a hand toward Joe. "I am Master Donvah, sub-commander of Vanaheim's Tower of Defenders Expeditionary Force."

CHAPTER FOURTEEN

An awkward silence stretched between the two as Joe stared at the offered hand, fully unwilling to put himself in a position where he might not be able to move away quickly if those sausages the Dwarf considered fingers clamped down on him.

Slowly, the limb dropped down to the Dwarf's side, though Joe didn't miss how his perceived slight caused the others to shift their positions, bringing their shields slowly in front of themselves in preparation of defending against whatever his next move might be.

The corner of Donvah's lips curled upward ever so slightly, his eyes glimmering with interest as though the idea of diving headfirst into a fight was the most exciting moment of his day so far. "Well? I've introduced myself. You going to stand there and be rude like this, or... are you deaf?"

"No, *you're* DEF." When in doubt, Joe always defaulted to humor, though in this case, he only elicited confusion. "Defenders Expeditionary Force? You know? D.E.F.? Nothing? Well, I tried."

"How about just a *name*?" Donvah's face fell slightly as he realized that Joe wasn't reaching for a weapon. "Or maybe you tell me exactly how hard you hit your head. Do you require medical attention before being debriefed?"

"Debriefed? Why would you want to take my underwear-"

"*Medic!*" Donvah called in a bored tone, "Someone check for a concussion; I need to know if he's playing dumb and has actually had some sort of breakthrough in the hunt for the Jötunn, or if he's just outta his mind."

The Dwarf's voice was as hard and unyielding as the cumulative thousands of pounds of metal the team was clad in. Even as the other armored figures shifted to the side to allow one of their number to hurry forward, Donvah himself never moved his hard gaze away from Joe. Seeing the human become agitated as the medic approached, the weathered face began to set along grim lines. "You're welcome to spare us some time and give us whatever it is you've been working on. In fact, we'll pay you, even reward you quite handsomely if you've truly managed to secure a method for hunting down the World Boss."

"I've absolutely no intention of hunting down the World Boss at this time, nor have I created a way to do that," Joe replied earnestly, surreptitiously slipping his newly Enchanted token into his spatial storage ring.

"Truth," a voice murmured into Donvah's ear. "Though the intentions are murky. He's being intentionally misleading."

Joe's eyes flipped to the person standing just behind the Dwarf, noting the crest emblazoned on his armor with a grimace—the man was a paladin of some kind, likely one dedicated to defending 'truth' or some other such concept. The Ritualist spoke in a dry tone. "You're reading my *intentions*? You must be lots of fun to be around. Know what? Sure, let's talk about intentions. First off, what makes you think I owe you anything? Simple answers, let alone proper explanations? You're a bunch of random people who invaded my camp in the middle of the wilderness and started making demands of me-"

Flinching away as a spell was cast on him, Joe took a sharp breath as he realized the medic who'd stepped forward had only cast a diagnostic spell on him. "Abyss, you didn't-"

Blaauurgh. The medic turned to the side and began vomiting, his visor acting as a strainer as he emptied his stomach and simultaneously nearly drowned himself in his own armor. Everyone stepped forward in an instant, closing ranks around the heaving medic as they tried to figure out how Joe had managed to attack without their knowledge.

"Wait! *Wait!*" Joe held both of his hands up and to the side in a universal show of surrender. "That's not my fault, it wasn't even a protective artifact-"

"How are you even walking *around* right now?" The medic finally managed to choke out as he yanked his helmet off. "I haven't had that amount of feedback since pulling someone off a monster who had injected his bones with acid and lit him on fire from the inside out!"

"Just a regular Thursday for me, buddy." Despite the situation, Joe felt a grin form on his face, a bit of dark satisfaction flowing through him thanks to knowing there was someone who fully understood how he was feeling these days. "In the future, I highly recommend checking with your patient before trying to do a diagnostic like that, if they're conscious."

"Two hundred years of practice without having any issues using it," came the somewhat defensive answer as the medic upended his canteen into his helmet, trying to wash away some of the mess he left behind.

Joe's eyes went wide as the medic shook his gear, then unhesitatingly slipped it back on his head. "Are you... that's disgusting. You only rinsed it. *Once.*"

"He already broke protocol by taking it off in the first place." Donvah smoothly stepped back into the conversation, shooting a glare at the medic that promised *words* after this meeting. "As I was saying, if you have information on the World Boss, I need you to hand it over. I swear on our honor, you will be compensated properly for your efforts in assisting us, but we *must* be the first to find and slay it."

"I really can't help you." The Ritualist shrugged helplessly, his eyes sweeping across the ground where a few stacks of notes lay pinned beneath stones. When he glanced back at the dwarf, Joe took a deep breath and prepared himself for a fight—it was obvious the sub-commander wasn't going to take 'no' for an answer.

"Can't…? Or won't?" Donvah's inquiry was dangerously soft. "Perhaps we weren't as fast as we thought we were. Could it be that you've already found someone else and promised your research or method to them? Someone like the Stormbinder's Tower?"

Joe did his utmost to remain absolutely neutral as the Dwarf questioned him, but it seemed Donvah had already made his conclusions.

"What I see here is clearly not the full story, and this is neither the time nor place to learn what trouble you are making for my tower." For just a moment, Joe thought that meant the Dwarf was about to simply leave, but his next words crushed that fragile hope. "In that case, I demand you turn over all of your research immediately, then you will come back with us and meet with the Grandmaster in command of our expedition. If you refuse, I can't guarantee a good end for you."

"You *demand*?" Instantly, Joe's left eyebrow quirked upward. Taking a deep breath, he felt his jaw working as he chewed on the words he was trying not to spit out. "I owe you nothing. I don't need to explain a single thing to anyone, especially when it comes to my *own* research. You coming here and threatening me? Well. In cases like this, threats are just invitations."

The ambient mana field quivered with scores of tiny shockwaves as Joe connected to and activated every ritual he had set up around his campsite. Ritual diagrams sprung into existence, shimmering light blazing as they began unloading their prepared power into the physical plane. For his part, the Ritualist leaped up and back just as the bottom tip of Donvah's massive shield passed through the space he'd been standing, sharpened and serrated like the blade a sadistic cultist might carry.

Elemental effects, big and flashy, targeted the group's faces, even as the more subtle machinations came into play, frost appearing and creeping over the joints of the articulated armor, the inside of the metal boots rapidly heating up, roots from the immense grasses growing around them bursting through the soil and tangling to create physical restrictions. Nothing Joe had activated was meant for intimidation purposes; it was all designed to eliminate whatever was coming after him as quickly as possible, and, failing that, give him enough time to escape.

"A Ritualist?"

"What's a *prestige* class like that doing down on Jotunheim?"

"He's wearing Tower Robes! How did he manage to slip past the blockade?"

The questions came thick and fast, even as a shield wall *clicked* into place as the members of the expeditionary force worked to guard each other. They were catching the magical effects fairly easily and were barely impeded, even as everything collapsed in on them at once. But that wasn't the most worrisome moment: Donvah was looking at Joe oddly, his jaw going slightly slack as he blinked rapidly.

"A Tower Ritualist that escaped...? No. Bald. A Master wearing the robes of a Novice with barely any honor to his credit? That's... that's Joe the Ritualist. I guess I'll be here."

The man being described was rapidly sketching out rituals mid-air using Somatic Ritual Casting, fully uncertain as to why his name had just been said with such gravitas yet so little enthusiasm. As he prepared to empower his newest creations, he realized with a shiver that the shield wall had fully broken at that moment, and each of the members was staring at him with half-lidded eyes, their faces curiously blank.

Not wasting a single moment, Joe activated both of the rituals he'd been designing, and directional planes of force sprang into existence. To his great surprise, a third, weaker and shadowy version activated as well—the fully passive component of Haunting Shadows coming into play and creating a spectral echo of one of the rituals.

Not a moment too soon.

In the lightning-quick instant between hearing his name and the barriers activating, the defenders didn't just go on the offensive.

They went absolutely berserk.

Shields, previously raised in a neat, disciplined wall, dropped out of their hands as they charged at him, half of the group running face-first into his barriers, only to be flung backward and into the midst of their fellows at breakneck speed. The formations dissolved, and strategy bled out of their thoughts like water through a sieve. Every last one of them threw themselves at Joe in a reckless, mindless bullrush, even as their eyes stayed curiously blank, any signs of fury or vitriol disturbingly absent from their slack expressions.

"That's new. Zero of ten, not a fan." Joe barely managed to roll to the side as a heavy gauntlet crashed into the dirt where he'd been standing, cratering the surface and reminding him that, even without weapons, these were physically focused, highly dangerous individuals. Leaping and twisting over another, who dove face first like a battering ram into a tree-wide leaf of grass, Joe quickly made a call and rushed back toward the center of his encampment. "If you follow me here, you're eventually going to be broken down; I don't care how much health you have! I have over a hundred total effects from my rituals targeted at this exact spot-"

The Paladin of the group hurtled through the air, having been sent at the Ritualist as a projectile, hurled by Donvah as though he were nothing more than a javelin. Joe's instincts screamed for him to get out of the way. With a surge of intent and a flick of his wrist, he sent three Ritual Orbs out and up, the triple strike sending the Paladin up and over—though the tips of his metal-clad fingers swung down and managed to painfully graze the back of Joe's head.

Eyes watery from the natural reaction to being struck in such a sensitive area, Joe almost missed his next movement, his upward bound shifting to a lunge to the side as one of the discarded shields was grabbed and hurled like a bladed frisbee, slicing into then *through* the flora he'd set up his shelter in. A defender bounced off the ground and rolled forward, scrabbling against the dirt as he arranged himself upright with near-inhuman urgency.

"Just a little more…" Dodging, ducking, rolling, sliding, and jumping beneath shields and people that would have popped his body if their blows had landed, Joe did his utmost to allow his rituals to continuously wear down the attackers, using his orbs infrequently, and even then mostly to either reposition himself or deflect and attack he otherwise would have succumbed to. Waving his weapons in front of their faces did nothing; the attackers recklessly took blows to the head without concern if it meant getting to him faster. "Got it! Next attack coming in from the left, then chest-level, since the next guy likes to throw himself as soon as he gets within seven feet of me."

It was moments like this where Joe truly felt the effects of his peak fifth-tier Characteristics: after merely a short span of minutes, he'd managed to map the attack patterns of the entire force arrayed against him. Obviously, if they'd been in full charge of their faculties, and varied up their attacks with skills, spells, or even planned tactics, his efforts would've been in vain.

But, as they were practically mindless and simply using the most expedient attacks possible, Joe soon found himself weaving among them with far less effort required, allowing his rituals to rain down lances of fire, swaths of chilling frost, and massively impactful columns of stone hurled at high speeds.

Dodging a roundhouse punch that would have ripped his abdomen open with less than half an inch to spare, Joe regarded Donvah with curiosity, even as yet another layer of roots burst from the ground and wrapped around the thick armor, further stiffening the leg joints and applying yet another debuff to the Dwarf. "This goes beyond rivalry. I can tell you're under some kind of compulsion, so I'm sorry that I'm going to have to put you and your team down like this. If you're in there, try to let me know who to go after to seek revenge on your behalf. Is this the Tower of Blood Rites? Did they take over your bodies from a distance?"

Casually sidestepping the Paladin, who had defaulted to throwing himself into the air every time he came close, Joe considered the facts and firmly nodded as his assumption settled into certainty. "Yeah, not many people I can think of who could put a compulsion trigger into someone's head like this, least of all a *group* of Masters. Plus, that's something they would've needed to make happen on Vanaheim. It's not like I've had enough time to form a grudge with someone else up there, right?"

Remaining within the same five-foot radius, Joe allowed his rituals to continue bombarding the constantly attacking expeditionary force, and slowly his stomach sank, and his mouth went dry as they just *kept coming.* They had no instinct for survival, no coordination, just a blind need to latch on to him long enough for the others to beat him into a messy, pulpy ointment out in this rural location. Even worse, each of them was declared for defense, not just specialized in it. That meant high armor, magic resistance, *and* health.

When the first set of rituals faltered and began to power down, Joe began to breathe heavily, working through how he'd need to gain some distance so that he could get a few more diagrams set up and working. Lagging just behind this moment was a shift in the battle, as the rituals finally began to prove that, though they may be individually useless, they were oppressive as a collective.

The environmental hazards reached their peak, the damage over time effects of bleeding and burning hit their most frenetic gnawing at the defenders, and the burst damage began leaving gaping wounds instead of rapidly clotting-over scrapes. The defenders bled freely, smoke pouring through the joints of their armor, and their sprinting was forcibly slowed to a staggering lope; yet they never stopped.

Instead, between one heartbeat and the next, the weakest among them buckled as his legs gave out, and his armor flashed with runes that covered the entire surface in blinding light. Even as Joe stepped away to avoid the attack that should've been there, that member of the force vanished, a soft clap of air collapsing in on the suddenly vacant space signifying that an emergency teleport had been activated. Eight seconds later, another blinked out of existence, then a third.

One after another, lifesaving artifacts activated, significantly easing the pressure Joe was under. "Don't know if that's chucking you back to the base of the bifrost or something, but if any of you remember what happened here, do your best to stay away from me so you don't get put under your compulsion again! You don't seem like bad people, so I hope you make it. Still, I care about *me* living more than I care about you surviving, so don't come back!"

Finally, the field around him was empty, with only a few oversized shield souvenirs to remind him of the impromptu raid on his camp, along with sticky sap flowing out of damaged, sliced grass forming a shallow pond and ruining the few stacks of notes he'd left out. Double-checking to ensure none of the group had remained, simply knocked out or something of the like, the Ritualist eventually interacted with his circles and deactivated them—allowing the area to return to a quiet, if heavily altered state.

Finally stumbling to stop, Joe bent forward as his chest heaved for air, sweat pouring down his head and mixing with the blood and filth he was coated in. A glance around showed some of his largest stabilizers sparking and interacting oddly with the environment around the areas they'd been cracked or chipped by the wild assault. All of his ritual tiles were exhausted, down to the last dregs even before he had turned them off. "What a giant waste... at least I lived through that, but I definitely have a few questions I'm gonna need answers for."

Joe was deeply disturbed at how such a powerful force of people, already resistant to magic, could've been under the sway of some unknown enemy. Sure, he'd seen plenty of people form grudges against him, but this went beyond the pale. "There's only two things I can think of that would make someone put this kind of effort into coming after me, and I'm not involved in politics. That just leaves a personal vendetta, but was my little spat with the Tower of Blood Rites really so... I don't know, *offensive*?"

Frustrated that he didn't have an answer readily available to him, Joe quickly rushed around the area, saving what he could, tossing the spoils of battle into his storage rings, and preparing to move out. While it was unlikely the expeditionary force was in any state to rush back here and try to hunt him down once again, he wasn't willing to risk any of their lives with that assumption.

Not when it was just as easy to press deeper into the wilds and set up a new camp among the megaflora and monsters; this time properly hidden.

CHAPTER FIFTEEN

Soft light filtered through the cave mouth, extremely dim by the time it reached Joe sitting with his back against the wall of petrified wood, which he found surprisingly comfortable. Darkness had never bothered him, at least not since he'd first gained the Ritualist class and the associated Darkvision which came along with the package deal. He took a deep breath as he looked down, the faint smell of resin a comforting shift away from blood, heated metal, and fresh growth.

Spread out in front of him were hundreds of pages of notes, gadgets, stabilizers both in perfect form as well as artfully damaged. It was unlikely he would need to worry about the rain damaging anything, and seeing as the opening of the cave—truly just a hollow in a skyscraper-sized tree—was barely large enough to allow him to pass, it was unlikely any monsters would make their way here, either.

"Unlikely... but if Cleocatra is correct, that just means it actually *is* likely, but with better rewards because it happened in the first place." He leaned his head back until it thunked into the wooden surface, and he had to wonder somewhat self-deprecatingly if the hollow sound came from the surface or his empty skull.

Joe was absolutely itching with nervous energy: there was absolutely everything to be done. He should've been sketching at his ritual designs, hammering away at blobs of aspects until they formed into forged items, spinning reagents to perfect his Alchemy skills, or perhaps studying the Sutra of Fragmented Oneness until it made sense.

Yet every time he reached for paper, pulled notes over, or manifested a hammer, he was filled with the same creeping exhaustion, the same thought looping back to the forefront of his mind over and again. "Randomly, impossibly, those people found me *right* as I was starting to have a breakthrough. What's the point of starting up again when I'm just going to get interrupted, have my work destroyed, or need to fend off a group of thieves who would take what I've made for themselves? Fifteen Masters at a time? If they hadn't had their minds wiped away right in front of me, I'd be getting frog-marched in front of a Grandmaster by now."

His fingers drifted up, gently nudging the bell of the Karmic Shroud Collar nestled tightly around his throat, the silvery chiming echoing impossibly loud in the small space as he did so. "Two charges to use before I can let it regenerate, but is two days enough to get done with everything I want to do?"

He knew the answer to that: of *course* it wasn't. Even so, the thought of activating the shroud and pushing away the never-ending attacks and random encounters at a volume no one else seemed to encounter—which were all apparently a manifestation of the system attempting to guide ever-better rewards and resources to him—well, frankly, the break sounded nice. "Actually, maybe that's exactly what I really need. A two-day break. No random quests appearing because I'm playing around with trinkets. No enemies finding me while I'm lost in thought. Just some *me* time."

Not allowing himself to overthink, Joe activated the second charge of the shroud, and a wash of... stillness? Peace? *Something* moved around him between one heartbeat and the next as the cave went quiet. The wind was still blowing outside, he could hear all sorts of natural sounds, but it was as though there'd been a white noise machine blowing around him, and now it was just suddenly... off. A tension he didn't realize he'd been carrying in his shoulders eased suddenly, the soft edge of paranoia mixed with overstimulation bleeding away with each breath.

With the weight off his shoulders, his mind was suddenly far clearer, and as Joe reached out to store away his notes, he noticed a slight angle on the diagram that had seemed... *innocuous*. "You little... that would've blown the whole thing up!"

Eight hours later, Joe sat in the center of a triple ring of discarded projects, stabilizer stacked to one side, notes on another, his Abyssal Bloom Alchemy Furnace tilted up with a thin trickle of smoke streaming off of it from where it had just finished cleaning itself. He had written, revised, repurposed, pushed, and stepped away a half dozen times with each of his projects, but every time he got close to eking out just a little more, the path forward he could see *so clearly* in his mind collapsed.

It was only a skill issue in system terms, as Joe could absolutely find success with his projects *if* he'd been fully healthy. But external Mana Manipulation could only stretch so far. Without clean channels threading through his body, allowing him to handle the immense stressors he needed to be able to work with in terms of his next rank of aspects, the energy patterns tangled and burst. Metal turned to slag on the cusp of becoming cohesive. Syntax collapsed, shifting from a planned mantra, a ballad, to a haiku made of groan-worthy puns. Even his attempts at condensing the problems down using Calculus and Number Theory turned them into little more than sudoku puzzles instead of proper matrices.

"Every time it's the same. I can build scaffolding until I collapse from exhaustion, but the problem is that the foundation itself is fractured. The damage is too deep. I..." Joe stood up, swaying on his feet as he accepted the truth that Jake the Alchemist had warned him of. "...why'd I think I could prove him wrong? Actually creating anything Master rank or above is beyond me until I fix myself. He's never lied to me. Abyss, he's usually so blunt that I'd *prefer* he gives me some comforting lies."

As he returned to his original spot against the wall, allowing the cool, wood-based petrified stone to suck some of the heat out of his over-taxed body, Joe decided to go back to his original plan. "Way too keyed-up to sleep, I feel like I just had a dozen shots of espresso-"

B-burble? A tiny, enraged Elemental poured out of Joe's mug, looking around for the coffee shop that would dare cross into *its* territory.

"Ehh... sorry, Mate, just a figure of speech. You know you're the only coffee for me." As he spoke, the Elemental noticeably calmed down, though it manifested a pseudopod arm, shifted to point at its coffee bean eyes, then at Joe's face, then twice more to ensure he got the message. It wiggled back and forth then sank down into the mug, vanishing into... wherever it went after unsummoning itself.

The unexpected companionship shook him out of his funk slightly, though he felt frustration physically pulsing in his temples. "I can't work, I can't sleep, my body is all but broken. What would someone else do in this situation? Maybe I'll try meditating?"

Joe had spent long hours each day over the last year getting into a highly focused state so he could work with Grandmaster Snow to rebuild his Mana Channels, but having learned his lesson from the last hours of being confronted with failure at every turn, he instead attempted to dive deeper, aiming for a trance-like state instead of focusing on particular problems.

Over the next few minutes, which slowly dragged out into half hour, then an hour, Joe allowed his breath to slow down. His shoulders unclenched, and thanks to the now-silent chiming of the bell on his karmic shroud, no monsters rushed him from the darkness where they shouldn't be. No random people on an unrelated mission sought him out. No trainees knocked on his door to get some tips for progression. Slowly, the light pouring through the mouth of the cave dwindled further as the clouds outside thickened, until even the stabilizers scattered around the room were indistinct reflective surfaces, and the papers laid out melded with the ground, indistinguishable from their surroundings.

His thoughts slowed down as his vision tunneled, then slowly faded away as his eyes fluttered shut.

Then, completely unexpectedly, he blinked as he found himself in a cavernous space not entirely dissimilar to the void he'd found himself in while creating his Enchanted token.

Directly in front of him was a bright red set of numbers, a simple one and zero. There was no explanation, no label. At first, Joe simply acknowledged the numbers and didn't worry too much about why they seemed so sharp and real, while everything else had a bit of a fuzzy, dreamlike blur hiding their finer details.

Then the two numbers vanished, leaving behind only a nine. His eyes widened, and Joe felt his stomach sink as he realized this wasn't just random numbers... it was some kind of a countdown. "Great. Random countdowns have never been a bad thing, especially when they're written out in bright red and oddly danger-shaped."

Taking his eyes off the digit, the Ritualist swept his vision across the open area, feeling oddly comfortable and at peace in the space. In the distance, he noticed enormous shifting ink flowing up and down a curve which had to be a wall, or at least a distinct edge to the space he found himself in. Joe took a few steps, or at least tried to, only to realize with a start that he didn't have any legs. A glance down only revealed clutter, building blocks and patches of 'land' covered in some kind of fluid which didn't seem to belong where it was pooling.

"Ah. I'm in my mind." By taking a few moments and really *thinking* about what he was staring at, the Ritualist realized that, not only did it become more and more detailed, he had gained a surprisingly large amount of information on it. "No, I just *know* what it is. That's adrenaline, but it should be in that pipe over there, not just leaking out like it is. That can't be healthy, right?"

He struggled to move closer to the leaky pipe he just absolutely knew was under that piece of rubble, but realized with frustration that he was wobbling back and forth in place like an astronaut out of arm's reach of a surface. He was just stuck in midair, unable to properly navigate the area. "All right, there has to be some sort of trick to this. Think, Joe. You're obviously in your own head, now just literally instead of *figuratively* like earlier. How would someone go about moving without legs? I'm a floating ball—wait. I move floating balls around all the time. Can I treat myself like a Ritual Orb and use psychic-"

At the speed of thought, Joe was suddenly near the edge of the space, having hurled himself across the vast distance with a tiny application of intent. Even then, he didn't manage to catch himself before slamming into the wall. He simply slowed to a stop, unable to approach the massive shifting characters flowing along what now appeared to be an ossified layer of curved bone. "The inside of my skull? Okay, I know I don't actually have this sort of space in my head, which means this has to be symbolic of my thoughts somehow. With that in mind—heh, in mind—what am I *looking* at?"

Spinning himself around, Joe looked back the way he'd come, only to flinch as he saw the countdown timer shifting from one to zero. He grit his non-existent teeth, fully prepared to feel himself thrown out of this trance-like state and back into his normal body... only for the zero to shift into a ten. A few moments later, it dropped back down to a nine once more.

"Right, maybe it's not a bad thing? Some kind of internal timer, maybe?" A shiver passed through him, an ominous whisper telling him he was wrong. With an effort of will, he turned away from the far-too-clear numbers and tried to simply focus on his thoughts, as he had planned to do when attempting meditation.

"Not here to test things or do stuff, just because it's a space I've never been in before," Joe promised himself, though he continued to peek at the open space which was covered in rubble, dust, and all forms of goo. "None of this makes sense in the first place. I'm just going to center myself, think calm thoughts, and relax, like I promised."

As he calmed, he found that some of the dust lifted from the ground, pouring into the cracks along the edge of ruined structures. Until that moment, he hadn't even realized where the rubble had come from, but now it was impossible to look away from the gargantuan palace which took up the entire space. He *knew* it had been an open cavern only moments before. The edges of this inner world were gone, indistinct, no longer simply his skull. Instead, the massive shifting symbols now ran along the edge of the palace, and he found himself being pulled into a representation which made far more sense to him.

Twisting hallways of thought looped back on themselves multiple times if he let them. Shelves stood filled with memories, a doorway which led to an open caldera filled with dozens of buildings. Each of them was representative of various skills built into the palace itself. At the core, central areas were firm, perfect buildings with minimal damage, but with clear add-ons growing out of them. It was as though traditional buildings had modern engineers come in and put a machine-made shingled roof on hand-carved stone. Nothing wrong with that, though it created a pieced-together picture instead of a cohesive whole.

"Bonuses?" Just like before, when Joe devoted his attention to a certain area, he simply *knew* more about it, as this was his own mind. "Is that how my mind thinks of them? Just power tacked onto the original, not quite a cohesive whole until it reaches a certain threshold, and they get melded together more perfectly?"

Keeping that line of reasoning alive, Joe widened his focus to the periphery. The outer structures—each fractured, each incomplete due to the rubble surrounding them—bled into the living script shifting across the walls of the mind palace. The two systems were linked, not separate, yet not the same. After several long minutes of deduction, the realization *clicked*.

"Those are my external skills! Active skills that form inside me, then move out to interact with the world." Glancing deeper into the palace, he recognized the symbolic edifices for what they were: passive skills, anchored deeper within his mind, perhaps even his soul. Their position made them less able to reach outward or be reached in turn, thus less scarred by the surge of Tatum's divine energy that had rampaged through him. As his gaze moved across the landscape, it caught on a structure reduced almost entirely to its foundation—a smoking ruin built solely from *foreign* materials that matched little else in this space.

Even *looking* at it pained him, psychic backlash causing the entire world around him to shiver and warp.

"Well, if nothing else, I found a major pain point." Once more moving before he could comprehend how fast he was going, Joe found himself in the center of the utterly destroyed structure. Oddly enough, now that he was inside the building, it felt nearly as large as the mind palace itself had been, with the shattered foundation of the building being the edges of his mental space. At least a dozen new, pristine buildings were rising up out of the rubble within the area, and as he looked over the various skills they represented, a clear picture began to form.

"Enchanting Lore? Alchemical, ritual..." A quick scan of the others returned only lore skills, each of them absolutely perfect and whole—even more so than the others outside of this nearly obliterated superstructure. "If that's the case, and these are skills contained by another, made entirely from a foreign source of materials, then that means this must be... *Knowledge*?"

The floor vibrated slightly as if his mind were acknowledging his words, and the Ritualist could only look around in dismay at how little remained of the deity-granted skill which had been instrumental in allowing him to advance his professions, find new paths to success in crafting, and act as support for his combat skills. "No wonder touching on this one caused a migraine every time I tried to put mana into its broken channels. That must've almost literally been like powering up a blender directly in my brain."

He went closer to the obliterated wall, a slight ache whisking through his mind as he did so. "Yeah, just like that. So, that must mean this is what my Mana Channels look like from the inside, at least according to my... subconscious self? What am I right now, pure ego?"

Moving ever so slightly away, Joe looked down as he thought, only to notice fragments of the wall scattered across the ground, broken bricks, plaster... then, reflexively, he did what he always did when faced with broken things—he started to clean it up. A huge chunk of rubble was floating in front of him before Joe realized that he didn't actually have hands to lift it. Before he could startle himself out of this state and drop it, he slid the jagged block into position. As he let go, the rubble stayed in place, not perfectly reintegrating with the rest of the wall, but not tumbling away, either.

Skill: Knowledge. Integrity: .005% → .006%.

The burst of information wasn't quite a system message, but instead had the same flavor as everything else here: dreamlike edges, an abstract haze that just made *sense*. The Ritualist, surprised at the lack of pain and success he'd just found in reconstructing the 'building' from the inside out, instead of the outside *in*, found himself looking up at the shifting darkness above. "How can I *possibly* fix this skill, when I don't actually know what the original looked like? Not to mention, doing it all by hand like this is going to take ages-"

Even as a slight inkling of 'hold up, I don't *do* things by hand' formed in his mind, Joe found an inscription tool floating in the air next to him. "Would it even be possible to fix this with a ritual? Could I even do that inside my own head?"

As he twisted the shining stylus, Joe sucked in a nervous breath as a bright circle of mana remained in the air behind the razor-sharp tip. "Seems that's a yes on making ritual circles; still haven't got any confirmation on if this is a good idea or not. It's… well, as long as I don't burn my brain out, it's not like I can do much more damage to this skill. Hopefully, if I blow my head up, it'll at least clear out after I resurrect?"

Long past the need for a reference, at least for this particular ritual, Joe simply twirled the quill-like tool and let muscle memory take over as he began sketching a circle in the air. He could feel a structure in the distance begin to glow, and an odd psychic resonance flowed through the air with every motion that burned mana directly into his brain. "That's got to be Somatic Ritual Casting activating. Abyss… this is seeming more and more like a terrible idea."

Even so, he didn't stop as his lines connected and the circles overlapped. A Ritual of Repair slowly took shape in front of him—only taking this long because Joe wasn't certain if he should make it purely out of mana, or if-

Aspects bubbled up from the base of the damaged foundation of the building, having traveled through his spatial storage and flowing to where they were called. "Right, this just got *very* dangerous. If I just let these go in here, that's *True Damage* I'll be taking straight to the brain. Slow and steady here…"

With each circle he drew, Joe used aspects from a higher tier, going so far as deciding on using Common aspects for the Novice circle as he didn't want to associate anything 'Damaged' with his mind. For the fourth circle, as he was using Special aspects instead of Rare, the Ritualist hesitated for a moment, caught between two possible choices. "I could go with Anima aspects, as they boost healing, but I think Arcane aspects just make more sense here. Even if this is how my brain perceives the skill, this is still technically work on my Mana Channels, and these aspects boost magical conductivity. Maybe it'll help."

As the last sympathetic line was drawn, Joe began the process of targeting the 'building' in his brain and ran into his first major hurdle. The fact was, this was a ritual meant for repairing real, physical buildings, and this simply *wasn't* one. Even so, the ritual was completed, and spinning around *inside* his skull. Joe stared at the circles, the innermost one being a pearly white, followed by silver, light blue, then a steely purplish representing the Arcane aspects.

"If I try to just dispel this, where does all that power go? Probably straight into popping a blood vessel or blowing out a lobe. This… if I can do this much, it *has* to be possible to figure this out!"

In the distance, as if in reply to his agitation, a crimson number dropped to zero, then reset to ten once more.

CHAPTER SIXTEEN

"Do I cut the white circle, the silvery purple, or just do my best to pretend this isn't a problem and see what happens with the bomb I just built in my own brain?" If Joe had been able to manifest fists, he would've been throwing them at his own face over his sheer recklessness. "How do I gracefully shut down aspects made of plasmatic fire, when I've never been able to simply pop a ritual without literally making it *pop* and expend its resources as a burst of power releasing?"

Happily, the ritual wasn't unstable, which was another consideration he hadn't even thought to protect against. "Okay, I definitely need to figure this out before I lose the Karmic Shroud, and it starts melting down in an effort to give me 'better rewards' by figuring this out during a combat situation. Don't panic. Look at me not panicking! I'm just workshopping options while maintaining escalating situational awareness!"

Looking anywhere except at the floating ritual, Joe's attention returned to the hazy block of rubble, which was maintaining its position without any seeming support. It rapidly regained detail, and with clarity came new information. There were tiny threads practically bleeding off the block—flows of energy thinner than hair drifting along unseen currents before going taut, one after another.

Following one of the lines of mana, he found himself traveling outside of the superstructure into the open caldera of skills. Ever so slowly, the line approached the enormous shifting ritual inscribed on the mental palace then threaded into and firmed its position in relation to the Sage-ranked ritual before fading to almost perfect transparency.

"Oh." Joe had absolutely zero experience with Sage-ranked rituals, besides trying to read this one while using Essence Cycle specifically to cause his head to explode as an act of desperation. Even now, inside his own thoughts, he didn't dare look too closely, not with what all else he had going on at the moment.

Yet, the integration of the skill into the ritual made sense, as it was integrated into his physical *and* mana body. "That makes sense; these are leach lines, ways for my Akashic Record to interact with my class then my various skills without interfering. It's not welding itself on, it's more like... the roots of a plant finding gaps in a stone and sinking through them."

In a blink, Joe was back in front of his Ritual of Repair, a grim determination filling his gaze as though the circle had personally offended him. "Maybe I don't need all of this? Perhaps I just need *an* effect and to hook it to the greater system. What if I used the skill as an *input* to the ritual instead of as the target? Then maybe I can hook it to the greater system, and my Enchanted token could be positioned so that I break off everything except the 'repair' portion?"

It certainly wasn't the full effect of the Sutra of Fragmented Oneness, far closer to an organic layering of an enchantment inside himself. "Just need a tiny proof of concept, not a Master-rank ritual. On the plus side, concepts don't explode, right? Wait... maybe they *do* explode when you're a psychic entity?"

Pushing that thought away *firmly*, Joe reached down and lifted a chunk of the original skill, mentally applying pressure all around it until the fist-sized chunk of conceptual skillstuff began breaking down, shredding further until it was an incredibly fine dust. Already slightly tired from the effort, Joe wove the particles into a stream then carefully arranged them at one of the inputs of the ritual diagram. Happily, everything seemed perfectly content to hover wherever he left it, so long as he didn't act on it again.

Next, he focused on the token stored away in his ring, and though it didn't truly appear where he was, a glowing mote of sparking, chaotic energy manifested exactly where he was trying to place the enchantment. From there, Joe moved to the ritual and began running his thoughts along it, pushing on the surface and, for lack of a better descriptor, began *sanding* it. Seeing as the edges were already perfectly smooth, being energetic representations, the slow oscillations didn't change the ritual so much as shave away purpose. "Just need to make you a little weaker here, then here… a natural breakpoint when this activates."

Joe worked at the circles for triple the amount of time it had taken him to actually create the ritual as a whole, even as he left the final ring exactly as it was. No need to mess with the highest-ranked aspects, especially as they were already geared perfectly toward being conductive toward Arcane energy. "This is a terrible idea. I know it is. Hah! When's the last time I did something like this? I feel… terrified. No. *Exhilarated*. Eh, this is a 'both' situation. If this works, I'll be thrilled, and it'll be the start of my relapse into pushing the boundaries of my magic again, I just know it. If it doesn't… I might not be able to care."

Just before he activated the ritual, he felt a… *nudge*. A slight push had him biting his lip then carefully moving the token a millimeter to the right and shifting its angle by a tiny margin. "Really hope that was a Query Echo activating and pushing me toward a slightly more effective equation or structure… and not just my nerves."

The variegated circles normalized, white, silver, light blue, and steely purple all fading away and leaving behind the pale, shimmering blue of actively flowing mana. The powdered skill-stuff was *slurped* into the input, a tendril of mana immediately flowing out and creating a connection to the overall structure of the skill itself. Power flowed slightly faster, and the ritual began to spin.

Then the rings swirled far enough to touch the spark of enchanted energy hanging in the air, and it cut through them like an acetylene torch through butter. The Novice ring had a chunk carved out of it but was already moving fast enough to continue onward. The Beginner and Apprentice rings were sliced at nearly the same moment and began slumping inward as the entire ritual began destabilizing, clearly on its way to full collapse.

Joe gripped the ritual with his mind, barely managing to force it to continue spinning as he held the circles together through sheer force of will. Instead of crumpling, the rings continued moving, the Enchanted token erasing swaths of it along the breakpoints he had hoped it would hit, no... had *planned* for it to mangle. Then, all at once, the innermost three rings dropped down, the Novice circle becoming a crescent moon instead of a perfect circle, while the second and third rings combined into one overly thick diagram.

The balance was completely off, and each time the ritual shook too hard, small sections were clipped off by the sparking enchantment still remaining serenely in its space. Acting like molten slag, the snippets of the ritual drifted out of the spinning circles, then touched the foundation of the skill below.

Then began to burn.

Knowledge Integrity: 0.006% → 0.004%

Every ounce of Joe's focus turned away from the outside world as the skill lit aflame. Pain that had no right to exist took over his mind and began to rule him, and Joe let out a shriek of pain that would've done a tea kettle proud. He tried to return his conscious thought to the ritual he'd left spinning but was only able to free his paralyzed mind after long moments of accepting the pain and becoming one with it.

The ritual was fading, but now that he'd let it loose, it was at least spinning correctly on its axis, no longer clipping against the token energy that was hovering within it almost *hungrily*.

Then a tiny tendril of darkness whisked past Joe and connected to the ritual, and the mutated diagram stabilized. Power and mana began flowing in *three* directions.

Powdered *Knowledge* flowed into the ritual. Mana into Knowledge. Lastly, a thin streak of power burst *through* Knowledge then into a secondary input.

Unfortunately, the integrity of the skill continued dropping, due to the burning True Damage, now even faster as the connection to the greater ritual was being partially cannibalized by Joe's creation.

"It's stable! Why's it still killing the skill?" The foundation had cracks spreading across its surface, clearly on the verge of absolute destruction. "I knew the loss of the skill was possible, but why would that happen while the ritual is *working*? Worse, what's going to happen if that causes the ritual to burst? It won't be just this skill, it'll be whatever else is caught up in the-"

A huge pile of dust and shards were consumed by the rampaging aspects and power that had been cut out, then the still-burning plasma dropped to the floor after the thin veneer that had been shielding the foundation was eaten through. "Aspects! That's why! I didn't give it any resources to work with to actually *rebuild* the structure!"

Joe had already proven that he could pull aspects to him here and quickly began yanking them through his spatial storage and into his physical body. Distantly, he felt pain as the power burned through him. Thankfully, since he had an intended destination for them, the actual self-destruction was minimal. "Novice mistake, Joe! The foreign energy that made this skill isn't even here anymore. Tatum probably broke this one during his little spasm then yanked all of it out along with the rest of the divine energy he had flowing through me at the time, since it was all the same power. No wonder there was practically no debris left in here!"

Knowledge Integrity: 0.004% → 0.004%

The notification caused Joe to suck in a sharp breath, as it was clear to him that damage had occurred, only to be repaired at the same time. The flames were still coating the floor, and until they burned themselves out, Joe could only hope the natural regeneration of the ritual would fight against the destruction and eventually win. "Abyss, there's practically nothing left of this skill in the first place. What rank would a skill made of divine energy be? Mythical, at least?"

Finally the Common aspects he'd been shoveling in started to appear instead of being directly sucked into the ritual and used to fight the burning. Oddly enough, as soon as they crossed through the threshold of his mind, they stopped being plasmatics fires, and instead his subconscious shifted them into safer iconography. Enormous piles of bricks and wood began appearing, filling the space until Joe had a sudden surge of dread fill him—he cut off and reversed the flow of aspects, storing them away as the feeling subsided.

"I guess that's enough Common..." Bracing himself for more pain, Joe began pulling in Uncommon aspects, the silver flames shifting into massive spools of wire, nails, screws, all sorts of connective materials that would line the interior of the structure. All the while, his ritual drank them in, their symbolic form vanishing as they were used and expended nearly as fast as they appeared.

Knowledge Integrity: 0.004% → 0.0041%

Once again came a despairing certainty that he was about to bring too many of the deadly flames into his skull, so with an effort of will, Joe moved on to Rare. As steel beams stacked, and Joe approached the threshold of Unique, he decided *not* to skip Special aspects, as he usually did. "Already have these in the ritual, might as well use them on the skill."

Arcane aspects flowed in and became buckets of silver goo, a polish ready to be applied wherever needed. The Ritualist could only hope the ritual would figure out what to do with them, and he wouldn't need to handle another issue down the road. His concern grew as more and more Special aspects flowed in, the buckets turning into enormous cauldrons, then open-topped tuns.

There was *never* a feeling that it was too much—in fact, eventually he simply ran out and was forced to begin pulling in the indigo-colored, Unique aspects. Strangely enough, these turned into sconces ready to be set into walls, light sources, and tempered glass panes ready to be set into the currently non-existent walls.

Knowledge Integrity: 0.004% → 0.0039%

Glancing over, Joe saw that the ritual clippings had spread across the surface of the floor, like a viscous oil with no surface tension. "Nothing to do but keep going! Making a second ritual would only make it worse... right?"

Overwhelming fear struck him at the thought of trying to recreate that ritual, his subconscious clamping down on the idea with the weight of a mountain being dropped on his head. Swallowing bile, though a fragment of his thoughts wondered what would happen if he vomited *in* his brain, Joe pushed onward and finally began pulling on his as-of-yet untapped Artifact-rank aspect Jar, slowly, *ever* so slowly drawing the bright orange aspects into himself.

They became enormous pillars, load-bearing columns that stretched from the ground they were created on and off into the shadowy shifting sky; their details becoming hazy at that point, though they still seemed more *real* than almost anything else when he looked at them. One after another they formed, far more than Joe had expected to be able to need. "Makes sense, I suppose. A skill this powerful has to have a framework, but... I really hope I don't need to figure out a source of Mythical aspects. This next step is going to be hard enough as is."

As a silver lining to this whole process, as Joe was only essentially granting access to the components and leaving them for his ritual to somehow manage, he didn't need to struggle to bend them into shape. There was no adjusting them with Mana Manipulation, none of the metaphysical weight he'd come to associate with these potent sources. As he finished with the columns, the Ritualist could only hope the trend would continue with the Legendary aspects he was about to start pulling in.

He gripped the solid gold aspect and began gently tugging at it. The unyielding essence of reality began moving through his body like a literal bar of gold being injected through his veins, burning a physical hole where it passed until it reached his head and was thankfully directly shifted to the conceptual premises. Soon Joe was gasping for air, sweating profusely as the aspect continued pulling in, though as of yet, there was no sign of what it would become.

"Where is it?" Continuously drawing in the power he had no method of controlling, Joe began glancing around frantically, wondering if the Legendary aspects were turning into a roof or something that would be placed at the very end. Minutes stretched as he continued pulling singular motes of the energy at a time, knowing that even a *single* fractional too many would be enough to obliterate a good chunk of his mind if it went out of control.

Finally, mercifully, he was filled with the sensation of being *done* with the needed components. An odd acknowledgment passed through his conscious and unconscious self, the full understanding that if he'd been able to source Mythical aspects, he would've been able to use them. Even so, a wash of relief went through him as he realized this was *enough*.

All at once, the floor of the gargantuan building *shifted*. The cracked, barely quarter-inch-thick foundation that remained was replaced by a single massive slab of Legendary material. The flames continued to burn along its surface, but now they had no effect, eventually expending themselves as they found nothing to eat into.

Knowledge Integrity: 0.004% → 10.0042%

"A Legendary foundation for the skill." Joe wobbled back and forth, unable to focus on any one portion of what was happening around him anymore. The solid gold floor was positioned with weight and intent, immovable and guaranteed to stand the test of time. "Even if all else fails... now *this* will remain."

The world tilted, and Joe was forcefully ejected from his trance.

He expected to be rendered unconscious, but instead merely opened his real eyes, feeling fully refreshed in body, though his mind was heavy with the need for sleep. Knowing he was well on his way toward going under, willingly or not, Joe quickly flicked the bell on his collar and activated the final charge of his Karmic Shroud as he read over the notifications the system had waiting for him, allowing himself a single pleased smile before closing his eyes and passing into a dreamless sleep.

Skill increases.

Artisan Body (Journeyman VI → Expert 0). You have reached the Expert rank, after managing to fully experience the fact that a powerful body is nothing without a powerful mind to guide it. Your reward is guided by the method in which you demonstrated Expert-rank mastery: you are now able to intentionally enter a trance-like state and view your mind and Akashic Records in whatever method your subconscious designates.

Battle Meditation (Expert VIII → Expert IX).

Combat Ritual Orbs (Expert V → VII). You became an orb in your mind and controlled it by entering combat... with yourself! What a truly novel way of controlling an orb with your mind.

Magical Synesthesia (Student V → Journeyman 0). None of that was really there, you just assigned concepts to the magic you were immersed in. Okay, some of it was there. Like the fire you placed inside your brain. I suppose the ritual counts, too.

Somatic Ritual Casting (Expert IV → Expert IX). You need pretty steady hands to operate on your own brain. All that luck sure seemed like skill to me.

Mental Manipulation Resistance (Student I → Journeyman III). You're not supposed to be able to do what you just did. From now on, it's going to be harder to do it. Ten after ten in your head, a skill is sown. The fiercest fight is the one you don't own.

Though he heavily disliked the eerie nature of the message that came along with Mental Manipulation Resistance, it was still somewhat of a relief to understand what the countdown timer had been all about. Still, there was missing context. Barely able to remain awake, Joe mumbled sleepily, "Ten… *what?* Minutes? Hours? How long was I actually in there?"

With no answers forthcoming, the Ritualist finally looked to the message he'd really been waiting for, only to realize he wasn't sure how he felt about what he was seeing.

Skill Devolution in progress! Deity-granted skill 'Knowledge' is becoming a Legendary skill! Once skill integrity reaches 100%, the skill description will shift. Components allocated to (Legendary rank) skill: 100%. Mana requirements: 1.021%.

All Mana Regeneration will be devoted to the skill devolution until it is completed.

Damage taken: 1,111.

Current health: 1,334/4,546

Mana: 172/3,901

Mana Regeneration: 0 (42.98)

Finally unable to keep his eyes open for another moment, Joe slipped into a deep, healing sleep.

CHAPTER SEVENTEEN

Time remaining until Karmic Shroud goes on cooldown: 2 minutes, 39 seconds.

"Not the message I was expecting to wake up to, but still cool with it." Joe stretched, body aching at every joint, head throbbing, but eyes bright and excited as he saw that he was regenerating mana again. "Looks like I slept for almost a full day, but celestial *feces*, did I need it. All right, Knowledge, show me what you became!"

Skill devolution complete. 'Knowledge' (Expert I) has decreased two rarity ranks and has become...

Loremaster (Master IX). Accrued understanding no longer instantly floods your brain and neatly collates itself into a proper understanding. Instead, it filters through you like sediment settling in a vial;:slowly, yet inevitably. Though you can no longer force insight, clarity always arrives over time.

Effect:

1) Choose a single lore skill to gain passive understanding of. Over the course of a period of time required to gain Master rank zero, 10,000 hours, you will gain levels in the skill until reaching that threshold.

Each level of Mastery after that point requires an additional 246.5 ×

(1.2458^n) *hours, where n = skill level in the Master rank, with '0' being considered as a '1'. This is capped at the level of Loremaster. The ninth level can be fully 'researched' with the time requirement of 2,219.7 hours, which will serve as the Enlightenment needed to achieve Grandmaster status with the lore skill.*

2) For every Master-rank lore skill you possess, you generate passive upward insight pressure, reducing the amount of time required to increase a separate lore skill by 15% per Master-rank lore skill. (Max reduction: 90%)

3) Active effect: Loremaster's Gift. You may create physical system-quality lore books for any lore skill you have. Each lore book must be studied and understood in sequence to apply its full effect. Otherwise, it may be absorbed instantly for a partial, instant skill level gain and a temporary comprehension buff.

Novice: Unlimited Production. Requires 30 seconds to create.

Beginner: Up to 1,000 per month. Requires 5 minutes.

Apprentice: Up to 500 per month. Requires 15 minutes.

Student: Up to 250 per half year. Requires one hour.

Journeyman: Maximum of 125 per year. Requires 4 hours.

Expert: Maximum of 70 per year. 12-hour creation time, requires 8,000 experience or one Unique core.

Master: Maximum of one per year, per lore skill Master rank of skill. Requirements: 40 dedicated hours. 12,500 experience, or one Artifact core. 1,000 Artifact aspects.

As this skill is technically self-created, it automatically achieves the Master rank. The remnant divine energy was fully absorbed by the new skill as skill levels. Due to the method of this skill's creation, it was formed with the foundational requirements of a Grandmaster-rank skill, therefore all needs for Enlightenment have been met. Apply 100 Mastery Merits to achieve Grandmaster rank!

Due to gaining 9 Mastery levels, you have earned 50 characteristic points per characteristic. (Deferred until passing the characteristic threshold.)

Caution: additional direct alteration of your Specialization (Reductionist) may result in your class collapsing. Potentially explosively. It is <u>highly</u> suggested you find a different, less permanently-lethal method of altering skills in your mind and soul than by siphoning power and stability from *your class imbuement. External adjustments, while costly and potentially time consuming, are less likely to have permanent negative effects.*

Reductionist class experience: -3,593. Experience gain with this class is reduced by 85% until the lost amount has been recovered.

"Well. That's… a lot." Joe's mind whirled with ideas, chiefly among them a war with himself over whether he should pursue fixing his Mana Channels and restoring his skills, or if he should instead plan on rebuilding each of them on his own, *perhaps* with a safer method. "Instant peak Master in that skill by rebuilding it without the system's help. Now *that*'s a sweet benefit… is that what Jake meant when he told me to use this as an opportunity?"

Then he realized the likely outcome of fully restoring his Mana Channels using his self-created Core Class Skill method and nearly began salivating at the thought of potentially bringing his Coalescence and Mana Manipulation to peak Mastery as well. "New plan. Hand off every part of this project to someone else and focus on rebuilding as many of my individual skills as possible while they all work to bring it together. I'll get as many benefits out of this admittedly painful trial as I can grab."

An odd sensation collapsed around him at that moment, and Joe shivered slightly as his karma reconnected him and the world once more. In the distance, a monster roared with hunger… but he was *pretty* sure that had nothing to do with him.

Sweeping his notes and gadgets into his spatial storage rings and codpiece, Joe turned to leave, only to pause and look back at the wall he'd been laying against. There was an odd… *fluctuation* there. Pulling out his inscription tool, Joe decided to use Common aspects to burn a message into the wall; the realization he had attained here meant he would always remember this spot. Perhaps he could give anyone who found the place something to think about as well.

'Do something noble with your suffering. The pain may pass, but the nobility will always remain.'

As he stepped away and looked over the message he had burned into the petrified stone, Joe took a long moment to think over several poignant times in his life when his suffering had faded. Each time he had pressed on through the pain, he'd become a better version of himself.

"I hope I can eventually look back and think of this as one of those times," the Ritualist murmured as he turned away and hurried to the exit, fully aware that any passing monster could trap him in this cave if he lingered too long. Just before he exited, Joe glanced at his skill list and applied his new Loremaster skill to Magical Syntax Lore. "If I'm reading this correctly, only about sixty-four hours until that hits Expert nine, then another sixty-nine—*heh*—until it reaches Master. Five and a half days until I have my next Master rank skill... I can handle that."

Then he was out of the cave, falling a dozen meters to the loamy ground below. He impacted the surface, kicking up a mound of soil as he immediately broke into a sprint. Joe ran like a man who had exactly zero interest in searching for hidden treasures, seeking out powerful monsters, or interacting with lost adventurers.

His slippers *squelched* against muddy surfaces, only their self-cleaning enchantment allowing them to have survived this long out in the frontier of Jotunheim. Every step he took sent a wash of pain through him; his minimal health regeneration had barely scratched the surface of the damage he'd taken since leaving the sect territory that he was now rushing toward.

"Why didn't I choose my Neutrality Aura to rebuild instead of Knowledge?" Joe grumbled at himself, though he wasn't truly upset at how things had worked out. "I've got bright white, clean robes on, but every inch of exposed skin has a quarter inch of blood and filth coating it. Abyss, I don't think I've ever been this happy not to have hair to worry about. I can't imagine how long it would've taken to scrub this out if it had gotten matted down."

Zigzagging between towering grass stalks thicker than trees,

Joe suddenly stopped on a dime, turning around in an instant and hoping the small pride of prowling Leopards hadn't noticed his sudden arrival. His route turned circuitous from then on, a constant set of switchbacks, suddenly altered motion, and back-tracking each time he ran into monsters, found terrain he couldn't easily cross, or noticed signs of other people having been in the area recently. Now that he was aware of the cata-strophizing effect of the karmic imbalance between him and Tatum, he could feel a subtle nagging sensation, practically a magnet for trouble that painted him with a beacon that screamed 'monster buffet, open all day, *every* day!'.

Inevitably, Joe ran into a situation where the monsters saw him and latched on hungrily.

As he burst onto a path he knew would give him a fairly clear route back to the Sect territory, he felt his heart sink as three hulking penguins paused in their waddling and snapped to attention as they stared him down. These creatures had seen better days: their feathers were patchy where flame and mana had ripped chunks out of them and had open wounds still leaking blood from where they'd been kissed by a blade.

"Looks like you three are survivors of the Sect's purge of the Tyrant, huh? Hopefully that just means you were on the outskirts, not that you were some kind of *smart* birds that recog-nized a losing situation and legged it?"

Squwaaak! The largest among them screeched out what was clearly a command to the remaining duo. Wings raising for balance, they rushed out to either side of Joe in an obvious attempt at a pincer tactic.

"Abyss…! Why *wouldn't* they be smart birds?" The Ritualist grumbled as he rushed headlong at the biggest one, barely avoiding the headlong charge of the others who were able to move far faster than their bulk should've allowed. "Let me guess, you got upgraded by that Tyrant; maybe you were some kind of lieutenant?"

Proudly arching its back, the bird spread its wings wide and tracked Joe's movement as he raced toward it, lining up its razor-sharp beak in an obvious attempt to spear him and finish the fight with a single blow. Just as it lunged forward, the Reductionist tossed his Ritual Orb of Strength up, the crossbar of the dumbbell-shaped weapon fitting perfectly into the slightly open mouth of the bird and catching the blow for him. The penguin's head was awkwardly parried, though it merely grumbled in minor pain and annoyance, just as Joe would've if he'd stubbed his toe on a door frame.

"The creatures on this world have a ridiculous amount of health," Joe grumbled as he took the opportunity to leap up and to the side, running along a blade of grass even as his weight caused it to tremble and shift. His feet hit a slick patch, and he barely managed to shove off the plant just before he would've otherwise lost his footing and fallen.

Once more hitting the ground at a sprint, Joe paid no further attention to the penguins smashing through the plant life behind him, their massive bodies and anger allowing them to rip up a path as they rushed after him, beaks snapping as they came within striking range of the tasty human who was *ever* so slightly faster than them, thanks to the warm environment and firm surface he was running along.

Ritual Orbs darted in and out behind Joe, orbiting out and around enormous plants before using the momentum they'd built to *ping* off of beaks and eyes. Every hit only shaved off the smallest sliver of health, but the flinches he inflicted allowed him to gain a few more feet of distance with every impact. Finally, the heavily damaged monsters slowed down, screeching after him in anger, even as their desire to pursue him began flagging.

Joe finally chanced a glance backward, meeting the eyes of the largest of the penguins before they jerked to the side and broke off, waddling back into the underbrush and vanishing in the distance. "Smart monsters are never a good thing to leave alive in a place like this."

Letting out a slow exhale as he continued running, the Ritualist wondered if he should have stayed and finished the job.

"Eh… they survived the Tyrant purge and decided to back off. Maybe they're more focused on survival than becoming a problem. Still, if I ever run into them again, I'll have to be less polite about them trying to eat me."

By the time the Sect territory came into view, Joe's headlong run had devolved into a combination of hard jogging and limping, his heavily damaged body on the verge of breaking down. His Stamina was bottoming out, and he noted with great concern that his Stamina *Regeneration* had begun taking a major hit—now it was down to less than a third of its usual rate. As he staggered across the clearly demarcated boundary, he was greeted by a blood-chilling shout from a watch post in the distance.

"Monster incoming! Looks like some kind of skinwalker that doesn't quite know what humans are supposed to look like! Spells at the ready! Shields up-"

Joe glanced down at himself, reaching a hand up and scratching a single finger at his face… only to have nearly a full handful of grime flake off; mud made of a foul combination of coagulated blood and dirt. Still, his clothes were pristine, which probably only added to the incongruent effect which caused the guards to prepare to attack him. "Fair point, I'm gross right now! Still, not a monster. I understand, normally I'm a dashing Ritualist in the handsome and charismatic sense, but right now I'm just dashing in the 'running for my life and trying to get back to my house and take a shower' sorta way."

An extended pause followed his words, then a somewhat familiar face popped out of seemingly nowhere, a scout with some high level camouflage skills no doubt, and took a closer look at him. "Abyss, would you look at that, it really is Joe! Thought you were a local Tilbane that got a hold of some fabric. I've seen weirder things, trust me. *Woof*, you *smell* like one of them, too."

"Demoted," Joe replied in a deadpan voice as he marched past the chuckling scout. A few more comments were tossed his way, all of them a good-natured ribbing at his expense, as it was well known how much he valued his personal hygiene. To see him this... *crusty*... was a rarity for sure, so the Ritualist refused to stop or speak to another soul until he'd slammed the door to his house behind him, stripped off his gear, and stepped into the shower he had practically built his bedroom around.

Water sluiced away grime, blood, and sweat both dried and fresh, though it took three rounds of scrubbing for Joe to feel properly cleaned once more. Finally, he was left sparkling, though he was still covered in a variety of festive colors, thanks to the immense amount of bruising across his otherwise pale body. Reaching a slightly trembling hand out for his clothes—which had fully purified themselves of any remnant gunk after he had tossed them to the side—Joe got redressed and slowly made his way out to the training field, trying to recapture some of his dignity by walking with his nose in the air.

He settled into a comfy chair in the recovery section of the field, where a low-grade healing ritual was always up and running. Letting out a sigh as he felt his health beginning to trickle upward, Joe had to pat himself on the back. "Don't think I've ever been happier that I've handed off all of the mainte-nance of these rituals to the trainees under the guise of 'helping them learn how to do' the work. This is why I need schools instead of apprentices—way easier to drop scut work on a group than a person."

His surface wounds healed quickly, the bright bruises fading away before his eyes, but as the deeper wounds were touched upon, Joe could only let out a low *hiss* of pain. "Yep, they forgot to use the numbing variant. Not a huge fan of feeling my tendons getting pulled back in place to fix sprains. Ouch! Try to be patient, patience is... today let's call it a survival skill instead of a virtue."

As his body slowly knit itself together, Joe took the time to work through the next steps for himself, quickly building out a roadmap to recovery that he was intent on following to the letter. "Jake is working on putting together a proper Ichor for me to use; I can't imagine that'll take him too long to formulate and produce. Who can I trust to get the rest of it running? The metal components need at least a high-level Master. Should I... actually, I think I have some training and favors remaining with Grandmaster McPoundy. But I've been avoiding him pretty hard over this last year, since I still owe him a proper smithy."

Sucking in a sharp breath at how behind he was in his commitments, Joe considered asking someone else, only to reluctantly shake his head. "Better to just bite the bullet on that one. I can't think of any other Master-rank person or higher I could afford to work with on something like this. We'll see him first, since he's just a town over. After that... I'd go to Havoc for my enchantment, but something tells me he would give me a version that would work *bu~ut* would *also* turn me into a mobile fortress if I didn't break through a threshold or something within the next month. Don't want to accidentally turn into a golem, so maybe I'll take a quick jaunt up to Vanaheim."

His thoughts wandered to the Ritualistic Enchanter he'd met at the Ritualist Tower, Master Darling. A slight smile touched at the corner of his lips as he remembered the accidental gaffe he'd made during their conversation. "Maybe Darling would be open to trading favors if I brought her something unique like this to work on. Going to need to get up there and chat with Cosmo Hollows, either way—no *idea* who else I could even try to work with to get the matrices I need for this. I wonder what he would request in return...? No matter what, I *can't* commit to going to the math club twice a week."

Pondering that for a long moment, Joe could eventually only shrug and shake his head. "Nothing I can do but ask. Oh! I know! What if I give him Lore books from Calculus and Number Theory once I have that skill reach Master? I bet an easy introduction for anyone who wants to join his club would be worth more than one person popping in intermittently! That would be a win-win for me, since I can't think of anyone else who'd want to get access to that *particular* skill set."

With four of the five class skills accounted for, Joe turned his attention to the fifth and final, the only one he planned to be working with directly. "Ritual Circles... once I have each of the other components, there's nothing saying I can't create the design on my own. I should be able to figure out how each of them will interact, then make a... no. That's right, I'll need a Grandmaster ritual to control each of the Master portions. That's... hmm. There *aren't* any Grandmasters of Ritual Circles, are there? How am I..."

Joe's mind went blank as he encountered this unexpected obstacle, and he blinked furiously, realizing he might've just painted himself into a corner by going all-in on this plan. Ever so hesitantly, he opened his skill sheet and tried to cobble together a plan of action for that particular component. "Maybe if I finish getting Magical Syntax Lore to Master, then work on my Ritual Lore directly, that'll be enough to support my growth in Ritual Circles up to the Grandmaster rank? I can perhaps get there just by designing more and more powerful rituals, without activating them myself?"

It was a long shot, and he knew it, but until he had a better option, Joe had nothing else to go with. As he mentally reached out to close his skill sheet, he noticed an icon blinking. "Quest update? What's that all about?"

Quest update: Dulling the Sword of Damocles. You have made significant progress in slowing the ever-increasing karmic debt between yourself and Occultatum.

1) Let go, even if just for now. Remove the title 'Tatum's Chosen Legend', formally placing your granular bond on hold. (1/1)

2) Take three steps into the light. It has become easy for you to complete projects using the gifts given to you by your faction leader. You must complete at least three major workings under your own recognizance which would be easier to complete by using the resources on hand. Do not invoke or empower him. (0/3)

3) Convert at least one of the divinely granted skills you have been gifted into an arcane version which works entirely off your own understanding. (1/1)

Reward: Speak to Queen Cleocatra for an external Karmic remapping of one of your skills.

"Karmic remapping? That sounds like having her fix one of my skills for me. Is that possible? I suppose that means turning Knowledge into Loremaster was enough to count for this? Nice, a double win! And... maybe *two* skills fixed? I love it when I make major progress just doing what I'd normally do anyway."

Feeling emboldened by the unexpected success, Joe stood up and prepared himself to meet with McPoundy, his spine popping in several points as it finished realigning, the last bit needed before his health fully topped off.

CHAPTER EIGHTEEN

Grandmaster McPoundy's forge wasn't hard to find, but then, *getting* to it had never been the issue.

Joe looked at the structure, an Expert-ranked smithy that looked like it had been cobbled together from whatever material that could be found on this world. The walls were held together with support beams of Verglas Leopard bones coated in an unrecognizable metal. The floors were comprised of bedrock hauled from deep in the mine far outside of Novusheim, and the roof? The roof was thatched penguin feathers pulled from elites among their kind.

Taking a deep breath, he stepped toward the entrance confidently, only to immediately be stopped by a pair of axes crossed in his path.

"Got an appointment with the Grandmaster, uhhh… bro?" A Legionnaire questioned Joe suspiciously, eyeing him up and down, his gaze becoming uncomfortable as he took in the Ritualist's clean-shaven face and bald head.

"I don't, but I'm certain he's going to want to see me," Joe replied with a warm smile. "Why don't you let him know Joe the Ritualist is here to see him?"

"Joe the Ritualist? You sure?" The other Dwarf perked up considerably. "That's you, right? The Grandmaster left a message for you for when you eventually showed up."

"That's me," Joe brightly proclaimed, only to have his view of the world suddenly spin as he landed heavily on the ground, a clean sucker-punch sending him sprawling.

Slap!

For a moment, Joe was certain his Haunting Shadows had somehow fixed and reactivated itself, only to realize that the other guard had whacked his fellow across the back of the head. "Boulder-for-brains, that's the message we were supposed to give him if we found Joe out and about, not if he came to see the Grandmaster on his own terms! We were supposed to kick him in the chest if he came here, not punch him!"

"Well, I mean, he's right there. We can give him both messages."

"*McPoundy!*" Joe roared over the din of hammers beating metal into shape, on his feet in an instant with his Ritual Orbs hovering dangerously around his head as blood trickled from his freshly broken nose. "This is incredibly unprofessional!"

The air suddenly went dangerously quiet, every smith within the building freezing mid-swing. A low chuckle rolled out of the door, dark and mirthless. "Oh-hohoho. *I'm* over here being unprofessional? Where have *you* been for the last year and a half while I've been languishing away, working at someone else's forge instead of in my own... like we *agreed* upon? Know what? Let him in! I want to see his face as he answers me."

Strolling into the building without giving the Legionnaires a second glance, Joe tried to glare at the dwarf standing next to a flame hot enough that the Ritualist's skin went tight even at this distance. Unfortunately, his righteous indignation was interrupted by McPoundy's. The Dwarf was glaring at him with an expression that could melt steel on its own. The Dwarf crossed his corded-with-muscle arms and firmed his stance so that he looked like nothing so much as a fortress in the flesh.

"Joseph." That single word rumbled out like an earthquake,

less moniker and more abject judgment. McPoundy slowly raised a thick eyebrow, glistening with work-earned sweat as he stared the human down. "Glad to see you finally remembered that I still exist. Finally here to do right by me and fulfill your long-overdue obligations?"

Coughing into his hand, Joe felt all of the fight go out of him as he shamefacedly lowered his head. "About that-"

"Baldy, I *swear*, if you came here to ask me for a favor, I'm gonna call Stu and set him loose on you." McPoundy moved in a flash, his hammer rolling out and slamming onto the anvil in front of him, a hairline crack appearing in the massive block of metal with the casual strike. "Look at what I have to work with here. I have to be as delicate as though I'm forging in a glass-blower's hot shop. A *fifth* of my profits go into repairing the walls where I'm working, let alone the anvils. You told me that, when you had the resources, you'd remake my forge for me."

"Pretty sure I never actually agreed to anything. Look, is there any chance we could speak privately?" As Joe dabbed at the blood still dripping from his nostrils, his hopes to get out of view of the dozens of Dwarves pressed into the forge were dashed as the Grandmaster's head moved in quiet refusal. No hesitation, no room for argument.

"You can handle a small taste of what I've been working with. Let me promise you, there's nothing you can say that'll lower their opinion of you any further than what *I've* said about you." When Joe didn't immediately leave, a small smirk caused the Dwarf's beard to jingle ever so slightly, the metal trinkets and strands woven in bouncing against each other. "Oh? Maybe you're here to *grovel-*"

"First, I'll politely remind you there *was* never any formal agreement between us." Joe held up both hands in a placating gesture as the dwarf practically swelled to twice his size in preparation to launch into some tirade. "But I *did* come here to try and get into a position where I can actually fix all this. I can remake your previous forge, down to the scratches in the walls. You know I took a scan of that building."

"Didn't realize we needed to make a formal questline for you to follow through on something you *said* you'd do. I figured your word was enough, or at least that you'd be man enough to come and tell me you couldn't or wouldn't do it." McPoundy shook his head disbelievingly. "Well, don't feel the need to darken my doorway any longer. You want there to be nothing between us, that's fine by-"

"We talked *once*. It was a passing conversation, not a deal! That's beside the point—I haven't been avoiding you because I don't *want* to build the building; I've been avoiding you because I haven't been *able* to!" Joe spoke over the Grandmaster, eliciting a series of shocked gasps from the other Dwarves in the room, who looked between the two disbelievingly. "I know you've been in contact with Grandmaster Snow, and there's been no hiding that I'm a wreck currently. That's what I'm here to talk about with you, and yes, I will humbly *grovel* if that's what it takes."

Ever so slowly, the Dwarf deflated, though his eyes remained narrow and suspicious. "Keep going."

"I need an Artifact-rank item that can hold me in place and interact with a ritual and other Master-ranked items. I'm going to go in and physically redraw my Mana Channels inside my body." The room went very still as Joe plainly announced his plan, with more than a few of the occupants shaking their heads at his audacity. "The only person I feel comfortable asking for help on this is you, because I need this to be the best possible Master-rank gear. Absolute peak."

"Full price, and you're right at the back of the line." The Dwarf turned away, picking up his hammer and clenching it tightly enough that the leather grip popped along the stitches. "You'll *stay* at the back of the line, too. Every order and commission I get goes in front of yours. I've already waited a year for you to come through, and I've stagnated *hard* because of it. You worked through your promises with everyone else first, then kept me waiting this long? Do you think just because you need something you can say a few words and smooth over that insult?"

"No." Joe let out a long sigh, rubbing his freely sweating forehead. "I also know there aren't many options for getting a forge you can use properly. Besides finding someone who can actually build it for you, stockpiling the materials alone is probably the work of at least a decade."

"Only a few years on a world crawling with powerful monsters like this." Though his back was still turned toward Joe, much of the heat had vanished from McPoundy's voice. "Making a peak Master item for you will only slow that down. But fine. Out of recognition of what you've done for my people, I'll give you one more chance. But I'm also going to take an oath from you. One week after you've fixed your Mana Channels, my forge is built by you. No more delays. Swear it, and I'll take a look at your design."

"You'll also swear to make my-?" Joe had to drop to the ground to avoid the hammer that sailed through the space his face had been occupying only a split second previously.

"*My* honor has never been in question here!" Spittle rained across the floor, and it was clear the only thing keeping McPoundy from actively attacking was the deep desire he had for a quality forge.

"Yeah, that was dumb of me," Joe admitted with a bitter smile as he got back to his feet. "I'd never mean to impugn your honor; I'm just used to reflexively making mutual agreements. Look... I didn't realize you were having such a hard time, or I would've come and explained things otherwise."

"It's been a rough year, Joe." McPoundy hammered the words out, fiery and unfiltered. "Especially for the crafters among us. Many of us have the raw material to push our craft forward, but without a proper *place to do the work*, we can't push ourselves through the thresholds."

Just as he was about to respond, the Ritualist choked slightly. His eyes went wide as he was struck by the realization that he *could* create a Grandmaster Ritual Circle; he had the Legendary-rank Ritual Hall to work in, which could potentially allow him to at least *design* the ritual itself.

With that in mind, the realization hit: of *course* the Grand-master was irritable. No proper workspace, no stable footing, just chaos and trying to keep his people afloat through it all. The thought stripped the heat from Joe's temper in an instant, crushing every last bit of anger he was feeling. "Hey. Listen. We lost touch there for a while, but going forward, if you have *expectations* of me, send a message or something. Don't just sit in a hot room and be mad at me."

Snatching the schematics out of Joe's hand with a snort, McPoundy spread the pages out on a nearby workbench and scanned the diagrams, his pupils flicking over the concept with perfect precision, as though he'd already seen through every flaw. After several minutes, he shook his head and threw the pages back at Joe, allowing them to scatter in the air. "It's clever. It won't work, and it's *wrong*, but at least it's clever."

Bristling as he dove for the fluttering pages before they landed on the floor, or worse, an open flame, Joe growled out, "Care to explain instead of throwing other people's things around?"

"I'll tell you *one* of the flaws. Any more than that, and I'm charging you for the lesson." Before Joe could try to persuade him differently, the Dwarf waved his hand at him dismissively. "Making this for you makes us square. No more lessons; you barely need them anymore, anyway. I'll redesign this from scratch and build it for you for free. You just make me a proper forge when you can. I... *suppose* I can understand how working with such powerful materials is outside of your capabilities at the moment. Can't expect someone to build a Masterpiece with the tools of an Expert, when even I, a proper Grandmaster, have trouble with it."

"Yeah, it's not like the ritual I use to build a building is... is..." Joe's mind went blank as he slowly, inch by inch dropped his head down to look at the ritual he'd pulled from his storage, the *Student-rank ritual* that he'd used to build practically every structure he had put together since the beginning. "Grandmaster, I have some good news and some... um... have you ever planned to do something, then kind of forgot what all it entailed? Perhaps because you were in a lot of pain and focused on that part instead of what you were actually capable of?"

"Blast it, man, how far are you going to push this? Didn't you already get me to agree to everything you wanted?" McPoundy's teeth were clenched, and his eyes pressed shut as he tried not to lose his temper in front of his people... again. "Can you just say what you mean to say, instead of playing all these word games?"

"Let's go with the good news, then. Any chance you've already picked out a place you'd like your smithy to be set up? Because..." Joe held up the ritual sheepishly. "As it turns out, I should be able to put that together, *ahem*, now... if we can get a large enough group of people to help us out."

"I'm... I'm..." The Dwarf's mouth was working like a fish trying to breathe on land. "I'm going to go for a little walk. When I get back, I want to see my new building. One of you... just... someone take him over to my estate and show him where to set it up. The rest of you, go find two friends, have them find two more, and haul them over for a few hours of work."

"One second." Joe's voice was barely a squeak as he raised a hand, "Any chance you could spot me a Master-rank core I can shape the building around?"

The sounds coming out of McPoundy's mouth turned unintelligible, and he blinked rapidly as he swayed over to Joe, then pressed a core blazing with light into his palm. The Dwarf gripped both of Joe's shoulders and stared into his eyes—a deep, intensive desire to *hurt* him shining through.

"Stop toying with my heart and my livelihood, or I might accidentally kill you for real."

"Noted and understood." Joe gulped as the Dwarf let go of him, stepping out into the cool evening air and walking away while running one hand through his beard and another across his beaded hair. The Ritualist watched him go as another Dwarf sidled up to him. "Feces, I think I might've accidentally broken him."

"It's been a tough year," the newcomer echoed what McPoundy had been saying. "Between the chaotic mana fields making precise forging unreliable, unstable heat sources making our metals cool unevenly, unfamiliar metals getting pulled out of the ground, and an until-recent scarcity of fuel… everything has been harder. Then consider how his hammering pattern is designed to destroy and rebuild better, and you might see a fraction of what's been weighing him down."

"The mana is unstable? I have a ritual going, though-"

"Yeah, and when it goes down, it takes up to a few days for one of your teams to come around and get it up and going again."

Joe blanched at the realization that he hadn't come and personally checked on that ritual since he had initially set it up, leaving him wondering how many times it had dropped and crushed people from lower worlds like a bug—let alone caused havoc among the craftsmen's projects.

Seeing his expression, the Dwarf clearly wasn't certain how much more he should say, but pressed on after a moment of reluctant hesitation. "As the highest-ranking smith, and being on the council, he has a huge burden on him to train us, or at least guide those who train us. Not to mention the massive forging needs of Novusheim as a whole. Keeping the city stocked with weapons and armor, let alone wires and nails? At the end of the day, it's *all* his responsibility—even if he isn't the one who has to do the work himself. Don't take his attitude to heart; I can tell you it'll probably flip a hundred and eighty degrees as soon as he has somewhere he can retreat to for some personal time."

"I feel that." Joe sucked in a breath as he thought over how *he* had been acting before he ran away into the wilds for a few days. "Yeah, let's go get this structure in place. Then, maybe, I'll check on the infrastructure I put in place before I head out again."

The duo walked slowly across the paved stone roads through Novusheim, Joe's slippers scuffing softly as they strolled. It felt odd to be led along at what seemed a snail's pace, especially since he knew the Dwarf with him was practically vibrating at the thought of doing something to help the Grandmaster get into a better mood.

Finally, they walked along a winding offshoot of a road, to a flat section of land near the southwestern wall of the city. Unlike the rest of the space, which had been mostly claimed for various structures—habitation, workshop, or storefront—there was simply nothing there for a huge stretch. "McPoundy's estate, I assume? At least the land for it, since he hasn't even built a house here?"

"He likes to say that he likes to sleep next to his forge. Since he's always around fire, anytime he isn't... well, don't tell him I told you this, but he really hates the cold."

Joe chuckled at the mental image of the hugely muscled Dwarf bundling up in a thick coat and scarf just to go out in the current weather, but he went quiet, and his jaw dropped slightly as they came to a rise in the road and saw what was waiting for them.

Spread across the flat area were hundreds of smiths. Many of them had clearly been pulled directly out of their forge, coated in soot and grime, still wearing thick leather aprons and gripping hammers as they stood blinking in the dying daylight. The more Joe's gaze traveled, the more the odd scene struck him.

It wasn't only Dwarves waiting; there were plenty of humans in the mix as well. As Joe and his escort were noticed, the air began to fill with eager voices.

"What's all this?" the Ritualist murmured as he looked out at the small army of people waiting for them, slightly on edge since the vast majority had hammers out and ready to be swung. "Ambush?"

"That's just the volunteers," came the confident reply from the Dwarf next to him. "I'm sure as soon as notice went out that McPoundy was about to get something nice for himself, every single smith in the city came running to show their willingness to do whatever was needed to help him out. He's done so much for us; how could we do less?"

Joe was immediately filled with a deep sense of shame for having allowed such a beloved figure to languish so long. Bobbing his head, he rubbed the back of his neck as he swallowed thickly, his throat suddenly surprisingly dry. Muttering just loud enough to hear himself speak, he admonished himself, "Should have done this *months* ago."

"Yeah, that would've been pretty great of you," his traveling companion agreed lightly, clapping him on the shoulder and nearly knocking Joe over. "Still, you know what they say, the best time to start was a year ago. The next best time to start is right now. Shall we get to it?"

"Absolutely." Manifesting an inscription tool and pulling out a large ritual tile, Joe straightened his back and strode forward powerfully, soon finding himself deep in the crowd of people eager to assist. With hundreds of people surrounding him and eagerly looking on, Joe dropped to one knee and placed the tile, laying out both the ritual itself and the blueprint it would be creating the building based on. Next came an Ascendant Matrix and each of the aspect jars necessary to complete the project.

Once everything was prepared, he stood tall, took a deep breath, and faced the crowd. "I'm going to need three people here, here, and here! Good! Everyone else, back up! The next ring requires…"

CHAPTER NINETEEN

"Joe! *There* you are!" McPoundy lurched close, hand stretched into a claw as he reached for the Ritualist. Closing around the bald man's shoulder with a viselike grip, the sausage-fingered smith drew Joe close, and the Dwarf released a sigh so filled with fumes it nearly knocked him over. "Ya did all this? Fer *me*? I'll say it right in front o' *ever*'one! *Hic!* I was too harsh with you! I'm just a bitter old smith, but we-wheve all got our own burdens to bear, right?"

After a few diplomatic, yet ultimately futile, attempts to wiggle out of the crushing hold on his arm, Joe instead leaned into the swaying smith and tossed his arm around the stocky man. "No, *buddy*! You weren't wrong to be upset; I should've come sooner. I got all in my own head about-"

McPoundy blinked his glazed eyes owlishly, shifting his head so he could stare more fully at the masterpiece of a smithy that had been raised in the center of his estate area. When he spoke, it was clear he wasn't really able to internalize any of the words coming out of Joe's mouth, "Ahn *look*! Look at what you all did fer me, even after I tried to beat you into shape like an ingot of slag iron! Do you see *that*, Joe?"

The Dwarf pulled the Ritualist in closer, his voice dropping to a whisper as he spoke in a hot, breathy stage-whisper that almost had the human gagging as turned his face away. "Do you see her? That's my forge! My hhaa-*ome*, Joe! She's back. Down to every last dent in the main anvil. But you know what? I'll never admit it... she's even *better* than before."

On that part, they could both agree. Doing his best to ignore the full-blown party that had erupted, Joe swept his own gaze over the smithy, proud of the establishment he had erected. Thanks to a quick re-equipping of his Architect of Artifacts title, he'd been able to remain true to the design, while at the same time increasing the stats of the building by a full ten percent across the board. It would be easier to make stronger gear, less materials would be wasted, and it would survive attacks or failed products which would've taken down the previous version back on Alfenheim. "I'm just glad you're happy, McPoundy. It's long overdue."

"*Happy*?" The smith's face contorted as his eyes suddenly misted over with tears, and he shook Joe back and forth so hard that his teeth rattled. "I *love* it! Look how I treated you, even though you're Extended Family to my entire people! But... but *ffha-amilies* fight, don't they? Don't they, Joe? I had no good reason for it, all I had were excuses. Thinking I been taking on too much, then all a' *youz* came here and reminded me why we do it!"

His final sentence ended as a heart-pounding roar, returned instantly by the crowd of professionals in the area letting out an incoherent shout and raising their own unsteady mugs to the Grandmaster. Someone deep in the crowd broke out into a song Joe couldn't quite follow, which was quickly picked up by the rest of the group. Seeing that the Dwarf was distracted, a massive smile on his face and half the contents of his mug running down his shirt as he tried to take a drink while seeing double, the Ritualist twisted and escaped, leaving a few inches between them for safety sake.

The Dwarf swiped at him, a confused frown touching his

lips when he didn't feel anyone right next to him. His expression cleared up as he looked at his bald companion once more. "That gear you want? It's *done*. Eh, that's... *consider* it done! I'mma make you the best iron maiden you've ever seen in your *life*. You want to stab yourself down to the marrow and dump goo in? I'm going to make sure it happens! Not a single bone left unbroken! Blub-blub, gooey bones."

"Uh, that's not quite-"

"Is~ss fine." The Dwarf waved him off, not interested in being convinced against his plans. "Going to do exactly what you wanted it to do. Now..."

Trying to take another drink, the Dwarf seemed utterly dumbfounded by the idea that his mug was empty, but as he tossed it aside with a shrug, another person slapped a full one into his hand. Brightening instantly, the Grandmaster went to speak again, but Joe finally managed to cut in properly. "I'm glad we're better, McPoundy. Look, while I'm on a roll with all this, I need to go see a man about a math problem. Enjoy your proper forge, and... well, maybe don't try to use it tonight. If you get too close, I think your breath might catch on fire and burn you from the inside out."

Three slow blinks later, the Dwarf's mouth shifted into a radiant smile, and he roared out a deep, booming laugh that echoed through the city. "See a man about a math problem! Good one! Latrine is *that* way-"

Joe had edged away and was doing his best to quickly make his way through the crowd of hundreds that had gathered around them. Heavy hands swung out, clapping him on the back over and again, guaranteeing deep bruises. Even so, he didn't begrudge the people their fun; the fact that they'd come together without complaint and literally *fought* for the honor of being the one to help get the Grandmaster his own place spoke volumes to their temperament and loyalties.

"Good people deserve good times." His murmur was lost in the revelry, but that didn't make his statement any less true. As he finally broke free of the crowd, and started moving through the darkness of the city toward the shimmering light of the bifrost, the Grandmaster's slurred words reached his ears.

"With this, when the day comes, we'll be the ones makin' the weapons and armor for the legions to wear as they march on Alfenheim! *We'll* be the ones to outfit the army that takes the world back!"

The responding roar of approval would have shattered the glass of any Common-ranked building in the area.

Joe passed hundreds of people streaming through the city to see what the commotion was all about, though some of them were actually on their way back with additional party supplies in hand. Though he felt a strong urge to participate, it was easily ignored—he wasn't about to waste the momentum he'd started accruing. Stepping past the guards on duty, he took a deep breath and plunged into the bifrost, flung into the sky at what felt like the speed of light as he spoke his destination.

"*Vanaheim!*"

The World of the Sage's Ladders soon appeared in the distance, the towers looking like nothing so much as a thousand lances aimed at his heart, racing to impale anyone coming in with hostile intentions. Then he was among them, blasting past the black spines toward the landing point of the bifrost.

One moment he was streaking through the light, the next he hit the ground surprisingly hard, forcing him to stagger out and onto cold stone. Taking a few shallow breaths, Joe straightened and brushed his robes in annoyance. "Ugh. That trip had all the gracefulness of a cat coughing up a hairball. Does *everything* have to feel awkward without my auras being active?"

Then he froze, going so still that he even forgot to breathe for a few moments as he looked up and found himself ringed by grim-faced Masters, each of them radiating power and holding weapons held at the ready as they assessed him.

"You're wearing Tower robes," a haughty, high-pitched voice called out, "Are you with the Stormbinder's Tower?"

"Or the Tower of Defenders?" another instantly countered in a rough, rugged tone. "It's clear you're not new here."

"Neither?" Joe felt an odd moment of deja vu, as this was almost the exact situation he'd found himself in when he had first arrived on Alfenheim. A large amount of the tension in the area faded away, as the two groups stopped focusing so intently on each other, ready to start cutting down their opponents if one of *their* chosen Champions had returned with a Mythic Core. "Just popping in for a few minutes to get some guidance, then I'll be on my way again."

"Not sure how you got off world before the blockade went up, but don't expect to leave anytime soon," a massively armored man stated as he peeked through a tiny gap between the pair of tower shields he was hefting. "No one's supposed to be allowed to leave besides pre-approved expeditions. I'd *highly* recommend getting to your tower and staying there for a few years."

"Thank you for your recommendation," Joe replied neutrally, unwilling to verbally commit to anything, just in case someone among this group had a way to magically hold him accountable to his words. He had seen far stranger magics on his travels. "I'll just go ahead and get going, in that case."

Pushing through the blockade, Joe didn't ask any questions, doing his best not to look anyone in the eyes as he moved forward—small steps, as he seemed to be endlessly waiting for people to begrudgingly step aside. Whispered conversations erupted all around him immediately, the ambient manifold flaring as skills were activated, and spells were cast. Tingles raced up and down his spine as he was subjected to countless, exceedingly *intrusive* scans. His face went red with anger, both at the fact that he was being subjected to this treatment, as well as a surprising amount of shame over being fully unable to do anything to stop their prying.

"Is that *Joe?*"

"Mak? The cheese guy?" Joe's instinctual shift into a defensive position relaxed as the brightly garbed Kraftsman waved him over.

"The cheese *man*, thank you very much," Mak corrected

with an easygoing chuckle. "Did you get turned away from the blockade? They're getting pretty tense, with no word from Jotunheim on that World Boss they've been after. On the positive side, they say they are hoping for good news any day now."

"Maybe wouldn't get my hopes up about that too much," Joe stated under his breath. "It's good to see you, and thanks for your help when I first arrived."

"Happy to help, happy to help!" Mak cheerfully waved, his eyes already turning back to the prospective clients clustered around the bifrost. "Remember to come directly to me for all of your cheese-related needs. If you've got a need for cheddar, there's nowhere better!"

Just as he lifted his foot to resume his journey, Joe paused and actually considered Mak's words. Turning, he went over to the enormous wagon and reached for his codpiece. "Actually, I do have some cheese I was hoping to get your opinion on."

"Not this again." Mak leaned away, a hint of anger in his eyes before he realized that Joe was actually lifting a small round for him to look at. "Ah. You are being serious; sorry, I have heard *certain* jokes so many times... let's take a look. What is...?"

"Goat cheese." Seeing that the merchant was looking at the chunk only reluctantly, Joe plopped it on the counter and took a casual half-step backward. "Turns out I have a place that makes a bunch of this, so you can have this one for free. Any idea what you'd be willing to pay for it?"

"You're joking. Someone looked at a creature other than a Mooncow and thought 'you know what I should do? Ferment whatever comes out of this thing.'?" Mak poked at the cheesecloth, a few calculations showing behind his hooded stare. "On the house, huh? I can make a few inquiries, but I can't promise anything. Cheese is *supposed* to be made from milk, specifically *cow* milk. If this isn't useful, it doesn't matter how plentiful it might be."

"Useful." Joe toyed with the word for a moment, not sure how to put his thoughts into order. "What do you mean by that?

Wasn't it just that cheese had a particular way of aging well, and that became the standard for currency here?"

"There's more to it, but that's not my place to talk about." For the first time since meeting the man, Mak turned deadly serious. "Let's just say there's a *reason* our currency never becomes inflated and leave it at that."

Seeing that the conversation was most definitely over, Joe politely inclined his head at the untouched cheese. "I think that's really going to grow on you; let me know what you think the next time I see you."

"It *grows* on people?" Surprisingly, the merchant seemed intrigued by this thought instead of disgusted.

Joe decided to allow the misconception and started walking again, only to see his favorite Nyanderthal on the planet. Immediately, he detoured to the small cart-kiosk selling flowers, chocolates, and coffee. "Beth! How goes the sales? I was thinking about you recently. I met up with your queen again, Cleocatra? She found me on Jotunheim, and what she was telling me made me realize how difficult it was for people like you to get off-planet. Anywhere you want to go? I don't mind giving you a ride!"

"Welcome back to my little shop, customer. I have flowers, chocolate, and coffee. Feel free to browse. If you need something, I guess I'll be here." The orange-haired Nyanderthal's ears had perked up and were pointing at him with immense interest, belying her neutral, apathetic expression.

"Really, I'd be happy to help." Joe leaned forward when she didn't say anything else, speaking in a low tone. "Any chance you are cursed or something? My class has some really potent curse-breaking abilities-"

"*Welcome.*" Her ears had flattened, the cat equivalent of being furious, and the Ritualist realized he had perhaps been prying into someone else's life a bit too directly, especially when he didn't actually have any connection to her at all.

"Sorry, sorry." Joe held up his hands, "Just trying to be polite, you know me, always *kitten* around."

Beth recoiled ever so slightly, a green tinge on her face as though Joe had just made her feel physically ill. When she spoke again, the words were strained, as though she were holding herself back from being sick. "I have flowers, *chocolate-*"

"I get it, I'll go." Joe heaved a sigh, "Look, maybe someday we'll be friends. Maybe I just don't speak your language or understand you very well. Oh! I know! Next time I see Cleo, I'll ask if she could come along with me and chat with you. Maybe you'd be more comfortable talking to someone from your own Nyanderthal group?"

He didn't get an answer, though her ears were slowly moving from side to side once more as she stared at him blankly. Joe waited a few moments, but with a slight roll of his eyes, he turned and got back out on the road.

As he left the heavily populated area, the weight of dozens of stares boring into his back left tingles racing up and down his spine. He did his best not to break into a run, as he knew that would only entice those gauging him into direct pursuit. "Whew... people are getting pretty *feisty* around the blockade. Abyss, if I'd come out holding a page torn from a book or wearing a helmet that was made of extra-thick metal, I might've just accidentally sparked off a civil war. Ha... if I wanted to cause trouble, next time I'll just be holding an Artifact core in my hand when I pop off the bifrost. That should cause some drama, since it's unlikely any of them have seen a Mythic Core in person."

His brisk pace soon had him almost in striking distance of the Tower of Ritualists... and of course, that was the moment a group finally moved to block him.

Joe had been expecting this, as even with keeping his head down, he'd felt more eyes turning his way with each intersection he'd passed. Word of his arrival had clearly spread across the planet, and there was sure to be information and images included in the dossier. His stomach dropped as he realized there was a full squad casually standing in parade formation, obviously waiting for him to make an appearance.

Before the Ritualist could spin around and look for another path, one of the crimson and black-robed Masters stepped forward with a swagger. "You can *try* to run."

A gust of wind swept down the road, setting the combat robes fluttering. Yet, not a single strand of the towering pompadour—sculpted to an impossible height—moved even fractionally as the breeze picked up. "But believe me when I say every path has been accounted for. The cowardly members of the Tower of Ritualists won't be sending anyone out to save you or support you; all of their strength is fully converged around holing up in the tower itself. Submit yourself to honorable combat and fall here, or run only to die tired."

"Look, I didn't mean to be so rude when I first met you guys." Joe let out an irritable sigh as he pulled a stack of ritual tiles out of his ring. "What's it going to take to go back to neutral? We can still be rivals tower-wise, I just don't want this kind of personal grudge that follows me across worlds."

"We'd never *lower* ourselves to hunting you off Vanaheim." The instant, snapped-back reply caught Joe completely off guard. "Honorable combat only has meaning *here*. Elsewhere it's just bloodsport, and if there's one thing the Tower of Blood Rites will never do, it is make *games* out of the sacred power of blood."

"You mean to tell me you guys had nothing to do with causing the expeditionary force from the Tower of Defenders to lose their minds and attack me like rabid dogs when they found out who I was down on Jotunheim?" Joe could only shake his head incredulously at the claim. "No one else up here even knows who I *am!*"

"Now you're just trying to distract us, and it won't work." The Master settled into a horse stance, one arm outstretched at Joe, palm flat and aimed directly at his heart. "For someone to put an effect on someone that isn't canceled by the movement through the bifrost, and such a powerful group at that, they would've needed to have been at least a Sage—if not a Class Sage directly. No matter how highly you think of yourself, you aren't worth the time nor attention of a person that powerful. Now. Do you accept an honor duel, or do I have to break a few bones to *get* you to agree?"

The group fanned out, moving to block escape routes, though Joe kept pace with them, ensuring he had space to make a break for it.

"You stand before Master Surge of the Tower of Blood Rites! I *demand* you accept my duel!" Surge shuffled forward, not breaking his stance as he closed in on the frustrated Ritualist. "I will not ask-"

"Do we *really* have to do this right now?" Joe grumbled as he scattered tiles around himself in preparation of a fight.

"Yes. We *really* do," Surge replied in a slightly mocking tone. "We cannot allow the possibility that you carry that which you should not. A Mythic Core will always drop on death, no matter what container it is being stored in. No matter how secure you think you've made it-"

"I don't have a *Mythic* Core on me!" Joe half-laughed in surprise at the absurdity of the comment. "Is *that* what this is about?"

"That, and the fact that you're on the priority kill list and currently without an escort," Master Surge spoke with the unhurried precision of someone who had already won the upcoming battle. "As I said, though the possibility is low, we must know for sure. The easiest way to check is by putting you down and sifting through what remains. I will not ask again. Accept my challenge. Submit and die."

"Isn't that supposed to be submit *or* die?" Joe allowed mana to flow out of him, simultaneously activating a half-dozen barrier rituals in a ring around him. His attempt at feigning a casual attitude was easily seen through, especially as his pulse was hammering in his chest, the veins in his neck and head bulging and pulsing in time, and thin rivulets of sweat were running down his skin.

Frankly, he knew this wasn't a fight he could win. His only hope was to stall long enough that someone came along and pulled him out of this situation—without the ability to empower his external spells and skills, he was left to rely *entirely* on the rituals he had on hand. Seeing his opponents tensing up and closing in, Joe uttered the last thing they'd been expecting to hear: "Fine. I accept!"

"Cowardice is unbecoming-" The statement died on Surge's lips as he registered the actual words that have been spoken. "That is... very well, then!"

"On one condition!" The Master stumbled in his lunge at the Ritualist as the bald man lifted a finger in the air, then slowly lowered it to point at Master Surge, then each of the others that had come along with him. "I want to fight *all* of you... at the same time."

"Are you..." Surge began laughing, though he quickly sputtered out, "We accept! Now only *one* of us needs to defeat you in order for *all* of us to pull honor from your tower."

"Perfect. As the one challenged, I only need to survive until the timer runs out, right?" Without waiting for an answer, Joe spun on his heel and *sprinted* away. An explosion of shouting erupted behind him as the black-and-crimson-robed combatants gave chase.

From the arguments going on among them, Joe learned that they weren't entirely certain if he was correct. As he'd hoped, generally no one tried to run after accepting an honor duel. Yet, he'd seen firsthand how the Grandmaster of his own tower had merely needed to run out the clock in order to secure a technical victory.

"Your actions only prove we are justified in our actions!"

"Say 'actions' again!" Joe bellowed over his shoulder as he took a sharp turn. The first... tower member? Disciple? While he wasn't certain what each individual member should be called, one thing the Ritualist did know was that the first of them to round the corner after him caught a Ritual Orb to the face.

The man went down, *hard*, wheezing for air through a broken nose that was already fountaining blood. An instant later, Joe landed on him feet-first, driving his heels into the downed blood-user's chest.

Every bit of force from where he'd jumped off the street, then pushed off the wall surrounding the nearest tower was directed to crushing the man like a bug... but in reality, it did almost zero damage. Instead, Joe bounced off of him, stumbling and finding himself among the crowd of robed fighters who seemed just as surprised to see him as he was to be in the middle of their group.

"Juke?" Joe shot forward as if this had been the plan all along, going back the way he'd come and leaving the startled platoon scrambling to spin around and close the lead he'd gained.

Just as he thought he might actually have a chance at making his plan work, the Ritualist was painfully reminded that he wasn't trying to outrun a group of delinquents—he was fleeing in a straight line away from Master Mages specializing in blood magic.

Splut.

Damage taken: 2040 arcane. Debuff gained: Bleeding (Catastrophic). -65 health every 2 seconds.

Joe dropped to his knees, skidding along the stone surface for a few feet as he stared down at the thick spike of hardened blood that had just burst through his abdomen. In shock at the massive amount of damage he'd taken from a single hit, Joe blurted out the first thing that crossed his mind. "Huh. Spleen... *huuhghn*... on a skewer. They ripped that out... *uughh*... of my body in one piece?"

"How is it possible that you're *this* weak?" Master Surge's voice had barely entered Joe's ears before a harsh kick to his upper back sent him sprawling to the ground. Then every member of the battle group was surrounding, kicking, and stomping on him. "You tried to humiliate us with underhanded tactics? We'll remember this for the next time we meet each other, Ritualist. You should take a moment to engrave in your heart that, if you drag us into a chase, we'll end it by dragging you into a beating!"

As his health rapidly dwindled, Joe frantically tried to bring rituals to bear to attack or defend himself, but the group of Masters all but *contemptuously* broke through his low-ranking diagrams. As they were on Vanaheim, none of his assailants were restricted from using their own Master-rank abilities, and eventually Joe realized the only reason he was still alive was so they could brutalize him a little longer.

Finally, Surge snapped his fingers, and the rest of his people instantly stopped and took a single step backward with military precision. "Believe it or not, you're *lucky* you came back alone. We can't have a new Sage rising if they aren't going to serve *our* interests. That means any companions you bring with you will be cut down where they stand. Person, summon, or pet... every last one of them-"

Before he could finish his monologue or deliver a finishing blow, the debuff took the last dregs of Joe's health, and he felt his vision beginning to fade. Then, as he hit zero, his eyes snapped wide open. He felt a manic grin shift his expression as energy began crackling along his teeth.

Skin starting to glow, Joe's eyes fluttered shut. "Whoops. Looks like I died. No external control needed for this one, so let's see if I got the rules correct."

Joe's entire mana pool detonated as his Monarch of Mana title activated, creating a sphere of deadly energy that obliterated his body and washed over everything—and everyone—within a dozen feet of where he had fallen.

CHAPTER TWENTY

Oddly organic stone wall.

Joe blinked several times as he tried to reconcile the previous moment with the current one. "What's…? I died. I exploded; where's my respawn room? Probably owe Mom a message or three."

A low murmur of voices reached his ears, and he pivoted on the spot as his instincts snapped him to full alertness. Joe noted almost unconsciously that he was… not pain-free, but free of the new pain he had earned from combat. Almost as importantly, he was *grime*-free. The smell of the room hit him next: a faint ozone of spent mana, charged inks, and the cloying scent of reagents being used for various purposes. "I'm in the Tower of Ritualists? Oh! *Right*! Getting killed in an Honor Duel doesn't cost experience, it just-"

His face went pale as he pulled up his notifications, hoping he'd made a winning bet when he gambled with the tower's supply of Honor.

You have died! Honor duel x10 concluded!

Honor lost for the Tower of Ritualists: -10,000 (1,000 per duel, at equal Master rank)

Honor gained for simultaneous victory: 10,000.

Modifier for defeating multiple duelists concurrently: 1.1x.

Total Honor gained: 1,000. (Disputed // source: Tower of Blood Rites)

No Honor shall be gained or lost until an Arbiter makes a final decision.

You have earned a patch for your Ritualist Tower Robes: Decury Duelist. By defeating 10 equally ranked combatants at the same time in an honorable manner, you've earned the right to proudly display this patch on the shoulder of your robes.

Effect: When fighting an Honor Duel while either outnumbered or outranked with an average tier difference of at least 1, gain a 10% additional resource allotment based on the Honor you bring to your tower.

Congratulations! You are the 10th still-living entity on Vanaheim to earn this patch! Resource allotment has increased to 11% (10% increase.) Wow! Look at you, being the first highly Decury-ated Ritualist!

Quest gained: Mastering Ritual Combat III.

Quest completed.

Quest gained: Mastering Ritual Combat IV.

Quest completed.

Quest gained: Mastering Ritual Combat V.

Quest completed.

Congratulations! You have completed the 'Mastering Ritual Combat' chain Quest by fulfilling a hidden condition: Defeating at least 10 other Masters during an honorable duel on Vanaheim while representing the Tower of Ritualists and relying entirely on rituals during combat! You have proven yourself a Master-ranked combatant.

Reward (Aggregated).

Reward: 1) Choose one of the skills used in the creation of any of the rituals you used in combat to receive, three times: +2 to the skill, if it is in the Expert rank.

2) Gain a Seven-circle flourish along the cuffs of your Ritualist Tower Robes, denoting you as a Master combatant. The circles will be embroidered in 'Endlessly Orange' thread and will blaze reflectively in direct light when you are not attempting stealth. Though almost entirely ornamental in design, your portion of the spoils increases by

7% from successful combat challenges on behalf of the Ritualist Tower.

Please enter the unified supply room or see an attendant in your Tower to gain your new robes.

Fully aware that it was far harder to retract skills after they'd been assigned than to deny him access to the reward during a review of the situation, Joe didn't hesitate for even a moment. He practically *ripped* open his skill sheet and swept his gaze over the skills he could increase... all while doing his best not to burst into maniacal laughter. "I'm so glad I got in the habit of using as many of my core class skills as possible, thanks to that chain quest! *This* is why! Preparation pays off!"

Alchemical Rituals (Expert IX)

Enchanted Ritual Circles (Expert VII)

Magical Matrices (Expert VIII)

Ritualistic Forging (Expert VI)

"If I got Alchemical Rituals to Master or Enchanted Ritual Circles, that would waste at least one of the boosts. Easy enough, that leaves Magical Matrices and Ritualistic Forging. I can Master *both* of them." With a simple flicker of intent, he assigned the rewards, allowing him to bypass any need for Inspiration by directly achieving Master status in both skills.

Congratulations! Two of your skills have reached the Master rank! As they are both Core Class Skills, and you did not have a moment of variant inspiration to cause them to evolve, they are directly increasing in power and capability. Calculating...

Magical Matrices (Expert VIII → Master 0). A single equation, infinitely layered in parallel.

Effects: 1) **$+1.1n\%$** *effectiveness of the high-order mathematics Lore skills when applying them to the creation of magical diagrams which require any form of higher math, where n = skill level.*

2) Multithreaded Master: You may now stack multiple matrices simultaneously, so long as they share at least one lore discipline.

3) Three times per day, while working through complex magical calculations or ritual construction, you may experience a 'Query Echo'—a brief moment of insight that subtly nudges you toward a slightly more effective equation or structure. This nudge may manifest as an intuitive twitch of the hand, a visual overlay, or a momentary realization.

Ritualistic Forging (Expert VI → Master 0) Even in failure, you begin to create success.

Effect:

1) No external heat source required. Activating the forging process engulfs your hammer in infernal fire, fed by consuming impurities while preserving the usable material.

*2) **2**% chance to apply an Infernal Modifier to any item created—this may manifest as affinity, aesthetics, effects, or cursed qualities.*

*3) **2**% chance to consume the supplied materials consumed entirely, taking as much as it can grab before being cut off. **After the Materials are consumed, the flame leaves behind infernal residue, a Unique-rank component.***

You have become a Master in <u>three</u> of the core skills associated with the Ritualist class! Please enter the unified supply room or see an attendant in your Tower to gain robes reflecting your new status as a triple Core Master... better known as a Tri-hard.

Joe squinted through the swarm of notifications, realizing only then that he'd been standing still and staring into the distance for the past several minutes as he allowed the rush of emotions to flow through him. Taking a deep breath, he settled on a warm smile and began searching for an attendant. It didn't take long, as the supply room had been one of the only places he'd visited the last time he was in the tower.

Stepping into the small space, where a surprisingly young woman was seated behind a counter reading a book, the Ritualist opened his mouth to make his request... only to close it and frown as he had a strange sense that he *knew* this person.

Unable to place her immediately, he pushed the thought to the side and tried again. "Hello! I'm here for some updated Tower Robes. Are you the person I should be speaking with?"

"Hello, *Joe.*" As the familiar voice washed over him, Joe had to stop himself from turning and sprinting in the other direction. The young woman snapped her book to the table and looked at him with all-too-familiar eyes. "It's good to see that the ones you're wearing have survived this long. I think a full year is a new record."

"*Minya!*" His voice came out as a strangled yelp. "What in the blue abyss are you doing here? I mean, uh, good to see you!"

"I'm on *every* world, Joe," she informed him patiently, as if he hadn't just come to this conclusion on his own. "I simply am able to display different levels of power due to the restrictions they have. Let's have a little talk about how you treat your equipment."

Physically cringing away, Joe offered a small, defeated bob of his head. "If you've been keeping tabs on me, I hope you'll take into account that I really have *tried-*"

"You wear your clothes so hard I'm surprised they don't scream in fear when you open your dresser drawer."

"Look, more than half of it wasn't my fault," Joe tried as she crossed her arms, clearly unwilling to hear excuses. "I was literally dressed-down by a Dwarf with a grudge against me just because I was a human—his attacks actively destroyed most of what I was wearing."

"I'd say I was surprised your wardrobe hasn't unionized against you to get hazard pay." Minya shook her head at his rolling eyes. "But I know how you feel about organization; you'd probably start walking around naked out of sheer pig-headedness, just to spite them."

"That's... I suppose that's fair?" Joe raised his hands in surrender, though he stopped the reflexive motion and forced them to his sides. "Look, I *like* my clothes. It's just that-"

"Take them off." Minya heaved a great sigh, motioning for him to pass over the Tower Robes he was currently wearing. "Don't look at me like that; I'm going to see for myself how you've treated this set. After that, *I'll* decide if you're getting an upgrade or not; I don't care what the *system* has told you."

"Why are you even *in* the tower?" the Ritualist grumbled as he reluctantly pulled off his robes, only to awkwardly stand in the center of the room clad only in his spiked codpiece and choker-style collar with the bell lightly chiming. "Isn't this a place for *Ritualists*?"

"You're not currently *in* the Tower of Ritualists, Joe," Minya offhandedly informed him, not giving him any additional information after dropping that bombshell. Instead, she was entirely focused on his clothes, her fingers slowly creeping up the fabric as if she were reading a book in braille. When she got to the collar, the merchant slowly looked up at him with a complicated expression.

"You... you've *only* worn this? Exactly *this* outfit ever since you first got it? More than a year now? Do you have any idea what that does to the fabric? Let alone... do you have no fashion sense at all?"

"It's practical!" Joe swung his hands to the sides, as if to make an obvious point, the bell in the hollow of his throat chiming loudly at the motion. "Also, there's nothing wrong with wearing the same thing over and over. It's self-cleaning; that means it's perfectly sanitary!"

"Self-cleaning... that particular enchantment is crying to be refreshed. Did you drag it through a swamp? Look at these slippers!" She lifted the strangely sad-looking shoes into the air and waved them back and forth in his face. "Slippers are indoor articles! They're made for hallways, rugs, and being put up on ottomans while you're reading a book next to a fire! Why didn't you take the outdoor set with you when you were here last time? The boots are perfect for... whatever it is you've been doing outside."

"To be perfectly honest, I didn't know that was an option. Someone gave me one set of clothes, and I figured that's what I was supposed to wear all the time."

"You're such a... *boy!*" Minya raged, looking as though she were about to throw the slipper at him, but managed to catch herself and place them on her counter gently. "The Self-Repair Enchantment is actively in recovery mode, meaning it's barely remaining viable by absorbing the mana the set reserves from your mana pool. Yet..."

She faltered for a heartbeat, then murmured like someone confessing more than she wanted to say, "Yet, though your constant usage frankly constitutes gross negligence of your gear, the endless mana being pushed into it, and being used for its intended purpose, has pushed this set toward intelligence far faster than any I've ever examined before. Somehow, you've managed to birth a nascent mind into this cloth simply by dint of refusing to do your laundry or dress up for formal occasions. A remarkable method, I must admit, even if it is more than a little unsavory."

"I'm not sure if you're still mad at me or giving me kudos. Either way, I'd really like to put something else on before someone else walks in here. I look a little more, uh, *outgoing* than I'm comfortable with." Joe rubbed his arms to emphasize his point, but when she glanced his way, Minya's eyes remained on the silver bell on his collar then traveled *down*. After she'd stared at his codpiece long enough for him to begin shifting uncomfortably, Joe loudly coughed into his hand to bring her attention away. "My eyes are up here."

"Brat. As if I'd be interested in anything other than that Legendary codpiece you're wearing alongside that Mythical collar. What's next? Deity-gifted socks?" She vaulted over the counter, squatting down and leaning in to get a closer look at the storage device even as his face went red. "Ancient in design… and long past due for an upgrade."

Joe perked up at that, standing slightly straighter—only to once again realize how unfortunate it would be if someone walked in to see them standing like this. "When you say upgrade, you mean bringing that up to the Mythical rank?"

"No, I mean it deserves an upgrade in who gets to wear it." She rolled her eyes and stepped away. "Of course I mean a rarity upgrade! That gear has a full-blown intelligence, and you're only using it to store basic items and… other junk."

"It can… think?"

"Don't get so excited; all it wants to do is store more important items, arrange them meticulously, and find ways to make what it's holding better in every way. A Mythical storage item might be the only way you'd be able to get around Vanaheim's restrictions on something like aging cheese naturally—if you want to know one of the most basic, blasé potential uses."

"Neat. A currency-creating device." Joe glanced at the counter longingly. "About those robes-"

"Yes, you can have new robes. *This* set will be staying here with me for some long-term recovery, before being handed off to..." Minya frowned as the embellishments along the robes on the counter glittered brightly. "Or not? Despite your man-handling, it seems to have taken a liking to you. Fine. This set will be staying here until you earn your next upgrade to your Tower Robes. Until then, I'm going to give you *four* sets to use. Two for outdoor use, one for formal occasions, and one for comfort wear, such as in a house or to be used as pajamas. *Alternate* their usage, Joe. At least daily."

"Understood," he agreed impatiently. In return, she *harrumphed* and got to work, pulling out multiple pieces of equipment and stacking them along the counter, only to seem to shift and blur as a needle and thread appeared in her hands.

The next thing he knew, Joe was staring at a gorgeous set of Tower Robes with a whole assortment of embellishments his previous ones didn't yet have. First was the Decury Duelist patch on the shoulder of each of them, a roman numeral 'X' that glowed a dazzling, eye-catching orange sitting on a hexagram background. Next was a series of seven bright orange layered embroidery circles along the cuffs of his robes, marking him as a Master ritual combatant.

But it was the gloves that had the most dramatic change. While it still had the seven golden, stitched circles marking him as a Master of Ritual Circles, they now had a strange depth to them. As he shifted the material back and forth, it created an optical illusion as though he were looking into an endless well. Along the knuckles were metal studs, each of them clearly a high-end stabilizer in their own right, though the index finger had an oddly malleable groove in it.

Joe glanced at Minya, and didn't even need to voice his question before she was offering him answers.

"Master of Magical Matrices adds the depth. It's meant to show you have an endless well of knowledge and power to draw on, allowing you access to rituals far beyond the strength you should be able to exhibit. The metal adornments are obviously meant to be for Masters of Ritualistic Forging and will all but guarantee success of any of the rituals you personally activate up to the Expert rank—up to seven each day—so long as the environment is generally stable for whatever world you're on. The groove over your index is for a weapon augment, as people from your tower tend not to have standard weapons with easy augment slots. Should work for just about anything."

Joe quickly put his new gear on, immediately feeling calmer and standing confidently now that he was dressed. He felt his mana connect to the set and slowly drain into it, filling the internal reserves of his new clothing. "Thank you for these."

"Yeah, well, you've earned them. Now take care of this set... and get out of here, I have more customers coming. Your mother says hello and that you need to come get your cheese. It's overflowing."

"Hi... back?" Unsure of what to do with that last piece of information, Joe quickly left the room behind him, eager to seek out his fellow Masters and surreptitiously show off his new achievements. Still, he couldn't help but look over his shoulder at the innocuous doorway that led to Minya and her judging glare. "Pretty sure that was a subtle warning that she can go tattle on me to my mother."

CHAPTER TWENTY-ONE

Conversations died as Joe walked through the halls, the adornments on his robes catching the eye of every person he passed. He didn't say a word as he searched for Master Hollows, knowing from his time in the military that his new robes would do all the heavy lifting for him. It was a rank signifier and various badges of honor all in one; only now, when he had spent so long solving problems for everyone around him, did he truly appreciate the way the implied status got people to move without *asking* for things.

Joe chuckled to himself, remembering the times when he'd looked at high-ranking people and had been annoyed at how they always seemed to be in a rush moving from one place to another. "Can't *believe* it took me so long to figure this out."

The implications of his gear certainly made him begrudgingly understand why Minya had such a fascination with enchanted items, but clothing in particular. His previous robes, with a single Mastery symbol on his gloves, certainly whispered 'competent' when he moved from place to place. Still, perhaps he *had* been far too comfortable in the past wearing the bare minimum, or clothes that had become ragged. Now that he thought about it, even the set he'd just given up had been fraying at the edges—he'd just assumed it would be an issue it took care of on its own.

"Master Joe, err, that is, *Tri*-Master Joe, I don't suppose you're looking for a student in one of your disciplines?" A young lady in Apprentice-rank robes flushed as she tripped over the honorific Joe hadn't even been expecting in the first place. "I've been following in Grandmaster Pete's footsteps-"

"I'd love to help out, but I don't know enough about the politics of the tower to accept anyone at this moment," Joe gently interrupted the stammering apprentice. "Does accepting someone such as yourself take away from someone else's plans? I just got here, and I don't want to be stepping on toes. I've had my fill of that, and I'm trying to cut it out of my diet entirely."

"Toes?" the frazzled young woman muttered as Joe swept past. To her credit, she shook off her apparent confusion and hurried after him, walking alongside him as he glanced around and tried to get his bearings. "You wouldn't be impacting anyone else's Mastery Merits! As I was saying, my focus is Alchemical Rituals, but you're the first Tri-Master I've seen in the tower. Everyone else is, at *most*, a double Master. But even then, they put almost the entirety of their attention on their chosen specialty. I could help you find your way around, set up interviews with candidates that want to train under you-"

Joe glanced at the Apprentice, flattered by the sudden surge of attention, yet uncomfortable with the fact that she was trying this hard with only having met him a single time. "Hey, all of that sounds very helpful, but I don't know you and you know nothing about me-"

"False!" Her tone hardened as she swept a hand at his gloves, cuffs, then shoulder. "You've mastered three core skills, are a Master of Ritualistic Combat, and managed to take out at least ten opponents of equal strength at the *same time*. With accolades like this, and if you keep pushing forward with the rest of your core skills, you might even become the very first *Class Sage* of our tower. No one's going to fault me for trying to be the first person to join your coven on Vanaheim; they're only going to be kicking themselves that they didn't get here before *I* did!"

"Okay... fair enough. Sure, welcome aboard, but I can tell you the hours suck and there's no pay." Joe chuckled as she unexpectedly beamed at his words. "If you want to put together a short list of people you think would want to learn from me—specifically and *only* the core skills they aren't already learning from a different Master, mind you—I'll think about it. Otherwise, I'm a big fan of teaching people that want to be taught, so figure out some times you can get people together and ambush me whenever you see me around to get me to teach for... let's say an hour at a time?"

"An entire *hour* at a time?" By the way her eyes sparkled, Joe knew he'd just seriously overcommitted himself. "I'm Jenesequa[1] , please call me Jenny! I'll start organizing a schedule immediately. That is... if you can confirm me as one of your students in... Ritual Circles?"

"Good pick. That's the one I'm planning to get to the Grandmaster rank first." As he lifted his fist and gave her a thumbs up, Jenny let out a strangled squeal of excitement then turned and rushed off with as much dignity as she could muster. He shook his head and resumed his search, not calling after the Apprentice to remind her that she'd offered to help him navigate the tower. "Careful, Joe... someone's going to have to come along and pop your over-inflated ego if this keeps up. Now, if I were a math club, where would I be?"

He looked up at the tower, with its hollow center allowing him to see all the way up to the penthouse area, and slowly shook his head. Glancing around, he found a staircase leading downward and decisively started moving toward it. "Yeah, math club is definitely in the basement."

As Joe searched the lower level, he became less sure of himself, all the way until a sudden burst of noise flowed out of an open doorway at the end of the hall.

The slightly snarling voice Joe associated with Wolfmen was leading a chant, "What do we do?"

"Solve for X!"

"What do we seek?"

"Truth in technique!"

Then, all together, the group finished, "M-A-T-H! Subtract the doubt, multiply the *jo~oy!*"

A small crowd of people poured out of the entryway a few moments later, passing by a very bemused Joe. After the flood had turned into a trickle, he slipped into the room, watching as Master Hollows tidied up some papers on a desk. His fellow Master only noticed the bald Ritualist as his clawed paw reached for an eraser to clean the chalk off a blackboard. "Joe! You came! Even after we lost our spot on the fourth floor, you sought us out? Oh, I'm so sorry, we just let out for the day. Wait! I'm certain I could call them—Celestial feces, man! Your robes!"

Cosmo's ears perked up as his eyes traveled from the patch on Joe's shoulder to the circles on his gloves, pupils dilating as he realized there was an illusion of depth which mirrored his own circles. His back hunched fractionally, his body language becoming ever so slightly more submissive, as was the norm in Wolfman culture when standing in the presence of someone of higher rank.

"Oh, don't do that." Joe stepped forward and gripped Cosmo's shoulders, forcing him to lean back and stand straighter. "A good friend of mine would take great offense at you intentionally hunching. Besides, I'm here as a peer to ask for help, not to show off or… I don't know, try to build a faction of my own in the tower?"

"Huh. Well, that one's going to happen with or without you." Cosmo showed a wolfy grin, calming down now that Joe had shown open familiarity with him. "You're the first Tri-hard in the entire tower. I'd be surprised if there wasn't already a queue waiting for you when you leave here after word spreads. You need a *favor*, you say? I'd be more than willing to help you out... if you wouldn't mind committing to a few weekly sessions with the club! Can always use a fresh perspective from another math Master!"

Wincing at even the *thought* of committing to additional tasks, Joe quickly shook his head in the negative. "No, I was hoping to only *pay* you for your services. I *just* became a Master in Magical Matrices, meaning I need someone far more potent to help me with a problem I'm having. I was hoping that someone would be you."

"Pay?" Cosmo scratched at his furry neck. "Do you have the Parmesan for it? Sorry to say I'm far beyond cheddar at the moment, and even gorgonzola isn't going to do the trick. Full wheels, properly aged. I apologize for the cost, as much as I'd like to give you a discount, but I'm sure you've started to realize what *your* time is worth, and I've been in the Master rank for nearly a decade at this point."

"Cheese. *Right.*" Joe pulled a face as he was reminded of his lacking actual currency on this world. "I'm a triple-Master and somehow a pauper at the same time."

"Perhaps we should talk about other things for now?" Cosmo gently offered an escape, awkwardly realizing Joe didn't have the funds available to pay for his services. "Tell me about that shoulder patch. Decury Duelist, is it? I'm not overly familiar, but from what the system is telling me, that's quite the impressive adornment."

"According to the notification, I'm the tenth still-living person to earn it on Vanaheim." Joe rubbed at his head, eyes distant as he tried to decide how to make his pitch. If the mathematician would only consider being paid properly... well, he could only hope Cosmo would be open to bartering. As he opened his mouth to make an offer, the Wolfman's muzzle twitched in interest as he spoke first.

"You're one of ten on the planet. An *impossible* fraction, and exactly what we need in a place like this. If we had *two* Masters in this club, our funding would increase exponentially, and we could finally get out of this basement." Cosmo's tone turned cajoling. "Especially such a decorated member, a *Triple Master* of the tower? Why, recruitment would *surge!*"

"As much as I love the hard sell," Joe intentionally kept his teeth from showing in an approximation of etiquette among the Wolfmen, "I was hoping you might be willing to make an exchange? If having additional Masters of Magical Matrices is what you seek, I might be able to help with that. I recently gained a skill that'll allow me to generate Lore books for my Mastered Lore skills."

Cosmo stared at him consideringly, and when he finally spoke, the words weren't what Joe had been expecting. "You've Mastered... the *lore* of Magical Matrices? Calculus and Number Theory? That's, forgive my disbelief, but that's quite unlikely. How old are you? *Under* a century? Math is far more difficult to Master than-"

"Let's just say there are, uh, extenuating circumstances," Joe hastily interrupted before his fellow Master could solidify his thoughts into firm disbelief. "I'll be able to bring you an Arti-fact-rank Lore book—perhaps multiple times over the next year, if I gain additional levels in it—and lesser versions far more frequently. All in exchange for you helping me with the formula of just *one* ritual."

"Hmmm." The Wolfman flicked his ears uncertainly. "If I didn't allow people to absorb them, I'm certain we could create lesson plans off of those that would help everyone's progress increase exponentially. I *do* love exponents. Know what? Sure. One equation, Master rank, for one Artifact-rank Lore book and a set of lesser versions for each member of the club."

"Each member currently *in* the club." Joe's grin stretched across his face, even as Cosmo had a matching smirk up here on his. "Just as you said, I'm certain your membership will be surging soon."

"Best place to find Mastery Merits is in a group that wants to learn what you have to teach." Cosmo hesitated for a heart-beat. "I'm certain you won't be opposed to them staying as *my* Mastery Merits?"

"But of course."

"Excellent. In that case, show me what you need done, and I'll get to work on it as soon as you hand over the Master-rank Lore book as a down payment."

Joe froze in place, suddenly exceedingly aware that his Calculus and Number Theory skill was currently only at Expert rank two. Pulling out his formulae, he handed off the document and explained what he was attempting. For the first time, instead of derision being returned to him for his efforts, Master Hollows simply read over the scribbles and nodded in understanding.

"A good base here, but as you're looking for an open formula version of this, it'll need some reworking. How many inputs will you be managing with the final ritual?" The duo spoke for a few more minutes, with the Wolfman taking some casual notes. As they wrapped up, and the conversation faltered, Joe felt the weight of expectation settling onto him.

Coughing into his hand, the Ritualist looked at Cosmo sheepishly. "It'll be a couple of weeks before I can get you that Lore book."

"Ah. No problem. It'll be a couple of weeks before I can start on this, in that case." Cosmo tucked the document away, casually meeting his counterpart's eyes as he did so. "I am greatly looking forward to working on those projects; it seems quite fun. Now, unless there was anything else…?"

Joe grit his teeth and swallowed his frustration, then made his way out of the room, a soft grumbling twisting like a knot in his chest. This was the first major roadblock he'd been unable to navigate immediately when making the design he needed, but he took a deep breath and reminded himself that the only real requirement at the moment was *time*. "Two more weeks, and I'll be able to pay the man. Can't get salty just because he's not willing to work for free. That's actually normal and admirable, when I think about it."

"*There he is!*" The words pealed across the open tower area as Joe reached the top of the stairs and stepped onto the main floor.

He froze in place, Ritual Orbs popping into the air off his bandolier almost on their own as he stoically resigned himself to fighting off the ambush. Yet, instead of attackers, Joe's expression morphed into one of great confusion as a tide of robed individuals rushed toward him, each of them babbling requests and gushing their personal accolades in a cacophonous attempt to persuade him to be their mentor.

"Please, just one lesson on forging! I'm *this* close to Expert-"

"-You just come from the math club? I'll join if I have to-" Joe's lips quirked as he heard this voice rise over the others, which he knew would be taken as confirmation by at least half of them.

"How did you get so good at dueling? Can you sign my-"

Requests, flattery, self-promotion; it was an entire chorus of ambition washing over him, each of the lower-ranking Ritualists desperate to be the first to capture his attention. Joe stepped back as the crowd pressed close, *almost* falling down the stairs yet managing to catch himself at the last moment.

Congratulations! You have managed to put the foundational principles of Dexterity into every aspect of your life, from combat, to creation, to casual movements as you go about your day.

Your Dexterity Characteristic has been influenced by these actions and has been adjusted accordingly. Please choose one of the following.

1) Combat shift: Geometric Dexterity. Combat is a series of equations waiting to be solved. Effect: Angles and trajectories gain immense clarity while you are in combat.

2) Crafting shift: Fractal Dexterity. Your movements become a dance harmonizing with the world. Effect: Improves all fine-detail crafting when rhythmic motion is used.

3) Lifestyle shift: Dialectic Dexterity. Every movement you make is a question answered by your following motion. Effect: While moving, when confronted with resistance or impediment, the action to overcome it becomes inherently intentional.

With people still clamoring around him, and now an invasive system notification flashing in front of his face, Joe found his jaw working back and forth as he tried not to say the wrong thing and accidentally disillusion a large group of people, or accept a suboptimal choice. Just as he was about to start shoving his way out of the crowd so he could dig into his Characteristic shift a bit more, another voice interceded on his behalf.

"*Hey!*"

Just like everyone else, Joe's eyes flicked to the interloper, but unlike them, who simply saw another competitor, he was filled with genuine thankfulness as his savior marched toward him.

"*Your* apprentice, Jenny, reporting for duty, Tri-Master Joe!" She stopped directly in front of him, though she had needed to push a handful of people out of her way to make that happen. "As we discussed earlier, I'll start directing anyone who wants to learn from you to do a proper sign-up. I haven't forgotten your *very* clear instructions on being accosted out in the open; anyone who knowingly approaches you improperly will be put at the back of the line, at the *minimum*."

"A-*hem*." Joe coughed his hand, then distractedly murmured, "Ah, yes. Very good. See to it, then."

As Jenny's expression turned to one of triumph, she straightened up and began addressing the immediately more subdued mob. For his part, Joe rushed over to the staircase and began bounding upward, not at all paying attention to where he was going as he quickly read and reread the options he'd been presented with.

"It's never given me choices before... does that mean something different? Or was I simply not using my other Characteristics in a wide enough scope that I *earned* choices?" Sucking in a breath through clenched teeth, Joe pushed his fretting to the side and focused on the actual decision he had to make. "Combat, crafting, or quality of life. Well, in order, having an innate sense of angles and trajectories would make it easier both to land hits with my orbs and magic, as well as avoiding incoming attacks. The question is, should I really worry about that as a *Characteristic*? The core of who I will become?"

The frustrating part was, that question rang through his head with *each* of the options.

"I do a lot of crafting; I'd be a fool to say anything other than that's my main focus, but how much of it is done with rhythmic motion? Basically just... forging, right? Maybe placing components during Alchemy counts? Oooh... what if the motions I'm making while drawing out ritual circles count? Especially with Somatic Ritual Casting? It doesn't specify that, but it *should* impact those, right?"

Yet, it was the third option that kept drawing Joe's eye. If he were being fully honest with himself, he was... tired. He'd been attempting to optimize all of his choices the entire time he'd been in Eternium, and the option to take a quality-of-life upgrade was *drastically* appealing. Letting out a soft sigh, and not giving himself another moment to hesitate, he selected the third option. "What's the point in all of this if I don't enjoy it, right?"

Congratulations! Dexterity has become Dialectic Dexterity!

Every movement you make is a question answered with a counterpoint motion, a challenge immediately taken up. Your body responds with effortless adaptation, ensuring you are never failing due to remaining static. While moving, when confronted with resistance or impediment, the action to overcome it becomes inherently intentional. This manifests as a dialectic adjustment. When a dexterous action fails due to poor execution, miscalculation, or opposition, a corrective or alternate action is instantly performed at 50% reduced efficiency, but without additional cost.

As an example: stepping backward off a staircase due to failing to account for the drop. Instead of tumbling down and potentially breaking your neck, you may instead tuck and roll, leaping the entire stairwell and landing on your feet at the bottom. You will remember both options as having happened.

Beyond the actual effect of the shift, the Ritualist felt a subtle shift in his center of balance. He wasn't moving faster, exactly, but every time his toes landed on the stairs, the motion felt cleaner, crisper, as though each point of contact was just half a percent more efficient.

"Half a percent..." Joe mused to himself as he found

himself practically flying up the stairs. "Maybe a couple seconds shaved off my climb here, so what? But... what's that going to look like over time? I've heard that compounding interest is the eighth wonder of the world. *Definitely* think I made the right choice here. I'm not always fighting, nor am I always crafting..."

"...But I've always got to move if I want to go places and get things done." Joe turned on his toes as he reached the landing, leaping out into the open air and crossing to the other side, where a surprised Ritualist looked up at him with startled blue eyes.

"Master Darling! Hope you don't mind if I... drop in?"

CHAPTER TWENTY-TWO

Having learned his lesson from the last time he'd jumped to an open platform such as this, Joe made sure to watch where his feet were landing. Thanks to his newly upgraded Dexterity, his toes kissed down with just enough force to fully arrest his momentum, yet not even slightly disturb the remnant chalk dust spread across the huge slab.

Even so, Master Hilda Darling had a soft gasp startled out of her as she went stock-still, eyes as wide as saucers. When nothing detonated, she slowly let the breath out, speaking in a tone gentle as if she were trying to entice a squirrel to eat from the palm of her hand. "Watch your slippers. If you disturb that diamond dust to the left of your right foot, it'll latch onto you and activate the incomplete ritual. Frankly, I have no idea what will happen-"

She froze mid-careful admonishment, and when she spoke again, her voice wavered between forced composure and downright shock. "Triple Master? Decury... my, my. You sure have been busy since the last time I saw you. I was wondering why I gained a Mastery Merit a short while ago; I hadn't thought any of my Experts were at the cusp yet."

"Oh good! I suppose the fact that I accepted you as a sponsor was enough to get you the merit? Hey... I wonder if Cosmo got one as well? He didn't say anything about it, but to be fair, I ambushed him just as his math club was getting out. Ah... wait... I didn't Master Enchanted Ritual Circles?"

"So it is *brand* new, otherwise you would've never made that mistake." Master Darling's eyes twinkled as Joe goggled at her, completely taken aback by the unexpected tease. "How do you not know—without even thinking about it—which of your core skills you've Mastered? Now, I'd love to continue this conversation, but only after you have very, exceedingly carefully, stepped away from this circle."

Doing as instructed, the bald man sheepishly made his way to the edge of the platform, opening his mouth only for Hilda to raise her hand and shake her head. "I was only saying I could talk now so you'd move faster. I'm in the middle of something far too important to interrupt at the moment, so unless you're going to sit down and help, you'll need to schedule an appointment."

So saying, she immediately began *scritching* away at a token, mind fully bent to the task at hand. Joe let out a soft chuff —not *quite* a laugh at her audacity—and started examining the circle she was designing.

Crouching low, being excessively careful not to disturb the glowing lines formed from imbued chalk, Joe examined the Expert-rank circle spread before him. At first, he was annoyed —professionally, as a Master at Ritual Circles—at how much space Hilda had used in covering practically the entirety of the fifteen-foot square platform. The lattice of curves, sigils, and nested syntax seemed looser than it should be.

Then he traced one of the sympathetic links and felt his lips twist into a frown. "What in the abyss is going on *there*? Where's the tidy logic? The sensible design? This is unsettling. The anchor line should be creating a predictable transition here but... it must be the tokens!"

The ritual diagram *wasn't* sloppy, as he had assumed at first glance. Far from it, in fact. He hadn't expected anything else from someone who'd started with Enchanting as her main class and profession, but seeing how the tokens would be grafted in and therefore must plan to be altering the structure in a way *he* didn't understand... it made Joe's teeth itch. Tracing the outer circle with his eyes once more, he found himself muttering but made no effort to quiet down.

"That's a lot of emphasis on compression, and that sigil is particularly spiky. Obviously this is something drastically different from the last project you were working on. Some form of attack ritual, that's for certain. It practically screams its desire to lash out." Joe leaned back on his heels, pulse picking up as he wondered why Hilda's efforts had taken such a dramatic shift. "With those tokens, this is going to end up being Master-rank, but it's clearly a war ritual of some kind. Have things gotten so bad that they're making you build weapons?"

"You don't know the half of it," Hilda murmured distract-edly as she allowed a sliver of her concentration to remain on Joe and the conversation. "None of us can leave the tower without being ambushed by a squad, not since the embargo on travel through the bifrost. Most of the people whose duties were to keep the peace are either on an expedition or guarding the base of the rainbow bridge directly. There's a mad rush for Honor, and we've been piled on by people who like the look of our tower."

Joe pursed his lips, both relieved and annoyed to learn that the Tower of Blood Rites hadn't been out in force *specifically* to hunt him down. It was unfortunate for the other members of the tower, but seeing as how they'd been dealing with similar situations since before he got here... he didn't feel too bad. For a while, he simply sat in silence, enjoying watching someone *else* work instead of himself, for once. As Hilda was finishing the token she was describing, Joe found a pleasant surprise waiting.

Skill increase: Magical Syntax Lore (Expert VIII → Expert IX)

"Nice! Only thing left to do now is hang out for sixty-nine point two-nine, then-" Joe stop speaking as Hilda reached forward and placed her token in the final slot, and the entire diagram shuddered and condensed, the materials used in its creation being absorbed and leaving behind only shining lines of energy: a ritual ready to be activated.

After a few moments of perfect stillness, Master Darling let out a deep, shuddering sigh of relief, then turned to Joe with bright eyes and full attention. "You *truly* have the worst timing ever. While I'm happy to see you, please don't interrupt me while I'm on a privacy platform like this. That's *why* they're so difficult to get to, and I'd rather not have to start putting the privacy ritual up; it can mess with the flow of mana."

"Understood." Joe gave a slow, deliberate nod, doing his best to convey his respectful intentions. "I'll make sure to figure out who to book an appointment with to speak with you. Actually, no, I'll have my people talk to your people, and make it happen that way."

"Oh? You have *people* now? I suppose that's unsurprising, seeing as you've grown so rapidly in so little time. Did you start a riot down there? You were actively fleeing a crowd, and that's why you jumped through the open air and risked creating an Enchanted Simulacrum of yourself?"

"Is that what this one does?" Joe glanced back at the ritual with great interest, blinking in surprise at how the addition of the tokens had adjusted the design so drastically. "How *odd*! It suddenly makes sense? Oh, when you said simulacrum, I definitely thought you were going to create a copy of a person that would go and fight themselves. This is more like a voodoo doll generator, but for people on a large scale? Nifty."

Hilda deflated ever so slightly. "It seems my attempt at obfuscation did all of *nothing*. Yes, the idea is that I'll be able to take out two to three groups at the same time by making a doll of each of them, then subjecting it to a separate ritual. That way, it doesn't matter if they can dodge the effects or somewhat mitigate them, their magical representations will not have the same defenses, so they'll take the full damage. I actually got the design concept from Grandmaster Pete's battle, where his blood was used against him to act as the target of a variety of Rites instead of just one."

"The diamond dust gets into their pores then has a matched pair that forms in the doll? An interesting method of tying the targeting together. Then, even if they cut off their connection to blood or other material you've gotten a hold of, it won't matter. Fascinating!" Joe blinked rapidly and stepped away from the circle, before his grasping fingers could caress the magical surface or he lost himself in attempting to reverse engineer the design. "Obfuscation, you say? Mmm... I think there was some of that in the original design, but once it's solidified, the magic is the magic. You'll probably need an entire section devoted to that, or an outside ritual layered over it if you want to hide the design after the fact."

"Truly, I have much to learn about ritual circles." Hilda's eyes flicked toward him. "I don't suppose you'd have room in your lessons for another aspiring Master of Ritual Circles?"

"I'd far rather teach you one-on-one, if you're open to it." Joe smiled at her a bit nervously as he took this chance to make his request. "Since you brought it up, I certainly wouldn't be opposed to an exchange of services? I'm designing a rather *involved* ritual, and I find myself unable to generate the Enchanted section with my own skills."

Just as he'd done with the others, Joe laid out his plan and the challenges he was having with the design. She quizzed him with several clarifying questions but generally allowed him to continue speaking until he had run out of things to say. Then, rather pensively, she drummed her fingers on her chin as she gathered her thoughts.

"You need this to be an enchantment keyed not just to you, but specifically your mana pool and its flows through your body. Persistent under movement, modular with each of the other class skills, and not interfering with other rituals you may create or the skills already within your system. No, actually designed to work with what's there and whatever else you *might* get." She shook her head slowly, her expression unreadable but her clear intent making Joe's stomach sink. "No. Oof. That won't work. I could *perhaps* do this with some limitations, but they would be *very* hard limits."

"Could you... elaborate?" Joe pressed as she went quiet once more, trying not to let his desperation show.

"Yes. You must understand, an enchantment of that specificity would allow for some adjustment, but certainly not an endless number of new or shifted things piled onto it. It would collapse after... hmm, Master rank, so *seven* major shifts. This could be new skills, or it could be current ones which move through a tier. Perhaps you could get away with combining skills, which would count only as one change then leave you with additional space for new skills, but you'd still be faced with the same problem when ranking those up."

As she returned her full attention to him, the glasses she was wearing caught the light and sent a brilliant reflection onto Joe, which was taken up by his bald head and sent scintillating light reflecting across the inside of the tower. "I fully understand why you're doing this and what you're attempting to do, but I would be remiss in simply complying without explaining the dangers. After seven skill changes—level gains are fine, as are Characteristics—but the eighth skill would break the enchantment and cause a cascading failure."

Happily, Joe had a ready answer for her concerns. "I was told by one of my mentors that if I managed to breach the seventh Characteristic threshold, any of the issues I'm suffering from currently would be resolved."

"Ah. I suppose that would be enough, but that's an insane race against time. *Insane*." Hilda hesitated far longer this time, before speaking with carefully chosen words.

"Increasing your Characteristics through the sixth threshold is not as simple as it was before then. Think of it as your Characteristics reaching the Master tier. Simple grinding isn't enough any longer, and it's a true watershed, bottleneck—however you want to phrase it—to even reach the peak, let alone break through the seventh. If I complete this, and you successfully place this entire *system* of rituals into yourself, simply achieving *too much* might be enough to destabilize yourself. You'd end up doing far more damage than what you're dealing with currently."

"I'm one Characteristic shift away from having a completed set, and even though no one will confirm this for me, I feel that it'll be enough to push me through the sixth threshold and put me on the path toward the seventh." Bobbing his head more confidently than he actually felt, the Ritualist met her gaze. "I have enough deferred rewards that I should have a good head start, and I'll put off using this as long as possible. But-"

"-but you're going to do it either way, and you'd rather have it done by someone you think is going to give you the best chance possible at success." Hilda shrugged almost flippantly. "I've heard it all before. Certainly, I'll help you, but absolutely do *not* attempt this if you are trying to have a Characteristic shift. That would *guarantee* cataclysmic failure. Now, how many lessons with a Master of Ritual Circles would you think a design and complete set of the necessary tokens is worth?"

After some friendly haggling, Joe agreed to work next to her for the next three days, for at least eight hours, as a down payment.

"This will work well for both of us. For the most accurate alignment, I won't just need your blood or hair to target—ugh, I hope you at least have *chest* hair we can work with—we're going to need as much information about you as possible. Everything about you. Your mana pool, the dominant pathways you've created, how your temperament flexes under stress, how your mind and body interact with your skills."

"If you're using such a... customized option, why do you need hair and such in the first place?" Joe pointed at his face. "I have eyebrows... err, kinda. I hit the ground pretty hard recently. No point in trying to get me shirtless; I have no chest hair either. At least I'm not shy about donating blood where needed."

"It's fine, eyebrows tend to be far too tainted by keeping

things out of your eyes. Magically, not just physically. They have a different purpose, and therefore magical meaning than most other hair. Maybe we can run a razor along your back or legs? Armpits! Perfect."

Joe leaned away, face crinkling with disgust. "For *you*."

"As to blood, it's a quick and dirty targeting system, but to go past surface level, I need way more than can be captured with a knife and a pair of tweezers, or even a single session of measuring you." She sent him a winning smile, which he didn't return. "Perhaps just a week or two of study, nothing too egregious."

As she held out a hand for him to shake to seal the deal, Joe found himself smiling at the shift from serious and severe Enchanter to excited researcher. "Let me see if I have everything correct here. You want me to teach you all about my favorite subject for hours on end while you nod along and ask questions. There will also be a component of you doing your best to get to know me better. At the end of this, you're going to hand me a shiny new design, as well as all of the Enchanted Tokens I need to make this ritual happen. To me it sounds like a deal with no downside, so…"

He grasped her hand with his own much larger one, and they firmly shook on it.

Joe glanced down at her hand in sudden concern. "One more 'what if' before we get back to it. What about adding on a profession? Or upgrading them? How badly is that going to mess with the enchantment you're going to make, since I'm actively seeking… actually, a new and cool Enchanting profession. I have a very interesting option currently, since I have a maxed out profession that'll work as a prerequisite for a variety of new options."

Hilda slowly pulled her hand back, "Fifth to sixth tier? Not going to be too much of an issue, so don't worry. Professions are more like titles. They're just kind of added on to what you are, not a core part of it. Like a job, hence the term 'profession'. You should only worry about messing with what the enchantment will key into. Your fundamentals such as mana pool, mana flow, and the interaction points between body, mind, and Akashic record."

"Glad to hear that my side hustle is safe." Joe chuckled as he let his arm swing down to his side, then gestured at the platform. "On that note, any interesting leads on hard-to-obtain Enchanting professions?"

Her eyes crinkled with a hint of apology. "Afraid not. The rarest one I know of is Token Enchanter, which as you may correctly assume, I have. Most Enchantment professions have been standardized to the nth degree. As it turns out, when people are overly, let's say creative, while forcing massive amounts of mana through a contained area, they tend to detonate their project and themselves with it. Which led to, you know, standardization. If you want to find something truly rare, you'll either have to find it in the depths of a lost library or earn it from the system. Or... I do *not* recommend this, *found* the profession."

"As in, prove a new enchantment methodology that the system will recognize as valid?" Joe half-smiled and despairingly shook his head right alongside her. "Way more interested in the lost library option. The amount of learning and testing needed to create an entire profession on my own? No, thank you. I have other goals in life."

Seeing as he was officially on the clock, Joe buckled down with Master Darling and got to work explaining first the deficiencies in her current set of rituals, then spending time slowly leafing through and optimizing the hundreds of Enchantment-as-a-base ritual circles in her grimoire.

They only made it through three before his official required work time had ended for the day, but neither of them slowed down in the slightest, not even after it was obvious that most of the people in the tower had gone to sleep hours before.

What followed over the next few days wasn't so much a schedule as it was a constant tide washing away confusion and leaving behind polished clarity. Both in terms of their skills, as well as the lingering tension of not knowing someone very well. Hours slid into days like pages in a cozy book marked up by fans of a story; often, it was what happened on the margins that was more interesting than the actual content of the page.

Between sessions working with the Master of Enchanted Rituals, Joe ducked away to participate in Jenny's pop-up classes... only to start the first session with an unwelcome surprise.

CHAPTER TWENTY-THREE

As he was walking into a classroom setting, Joe'd expected to be delving into the topic of Magical Matrices, as it was the only class skill he thought of as blackboard appropriate.

Instead, what he found were neat rows of people standing behind tables, thin porcelain cups arranged in front of each of them, alongside a ceremonial teapot. Before Joe could turn around and leave, assuming he was in the wrong room, Jenny appeared in the doorway and gave him an overly formal curtsy.

"Master Joe! I'm glad you made it. Before we can begin any formal training, we would like to formally acknowledge you as our Master in the discipline of Ritual Circles, to ensure that you will gain each of the Mastery Merits you are due by granting us instruction. Before you ask, this will *absolutely* be the most sought-after class skill. As it stands, there are only four Masters of this discipline in the tower, with the vast majority having been lost through the years."

"Only four? I clearly recall someone shouting to me that they were 'nearly a Grandmaster' in Ritual Circles when I first arrived," Joe murmured to her as he smiled genially at the huge gathering of Ritualists. "Also, does it have to be a *tea* ceremony?"

"It's tradition. Also, I know *exactly* who you're talking about, and he's only there because he's planning to apply all his Mastery Merits from his other Mastered skills to that particular one." Jenny's smile faltered somewhat. "Frankly he's not the most... pleasant of people. He refuses to teach anyone about ritual circles out of fear that they'll surpass him and become the Skill Sage before he can. The other Masters have sworn oaths not to teach the skill before he becomes a Grandmaster or something more permanent happens to him."

Joe rolled his eyes, an uncomfortably familiar feeling of being stifled closing in on him. "Well, in that case, I'll make sure to run this class at least twice a day when I'm around. I absolutely *hate* necessary information being locked away so only a few people are able to benefit from it. No *wonder* this tower doesn't have a Class Sage yet."

As he settled into an oversized chair, which was definitely brought here so he wouldn't want to leave anytime soon, Jenny took a position in front of him and began brewing a simple tea. Happily, it was an instant powder, instead of leaves that would need to steep for long minutes, which was the only reason he didn't *insist* on coffee instead.

"As your first coven disciple on Vanaheim, I have the honor of being the first to perform the tea ceremony and lead the group in the phrasing." Jenny smirked at him, her eyes absolutely filled with excitement as Joe resigned himself to a *very* long day. "We acknowledge Master Joe as our specific guide in the class skill: Ritual Circles. We will accept no other Master in this skill unless released from this vow."

"*We acknowledge Master Joe-*" The rest of the people in the room parroted her words, and Joe had to close his eyes and breathe deeply so as to not want to make his way to the exit immediately.

Jenny lifted the teapot, prepared to pour into the first of the two cups. "In so doing, we vow not to teach others this skill unless the student first acknowledges you as-"

"*Wait.*" Seeing as his Characteristics were far higher than the majority of people in the room, it seemed as though Joe had cut her off instantly, but in reality he'd processed what she was saying and interpreted the likely remainder of the vow. "Instead of promising not to teach others, say this instead: 'When it comes to the class skill of Ritual Circles, I'll teach anyone this skill if I want to teach them and they want to learn'."

Seeing everyone staring at him in shock, Joe shrugged nonchalantly. "What can I say? Hoarding knowledge is just *boring.* If you're good enough to pass it on, there's no reason you shouldn't work on your ability to teach from the outset."

The room was instantly silent, but Jenny, blinking in surprise, quickly repeated the words exactly as Joe had framed them, cheeks flushed with excitement.

Everyone else hesitantly echoed her, though they spoke with more confidence as they realized Joe was serious about them passing on what they learned. When they finally finished, he picked up the delicate mug with a grimace, raising the porcelain above his head as he spoke in a dry tone.

"I accept your vow, and I'll be the best instructor I can in the limited amount of time I can give you. Now... drink up. I can't imagine that letting this hot leaf juice get cold would improve the flavor."

Everyone drank, and as they set cups down with a near-simultaneous *clink*, a ripple of relieved and excited laughter rippled through the room.

"Now, who wants to learn about Ritual Circles?"

Between Ritual Circles, the sudden massive increase in interest surrounding Magical Matrices, even a few Alchemy-focused Ritualists who worked up the courage to learn Ritualistic Forging under him—every last one of them an absolute Novice in the class skill—and working with Master Darling, the first three days of his short stint in the tower came to a close with an intense shift in his mind.

Congratulations! Magical Syntax Lore has reached the Master rank!

Magical Syntax Lore (Master 0). Every school of magic has its own dialect, and you are now a polyglot.

You now understand the linguistic structure of magic to the point that when analyzing, constructing, or deconstructing magical diagrams, taking portions from alternate magical fields, will be an order of magnitude easier to translate to the magical diagram you are creating. This Lore skill has gained an active effect.

Axiom Authority. Once per major diagram, up to the Master rank, you may declare an Axiom, a binding sigil which will overlay the final diagram. All future diagrams of the same type, when created by you, must contain this Axiom going forward. The Axiom must have high synergy for the ritual and be within an acceptable range of deviation, to succeed.

The declared Axiom has three effects.

1) The actual declared Axiom. Example: This ritual rotates in reverse of the standard but works the same way.

2) Master's Mark: The overlay on this particular ritual going forward will identify the ritual as created by a Master, adding an identifiable emblem as well as your individual power signature. When creating rituals of the same type, emblem-bound rituals are 5% more stable. (Not applicable to each first ritual created in this manner.)

3) Keyed to the creator: It will be 100% more difficult for others at the same tier of this Lore skill to discern the syntax of your created diagrams without specific permission, +50% per lower tier.

Before even a second had passed, Joe snapped out, "Set Calculus and Number Theory as the focus of the skill Loremaster. Look at that... the fifteen percent speed increase is already in effect. Instead of forty hours to Expert rank three, it's only thirty-four and some change."

He'd sat down before opening the notification, having been impatiently waiting for its arrival. As he read over each of the pieces of information, he found himself liking this shift more and more. "I can take general rituals and turn them into essentially branded rituals? That would be really useful if I needed to sell a few of them on Midgard... they sure like their commercialization down there, and people might pay extra just to prove they own something they got directly from the 'Dread Ritualist Joe'."

"As for the rest of this..." His eyes lingered on the example of the Axiom, not at all certain how simply declaring it could rotate backward and still work would even function. "Will that cause every part of it to be mirrored, or something? How will the clauses interact as it spins? Maybe that's what it means by 'range of deviation'. I bet that particular choice wouldn't work on anything above the Journeyman rank. Also, what happens if the Axiom *doesn't* work? Does it cause the ritual to fail as a whole, or does *nothing* happen?"

"I think this diagram is destabilizing!" Joe jerked into motion as Hilda's rising voice interrupted his thoughts. Exactly as she had warned, the Student-rank circle she'd been creating as quickly as possible was beginning to fluctuate dangerously.

With almost contemptuous ease, Joe injected his will into the ritual, along with a few hundred points of mana that poured from his open palm, and directly took control of the floundering diagram. He hadn't had much opportunity to use this perk of his Mastered Ritual Circle skill, but had found a fantastic niche for it—allowing people to create rituals outside of their comfort zone without too much fear that they would explode.

With a snap of his fingers for added flare, the circle disintegrated, the magic venting into the open air of the tower. The only downside was the components she'd added to the diagram consuming themselves entirely.

"Nice! You almost had that one, except you crossed a dangling conjunction with a grounding clause." The tip of his index finger began to glow, hiding the fact that he'd palmed his inscription tool, and Joe swiftly wrote out the entire ritual over the next handful of seconds—which had taken her nearly half an hour. "Look at this space—this is what you had."

Isolating that section, Joe overwrote it with another equation, then removed it entirely. "Essentially, what you'd put down was 'after energy is invested, shunt energy into ground'. These lines differentiate that, but if they get tangled, it becomes a short circuit that causes the whole thing to blow."

"Just like that, Student rank one." Hilda shook her head in amazement. "What a wonderful, *wasteful* teaching method."

"You jumped nearly two tiers in under a week. It would've been even faster if we hadn't gone through and fixed up all of the most commonly used rituals you have." Joe could only shrug at the implied discomfort at the cost of this training opportunity. "I only have a little over another week here before I have to get back to work on my other projects, so just gain every benefit you possibly can from learning from a Master while you can. When you're too tired to keep going… we can switch, and you can teach me about Enchanted Ritual Circles."

"You can't afford my time," she immediately deflected with a neat verbal sidestep. "I suppose, if you get me up to the Expert rank-"

"*Now* who's reaching?" Joe dryly cut her off. "Tell you what, we can make a separate deal later. You help me become a Master of Enchanted Ritual Circles, and I'll do the same for you for regular ol' Ritual Circles. Until that becomes an issue, let's just focus on what we're doing, yeah?"

As the bantering faded away, and Hilda once more got utterly focused on her work, Joe glanced down at his hands, staring at the skill that had increased over the last several days.

Calculus and Number Theory (Expert II → Expert V).

That increase alone had taken nearly five days, which meant his Lore skill would achieve Mastery in only ten and a half more. While it chafed to remain in a single location for so long —not to mention what would be required in order to generate the Lore book for Master Hollows—Joe could only grin and bear it. If he'd chosen a different path… no, he was certain *every* viable option would either increase the difficulty, time, or cost substantially. "That's okay… everything worth having is worth putting in the effort."

"Yeah, yeah, I get it. Burn money to gain skill levels," Hilda grumbled as she unspooled a wire made of electrum. Joe decided against correcting her, knowing full well that the advice he meant for himself was applicable to her situation as well.

A short while later, as he casually redirected a blast out into the open air, Hilda tossed her hands up and admitted defeat for the day. "I can't handle any more of this! Fine, you want some pointers while I wait for my hands to stop shaking? What have *you* been working on?"

Perfectly happy to have another set of eyes on his work, Joe pulled out his working theory on finding the World Boss and making a fast travel system to get to it on Jotunheim. "Take a look at this, if you'd like. No diagrams, so don't worry about your eyes melting."

"Always appreciated." Hilda spread some of the pages across the floor, fully unconcerned with getting them dirty.

"If you look here, the idea is to use a pared-down version of these shrines, leaving behind only a teleportation pad that isn't linked to the deity Occultatum." Joe pointed to his stick-figure sketches unashamedly. While his ritual diagrams were works of mathematically perfect geometric art, anything outside of that was *suspect* at best. "The idea is to have them constantly creating more along a grid, until the entire planet is mapped. Then I'll just figure out which ones are being destroyed and use the others to triangulate that position. It'll either get us to the World Boss or at least to some exceedingly powerful monsters."

"Yeah..." Hilda looked up at him with incredible doubt in her eyes. "The actual cost in resources to make all of this happen is practically *uncalculatable*."

"*In*calculable?"

"No," she replied without humor, "each time I attempt to scale it in my head, it breaks and undoes my math. It *un*-calculates. It's such a massive number of rituals working in sequence instead of pooling their resources together to create an effect that works in a single method. Right now, if any part of this got off-kilter even slightly, you would have to go to the physical location and adjust the output by hand."

Joe rummaged through his storage for a moment until he found a blank notebook then looked up expectantly at Hilda as his quill hovered above the page. "I'm always open to some feedback if it's constructive. Why don't you walk me through what you're thinking?"

"That's..." Hilda blinked owlishly as she took in his instant acceptance. "Rather surprising. Most people wouldn't be so quick to abandon something they've put *this* much work into."

"Only a few weeks of meticulous notes." Joe shrugged and swiped at the documents in her hand as if they were scrap paper ready to be recycled. "Plus, I'm not actually abandoning it; I'm certain there's going to be overlap. But if you have a better way of doing it, I'd rather not have to reinvent the wheel on my own."

Hilda's mouth twitched into a smile at the sight of a triple Master of their shared class excitedly hanging on her every word. "Perhaps I've misjudged your threshold for tedium. Yes, I do have a few thoughts on how you can adjust this sequential system. These are standard rituals you will be able to find in the Enchanted Ritual Circle section of the library, and—you're an Expert with that skill still, yes? Good, you'll have access to each of these with just a request."

Taking a moment, she tapped the page where Joe had set up what was essentially a conveyor belt, which would create large slabs with the fast travel enchantment inherent to linked shrines built into them. "This can be less intense. First, a simple Ritual of Recursion tied it to this means you will only need to build the initial teleportation pad, then the ritual will replicate that item until it runs out of resources. Specifically, it will create a ritual on an easily transportable item that can be dropped and activated wherever it needs to be, instead of a multi-hundred-pound slab."

"Why isn't this in widespread use already?" Joe's mouth and

hands were outputting different words, a process exceedingly difficult without a high Intelligence Characteristic. "Even if it's only useful for rituals, we could mass-produce them on a huge scale!"

"It's the problem of base-case instability." Hilda demonstrated her words with her hands as she spoke, making her fingers tremble faster and faster until mimicking an explosion. "Recursion requires a perfectly created base case ritual that creates a perfectly designed item. Once it's active, if either of those is flawed, every copy not only inherits that flaw but will *magnify* it. The only reason I think this will work for you is how these slabs are magically generated in the first place. If you were to use something carved or created by hand, eventually what you'd be putting down across Jotunheim is a chunk of stone that detonates like a Master-rank fireball when something brushes up against it."

"Ah." Joe made a note of that.

"The second reason is that any inefficiency in the design means you will eventually start having exponential mana and component consumption. A single mistake, then there's suddenly a sharp sound filling the air, and the last thing anyone in range smells is a hint of ozone and toast before they're caught up in the explosion." Hilda sounded more nervous now than when she'd started. "You'll need to adjust the ritual in the library before you use it; there are parts of it that... even when someone makes something, that doesn't always mean they did so perfectly."

"Check the syntax." Joe unconsciously had a smirk on his lips as he wrote that sentence on the page. "Fun fact, I'm absolutely *fantastic* at reviewing magical syntax."

"I should hope so." Hilda produced a slate a moment later, one with such incredibly fine details that as Joe looked at it for one second, five, ten... he still hadn't been able to take in all of the layers and attributes. "This is what I would consider one of the most important rituals anyone attempting to master

Enchanted Ritual Circles can get their hands on. It's called 'Robert Roswell's Happy Little Notebook'. This creates a slate you can draw on, while feeding it mana and components to create a ritual at nearly any scale. As in, you want a circle that actually surrounds a city? Or one that fits on the head of a pin? This is how you do it."

Still staring at the slate, Joe unconsciously reached for it, only for Hilda to pull it away and store it back wherever it had come from. "I definitely want one of those, but I don't understand how it's going to be necessary for this project? Actually, I think that was incorporated in one of my other rituals already; I just didn't realize it had a name and could be used for anything other than tracking and moving buildings."

"We'll definitely have to come back to *that* later, but for now, just remember that Jotunheim is *huge*." Seeing Joe fail to react, Master Darling shook her head. "It is at a scale that's very hard to comprehend, even for someone like me who has studied the historical records of it. If you don't take the time to map out the points where each of your teleportation pads should land, you'll drop them somewhere, and they'll get forgotten forever. With something like this, tied to the main ritual, after mapping them, you'll be able to see at a glance what is still in place and what needs repair. Also, you can give each of them a unique identifier so you can use your travel network effectively."

Bobbing his head, Joe wrote the ritual down. "I'd been trying to figure out a workaround on that, perfect."

"You would've had to hire something like a thousand masochistic cartographers just to keep up with what it was supposed to be, let alone how it will *actually* spread out, thanks to terrain and monsters."

Her eyes widened fractionally as she sucked in a breath. "Speaking of monsters, even before having a complete network, as soon as you start building out in the wild, every last one of these will be targeted and shredded by the first monster stumbling over it. Each of these slabs will need to be made with a Ritual of Obscurity built into them. The book in the library has information on how to blacklist certain entity types, monsters for instance. It'll only work up until a certain point of intelligence and power, but that's actually perfect for what you wanted, right?"

"The strongest ones find them and destroy them, which lets *me* find *them*," Joe agreed casually. "Cunning. I like cunning, when it's not someone finding tricky ways to take me down."

"Last one, and only because I think you put yourself in rather risky situations, 'Big Brother's Notification Service'." Hilda had a resigned look in her eyes as Joe paused to stare at her questioningly. "It's a simple ritual that—for good reason— I've never actually seen someone use. Admittedly, it was only kept in the library as a novelty."

"Sounds somewhat concerning? I'm guessing it's a monitoring ritual of some kind?" Joe almost didn't want to know more, but her casual attitude toward the ritual mollified him somewhat.

"It's an alert tethered to you, Enchanted of course, that pings your system mail whenever a ritual you have active completes itself. Every once in a while, someone monkeys with it, but even when it's functioning perfectly, there's no way to tell." She gestured at Joe. "Specifically, it only sends you those alerts as an ever-growing file when you're in a respawn room. For obvious reasons, we've never had someone who is part of the Tower capable of testing it properly."

"Not a part of the overall ritual, just something nice to have to let me know it's still functioning if I went out to see if the World Boss had spawned in a certain location, and it saw me first." Joe finished writing with a flourish, but as he stared down at the page, his feverish smile slowly faded, and his eyes grew distant.

"You know, you're right... I don't need a bunch of various rituals making a production line. I need a... a *swarm* of rituals capable of turning a single item into an enormous number of highly customized boutique, yet mass-produced..." Then, as though a switch had been flipped in his mind, it all came together.

The fleeting brush with enlightenment he'd encountered while watching the Penguins on Jotunheim collide on the ground, in the air, each one performing a single task, yet together generating a potentially world-altering effect. "Easily delivered items. Rituals that just need a burst of mana to be activated."

Hilda gasped and took a step back as golden light began collecting around Joe's head, his eyes shining with illumination that was not merely reflected. Luckily, Joe didn't hear her, or if he had, it wasn't enough to break the trance of Enlightenment he'd fallen into.

"What if the rituals moved on their own? Delivered themselves? If I add in the Ritual of Cloud Step... they move fast enough!" Joe's quill flashed across the page, line after line of text appearing perfectly as though it were being run through a printer. "I've got the delivery method, at the very least! The teleportation pad ritual is created, that attaches to a summoned fish; it's formed over a Ritual of Cloudstep, which binds to anyone or any *thing* moving through the area. Then the summons are directed to the point where the pad is supposed to be placed! When they unsummon themselves, or run out of time, they vanish in a burst of mana!"

He slapped his off-hand onto the ground, cracking the surface of the stone in his excitement. "That burst activates the ritual, dropping a pad wherever they are! *That's* how we can get around worries about uneven terrain or putting it out in midair and having it dropped to the ground just to break! The energy is just wasted otherwise, right?"

"With enough creatures, I could seed the entire planet with these. I'll need to set up major nodes, maybe every ten drops, then once every hundred for an even larger version. Shrines, temples, cathedrals... but paired down to just slab, then load-in site, then basically a parking lot. Then it won't exhaust people to travel massive distances, since the network itself will be able to sustain-"

Joe's breathing slowed, his words turning into frenetic whispers as he scribbled across the page. Hilda could only look on in amazement as she watched the Enlightened Ritualist generate what would almost certainly become a planet-spanning travel network based on arcane magics—the first of its kind across any of the worlds.

CHAPTER TWENTY-FOUR

Congratulations! Ritual Circles has formed a firm foundation and is ready to evolve and grow into the Grandmaster rank. Two of the three requirements have been fulfilled, and by supplying Mastery Merits, you will immediately be able to bring Ritual Circles to the next tier!

Enlightenment gained: True.

At least three other skills at the Master rank per skill attempting to become Grandmaster rank: True.

100 Mastery Merits applied: False.

Core Class Skill Enlightenment gained! Progress toward 'Ritual Magic' gaining Enlightenment: 1/5.

Joe stared at the message, then at the small notebook he had completely filled with his plans for what would ultimately get him a *supply* of Mythic Cores. Frankly, he wasn't certain which one he was happier to look at. Soft, happy noises kept squeaking from his throat as he swapped between the two over and over.

"I can't believe you had an Enlightenment that lasted an entire *week*."

Hilda's voice finally convinced Joe to look up from where he'd apparently been sitting for far too long, only to feel his jaw drop at the massive crowd of Ritualists absolutely *stuffed* into every available space in the area. The ones closest to him were sitting, but the strange portion wasn't how people were then standing—no, the award for bizarre went to the people sitting on their shoulders so those standing behind them could still see.

Every last *one* of them looked exhausted, but no one seemed unhappy with how the situation had turned out.

"Looks like the free lesson is over, everyone!" Hilda called out, only for those at the very back of the crowd to let out a soft groan and begin ambling away, while those nearest Joe waited patiently, contented looks on their faces. "Master Joe? You seem confused, but haven't you ever been able to learn something important from someone doing something either incredibly beyond you or simply by watching them work? Enlightenment is similar to that. It's good you have so many people who've given you an oath already, else much of that potential would've been wasted."

Only then did the bald man snap out of his stupor and realize that he did recognize, at least a little, every last face in the crowd. "They've gotten some benefit from me just sitting here and writing in my notebook? That's... good, I suppose? How about yourself?"

"I'm about ready for a nap. A full week of staring at an almost-unmoving person tends to tire a gal out." Hilda looked at him with bags under her eyes, though the intensity of her excited stare wasn't impacted in the slightest. "Managed to reach Journeyman during that state of Enlightenment you were in. I hope you got something *fantastic*."

"I guess we'll have to wait and find out?" Joe lifted the notebook and shook it, feeling rather hopeful. "It's only theory at this point, but I think I have an idea how to put *all* of it together. An aspect tower to supply raw materials feeding directly into a Master or even Grandmaster-rank ritual that controls the rest of it. Since I now know what all has to go into it, I should be able to start designing the control ritual itself when I have some time to work through it. Even so, with all that said, this is still just a story of a *possibility*."

"Well, that probably means you got a point or two in a Lore skill, if you have one. I'm off to bed. Oh... consider your payment for the Enchanted Ritual Circle paid in full." Without another word, she sent him a tired wave and wandered off, clearly deep in some contemplation of her own.

For his part, Joe still felt incredibly fresh, both mentally and physically. There was only one small issue—he surreptitiously sniffed at his pits, grimacing at the stale odor wafting off of him. "Find a shower and use it. Then..."

Congratulations! Calculus and Number Theory has reached the Master rank!

Calculus and Number Theory (Master 0). Sequences no longer hide in the infinite for you. You can see their limits and apply them to compress the impossible into the functional.

This skill has gained an additional passive effect.

Effect:

1) Improve the rate of skill increase in nearly all fields of magical crafting by $1n + -T\%$, where n = lore skill level and T = Tier difference.

2) Bounding of the Infinite Series: You may bind recurring sequences, forcing them to show as complete as if the otherwise infinite series had reached its limit. Any mathematical construct bound in this way, magical or otherwise, will take 20% more time to inscribe and be 10% more difficult for others to decipher.

-While you may never truly touch something, due to the repulsion of atomic fields, you'll be close enough for practical purposes.

"Seems it's not that I can find the last digit of pi, it's that I can tell an equation that *this* number *is* the last digit, and it'll accept that answer? Hmm. Not entirely certain how to apply that new effect to a ritual, but I'm sure I'll figure it out." Joe turned his attention to his skill list, trying to determine which of his other Lore skills he should attach Loremaster to, so as to not waste any more time in gaining another Mastered skill. "Ritual Lore it is. Only two levels to go... maybe I should've done that one first, just to reduce the total time-? No, can't undo it. Don't beat yourself up."

Applying the active effect of Loremaster to Ritual Lore, Joe felt a feeling of contentment settle over himself. Now that two of his Lore skills were Mastered, the total amount of time for the next one to achieve that rank was only ninety-three hours and some change, or just shy of four days. "If I settle in to make my first-ever Lore Book to pay off Master Hollows... I'll have a newly Mastered skill before I'm done. I *love* compound interest."

After finding a room to shower in and getting clean, Joe reached for his clothes, only to hesitate and reflect on Minya's instructions. With a sigh, he stored away the already perfectly clean clothes—what a waste—and pulled out the next set, which looked exactly the same in every way. After muttering about useless traditions, Joe descended the stairs of the tower into the basement, seeking out the classroom he'd last seen Cosmo in.

Instead of finding who he was looking for, Joe found himself suddenly face to face with Jenny, who was carrying a huge, leather-bound book around as she made her way over to him. "Master! Great to see you; fantastic session over this last week! I made sure to keep meticulous notes on who was there and credit the time toward the lessons they get. I rotated your oath-sworn every day to ensure everyone got some time. Now, I'm sorry to say, but since you never put an upper limit on who you were willing to teach... this is the current sign-up form."

"How many?" Joe questioned in a deadpan tone as he resigned himself to a few more sessions before leaving the tower.

"Pages?" Jenny ruefully chuckled as she dropped the book on a desk and started flipping the pages with a careless push. "I meant the entire notebook is full, or just about. There's some space on the cover sheets along the back-"

"Absolutely not."

"Are you sure? You just taught, in essence, for the last hundred and sixty-eight hours. Nearly two *thousand* total people came through and found themselves increasing not only their Ritual Circles skill, but the vast majority of them even got a Lore skill or three. There has to have been some benefit to that for you, and that means that this much of the book," She held her fingers against the spine of the book, covering seven eighths of its total page count, "doesn't need to get anything from you for the next... eight months?"

"Benefit?" It was true that Joe had a few more notifications blinking in the corner of his vision, but they hadn't seemed all that important in comparison to finishing his plans to finally fix his Mana Channels. Reluctantly, he pulled open the remainder of the messages.

Congratulations! The skill 'Teaching' has reached the Master rank and is ready to evolve, thanks to inspiration gained while teaching a massive number of students nonstop for an extended period of time. Unless they were forced to leave, not a single one of them found themselves bored or wanting to stop learning from the lesson you were teaching. Please choose from among the following evolution paths.

1) Pedagogue's Priming. You no longer simply teach based on your own knowledge; your lessons are encoded into your students beyond the classroom.

a) Effect: For each minute spent teaching a student or group of students a skill or spell you have a Master rank in, their individual skill gain will increase by 50% for half of the duration of the lesson during self-study.

2) Recursive Teaching. A single seed of knowledge can turn into a harvest feeding generations.

a) Effect: When you teach a student who themselves has the Teaching skill, that student gains the ability to pass on what they learned from you to others at 50% efficiency, as though you were teaching their students directly. This effect lingers for 75% of the time your student learned from you directly.

3) Idiomatic Instruction. Tune your lessons to resonate with your students, generating immense harmony between their learning style and your expertise.

a) Effect: Up to three students at a time learn from you at a 200% increased speed and efficiency. Up to 8 students at a time learn with a 150% modifier. For 24 hours after your lesson has ended, the students may apply what they have learned instinctively, granting them direct skill increases.

"See, this is why I didn't want to open my other notifications yet." Joe rubbed his head in frustration as he stared over the three options, each of which appeared better than the last, though only in specific situations. "Should I focus on large groups of students, a small group that I'll just have to *trust* will go out and teach others, or a handful that I'll be able to raise to my own level in half the time?"

"The last one, for *sure*! I volunteer to learn anything you want to teach. Forget these guys." Jenny immediately slammed the sign-up book closed, then slid it away from her where it neatly fell off the table and into a garbage can waiting near the door.

Slowly blinking at the eager student, Joe waffled between laughing at her antics or being concerned at how much he considered going with her choice, even though he barely knew this incredibly ambitious youngster. He settled on the former, letting out a soft chuckle and making his choice.

Teaching has evolved into Recursive Teaching (Master 0).

A single seed of knowledge can turn into a harvest feeding generations.

Effect:

1) Impart n-iT% of your skill level in a skill to those that you are attempting to teach, where n = skill level and iT = the inverse Tier of skill knowledge.

2) When you teach a student who themselves has the Teaching skill, that student gains the ability to pass on what they learned from you to others at 50% efficiency, as though you were teaching their students directly. This effect lingers for 75% of the time your student learned from you directly.

3) In a public setting, bystanders may also learn the skill being taught at a reduced rate of: $n/2 - iT$

Cost: $.1n \times T$ mana or stamina per second, where T is the Tier of the skill being transferred. No cooldown.

"Nice, even the mana and stamina cost was reduced to a fraction of what it was." Joe could only wonder at how many times those resources had bottomed out while he was undergoing Enlightenment, or if the strange energy that had filled him had kept those pools full on his behalf. Turning back to Jenny, he firmly shook his head. "Nice try, but I'll just make it a requirement that anyone who wants to learn from me is willing to work for it by helping others."

Even as she made light sounds of protest, Joe took in the remainder of the notifications.

Ritual Circles (Master III → Master V). Congratulations, you have gained 10 Characteristic points, in each characteristic other than Karmic Luck, for increasing a Master-rank skill twice. (Deferred.)

Ritual Duplication (Student V→ Journeyman I)

Architectural Lore (Expert II → Expert VII)

Celestial-Arcane Interaction Lore (Expert II → Expert V)

Staring at the skill increases, Joe could only theorize as to how he'd gained the new levels. As far as he'd been aware, his Ritual Circles core class skill would only go up with the actual creation of ritual circles, but... perhaps it was an effect of the buildup of Enlightenment energy? Maybe designing the framework for the ritual had more of an impact than he'd given it credit for? Shivering to anchor his thoughts in the present, Joe blinked away the haze and centered his gaze on Jenny.

"All right, I admit you've been doing way more work than I expected there to be available for you, but now *I* need something. I need to speak to Master Hollows, and I've no idea where to find him if he isn't here. Remember when you first signed on? You were going to show me around? Time to make that happen."

"You just need me to bring you to Master Hollows?" Jenny's lips twitched as she held back a smile, walked to the garbage can, and pulled the leather-bound book out with a grunt. "Done and done. Pardon me, Master Hollows? Master Joe is looking for you."

"He's finally decided to stay on Vanaheim permanently and become a regular member of the math club?" The Wolfman rumbled from the doorway as he stepped through the slightly too small frame. "I've been expecting this, but it *is* rather sudden."

"Nice try." Joe shot back, able to see it by the tilt of his contemporary's ears and how his tongue lolled out to the side that the mathematician was in a *fantastic* mood and simply joking with him. "No, I finally have the capability to produce the Lore Book you requested, and since the Enlightenment I just went through was so impactful on the people around me, I thought perhaps there might be something to be gained from watching this process as well. Perhaps, for additional rewards, if I managed to teach you and the club something interesting...?"

"Honor or cheese?" Cosmo shrugged, his hands waving helplessly to the sides in a distinctly human gesture. "Hard to make an agreement for payment without knowing what your offering is worth."

"Perhaps a favor, based on what you gain from it?"

"How about I agree to that, if you owe *me* a favor if this is a waste of our collective time?" The Wolfman renegotiated without hesitation.

Joe simply bobbed his head, not overly concerned with the thought of potentially owing the bulky instructor a favor. "Were you just getting ready for the club to start?"

"Everyone should be arriving shortly." Cosmo moved to the front of the room, setting a small box of supplies to the side. "I hope your lesson can compete with what I was going to teach. Pigeonholing is a *fascinating* application of discrete mathematics, and now they're going to need to wait until next week to learn about it."

"Ooh, yeah, I can see how that would be a hard lesson to miss." As the two Masters began chattering about foundational mathematical theory, Jenny slowly slumped in place, looking for all the world as though she wanted to melt into the floor.

The room quickly filled with people, the original members of the club gaining priority seating at the front of the room, which was soon over-stuffed and standing room only. Only then realizing she didn't *have* to be here, Joe's erstwhile assistant looked around in a panic, unable to find a clear path to the door to make her escape.

Too late.

"Hello, math club!" Cosmo's voice boomed through the

space. "I'm so glad to see everyone showing up for the sixth session in a row! One more day, and we can formally petition for a larger gathering space. I know you were all excited to hear about pigeonholing, but we have a special guest speaker today-"

The front of the room filled with low groans and sounds of disapproval, while those in the middle and back simply stared on blankly, completely lost.

"-Now, now! Our guest speaker today is Master Joe, fresh from his Enlightenment up on the eighteenth floor. He's going to show us some ability of his that he hasn't explained properly, except that at the end of the process, he will be graciously donating a *Master*-rank Lore book on Calculus and Number Theory to the club!"

That was enough to turn even the most disappointed student into an incredulous, enthusiastic onlooker. Suddenly nervous, Joe stepped forward and lifted his hands, not actually certain at all what the process would look like.

"If I end up just waving my hands in front of me with no obvious change for the next little while, uhh, that's supposed to happen." Joe's words earned a chuckle from the room, completely unexpected as he was being entirely serious. Quietly enough that only he should've been able to hear—though Master Cosmo's ears perked up in concern—the bald Ritualist murmured, "Probably should've done this with something else before going straight to this rarity. Hope it works."

Activating Lore Master, Joe was offered a selection to choose from and quickly went through the options to create the book he was after.

Resource requirements:
40 dedicated hours. 0/40.
1,000 Artifact-rank aspects. 1000/1000 available.
12,500 experience or one Artifact core. No core is available.
Proceed? Yes / No.

Only then did Joe realize he hadn't secured the necessary core, but as he looked up from the options with a leery expression on his face, only to meet the gazes of well over a hundred expectant students, he groaned and clicked on 'Yes'. As the numbers dropped out of his total experience pool, he could only let out a sigh of annoyance as he was knocked down to level twenty-nine. "Being capped on experience is *terrible* when situations like this arrive. No wonder people absorb cores for experience, even though there are so *many* other uses for them."

Unable to hesitate any longer, Joe focused on his goal of creating the book and immediately felt the system intervene. The scent of molten copper filled the air as a bright orange sphere of plasma appeared in the air between his hands, eliciting a gasp of surprise from those gathered in the room as they leaned away in instinctive understanding of the power, rarity, and therefore *danger* of the light he was manifesting.

"Good call, everyone. Don't try to touch anything here unless you want to make the fastest possible discovery of a logical *proof* of your mortality." Only Cosmo laughed at Joe's joke, making the Ritualist wonder if they hadn't gotten to the section on proofs in the club.

His experience points, which had already been removed from his total pool and reserved by the system, began flowing into the molten orange light. Even Joe gasped as scintillating fulguration flowed out of him, interacting with the aspect and forming into script. Numbers and equations written in machine-perfect writing etched themselves in the open air, dense formulae almost too tiny to read without a magnifying glass. As a full page's worth of data finished writing itself out, a slightly larger chunk of the aspect was pulled away from the tiny sphere, forming itself into parchment that the words imprinted themselves onto.

"Did you see that? He's *bleeding math*."

"How long do I have to be in the club before I can do something like that?"

There was very little for Joe to actively do, as it was the system that was pulling on his resources and generating the book. That gave him plenty of time to interact with the class, answering questions or just enjoying their own thoughts on what was going on here. Sometimes there was a chunk of information hanging in the air that was large enough to read, and it would spark fierce debate among those assembled. Only then, *after* the topic had died almost all the way down, did Joe or Master Hollows offer their own insights on the subject.

Another aspect appeared in the air as the first one was fully consumed, and so the process continued. Every theorem and concept he knew to work correctly was being dragged out of him and assigned to a neat row or column across the page. Minutes went by as Joe settled into a chair, only a fraction of his attention on the actual process of generating the Lore Book.

As exciting as the process was, seeing as no one present had seen something like this before, by the second hour, the conversation had generally shifted to simply silently watching for interesting tidbits. By the third, nearly everyone who had managed to get a chair when they first arrived was nodding off.

Then Master Hollows stood up and clapped his hands, and everyone jerked back to attention, especially Joe, who'd been pretending to meditate as he slowly drifted, unable to do anything other than wait for the process to be completed. Just as the system had stated, he needed to devote his time only to the creation of the item he was attempting to generate.

"Thank you all for coming. I think we've all seen more than enough for today, and I for one am immensely grateful for the conversations we've been able to have because of it!" People immediately began shuffling toward the exit, even as the Wolfman barked out instructions for the next club meeting, making sure to remind them in a cajoling tone that they only needed one more session with such a large crowd before all of them would be able to have their own seat.

Finally, only the two Masters remained in the room. To Joe's surprise, Cosmo didn't look like he was ready to leave. Not in the slightest, going by how, now that the rest of the room had cleared out, he was able to get as close as possible—without setting himself on fire—to the words writing out in midair.

"Truly, this is fascinating stuff," Cosmo whispered in excitement. "Can you keep it up for at least another hour? I feel like I'm right on the verge of gaining a level."

"For you, sure." Joe had long since realized that he could pause the process at any time, a welcome change from his usual crafting projects that would detonate with incredible destructive force if he ignored them too long. As the fourth hour came to a close, he finally decided he was done for the day.

"Just need a couple hours of shut-eye, then I'll power through the rest of it. Almost two full days' worth of time to go. Should I let you know before I start up again?"

"Absolutely. I don't want to miss a *moment* of this." Cosmo let out a low wolf-whistle. "Reading over someone else's understanding of mathematics, perfectly detailed and intricate, with footnotes and references included? *Far* too fascinating of an opportunity to pass up on!"

CHAPTER TWENTY-FIVE

Forty hours of dedicated effort felt a lot shorter when sleep was only a *suggestion* for up to a week at a time. On only the beginning of the third day after starting the project, Joe was holding a Masterwork Lore book.

When Cosmo eagerly reached a hand out for it, the Ritualist found himself oddly unwilling to part with it. Seeing his hesitation, Cosmo slowed slightly, but his hand didn't drop. Joe pushed himself to let go and gently lay the book in the enormous, outstretched paw. "It's strange, Master Hollows. I know for a fact that I won't gain anything by reading this book, as it's entirely based on the knowledge I myself have, and yet..."

"The allure of treasure only becomes stronger when it's treasure formed by your own efforts." Though his voice was gentle, the Master of Magical Matrices' movements were quick as he stored the book away. "Well, with that out of the way, I suppose I can give you this in return."

A thick document was deposited in front of Joe, and the bald man shook his odd moroseness off long enough to read the tooltip that popped up. Immediately, he felt his mood shift to pure anticipation—he finally had the first completed piece of the key to fixing his broken mana.

The Calcintsugi Continuum (Artifact). This is a unique formula created for a specific purpose, to mitigate a highly irregular situation. This continuum is designed to reclaim the exact coordinates of the broken flows of Mana Channels in a specific body, and repair them not with gold, but bound them via the medium of equations.

The book itself is a single, continuous Magical Matrix designed to work as the drivers which will integrate equipment generated through Ritualistic Forging, direct the magic from an enchanted ritual circle, regulate the flow of solutions created with Ritualistic Alchemy, and interface with the logic of the overarching control in the form of a ritual circle. At each input, the formula is open-ended, allowing for the possibility of additions and revisions to skills without interfering with their usage.

"I started working on this the first night you brought it to me," Master Hollows admitted with a rogueish flair. "It was far too interesting of an idea, a project, to pass up. Frankly, I haven't had anything this fun to work on in decades, and the fact that it was going to be put into usage directly instead of simply being another publication put on the shelf of the library? An actual *practical use* formula instead of just another half of a percentage efficiency upgrade to one of the standardized rituals everyone is using these days?"

For his part, Joe could barely look away from the enormous document, absolutely blown away by the fact that this was already ready to go. "I can't thank you enough, Cosmo. You need anything, *anything* I can help with, just know that I'm ready to get on board with it immediately."

The Wolfman simply shook his head back and forth, a knowing expression on his face. "Well, if the rumors hold true, it's best to find myself in your good graces sooner rather than later. Look at you. The first Tri-Master of our Core Class skills in the tower—at least still living—an acknowledged Master of Ritual Combat, and a Decury Duelist? Joe, Grandmaster Pete might end up being our first Skill Sage, but *you* are the only person even in the running to become the tower's *Class Sage*... and you just got to Vanaheim."

"You don't think that'll cause some problems among the others? I'm *very* sick of getting swept up in the politics of it all." Even before Joe finished speaking, Cosmo was shaking his head firmly.

"Not even a little. The fact that you even have to ask that question shows how little you understand about how desperately we need a Class Sage. Every last one of us would give away five levels in our Mastered skills if it meant we could donate them to someone and generate a Class Sage out of thin air. It would secure our tower permanently. Our *home* could never be taken from us. Plus, if we had a Class Sage, that would mean there's plenty of opportunity to have a handful of Skill Sages as well."

The Wolfman's ears perked up. "One last time, I can't quite tell you how thankful I am for this Lore book. I'm going to go and study it for some time on my own, then allow only the brightest among the club to study it as a reward for serious effort. Hopefully, the promise of such a spectacular reward will give even those who aren't as enthusiastic a proper taste for math."

"Just make sure to explain the rules well ahead of letting them touch it." Joe thumbed his nose while shivering at the thought of someone simply tapping the Lore book and absorbing it for a few skill levels. "You just know that someone without the proper *taste* for this would eat it raw."

"I have you to blame for my sense of humor becoming distorted over the last few weeks." The Wolfman growled even as the duo lifted their fists and slammed them into each other hard enough to be painful, the Wolfman way of offering a proper farewell to a friend. "I'm going to do my best to start stealing your students away from you as soon as you leave the tower."

"First off, correlation does not equal causation. Secondly... you want my students? Take. I have many." With that quick back and forth, along with the tacit admission that they were rather fond of working together, Joe quickly made his way out of the first basement level of the tower and began a long climb up the stairs.

As he went, the Reductionist pulled out a fistful of Common and Uncommon cores that had been rattling around in his storage devices—too weak for the type of rituals he now created and practically only valuable on Midgard as items for bartering. "Anywhere from one to two thousand experience in the Common, or two to four thousand in the Uncommon."

Seeing as he was passing by various people watching him with far too much admiration in their eyes, Joe lifted a fistful of the shining gems to his mouth and pretended to violently *crunch* into them, even as he simply was selecting the system prompt to absorb them. "Nom, nom!"

The shocked expressions on their faces were everything he could have ever hoped for, and as he passed them on the stairs, Joe leaned closer to the Journeyman Ritualists—going by the five-circle gloves they were wearing—and whispered in a hoarse voice, "No one will ever believe you."

He increased his pace without another word, powering up the stairs quickly. When he finally arrived at Master Darling's office, one of the only locations he had properly fixed in his head, he knocked politely instead of simply searching for a privacy platform and jumping over to it. Joe waited a moment, doing his best to be respectful, but still quite impatient to get on his way.

"*Come in!*"

The door itself vibrated with those words, sparkling ever so slightly as some form of magical protection deactivated itself. He walked into the room, expecting a minimalist setup, only to find himself looking at an office built as though it were meant to be a library. Warm wooden shelves were built into every inch of the wall, yet instead of books, there were various implements and shining cores under glass domes. But the centerpiece was a small rack of Enchanted Tokens set up like a rack of challenge coins.

Some form of privacy enchantment kept their details hidden from him, but Joe fully understood they were something extra special if they were put in such a pride of place.

"Master Darling?" His voice echoed through the room, and a moment later, he heard the wrestling of someone moving quickly in an adjoining room. Moments later, one of the shelves swung out, revealing itself as a secret door, and out came... a monster.

Joe recoiled, Ritual Orbs springing into the air as he prepared to defend himself. The creature looked at him with red-veined eyes, face shifting into a snarl.

"That's *incredibly* rude." The raspy voice only held a hint of familiarity, but it was enough for Joe to recognize the woman he'd come here to see. Shambling over to her desk, Master Darling tapped what looked like an enchanted bell someone would use to inform staff they were waiting for service. Immediately, her wild hair poofed out, then fell into perfectly coiffed layers, her wrinkled robes straightened themselves, and the exhaustion and various compounds which had coated every inch of her skin were eliminated.

When she turned back to him, her ominous glare practically *daring* him to comment, Joe merely noted that now she only appeared to have not slept in weeks instead of actively transforming into some fell beast. With a practiced motion, he manifested a coffee cup out of storage while pulling his own off his belt. Mate bubbled up happily, waving at the startled Enchanter before pouring a mug of hot, steaming joy into both containers and vanishing.

She chugged down the liquid without seeming to even notice the heat, then handed back the empty dish and waved off Joe's implied offer of a refill. "Thanks for that. Glad the messenger found you so quick; I guess you really *are* ready to get moving on this. Just know that you will be missed; there's been more excitement with you here over the last few weeks than we've seen in half a century."

"Messenger?" Joe shook his head and tried not to make any

sudden movements, worried that she would revert back into the sleep-deprived, grunge-coated entity he'd walked in on. "No, I was just coming to say farewell before I left to finish some of my other projects. Why did you send someone to find me?"

"Oh, just fortuitous timing, then?" Hilda pulled a small box out of seemingly nowhere, pulling back the sliding cover to reveal six shimmering tokens. "I've been using the inspiration granted by your runoff Enlightenment energy to get this project done. I was worried that, if I fell asleep I'd lose it, so... all done."

"This is... you made all of these in the last...?" Joe felt as though his brain needed to be restarted. "I thought you needed so much information, *and* the design?"

"I had the scaffolding of the design even before being bathed in Enlightenment energy for a week." Hilda snorted out a decidedly unladylike sound. "Now, to be clear, it's not *ready* to be used. There's one more token to be made, but that one correlates to your Characteristics. More specifically, it correlates to your *mutable* Characteristics, so your skills and such are included in that category. As soon as you're ready to actually activate the ritual, I'll only need a day or so of preparation to get it made."

Gesturing to the small box, she pressed on, "Still, I thought you'd appreciate knowing that I have everything else *Masterfully* made. The design for the last token is ready to go, as is every part of the enchantment on it that does not need your current mutable Characteristics entered. Perhaps two to five hours of total inscription work on my end when you're ready."

"Thank you so much." Joe took a deep breath, puffing out his cheeks as he let it go. "Wasn't expecting that, and... again, thank you. Now, you've repeated yourself something like three times in this conversation, so you should go and take a rest. I'll be back... eventually. The next time you see me, it'll be time to put it into place."

"Good, I'll need to write out the instructions, anyway..." Hilda blinked several times, each slow flutter taking almost a full second, then she continued her train of thought, "Three tokens placed in the circle, three tokens placed on *you*. Sternum notch, glabella, navel. Last one fed into the equipment to interface with what is going to be piercing your flesh and marrow to inject concentrated reagents."

"Can't wait," Joe dryly replied as she lost herself in her own mind once more. "Look, you're swaying on your feet and practically catatonic. Do you need help-"

"*Nahhh,*" Her reply was a long, drawn out denial. "I press that button, the desk folds away, and a bed pops up. We all know how long some of our projects take, and getting to a bedroom at the end of something like this is... is... a fool's prospect."

Thanking her and backing out of the room, Joe slowly closed the door even as she smacked a different service bell, and her desk began scooting to the side on its own. As a fluffy duvet erupted out of the floor, Joe fully latched the door. A shimmering light crossed it once more, activating whatever enchantment had been placed within. Turning toward the stairs, the Ritualist bit off an exclamation of surprise as he found himself face-to-face with Grandmaster Pete.

"Master Joe," the tower's foremost powerhouse addressed Joe in a formal tone, dipping his chin with restrained courtesy. "If I may have a moment before you run off?"

"That's—absolutely! You know you don't even have to ask, but-"

"But it's polite, yes." The air around them charged with power, flashing green brightly enough that Joe blinked, only to find himself standing across from the Grandmaster, who was on the other side of his desk and already sitting down. "It's come to my attention that you are planning to not only involve yourself with the expeditions clashing down on Jotunheim, but are going to be running a Grandmaster-rank ritual. An untested one, which may permanently alter your body and Akashic record. Is my information correct?"

Though he didn't know exactly where this conversation was

going, Joe saw no harm in being honest and forthright with his answer. "From what I've heard, yes. A component from each of the five core class skills, each of them working in tandem with each other to forcibly correct the... *issues* I've run into with my mana channels."

"What about the expeditions?" Pete's words hung in the air like a dark cloud.

"I'm planning a ritual on a similar scale, if that's what you're asking." Joe raised an eyebrow at Pete's lack of a reaction. "I made a deal with one of the groups for Mythic Cores over time. Essentially, it's going to be likely the best and fastest way that I can fulfill *our* bargain."

"Don't tell me another single detail about that bargain." Pete held his hands up quickly as Joe began to speak on. "*Especially* not which of the two groups you've aligned with. But, I now need to tell you about some interesting rumors that have been floating around..."

The Grandmaster's eyes flicked to the new outfit Joe was wearing, from the gloves which gave away his three Mastered class skills, to the embroidery along his cuffs that showed his overall competence with Ritual Combat, to the Decury Duelist patch on his shoulder. As his gaze traveled back to lock with Joe's, the man's entire countenance shifted.

"...and I'm absolutely *ecstatic* to see they're all true."

"Um?" Joe faltered as Pete suddenly launched out of his chair, hands on the desk as he leaned toward him.

"Can you believe it? The first person in our tower's history who has a serious chance at becoming a Class Sage, and *I* get to be the one who formally sponsored him!" Pete slapped the desk, a deep laugh bursting from his chest. "Well, don't let me get in your way! In fact, I'd like to make an offer, if you'd be willing to give me your trust. I'm not certain who you planned to activate and manage the ritual that will be carving you up from the inside out, but I'd love to fulfill my obligations as a sponsor. If you'll have me, I'd be *honored* to be the lead Ritualist."

Joe's mouth popped open, forming a small 'o' of surprise.

He'd considered the need for someone else to run the ritual, but hadn't given it too much thought as of yet, as he still had to put together the actual design *and* create the ritual circle. But to have Pete offer to operate it on his behalf? Someone who was bound by the system to have his best interests in mind? There was only one possible answer.

"Yes! That would be ideal! My only other real option was a Grandmaster of Mana Manipulation, but I don't know if her skills would translate as perfectly across as yours will."

"It'll be a festival day here, that much I can promise you." Pete grabbed Joe's hand, shaking it excitedly. "I'll obviously run the main circle, but we will select four others to be the lead on each of the other components, and... do you have any idea how many people we can get involved in this? Every last soul in the tower is going to be foaming at the mouth for the chance to take part in a brand-new, once-in-a-lifetime usage Grandmaster ritual. The sheer *bonuses* to skill gain and experience for being the first to activate something like this? We're not talking a few skill levels, we're talking a tier at a time for some of the lower ranks!"

Joe couldn't find it in himself to even pretend to be wistful about missing out on the benefits that would come from something like that, as he'd be getting something even more important in return—full functionality. "Then, the next time you see me... be ready to throw a party!"

"Absolutely. When you're ready, call on us, and we'll be there. Remember, one of our main tenets is that, if you want to go fast, you go alone. But if you want to go far..."

Pete leaned back, standing straight and proud, a goofy smile on his face, "...you go together."

CHAPTER TWENTY-SIX

Beam to Bifrost was the only active spell Joe could use without issue, though discovering that had taken quite a while. Most likely, it was only thanks to the fact that the spell didn't actually have any mana cost, though there was a ten-second channeling where he had to stay essentially as still as possible—a lifetime, if he was hiding from some massive beast and attempting an escape.

As soon as his conversation with Grandmaster Pete came to a close, Joe didn't wait to be sent away, nor did he want to risk running into someone else on the stairs and getting distracted for another week or six. Instead, he immediately activated the spell and was slowly coated in a shimmer of cascading light that began to resemble the energy of the bifrost more and more with each second that passed.

Then, as the tenth second was about to tick over into the eleventh, Joe simply ceased to be constrained by Vanaheim.

Barely able to register what he was passing due to the sheer speed of his movement, the Ritualist swept directly through the walls of the Tower of Ritualists, then through dozens of other buildings as he rocketed along the surface of the planet. He traveled through the blockade of Masters, who didn't seem to register his presence in the hundredth of a second that he was there—it seemed they were in the midst of questioning some new arrivals who had just ascended to Vanaheim for the first time. Then he joined with the bifrost proper and was launched into space.

Once he was traveling through the void, Joe felt a large amount of tension flow out of him.

"Not sure if I prefer Vanaheim over Jotunheim, or the other way around. Less actual monsters on the first, but far more responsibility on the second. Midgard might as well be a vacation planet at this point, at least now that I've destroyed that coalition against my Sect and me personally." Joe settled into the warm, energetic flow, pulling open his status sheet for the first time in a long time to pass the time, and munching on a few more cores to bring himself back to level thirty before doing so.

Name: Joe 'Monarch of Mana' Class: Reductionist
Profession I: Arcanologist (Max)
Profession II: Ritualistic Alchemist (15/20)
Profession III: Grandmaster's Apprentice (15/25)
Profession IV: Ritualistic Metalworker (16/20)
Profession V: Ritualistic Numerologist (10/20)
Profession VI: Arcane Enchanting Theorist (5/5) This can now be used as a prerequisite for any enchanting-based profession!

Character Level: 30 Exp: 465,000 Exp to next level: 31,000 (Locked.)
Rituarchitect Level: 14 Exp: 95,450 Exp to next level: 9,550
Reductionist Level: 12 Exp: 85,472 Exp to next level: 5,528

Hit Points: 4,546/4,546
Mana: 3,901/3,901 (Catastrophic Damage)
Mana regen: 42.98/sec (Catastrophic Damage)
Stamina: 3,229/3,229
Stamina regen: 7.39/sec

Characteristic: Score
Strength: 299
Dialectic *Dexterity: 299*
Stoic Constitution: 299
Light Intelligence: 299
Ritualistic Wisdom: 299
Dark Charisma: 299
Karmic Perception: 299
Red *Luck: 299*
Karmic Luck: 4

"Looks like there's just Strength left to shift, then I'll have a full set. Hah… gotta collect 'em all." Jotunheim came into view long, *long* before he ever got close enough to make out any details of its cloud cover. Even still, all too soon he was bursting through the turbulent atmosphere, rapidly approaching the only viewable part of its surface from so high up: Novusheim. Moments before he would've impacted the surface like a meteor, his speed was cut in half, then again, again, until he merely landed with a heavy yet survivable **thud**.

"Joe's back!" someone casually called over to a large group of passersby. Glancing over, the Ritualist saw a guard casually waving at him. "Good to see you again. Sorry you missed out on all the fun."

With a slow sinking sensation, Joe tried to figure out what it possibly could've been that he missed, but luckily the guard saw his expression and offered an explanation. "Your Sect had a big festival 'couple weeks ago, something about picking out a core mission? All of us were on high alert looking for you, to make sure we sent you along if you showed up, but they had to make a decision without you. Then there was a party. Lasted ten days, and everyone friendly toward them on the *planet* got an invite."

"Well, that's just…" Joe interlaced his fingers and put his hands behind his head, taking a deep breath as he tried not to succumb to the angst of having missed out on something so important. "I'm sure it was great. Thanks for letting me know;

I'll look into that when I make my way over there. Hey, have the blacksmiths been treating you guys right?"

"Oh, *abyss* yeah." The guard pulled out an oversized knife, nearly a short sword, and cut it through the air sharply. By the time the weapon came to a standstill, it was *humming* with energy, a bright glow creeping along its edge as the air above it started to waver with a heat haze. "Jotunheim alloy, now standard issue. Half price for people in service to the city, so that we can still afford to get our own enchantments engraved on 'em. Don't take this the wrong way, but it's been practically a nonstop party around here since you left."

"Because I did cool things before I left, not because I left... right?"

"Yeah, that's exactly what I meant." The guard's mouth was slightly open, a grin on his face—a picture-perfect representation of a moray eel—as he waited with bright eyes to make a joke.

The Ritualist got moving, not knowing the guard well enough to really want to hang around and get into conversation. "Well, if anyone needs me, I'll only be here for a day, two at the most. Feel free to spread the word, but I'm only here to pick up a few things. Hopefully."

Ignoring any other comments sent his way, whether they be silly or complimentary, Joe found himself drawn with inevitable swiftness to the Pyramid of Panacea. He clenched and unclenched his hands over and over, knowing that if 'mere' Masters had been able to create the designs he needed, certainly by now Jake the Alchemist would've long since finished his own project.

Sunlight pierced through the cloud cover broken by the bifrost funneling through it, glistening off the obelisks which now seemed to be meant more to contain the pyramid rather than hold it upright. The Ritualist followed the enormous chains binding the structure in place, squinting as light scattered off the crystalline surface. As he stepped across the clear boundary between regular cobbled street and marble surface, he was immediately inundated by the frost-chilled scent of burnt herbs and failed potion making.

"Now that's just *wrong*." The closer he got, the more acrid the smell became, until his eyes were almost watering from the intensity of the stench. "He had to have taken on some Novices or something, right? There's no way *Jake* is letting the world know that he failed at crafting something."

Stepping onto the long bridge that led to the front door, Joe felt a shiver of energy race through the platform, and the massive doors in front of him let out a low groan as they inched open of their own accord. For a moment, he thought he was being welcomed in. But just before he got close enough to breach the entryway, Jake appeared in a flicker of motion, resolving into a person standing stock-still as though he'd been standing there for hours, complete with his standard neutral expression.

"Welcome back, Joe. Here's your Ichor and the instructions on how to use it." The Alchemist stood with a green-tinted bottle carved from a single piece of jade, filled with a churning, volatile Orange Ichor that seemed to break every law of fluid dynamics Joe had ever even briefly encountered. "Go ahead and take it, and we will consider ourselves square."

As much as he wanted to grab the no doubt *extraordinarily* valuable item, the Ritualist could only force his hands to remain at his sides and slowly shake his head. "Jake... you know better than that. We never formally agreed on the cost of this, and you never even told me you were going to start making it. There was talk about favors being redeemed, maybe even Mythic Cores involved for *Artifact*-rank goods-"

"It's already *made*, Joe. It's ready for you. *Right now*." Jake's face twitched, showing just the barest hint of his canines as the man tried to hold back a snarl. "I'll make it easy. I'll even let you hold on to your Major favor, just let the upgrade of the Pyramid of Panacea commence. Take the *Ichor*, Joe."

Tch. Clicking his tongue, the Ritualist took a careful step backward. "I don't think that's in my best interest, Jake. You wouldn't have made that if you didn't want to be able to wave it in front of my face like this, and... if I have to be brutally honest, I don't think you have anything else you could use that for. Are you really going to just throw out a custom-made Artifact like that Ichor?"

"Perhaps you're right, and I was too hasty. Well, it'll be shelf stable for fifty years." The jade bottle vanished in a blur, stored away in some contraption as Jake's body language shifted back to completely relaxed. "Feel free to offer appropriate compensation for it, though I reserve the right to refuse all offers for the next forty-nine years and eleven months."

They stared at each other for a few long moments, then Jake took a step back and began closing the door. Letting out a heavy sigh, Joe lifted a finger.

"An Artifact-rank design and creation? For a Mythic Core? You *know* that's too much."

"I'm prepared to offer change."

The Ritualist paused, not sure how to react to that statement. "A Mythic Core isn't exactly something you can break down so easily, is it? There's only a few of them at a time on any world."

"Until it is *used*," Jake immediately rebutted, obviously having planned his arguments well in advance. "At which point the World Boss will begin respawning immediately. If you give me permission, I will allow the pyramid to absorb the core within the next few moments. The Lava Phoenix of Alfenheim will reappear within the week, ready to be hunted down and harvested once more."

"Magma Phoenix technically, until it surfaces." After a few heartbeats, Joe turned away, saying over his shoulder, "I'll come back when I have something else I think you'll like. It's too much."

"Two Major favors and ten Legendary cores. Payable immediately." Behind him, the world *thrombed* with such immense potency that the thin layer of ice covering the marble shattered, rising into the air for a few moments before sublimating directly into steam and drifting away. Pressure layered on Joe from all angles, the wind itself turning into a giant clot of turbulence around him.

Turning back, the bald man stared at the pile of cores in the Alchemist's open palm, intentionally stacked into a tiny pyramid to subliminally make his thoughts align with the alchemy hall. Taking a deep breath, he slowly nodded, and Jake's firm expression eased. "I'll take that deal…"

Jake's thin lips began to turn slightly upward, but crashed back into a deep frown as Joe finished his statement.

"But not yet." Taking a few steps away, so that he could force himself not to lunge at the accumulated wealth in Jake's hand, Joe swallowed hard and lifted his eyes to meet an unwavering glare. "Soon, though. As soon as I'm ready to accept and use the Ichor, I'll take your deal. I *swear* that, so long as you keep this deal intact, I won't seek out an alternate source."

"Why do you insist on *vexing* me so, Joe?" The cores vanished, and energy stopped collecting around the Alchemist. "Fine… but I won't wait forever. Eventually I will be able to source my *own* Mythic Core, then I won't *need* yours."

The doors to the pyramid slammed shut, and a wave of frosty air swirled around Joe, lifting him almost off his feet and sending him sliding across the re-frosted surface out and onto the far rougher cobblestone street. Thankfully, with his fine-tuned Dexterity, the Ritualist easily landed on his feet and simply continued moving, not looking back as he hurried over to Grandmaster McPoundy's forge and—hopefully—a far warmer reception.

He was not disappointed.

"*He's here!*" The call went out just as the Ritualist stepped into the Grandmaster's domain, having barely crossed the boundary of his estate. Joe barely had time to blink before a group of apprentices sprinted for the forge, throwing elbows and slamming into each other to be the first to arrive at the door and make the announcement.

Before he was halfway across the distance, the smith himself made an appearance, bursting into view as he threw the door open hard enough to send the winner of the mad dash tumbling into the others, knocking them aside like bowling pins. A booming laugh rolled across the area as McPoundy strode toward Joe, his arms going to the side as he prepared to embrace the Ritualist.

They slammed into each other, neither of them giving ground as the Dwarf pounded on Joe's back just like his name-sake. "Good ta' see you, lad! Come on in, we've just put the final embellishments on this beauty. You're going to love it! Smooth arcs of alloy folded over each other to form a lotus— should be auspicious symbology when you're trying to cleanse or renew somethin'!"

They walked into the forge, and Joe didn't even have a moment to appreciate the massive interior, the warm design, a veritable warehouse of ingots, weapons, and armor. No, his attention was immediately drawn to the massive pod in the center of the room, just as beautiful as McPoundy had promised. Even so, Joe found a deep part of himself quailing at the sight.

"Abyss, that... that brings back memories of the box they put me in to send me to Eternium in the first place. Prettier, I'll definitely give you that, but definitely have some dark memories associated with this sort of design."

"Yeah, you're not the first to draw the comparison." The Dwarf slapped Joe on the shoulder, far more gently than Joe knew he could. "Don't you worry, there's not another level to go down to another world. Eternium is the bottom from here."

"Prove it?" Joe wearily chuckled even as the Dwarf froze up and sputtered with concern. "I'm only playing, Grandmaster. Why don't you tell me about this gorgeous Artifact?"

The Dwarf brightened up immediately, turning and thumping the metal with his massive hand. "She's a right pretty lass, isn't she? Stronger than some of the weaker Legendary items I've seen out there! We're still debating on the final name; some of us are thinking the 'Hypodermic Chrysalis', but that gives an inaccurate view of what it can do. I'm thinking… the 'Intraosseous Cocoon'. The needles in there are as sharp as my wife and as inflexible as my last girlfriend!"

He leaned forward, giving the Ritualist a heavy wink. "They're the same gal."

"Wouldn't expect anything else." Joe could only laugh along at the re-energized Grandmaster. "Good to see you're feeling better these days, McPoundy. Can I see the inside?"

"Oh, aye, that ya can. Pretty sure you'll be getting a right close look at it in the near future." The Dwarf tapped a flowing symbol, and the 'petals' unfurled to reveal a comfortable bed which Joe knew at a glance would fit his body exactly—down to a fraction of a millimeter. "Like it was saying, this is filled with injectors I forged one at a time with my own hands and hammer. Each one'll pierce clean through your bones without the slightest give, then put out just a *hint* of abrasion to make sure they can't be jostled out if you flinch or the like. Not that you'll even feel them go in. Like I said… *sharp*. You get cozy, this closes around you, and every last drop of power and what-ever else you give it's going to be sent *exactly* where it needs to go."

"Sounds fun." Joe tried to deflect from the immense nervousness filling him at that moment.

Grinning knowingly, the Dwarf pressed the button again, and the pedals folded up. A moment later, there was a very faint sound from the interior, similar to a knife being pressed into a sheath, but repeated thousands of times in the same split second. "She's pretty, but I know where your head's at. Comfort is for the weak. What I'm giving you here is *certainty*. I can promise you this, lad, there's no more sure way of injecting whatever magic you need into marrow then the Intraosseous Cocoon. Decided on that name, officially now."

A cheer went up around the room, and small ingots of metal began being passed around. Joe raised an eyebrow at the clear signs of the intense round of betting that had gone into this, but he kept his mouth shut. He knew better than to demand that hardworking people *didn't* have fun in their free time.

"All right. Looks like exactly what I need, McPoundy. Now the only question is, how do I get the I.C. out of here?" Joe slowly felt a hint of a flush creeping up his neck as the Dwarf merely shook his head and snickered.

"Sounds like a *you* problem." The Dwarf took a step back, raising his hands in the air. "I designed it, we built it, *you* figure out how to transport it. Here's an instruction manual."

"A 'you' problem? The Intraosseous Cocoon 'you' problem?" Joe crossed his arms, but wherever he looked, he was met with unflinching, if somewhat mirthful expressions in return. "Fine. Then I'm going to call this the 'ICU', and that's what I'm telling *everyone* its name is."

"You're a *monster*!" McPoundy gasped in fake outrage, even as piles of items began appearing around Joe. Everything from papers, to notebooks, broken quills, piles of ingots, and small hills of low-level cores. "What in blue blazes are you *doing*?"

"Reorganizing." Joe grumbled as he swept everything into his storage rings, except the broken bits. Those he left littered around on the floor as an attempt at petty revenge. "I've only got one storage device large enough to hold all of this, so…"

Walking over to the massive item, Joe dropped into a squat position, wrapped his arms around the base, and *heaved* upward. As the pod cleared the ground, he thrust forward with his hips, tapping his codpiece against its metal surface, and the entire lotus-shaped item vanished with a soft *pop*.

"What…?" McPoundy shook his head in disappointment. "I know I called the ICU a lady, but even so, that's no way to treat a lass the first time you're meeting her. Tossin' her around and dirty dancing. We were only poking fun at you… we had a crate ready and everything!"

Joe covered his face and rubbed up over his head as the room erupted in laughter, then he looked around and made a few rude gestures as he backed out of the forge and into

Novusheim proper. "You *all* suck! See if I come here for custom work ever again… in the next eight to twelve hours!"

Their howling chased him all the way to the edge of the estate, but he wasn't truly worried or even thinking of them in the *slightest* anymore. It was all he could do not to jump onto the bifrost and vanish into the depths of the Grand Ritual Hall of Midgard, but there was a *tiny* bit to do before he could succumb to that desire.

"I'm going to pop into the Sect, see what I missed, pick up my Tyrant Penguin parts, and let everyone know I'm going into seclusion for a bit." The realization that he had missed out on the meeting to set the Sect's core mission was eating at him, and he could only hope that they hadn't decided on something *too* outrageous.

CHAPTER TWENTY-SEVEN

Step.

Step. Step.

Step. Step. Step.

Step. Step.

Step.

Letting out a soft series of curses as he huffed and puffed up the incline that absolutely had not been here the last time Joe was on this world, the Ritualist felt his boots scuffing over the raw stone that had replaced the soft, loamy soil. "I remember the system saying that a Sect needed to be built on a mountain, or the land would be converted to one, but I didn't think it would go this quickly."

What had once been an endlessly flat plane covered with megaflora and fauna, perhaps a gently rolling hill if he stretched his imagination, had been twisted into the jagged beginnings of a proper mountain range. Peering into the distance, he could see his destination. If he stared hard enough, Joe swore he could pick his house out on top of one of the peaks next to the main mountain, which had pressed upward higher than the others around it.

"Spontaneous Himalayan upgrade. Nothing like *altitude* to really give Constitution a proper test or three." Joe's muttering came through clenched teeth; the truth was, simple physical exertion would never impact him in this way, not with how much he'd been changed by the system. No, that fault was placed squarely at the fact that increased altitude brought them ever-more adjacent to the dense cloud cover surrounding the entirety of the planet and the oceans of turbulent mana contained within them.

The closer he got, the stronger the downward pressure and the harder it was to keep going. In other words, it felt exactly like how he would've expected it to feel back when he was reading stories that had similar concepts. It was a fun, thrilling thought in novels, but the reality was much harsher and sweatier.

As he hurried along the path—which had only become more well-worn as others must have been constantly seeking out the shortest distance between cities—he rounded a slight switch-back and came face-to-face with a startled guard sitting at an obviously hastily constructed outpost.

"Ahhh—*halt!*"

Raising an eyebrow, Joe tried to hold his smirk back as the startled man leveled a spear in his direction. "Solid transition from shriek of fear to giving orders. I'd give it an eight out of ten, but you can probably polish it a little bit and get a solid nine stars."

"Joe? That is... First Elder Joe?" The spear vanished immediately, and an awkward half-bow quickly followed. "I am outer disciple Vold Boulderbraid. It's a pleasure to meet you. I have two messages awaiting your attention. The first is that you can accept quests at this outpost, or you can make payments for completed quests that you issued. You have one outstanding payment due. The other message is simply to direct you to the Sect Hall, as there's information waiting for you there about our recent Core Mission selection."

"That was... very succinct." Joe had physically recoiled at

being bowed at, but it seemed this guard was heavily into the role play of being a Sect member, and he didn't want to crush the man's enthusiasm. Not to mention, he really was doing quite a phenomenal job, even if he was set up for failure, having been placed with such a blind spot just in front of his outpost. "You said I can pay here? Can I also collect the remains and such?"

"Yes, we have linked spatial storage areas. Anything above ten meters cubed needs to be collected in person, but I believe the Tyrant Penguin corpse was a little... *condensed*." The guard stepped into the outpost, coming back a moment later with a single sheet filled with details. "There's your initial offering, as well as a ten percent total increase due to the danger of the situation. Fifteen percent for the monster being an unknown variety. An additional twenty percent total for being composed of such high-grade materials. Lastly, a five percent bump for a relatively intact corpse."

"Relatively?"

"It was pretty heavily damaged along the skin and feathers, but it was a Team Alpha Strike to the neck that put it down. A single cut through its body, beheading it without further damage." The guard passed over the document, and Joe blanched at the final cost. "The Sect has graciously offered to make the payment on your behalf if you set aside any claim to the materials. They said you might've just put out the kill quest for the good of the members, but..."

"I *bet* they 'offered'. Nah. I think I can pay it? I just don't know. How do I check that?" In response to Joe's question, a thick stone tablet thumped down on a table. He could tell its purpose just by looking at it, so Joe went over and pressed his thumb to the block, and it lit up with only a small fraction of green light showing at one corner. "Is that...good?"

"Abyss..." The half-whisper immediately captured Joe's attention, but not as much as the guard breaking character. "That's *crazy*, dude. I've never seen anything like that. No, that's not just good, that's *awesome*. This shows the total amount of your contribution points that'll be used to cover the outstanding debt. As you can see it's... a teeny-tiny little fraction of the corner. What have you *done* to get that kind of-?"

Seemingly remembering himself, the guard blinked, flushed, and stood straighter. "First Elder, would you like me to deduct the funds from your account to pay for the kill quest you had issued and summon the remains here?"

"That'd be great. Thanks."

Pressing his index finger to the block, Joe watched in fascination as the tiny hint of green on the very edge of the block blinked twice, turned red, then gray.

"If you'd follow me?" They stepped into the outpost, and Joe was led to a vault door. With a few simple motions, it was pulled open, and an aroma of rotting fish washed over him, with just a tinge of the sickly sweet scent of decay overlaying the potent scent. Joe glanced at the corpse, then at the guard, a hint of judgment in his eyes, but the guard could only shrug. "It's been a few weeks since the kill. Take all the time you need to collect it, or use it for whatever purpose you need. I'll be at my post."

The Ritualist glowered at the stinky meat filling the cube, tapping at his codpiece, which was full of a giant metal ritual-forged body pod. "I guess I'll just have to break it down right here."

Stepping past the feathers still gleaming with oil-slick iridescence, and avoiding the beak that was serrated and sharp enough to cut through his Ritualistic Tower robes if he brushed against them too hard, Joe got in position and began setting up his Ascendant Matrix. Mana boiled out of him, and thankfully his Mana Manipulation allowed him to form it correctly. It took shape all too slowly, each line having to be individually crafted, instead of springing into existence like a pop-up tent—the woes of such a heavily reduced mana pool striking again.

Once the entirety of the Penguin had been wrapped in the net of light, Joe pulled out each of his Natural Aspect Jars, only to find that the vast majority of them had already refilled from when he'd put together Grandmaster McPoundy's forge. "Eh... it's probably fine."

He began pouring mana into the matrix, and ever so slowly the Penguin began dissolving from the outside in. Happily, the bloody brine which tried to drain out and wash over him instead sizzled into Trash aspects before it crossed the boundary of the matrix. Everything went fine as the beak and head were destroyed, as well as the wings, feet and feathers. It was only as the rib cage on down started unraveling that things went... sideways.

The remainder of his mana was suctioned out of him in an instant, and Joe barely had the presence of mind to yank a fistful of Mana Batteries out of his rings and slap them onto the Ascendant Matrix before his eyes rolled up in his head. He dropped to one knee, nearly passing out as he gasped for air.

Mana: 0/3,901

Health: 3,987/4,546 (559 health to mana conversion!)

"What the abyss was *that?*" When Joe looked up to glare at the Penguin, he had exactly one second to throw himself backward before the first of the Mana Batteries he'd connected to the matrix popped like a light bulb filament going out. Then the entire item shattered in a massive burst of structured mana converting into free power.

Every last drop was sucked up by the matrix, and the Ritualist found himself dazed, having failed to retreat as far as he'd expected. A glance downward showed that his codpiece was still connected to the matrix and leashing him to the construct, making his attempt at dodging a spectacular failure. Before any other unhappy surprises could make themselves known, the remainder of the Penguin vanished in a burst of liquid gold light, and a **clink** sounded through the enclosed space as a core dropped to the ground.

The intense orange light coruscating through the room marked the core as Artifact-grade. Joe licked his suddenly dry lips as he pulled open his notifications—and felt his jaw drop slightly.

Tyrant Penguin reduced.
First ever Tyrant killed.
First ever Tyrant harvested.
Rewards increased.
Aspects gained.
Damaged: 10,000,000
Common: 1,000,000
Uncommon: 100,000
Rare: 10,000
Special: 1,000 Tyrant.
Unique: 500
Artifact: 100

Each of those on their own was a shocking development, but it was the final piece that really caught Joe's eye.

Legendary aspects: 1.

"There was a Legendary aspect in there? Good thing we killed that bird immediately, if it had the potential to become a Grandmaster-level threat..." Joe found that his hands were shaking as he thanked whoever was in charge of this payout for not simply dropping the aspect on the ground or something similar. Joe had seen what Artifact-rank aspects could do when out in the open; the amount of damage a Legendary aspect being released could do was incalculable. "Thanks, whoever decided that a part of the reward should be 'no loss' as these were put in storage."

Scooping up the core, Joe deposited the shining gem in his ring and left the outpost, casually appraising the guard on his way past as he hustled up the mountain.

"Seriously, did it get steeper while I was in there working?" Joe's soft complaints were simply a way for him to try and find a balance between the realization of how wrong all of that could've just gone and absolute giddiness at having collected yet another Legendary aspect.

It hadn't been nearly long enough for him to be okay with how many Legendary aspects he'd needed to use to burn Gameover from the inside out. Worse, after that battle, he'd only been able to reclaim a small fraction of the total he had spent by reducing the toxic remnants mutating and corrupting the planet. In that single battle, Joe's original storage of twelve thousand nine hundred and two—which he'd gathered from reducing a chunk of Brisngr—had been sharply reduced to four thousand seven hundred eighty-two.

"Add one more to the mix!" Joe cheerfully reminded himself, looking at a crafting cheat sheet he'd made for himself a while ago. "Only a little over ten thousand more, and I'll be able to use all of them at once to create a Legendary Natural Aspect Jar. Ha! That'll... be great. Just have to not use any of them for *any reason* until then."

As he continued attempting to delude himself, the Ritualist finally came into view of the burgeoning city proper. Much to his dismay, his initial assessment had been correct: his home, specifically the entire area he'd claimed for himself, had risen up in the distance, yet the path between the main section of the city and what would apparently be his very own mountain had dropped away. Meaning that, if he wanted to get over there, he'd need to first descend, then climb yet *another* mountain. "Okay. That seals it. I don't think I've *ever* seen a clearer indication that I need to get teleportation up and functional on this planet."

He zipped into the center of the area, to the governmental building which had become ornate and... *flowy*, for lack of a better term. The previous utilitarian Guild Hall, which had served as the center of the settlement, had shifted into a three-tiered pavilion anyone could mistake as a spa or perhaps an old-school traditional martial arts dojo. Bracing himself for the likelihood of being pulled into meetings and talked at for a while, Joe walked into the sprawling, fortified courtyard and walked up to a reception desk, where he was met with another stomach-churning, deferential bow from the attendants.

"Honorable First Elder, this missive was left in our care for when you arrived." The attendant held out an envelope with both hands, his face nearly parallel with the ground as he offered the document over.

"Will someone please tell me what's going on with this *bowing* nonsense?" Joe snatched the envelope out of the hands of the man, who looked up with a startled expression.

"That's right, you don't know! Unfortunately, no one's here to explain anything to you in person." Joe felt a deep sigh of relief when he saw that the man's lips were twitching, and he was struggling to keep himself from bursting out in laughter. "First Elder, all of this will be explained once you read through the words of the Sect Leader. I'm afraid... I've been instructed to let the letter guide you."

"No need to be afraid." Joe stared the other man down until both of them felt their stoic expressions crack and they allowed sly grins onto their faces. "You're not trying to make me sit and be lectured for a few hours; you should instead be feeling light and free. I appreciate the help, and I'll see you around."

"As you say."

Instead of tearing the letter open and devouring it on the spot, Joe instead chose to race over to his own mountain peak. From there, he took a few hours to offer tips and tricks to the people working on the various crafting, utility, and combat skills that he had set up training areas for. Once he was certain that he'd done his duty in ensuring that the Mastery Merits would keep flowing, he took a deep breath and reactivated *Beam to Bifrost* for the second time that day.

As power built up around him, as well as a bone-vibrating grinding noise that he was sure would call all sorts of monsters down on him if he was foolish enough to start channeling this spell out in the wild, Joe sat in a meditative position—all the better to look mysterious as he was wrapped in energy and whisked away. The Ritualist couldn't help but let out a chuckle at the shocked and awed expressions on people's faces as he simply vanished from his seated position to parts unknown.

"No wonder people like to do stuff like this, just vanishing when someone blinks and the like. What's the point in having all these powers if you can't have some fun with them every once in a while?"

As he rode along the bridge between worlds, Joe finally pulled open the letter, which must have been written by someone *other* than Aten, going by the crisp and clear handwriting throughout.

It started fairly simple, basically just a breakdown of the differences between Guilds and Sects.

Essentially, the old Guild goals were to be made for casually adventuring, perhaps organizing raid groups, building up treasure, and going on adventures together. Mainly structured yet friendly terms for everyone involved. But now the priorities had shifted, and Sects were all about group power, Inspiration to achieve Mastery, Enlightenment to achieve Grandmastery, eventually becoming something akin to the towers of Vanaheim, where they were extreme hegemonies with a singular focus.

This also helped to explain the differences in how people had introduced themselves to him, as the leadership structure had been changed. There was still the Sect Master and Vice-Master, but now instead of the guild version where everyone *not* in a leadership position was approximately equal in the hierarchy, there were the outer Sect disciples, inner Sect disciples, and Core disciples. Standing slightly outside of that hierarchy were the Elders, in charge of portions of the disciples but having their own hierarchy based on *which* group they were in charge of.

"Kind of like how in the Army we had officers, but we also had warrant officers who were highly specialized and focused on their own stuff," Joe mused as he looked over the table of information, which took up an entire sheet, including diagrams of the new organizational chart. When he found his name, he blinked in surprise when he saw that he was technically on par with Aten in terms of power within the Sect. "Abyss, no wonder they were acting so deferential. Doesn't make me *like* it any better, but at least I understand."

Then came the actual mission statement, the '*Core* Mission' of the Sect. As it turned out, only those who'd been part of the original Guild, or came in and were aligned heavily with this mission, could ever become *Core* disciples—hence the name.

"*To take and rebuild a world worth coming home to after wandering afar.*" Joe read the mission statement twice, lips twitching in contempt at the ambiguous wording. "Yeah, I definitely shouldn't have missed that meeting. I can come up with three options better than that off the top of my head."

At least there was a helpful explanation underneath. As Joe looked it over, he admitted that perhaps he'd been a *tish* too hasty in his assessment. "The Sect exists to roam and explore, bringing back what we find and learn to enrich all of us. But, at the end of the day, our overarching goal has always been to return to, recapture, and rebuild Earth. This is going to require the ability to build not just weapons and structures, but safe havens, systems, as well as knowledge and institutions that will endure as we push back the monsters that are no doubt even now rampaging across our home world."

Blowing a deep lungful of air through his lips, the Ritualist considered that for a long moment. "I *guess*? Celestial feces, it's been a long time since I thought about that. I suppose there are some benefits to the phrasing; it absolutely precludes anyone who will be pushing for rampant destruction, attacking other people going about their Sect-aligned goals, and should let me have carte blanche on setting up defenses around libraries and such. Oooh… it's going to be really hard for anyone to hoard path knowledge, once I point out that would advance our Sect goals faster. Heh. That's going to really tick some people off on Midgard, I bet."

"Let's see, advancement in the guild." Joe quickly scanned over the majority of the information, not finding it too applicable to himself. "Extreme respectfulness to people above you in the hierarchy, sure. *Lifelong commitment*? I get it, but *yuck*. A tax on contribution points earned, and a minimum yearly amount due. Again, I understand, but I'm *definitely* going to go searching for exemptions on this one."

Then he got to one part of that finally made him laugh, "It was decided by a sixteen to fifteen vote, with First Elder Joe abstaining due to being unable to attend, that all future major Sect-affecting decisions, when it's possible that they can be voted on, must be decided at the Sect Hall of 'The City of Towney McTownface'. Doing such serious work in such an unserious location will help remind us all that we must account for... blah, blah, blah. Look at all these signatures. Most of them still live on Midgard, I'd bet money on it. They just don't want to have to travel. Smart, while being equally frustrating."

He finished reading through the document, finding it to be otherwise not all that useful, and so tossed it out of the bifrost as he approached Midgard—just to see what would happen. Frankly, Joe expected it to be instantly destroyed, not at all able to pass the energetic edge of the rainbow bridge, but instead it came to a near-standstill and floated aimlessly alongside. As it vanished in the distance behind him, he could only chuckle at how many people would see it while traveling and wonder what sort of Mythical item was sitting there, ripe for the taking, yet *just* out of reach.

"Someone's definitely going to make an overly convoluted plan to get their hands on that."

As Midgard began to fill his vision, Joe suddenly remembered that he was zipping in at the peak of the fifth threshold of Characteristics. He pulled out and equipped his inhibitor gear, locking his Characteristics at the Mortal Limit, barely in time to avoid causing a natural disaster.

His thoughts slowed down, his joints stiffened up, and the Ritualist grimaced and pushed himself to get into Ardania as quickly as possible. "Just have to get over to the Grand Ritual Hall... then I can store this away for the next few months, *ow*, that needle is bent at the tip! Gah. Where...? Right, I'll store it while I research my rituals. Maybe figure out how to do a few repairs on this thing at the same time?"

When the city came in sight, Joe vowed that he wouldn't be limiting himself again until he absolutely *needed* to do so. "I guess that means it's time to enter seclusion. Now if *that's* not a proper Sect Elder thing to do, I don't know what is."

CHAPTER TWENTY-EIGHT

Joe crouched on the slanted roof of a tchotchke shop, directly adjacent to a sign depicting him as a doll with angry red rituals for eyes. "'The official home of Joe the Dread Ritualist, get your plushie today'. Thanks, whoever came up with that, pretty sure I have you to thank for a good chunk of my contribution points."

Making his way across the shingles with feather-light steps was simple, as his Characteristics allowed him to move with the grace and stealth of a hardcore rogue; though certainly without the properly leveled skills to do so. It felt slightly awkward to Joe that he was sneaking around, and his mainly bright white robes with black embellishments certainly didn't help with his attempts at remaining hidden, but the Ritualist would rather have to slink through the town than deal with the various reactions he would get upon showing his face.

It had been an act of simplicity itself to jump over the wall, avoid the guards, and make his way across the rooftops of the quickly swelling city—something he would, no doubt, have to point out to the guard on his way out. For now, the lackadaisical precautions served his purposes.

As he leapt off the wall, Joe felt a slightly out of place hypodermic needle pulling against his skin, but even with the minor damage it had inflicted, he was grateful for the inhibitor gear. This way, at least he was able to feel like he was in control of himself on this incredibly delicate-feeling world. Landing on top of a building didn't shatter chimneys, blow out windows, or even leave a Joe-shaped hole when he tried to gently land or use a surface to push off to the next one.

Flashing across an open street, he realized there may be a secondary reason why things were going so smoothly: everyone here was just so *slow*. To them, he must have been an instant of white, a blur in the open air that would simply cause someone to frown and rub at the corner of their eyes.

Finally approaching the center of the City of Towney McTownface, Joe felt a swell of pride as his gaze landed on the Grand Pathfinder's Hall. "My little egg has hatched into a full-blown archway. Now it's time to get in there and make some hard-boiled plans."

Landing on the ground, he coiled himself down tightly before flinging himself up and over the road, a velvet rope, and a small kiosk with a bored clerk waiting to accept tickets for entry. The colossal archway filled his vision for a moment, the open area filled with nothing less than the void of space itself. Stars and celestial bodies shimmered as if someone had opened a portal into the depths of space mere feet away, then only inches. As he passed through, the world blinked and folded.

Apparently recognizing him, the Pathfinder's Hall had immediately deposited him in the Grand Ritual Hall, a secret location within the building someone could only gain access to if they were given direct permission. He walked along a floor he couldn't even see, continuing until he simply *knew* he was standing in the center of the space.

Now that he was here, the Ritualist had a slight conundrum to solve. "I have two major rituals I need to complete. Should I start with the designs to carve myself up and pump power in? That would make all future designs easier to create, right? Or…

should I perhaps use my first attempt at a Grandmaster ritual figuring out the problem of teleportation? I don't think either of these are going to be easy, but... yeah, maybe I should try out the one that doesn't have immense personal, permanent consequences for myself."

It was disappointing, as Joe wanted nothing more than to fix his mana channels, burst through the fifth and sixth thresholds for Characteristics, and know for certain that an issue like this could never impact him again. Taking a shuddering breath, he reminded himself, "Don't put the practice run inside yourself. A working prototype, sure. But the actual first ever Grandmaster ritual? Nah."

Now knowing for certain what he wanted to do, Joe pulled off his inhibitor gear and stored it away, taking a deep breath as his mind and body spun up to full working capabilities over the next few moments. Swinging his hand, he felt a deep thrum that rang through the building, but the wind generated simply vanished into... nothingness.

Whether it was absorbed by the walls of the Legendary building, or continued on into the seemingly endless space around him, Joe wasn't able to tell. "Perfect, no need to worry about Mortal Limit issues in here. Now, if I'm not going to start by carving myself up like a turkey dinner, what piece of the design should I go with first? I'm thinking... fish."

As always, the problem of setting up a teleportation network across Jotunheim was that the planet was ridiculously huge. He'd heard estimates that it was anywhere from eight to twenty times the size of Earth proper, but so far hadn't gotten any official documentation. "By the end of this, I might be the first person to fully map the planet and have an accurate number... maybe there'll be some kind of an achievement for that?"

Again, since the size was utterly brobdingnagian, Joe had to account for the fact that not only would it cost resources to create the infrastructure, but that teleportation itself wasn't free. That meant this system would absolutely devour aspects, guzzle down mana, and need to be scaled in a way that someone didn't need to move around and figure things out by hand. It was absolute insanity for a single person to try and create this on their own, but luckily Joe functioned best with a touch of madness flowing through him.

Connecting to the Grand Hall around him, he began pulling dark motes of an unknown substance into being, creating first a table, then a high-back chair to sit on. Probably not the most proper use of what was meant to be the material used to design rituals, but technically he *would* be doing that on these, just more comfortably than might otherwise be expected. Joe spread his notes out, flipping through his diagrams and pulling in the pieces from both his original conceptual setup, as well as the dense Enlightenment he'd undergone on Vanaheim.

"Only way to eat an elephant is to cut it into bite-size pieces and get to chewing. Step one is going to be all of my input." Taking several documents, he put them aside and contemplated their contents for a moment. "Essentially, after the initial setup, this just needs a constant feed of aspects and mana. No way for this to be a one and done burst; I don't have anything that could hold all of that, let alone the actual material to make it happen. Maybe I can convince the Sect to dump everything they aren't going to be keeping into an aspect tower? Abyss, we could be the solution for Novusheim as well, and even a few different cities across the worlds, if it's needed."

Writing down 'set up A.S.P.E.C.T. Towers and hire people to replace aspect jars', Joe moved on to the next piece. "Mana."

Tapping at his chin, he considered the features of Jotunheim and quickly had a solution to this issue as well. "The higher up we go, the more turbulent mana there is freely available. I've never used this design, but Havoc gave me all the pieces for a Mana Battery recharge station... what if I broke that into its three component pieces and had it set as an input for the various rituals *instead* of going to designated recharge pads for batteries? If there ever came a point where we managed to drain all of the turbulent mana out of the atmosphere…? Well, there's no way *this* would be enough to do that."

He wrote 'Mana collector, condenser, and output' out on the second page and stacked it on the first, though offset slightly. "Looks like at least two buildings working together, because I certainly wouldn't trust either of those to be left out in the open again. We aren't working in a field anymore. Something goes wrong with this, my mountain—at the very least—goes *boom*. We have input of power and components; how will we link those to the recursion?"

Tapping his quill on the desk, Joe read through what he had written out during his fugue state of Enlightenment. "Take the Ritual of Builder's Intent and feed it the design for a teleport pad as a building. That'll work for shrine-level versions; I'll need to take some time and go through mid and large-size temples. Gotta pare those down, strip out the divine energy, and make it run entirely on the arcane."

Putting words to action, his quill began sketching out plans, carving loops and clauses as Magical Syntax Lore spun up in the background, allowing him to optimize his notes and exceptions. Architectural Lore had a trait added to it he'd only ever rarely used, the 'Load Lattice Legend', which allowed him to create entirely new blueprints based on the concept he was going for. Seeing as he had the basic version in hand, expanding them out to become a cross between a foundation of stone and a teleportation-viable shrine wasn't quite simplicity itself, but it took far less of his time and effort then Joe had expected.

Time began to pass, marked only by the slow dance of planets, comets, and meteors blazing through space around him.

When he finally set his quill aside, he was looking at two blueprints he was almost certain were perfect for his needs. Moments later, a fresh notification appeared in his vision, joining a pair that had popped up as he'd been working.

Skill increase:
Architectural Lore (Expert VII → Expert VIII).
Ritual Lore (Expert VIII → Master 0)

Congratulations! Ritual Lore has reached the Master rank!

You are beginning to see that ritual magic is not truly separate from other fields. It is the diagram which ties them all together.

Effect:

1) Allows you to fine-tune rituals that you find or create.

2) Can be used to increase the potency of rituals and/or decrease their cost.

3) The associated levels of the lore skills for Ritual Circles, Ritualistic Forging, Alchemical Rituals, Magical Matrices, and Enchanted Ritual Circles are inherited from each associated discipline at half efficiency when being used in the same design.

As an example: Creating a ritual circle which uses enchanted tokens will benefit 100% of the levels from Magical Syntax Lore and 50% of the levels of Enchanting Lore, for a cumulative boost of (Master 0 + Expert II / 2) = Master rank 0.25. Additional disciplines create an additive effect.

Joe tapped his fingertips together, and a small amount of spilled ink spread across them. "That's... less revealing than usual. I guess I'll have to see how much of an effect it has over time? Certainly can't *hurt*, right?"

Looking over his skill list, the Ritualist decided to simply place Architectural Lore as the next to be boosted by Loremaster, seeing as it was already at Expert level eight, and crossing the threshold would only make the lower ones raise faster. With a smile, he realized that, whereas it would've taken nearly four days, specifically ninety-three point four one hours, with the newly Mastered skill added to the mix, that dropped to merely seventy-three point three nine hours—just *barely* more than three days.

"No wonder this skill is called Lore*Master*... this is the sort of thing I've wanted since I first got here. Passive, massive growth over time. I only had to work incredibly hard for a really long time and be nearly permanently destroyed to make it happen! A fair trade...?"

He paused as he weighed that thought, but after a few moments, gave a single, deliberate nod. "I guess the litmus test there is, would I do it again? For *this*? Absolutely. I could do without the constant pain, though." Moving on to the next piece, Joe began setting up the Ritual of Recursion, which would be required to make the teleportation pads he'd just designed over and over again, perfectly replicating the first without allowing for flaws to be generated and exploited.

Time began to blur as he went through various cycles of drafting, tossing pages aside, and trying again. Sleep was a necessity, less so thanks to Mate manifesting and pouring coffee down his throat directly so he didn't need to stop using his hands to write notes and draw diagrams simultaneously.

It wasn't just about the ritual itself, it was all about creating a version that functioned as intended *while* interfacing properly with the other functionalities he was trying to build into the system. Magical Syntax Lore allowed him to write the actual magical diagram, while Calculus and Number Theory handled the number crunching required for generating the requirements for the components of eight planets' worth of surface area, while *also* designing a throttle to ensure mana was coming in at the appropriate speed—instead of simply pouring into the designs and overloading them when aspects ran low.

Finally, the fish. Where he had *planned* to begin.

"If I use Hannah's Ritual of Marching Fishes and use the Special aspect 'Swarm', I should be able to get around the issue of making only a certain amount of fish per summon. Each one should turn into three, five, or seven, depending on availability of Swarm aspects." Without pause, he pulled out a core and began wrapping it in mana and aspects, holding it in place until every last drop of his Swarm aspects had vanished from his inventory, only to create a permanently accumulating Natural Aspect Jar. "Hopefully, all those bugs I had to fry at the place of power actually make themselves useful now."

The problem of delivering the fish, bound with the output of the Ritual of Builder's Intent, gave him pause for just a few minutes. Then his eyes lit up as he noticed a note he had written himself in the margins of his 'Enlightenment notebook'. "I can summon them on top of a Ritual of Cloudstep, then they can propel *themselves* through the air by 'swimming' along! Oh... that only lasts six hours. How am I going to get them to cross the planet in that—what am I even saying? I'll just have them teleport out to the farthest point closest to their final destination, using the original teleportation pad as the location they are summoned, only to be sent off from there. What does the mana cost of that choice look like-?"

Soon he had a tentative design ready to go. "Each pad becomes both a destination and a springboard, where each summoned fish is immediately teleported out and sent to start 'swimming' from there. I'll need every fiftieth one to drop a mid-size teleportation pad, and every two hundredth to create one on par with a grand temple. If I can set up Robert Roswell's Happy Little Notebook, I can essentially plan out the approximate spot each fish needs to reach. With that... it's time to test how fast these things can move when in the air."

Using these two rituals in conjunction with each other was exceedingly easy, and in no time flat—thanks in part to the reduced ritual-creation requirements of the Grand Ritual Hall —fish were falling into place, only to launch themselves into the air and happily swish their tails back and forth, leaving a stream of clouds behind them that slowly dissipated.

Joe kept up with them, carefully mapping the average distance they could travel and the speed in which they did so. As summoned creatures, they had apparently endless stamina until the end of their manifestation window, at which point, they'd vanish in a gentle burst of power if they weren't slain.

Quickly putting together an equation, he used it as simply yet another input and got back to work on the rest of the overall design.

Congratulations! Architectural Lore has reached the Master rank! You no longer work solely off of blueprints, you dictate the creation of a structure.

Effect:

1) $+1n\% \rightarrow 1.5n\%$ to the creation, enhancement, or reinforcement of *architectural elements, structures, and magical buildings, where n = skill level.*

2) 2% → 5% chance when constructing or altering any structure to add an inherent stability trait—doubling its resistance to damage, decay, or magical erosion.

3) Foundational Authority: Any structure you personally design can be fully restored, so long as at least 20% of its foundation remains intact. This will allow the building to fully retain its consciousness even if it would have otherwise been destroyed. The means of restoration are not included in this skill.

"That's probably something Minya would be happy to see. Three days have passed already?" Joe rubbed at his eyes as he leaned away from his table farther, farther, until he toppled backward, transforming his chair into a bed on the fly. "Set Loremaster on... Celestial-Arcane Interaction Lore. Five days to hit Master on that. I'm sure it'll help."

Burble? Want sippy-sip?

Waving off the offer, Joe let his head loll to the side while keeping his eyes closed. "Just need two to four hours of sleep, Buddy. Then I'll take you up on that."

It's go~ood!

"Just a little nap, then yes!"

The Ritualist opened his eyes a few hours later, only for the coffee Elemental to immediately pop up out of his cup and wiggle around excitedly. Taking a deep drink, the bald man rubbed his face one more time, unable to notice the mess of ink and such which had been smeared across his face and head during his casual movements.

"Just a few more pieces, then figuring out how to make it all work together." Joe glanced into the distance, and, squinting at an empty space, began forming ritual circles in midair with the Hall's assistance. "Then... then I get to make the actual ritual itself. I'll have a near endless number of people waiting to help me activate the initial version on Jotunheim... this is gonna be so much fun."

CHAPTER TWENTY-NINE

Just shy of twenty days later, Joe stumbled out of the Grand Ritual Hall, having run out of food three days previously and all excess water five days back. "Living off coffee as my only liquid for the last... *hurk*... few days might not have been the best of ideas."

Without wasting another moment, Joe sat down and activated *Beam to Bifrost*. As power began building up around him, and the teeth-numbing noise ramped up, people began to gather around and point at him, murmuring excitedly as they waited for something to go horribly wrong so they could see it in person.

"That's him! That's Joe!" someone shouted, and quickly a crowd began to form as the bald man grew brighter and brighter.

"He's going to explode!" Instead of the fear such an outrageous statement should've elicited, everyone immediately began clapping. "I get to be part of a 'Joe ground zero'!"

"We'll tell our kids about this someday, sweetheart!" One lady excitedly gripped her new husband's arm as they began jumping up and down together.

"Best honeymoon ever!"

The Ritualist opened his eyes and frowned. "I can't tell if all of you are extremely odd, or if my reputation is actually just that bad on this planet."

"¿Por qué no los dos?" someone called with a deep laugh that was taken up by the others. As the energy finished collecting around the bald man, there was a collective inhale... and he simply vanished without taking them all down with him in a fiery detonation, much to their disappointment.

As he was whisked away across the surface of Midgard, Joe could only shake his head in resignation. "At least I managed to finish the design and build out the ritual. Now I just need... *so many* people. The initial input of mana is going to be... yeah. Let's fill at least sixteen full inputs, not including myself in position one. What is that, two, three, five... fifty-three as the final prime in that sequence, so three hundred and eighty-one helpers at the minimum."

Taking a deep breath as he tried to rein in his excitement and nervousness over coming so close to finishing this project, Joe reached for his skill sheet to mentally catalog the *other* gains he'd made over the last slightly more than a fortnight.

Specifically, every single one of his current Lore skills had reached the Master rank. After the sixth had hit that threshold, reducing the total time requirements by a full ninety percent, the others had completed in only a few days each, giving him the final pieces he'd needed in order to put the massive, convoluted ritual together with a high certainty that he would succeed in its creation instead of just blowing up a mountain or two.

Congratulations! You have achieved Mastery in the following skills.

Alchemical Lore (Master 0). You no longer see the foundation of alchemy as mere transformation. It is not simply mixing or distilling, it is the knowledge that you can take the essence of the world and form it into the fluid that flows like blood in the veins of deities: Ichor.

Effect:

1) $+1n\%$ → $+1.5n\%$ to the creation success and quality of alchemical items, where n = skill level.

2) 2% → 5% chance while creating any alchemical recipe to double the duration of the effect.

3) You are now able to discern synergistic placement of aspects, even if the placement is not viable, according to the recipe. Altering the placement may cause deviation in the final product depending on placement.

Any new recipes created using this synergistic method will be automatically recorded and given to you as a recipe useful with both aspects and standard components.

Celestial-Arcane Interaction Lore (Master 0). Viewing how the universe interplays with magic has grown far more difficult. There is always more to be seen, stars beyond stars, planets hidden by celestial glimmers. While you may have mastered what you can see in your local area, it takes a far more discerning eye to peer deeper into the void.

Effect:

*1) +.5n% faster → +.5n% **slower** skill gain for Celestial Arcane Interaction Lore, where n = skill level.*

2) The creation of Arcane items using the star map of one planet within the same solar system will be equally as effective on any location of any planet within that same system, without needing to remap your bindings.

3) You gain an instinctive sense of the next favorable or unfavorable Celestial interactions which will occur in the next 24 hours.

4) Celestial Glimmer: When mapping an arcane creation to celestial bodies, the final product will glimmer with an inner, matching light.

As Joe passed through the outer membrane of Midgard, picking up speed as he rocketed out into the universe, he kept a careful eye out for- "There it is! Ha! I wonder how many people have managed to see that information packet floating there so far."

After allowing himself a short chuckle as he continued his journey to Jotunheim, much faster than other people traversing the rainbow bridge could, thanks to the benefits of having been the one to open the bifrost across three separate planets, the Ritualist turned his attention back to the few remaining notifications.

Enchanting Lore (Master 0). All life is filled with enchantment, and you have realized how this deeper insight can be captured with your inscription tool. Your inscriptions are layers of meaning that are being written, erased, and rewritten without end.

Effect:

1) Allows you to fine-tune enchantments that you find or create.

2) Can be used to increase the potency of enchantments and/or reduce the cost of creating them.

3) All enchantments now require 5% → 7% fewer components to craft.

4) You may rewrite the effect of an existing enchantment—once per enchanted item—without destroying the base enchantment, substituting the effect for one of equal potency at double the cost of the portion being rewritten. This has a 25 + relevant skill level% chance to succeed. Failure will always destabilize the enchantment, with variable effect.

Smithing Lore (Master 0). To you, smithing is no longer merely shaping alloys between hammer and anvil. It is rhythm, mantra, and infernal fire; your understanding has grown to encompass these concepts.

Effect:

1) +1n% to the creation success and quality of forged items, where n = skill level.

2) 2% chance while creating any smithing template to increase the final quality or reduce the material cost of the item.

*3) Hidden Chorus of Discord: They will learn to never take up your armaments against you. Each item forged by you will carry a note of discord hidden within its very structure. At any time, you may choose to have that note be sung aloud, detonating the item containing your forged handiwork for a total of (item durability * 1.5 * relevant skill level), where Relevant skills are any smithing or forging specific skills. Current: Ritualistic Forging.*

Skill increase: Ritual Circles (Master V → Master VI). Congratulations! You have earned 5 Characteristic points in each of your Characteristics for increasing a Mastery level. (Deferred).

Joe's mind was whirling with ideas for how he could use the additional bonuses his Lore skills now afforded him—especially the hidden note of discord when he created forged goods—and while he was somewhat put out that Celestial Arcane Interaction Lore would grow far more slowly going forward, he could only hope it would prove to have been worth the additional effort if it eventually it reached Grandmaster.

Barely giving himself time to reorient as he landed on the World of Giants, Joe blasted off at top speed toward the Sect. "Probably should've just built a shrine out there... actually, why haven't I? I know there was one at one point, but did a Penguin get it or something? Ohhh, *right*. The whole 'I'm not in a good place with Tatum having blown up my skills, and I just realized I could still build buildings with rituals' thing I had going on."

As the city of Novusheim fell away behind him, Joe felt his jaw drop as what he remembered as jagged mountains from his last visit only a few weeks previously were revealed to be mere *foothills* compared to the ridiculously oversized spine of mountains that would make the Himalayas feel inadequate.

"Is this a Jotunheim thing? Those aren't just mountains, those are absolutely *colossal*." On the plus side, any of his concerns over convincing people to help him set up a teleportation network faded as he realized how difficult travel had just become between the Sect and *anywhere* else.

Cliffs were stacked on cliffs, ridges curling back on themselves and practically *vibrating* with danger, hinting at the likelihood of packs of monsters having taken up residence in the new terrain features. The once nearly-flat plains were easily at a seventy degree angle, even *this* far from the central portion of the sect city. "No wonder the Council of Novusheim demanded we set up shop so far away from them. I used to be somewhat annoyed about that, but now I'm only concerned that it wasn't far *enough*."

His booted feet pounded against the ground as he shot upward, leaping across cracks wide enough to swallow entire trade caravans at once. As he gained altitude, each breath he took started to come laced with the oddly ozone tang of roiling mana. As he reached a plateau, revealing itself moments later as a valley around the newborn mountain, he found himself able to reach up and *almost* touch the lowest hanging of the clouds.

"Right, now, which one of these actually goes to my home? I know it's not gonna be in the valley; I have *peak* real estate." There were a series of taller mountains around the main population center of the Sect, though Joe wasn't entirely certain what they were used for. Thus far he'd only needed to interact with two parts of the massif, but he was fairly sure at least one of them would be reserved for Aten's uses, or at least his team's specific needs. "I wonder if more mountains will grow when we need them, or if we're going to have to allocate them based on whoever wants them the most? Or…"

His face fell slightly. "Never mind, most likely it'll be whoever can *afford* to keep them. Whether that means contribution points, status, or administration. I hope we never get one specifically for punishment or whatever. That'd be such a waste, when I could just teleport someone to the other side of the planet and make them figure out how to get back here as penance."

As he continued onward, Joe reassessed how much of a punishment he was willing to dole out on behalf of others. First of all, simply getting back to his own home was becoming quite the ordeal. What had previously taken a solid hour of full-blown sprinting had already turned into hours of mad dashes followed by searing exertion as each vertical movement pulled him into or through low-hanging clouds.

Now, after punching through the first layer and coming out dripping with sweat and trembling from the intense turbulence, he found that the path *absolutely* wasn't empty. Even though he was well within the Sect territory at this point, his earlier concerns of monsters being hidden among the rocks proved themselves well-founded.

Penguins slipped down the slopes, *squawking* as they noticed him. Enormous Leopards slunk across cliff tops, peeking at him whenever they thought he wouldn't be able to notice them in return. A harsh shriek caught Joe's attention as a

Wraith noticed him, pulling itself out of a cave carved into the side of a cliff and vanishing from sight as it glided into one of the clouds.

"Well, gotta hate *that*." Switching from traveling to evasive maneuvers, Joe began pushing himself to Omnivault whenever possible. He was able to use the skill only a single time before he would have to feed it with mana, through channels far too broken to do so. Even so, his infrequent massive leaps combined with Characteristic-fueled jumping and scaling of the terrain kept him well outside the range of even the fastest of the monsters—so long as he continuously moved uphill. "Ha! Penguins, you got stubby little legs!"

Ducking under an enormous cat, Joe decided to clamp his mouth shut and focus on running.

By the time he found the first outpost, he was absolutely filthy, streaked with sweat, dust, and blood that luckily wasn't his own. He rushed into the small edifice, startling half a dozen Sect members, who, to their credit, had their weapons in their hands in an instant and grouped together in an attack formation.

"First Elder Joe!" He gasped out his credentials, then waved behind him with his off hand. "Got a big pack of monsters on my trail, mind handling that? Mmkay, thanks."

He continued going, simply bounding over the startled guards as he hurried up an *actual* path carved into the mountainside by a stone mage of some kind. The sounds of combat quickly filled the air behind him, but he tuned them out without any great concern. "If they're there to guard this area from monsters, and now they showed up, welp… gotta love job security. Don't worry, friends! I'll *never* let you run out of work!"

From there, it was only an extended jog to return to the peak of the mountain, now a large flat space containing his small enclave, as well as perhaps a half-mile of empty space in a radius around it. "Half a day to get back here… that was rough."

Wiping the grime off his face as well as he could, the Ritualist squared his shoulders and tried to reclaim a bit of his dignity as he marched into the training areas he'd set up. When he finally came across another person, Joe waved them down and called them over. "I need everyone on this peak to gather and join me for an emergency mission."

"Absolutely, First Elder! How soon would you like them to-"

"As quickly as possible, thank you."

When his words were met with hesitation, Joe could only raise an eyebrow. The thickly muscled warrior's face quirked to the side, and the man stated with exaggerated care, "First Elder Joe... perhaps you'd like a short while to... freshen up?"

Suddenly Joe was eminently aware of the fact that not only had he just been running for his life across the world of giants, but he'd spent the last three weeks or so wearing this exact set of clothing. His fingers were still stained with ink, and by the way he was being stared at, he had to assume it was still splattered and smeared across his face as well. "Ah. That's... yes. Let's say an hour from now?"

By the time he'd cleaned himself fully, taken a *second* shower after looking in the mirror and still seeing ink, then gotten dressed in a fresh set of robes and boots—he had to admit the previous ones seemed *slightly* worse for wear, and perhaps there was a *hint* of relief hiding in the crumples of their fabrics—the space outside of Joe's residence was packed almost to bursting. Hundreds of Sect members, no, *disciples*, had come running at the announcement of an emergency task from the First Elder.

'Task' would be translating to 'quest', they were all but certain.

The murmuring and jostling for position died nearly instantly as Joe jumped to the roof of his house, cleared his throat, and raised a hand to gather attention to himself.

"I'm in need of *volunteers-*" He started in a powerful voice, only to be instantly interrupted.

"Pay us for our work!"

"Thank you, Gage, for your enlightened words." Joe glared down at the recently promoted Master of Skipping. "As I was saying, I need people to help me activate an enormous ritual. Something that hasn't been attempted on this world or *any* world that I'm aware of. I can't do this alone. I'll need people to help channel mana, supply it, and hold strong as the world fights back. As many of you as possible-"

Once again the silence was broken, though this time it was a wall of sound that made the roof Joe was standing on vibrate so hard he nearly fell off, even with his enhanced dexterity.

"Pick me!"

"I'm in."

"*I'll* do it for free!" This particular statement was repeated by dozens of mouths, only to be superseded by one voice rising over the rest, a Ritualist who'd been working like a madman to grind out their skill levels in the training yard.

"I'll pay *you* to let me be a part of it!" The desperation in this voice quieted the others for a long moment, and the sheer devotion in the tone gathered all of Joe's focus onto Devoe, the Dwarf standing proudly, a hungry expression on his face. "Massive ritual? I'm all but guaranteed some serious skill levels, right?"

This started an entirely new round of exclamations, with people nearly forming into a mob as they pushed to be among the first to help out with this project. Most concerning was the small contingent that simply dropped into full-blown kowtowing —a practice that the Ritualist was decidedly against, no matter how much they wanted to role-play this whole Sect thing.

Literally standing above it all, Joe saw thin strands of karmic energy beginning to take form, reaching toward him as people made promises he didn't want to have to accept.

"Stop."

That single word, laced with authority and a hint of a cold snarl, sent the entire group into silence, some even shivering as though he had dumped a bucket of ice water directly onto them. "I misspoke, it seems. As Master Gage pointed out, I'm not going to begin my tenure as the First Elder by expecting free labor. I also won't be taking bribes; I don't need whatever it is you're offering. What I will do is pay you properly, though hopefully you'll accept *benefits* over mere contribution points."

"I don't need a dental plan when I have magic!" Once again, the person speaking was Gage, though he was obviously attempting to disguise his voice.

"Alright, anyone *except* Gage is welcome to join." Joe chuckled as a strangled noise erupted from the hidden man. "Those who are part of this will get six months of free access to the instant teleportation network I'm creating today, which will eventually span the entirety of Jotunheim. Afterward, they'll get priority access and a large discount for the following year. That's on *top* of whatever skill levels you can earn for yourself throughout the process."

There were mixed reactions to his announcement; gasping, cheering, but generally positive excitement rippled outward as small groups began murmuring about the difficulties they'd faced recently, even trying to just get over to the main Sect mountain, let alone Novusheim proper.

Joe waved back and forth until the low roar died down. "Precedence in the ritual working itself will go to those working to become Ritualists. Hopefully, this might provide some insight or boost you to the next level, if not the next tier directly. For anyone who isn't chosen to help with that portion directly, don't worry! I'll need people to defend the area, hold off any wandering monsters, and at the end, I have a… special task for anyone with stone shaping magics. No one who is willing to work will be left out!"

Pausing for effect, the Ritualist waved somewhat vaguely at the crowd. "Except Gage."

"*Boo~oo!*" a solitary voice called back at him.

Hopping down from his house, Joe didn't bother trying to hide his smirk as hundreds of eager disciples surged into motion. They formed into a massive column of people trailing behind him as he left the mountain peak and guided them down the winding path to the valley. Within the hour, the Reductionist had used an Ascendant Matrix to carve out a huge flat space to work in, and he began positioning people in concentric rings.

When all was said and done, he would be at the center, and Devoe would be directly adjacent to him, along with two others the Dwarf had hand-selected to be the linchpin of the pseudo-Grandmaster ritual.

Once everyone was in place, including hundreds of guards of all classes forming a half ring with the mountain face at their backs, Joe pulled out an orb glowing with dense golden power.

"Are we all ready to get started?"

CHAPTER THIRTY

Glancing around to check the admittedly minimal preparations he'd been able to put in place—such as his Expert-rank mana stabilizers, which barely made a dent in the turbulence suffusing the area—Joe took a deep breath and slowly dropped his palm away from the golden orb. It remained hovering in place, flickering intermittently as though it were a living entity's beating heart.

It remained still and innocuously hovering in midair. Yet, as the seconds passed, people began shifting uneasily as the clouds drifting into the man-made cave above them began to swirl.

"Warriors and Mages on protection duty! Prepare yourselves!" Joe's sudden shout caused dozens to flinch, as his voice echoed around the perfectly smooth square walls of the cavern he'd cut out of the mountainside. "We've sent messages to the main Sect requesting reinforcements, but it'll likely be a few hours before you get any relief. This is all but *guaranteed* to ring the dinner bell and bring monsters down on us."

"Charming. Really, a heartwarming speech," Devoe murmured, his voice tight but also shaking with barely contained excitement. "What sort of odds are you giving this?"

"I'd... rather not say," Joe responded to him in a low tone. "If it doesn't detonate immediately because I made a math error, and also doesn't crush us into a fist-sized lump of carbon because of a syntax error, or simply destabilize because of the turbulence... I mean, worst case, it takes out *both* mountains at the same time and-"

"Really? That sounds great! *Such* a relief." Devoe's voice was far too loud and carried across the open space only to echo back. Then, murmuring so that only Joe and the closest people could hear him, the Dwarf pulled on his beard and shot the bald Ritualist a knowing glower. "Sometimes you can just try to put people at ease... First Elder."

Joe cracked a sheepish grin as he pulled out a brilliantly shining orange core, and every eye in the area tracked the gem as it was tossed into the center of the golden sphere of densely carved ritual circles. The instant the core was accepted, the valley itself seemed to *sigh*.

A gentle breeze blew through the open space, *thrumming* against the opening Joe had carved out of the rock as though it were an open bottle that had fallen into the hands of a blue-grass band. Then the light in the area fractured for a heart-stopping moment, only for the golden sphere to suddenly swell outward into a massive swirling orb of power that encompassed all three hundred and eighty-one now-linked volunteers.

Power continued accumulating, and Joe simply created a conduit between the people, himself, and the ritual, allowing their power to flow through his palm, along his torso, and exit his other palm along the *ridiculously* wide mana channels he'd carved into his arms for this express purpose. He supplied none of it himself, merely manipulating the flow to where it needed to be. With a deep breath, he spoke the activation phrase: "*Ex nihilo creare, de loco in locum mutare!*"

Every Ritualist involved repeated the activation phrase, a hundred lips whispering along—even though a few *still* managed to mangle the pronunciation he'd tried to drill into them while he'd done the initial setup. The strain hit immediately, causing every knee to buckle and a few people to curse softly as they struggled to retain their balance as the weight of such a potent power tried to drive them into the stone.

It was too much, too fast, and it took every *ounce* of Joe's concentration to keep the lattice from collapsing as people shifted out of position slightly, spoke phrases not part of the chant, or channeled their mana in spurts instead of smoothly, as was required.

Devoe barked for silence as he noticed Joe about to falter, one voice among many, adding to the cacophony for an instant before snuffing it out like a candle. Thanks to the sudden secession of noise and return of focus on their goals, the bald man managed to force the scattered initial activation into a cohesive whole. Too softly to impact anything, he subvocalized, "Five seconds in, and I'm already shaking from exertion. Let's hope it only gets easier from here on."

Instead of the standard ritual circles each of the people here had grown familiar with, the Grandmaster ritual was either moving too quickly or had passed outside of their scope of understanding. The circles that had acted both as guides and automatic positioning had been stripped away, leaving them simply encased in a dome of golden energy with the expectation that they would know where to stand and what to do.

Ever the analytical one, Joe was certain the dome was actually a sphere, with the remainder continuing unbroken through the ground. Still, that realization only captured a sliver of his attention—what truly captivated everyone was the brilliant emblem drawing itself out across the top of the golden surface like a barrier between themselves and the clouds above.

"Is that…"

"It can't be," another voice rose alongside the first.

"I've heard rumors about him, but I didn't realize it was *this* ingrained in everything he made."

The overlay that had shimmered into existence wasn't like any other magical glyphs, standard spellcasting diagrams, nor the ritual circles everyone was still expecting to make an appearance. Instead, a stylized image of a steaming coffee cup, almost cartoonish in design, with steam curling lazily from the surface as motion lines streaked behind it, held everyone's attention.

"Look, I was only able to make this thing in the first place thanks to Mate," Joe grumbled in the lull between initial activation and the actual focus-demanding requirements of the next stage of the ritual. "He literally kept me alive for most of a week and awake as much as possible. I thought it would be a nice way to recognize his efforts, and… to be perfectly honest, I'm going to be using this teleportation network for a secondary purpose, other than travel."

"What is it?" Devoe's question was spoken in an almost-dreamlike manner, but every last person was leaning forward, waiting to hear what Joe was about to say.

He bit back the full, honest answer of tracking and hunting down World Bosses as well as the most potent of the other creatures across the planet's surface, and instead went with an idea he made up on the spot. "I'm going to call it 'Joe To Go'. We'll get you fresh coffee anywhere on the planet within thirty minutes of you putting in your order."

"That's it? I can't… why is that so *believable*?" Devoe sputtered as dozens of other people simply nodded along knowingly. "Hopefully you'll also allow people to use it for transport between population centers, getting to the bifrost, caravans of goods, and other services that are deemed necessary?"

"Just coffee. Worldwide coffee." Joe couldn't hold back his laughter as the Dwarf physically recoiled. "*Rela~ax*, all that other stuff will happen, too, I'm sure. When we, as the Sect, control the means of transportation, we'll effectively have control of this entire planet. There's bound to be some big benefits in that for *all* of us… but I absolutely *refuse* to allow competing coffee services."

"You're absolutely *mental*." Devoe was grinning, though there was a spark of uncertainty in his eyes. "Even if you're only joking, it's honestly somewhat inspiring. I guess you really can only be number one if you're a little odd."

"Ha! I get it!" Joe's bantering stopped instantly as mana built up, sparking across his skin as the next stage of the ritual began. "Abyss, *brace*!"

As he struggled to push and pull on the power, massaging it into place as the vast ritual diagram slowly had its internal equations, runes, nodes and glyphs light up, Joe's words reached the ears of the defenders outside of the cave just in time for them to notice they were under attack. Shields were lifted and locked with their neighbors, oversized swords necessary for dealing with the monsters on this planet were hefted alongside twenty-foot-long spears, and it was *still* almost too late.

A colony of penguins arrived, sliding down the sharp, angled walls of the valley. Their serrated beaks were snapping, and when they realized they'd lost the element of surprise, they shoved off the ground, bouncing into the air and attempting to get over the closed ranks of warriors to the softer targets behind them still fumbling to get their spells in place. Leopards appeared in the nooks and crannies of the stone valley, and harsh whispers on the wind heralded wights drifting toward them, using the low-hanging clouds as cover.

"Monsters are just proof we're all doing something *worth* doing!" Gage called out from the front lines, making Joe's eyes narrow slightly, though he was mollified at the thought of the frustrating man raising his weapon in service of the Sect.

"Fine, you get free access, too, Gage." That was the last bit of attention Joe could spare for external events, the ritual demanding—absolutely *demanding*—the entirety of his focus.

Every few minutes, there was a new phrase that needed to be sung out, a new pattern of mana that needed weaving. Though he was keeping his own mana reserves entirely to himself, the absolute ocean of power flowing from the gathered crowd and into him would burn him to ashes if he allowed it to settle inside him for any reason.

"*Corpus in motu; mundus in ordine!*" With this phrase, each person involved was lifted off their feet, hovering a few inches in the air as they were ever-so-slowly cycled around into new patterns as required by the *essentially* Grandmaster-rank ritual.

Six hours later, the sheer volume of blood from slain monsters reached the point where it had begun soaking through the opening and flooding across the magically leveled area. As Joe was flipped upside down and noticed this, a sliver of concern for proper drainage crossed his mind, only to be pushed aside. "I'm going to need to install some drains or angle the area a bit so rainwater flows out and away."

By the tenth hour, there was finally a use for all of the cooling bodily fluids that had collected into a congealed gel below.

"*Sanguis pro structura!*" The words popped out of Joe's mouth unbidden, almost a surprise to himself. It was as though the ritual itself had decided it wanted to slurp up the offering of life essence, and *slurp* it did. Wherever the crimson fluid crossed the dividing line of the golden dome, it vanished. For long moments, a red mist hung in the air almost threateningly before *also* dissipating into nothingness.

The blood acted like a catalyst, and the red tint which had vanished from the edges reappeared at the peak of the half-sphere, seeming to almost pour out of the emblem of coffee and blaze across the top of the dome. From there it sprinkled down as a stream of red and settled on something which had thus far been invisible: the immense confluences of pure energy the ritual had been shaping out of mortal sight.

As though a ghostly presence had walked through a cloud of dust, a nearly transparent silhouette of a large, blocky building began to take shape.

Thrum~mm.

The golden dome rang like a gong that had been struck, rattling Joe's teeth as the three hundred and eighty-one volunteers inside the space were shaken around like leaves in the wind. A maelstrom of shrieks erupted from the monsters collecting in the valley, their anger and savagery reaching a fever pitch as they heard the figurative dinner bell being rung—just as the Ritualist had warned would happen.

Though he couldn't see it from his current-upside down position, Joe could perfectly imagine the penguins pushing themselves to shoot forward like knife torpedoes, leopards creating bridges of ice as they leapt from boulder to crevice. They were doing *anything* to bypass the protectors and sink their claws into the people performing such an immense act of magic in their presence.

"Hold!" The singular voice echoing back into the man-made cavern sounded as exhausted as Joe felt, definitely not what he wanted to hear from someone trying to rally other people. A sharp *clatter* drew the Ritualist's attention for a flicker of a moment, his teeth grinding as he saw the top of a broken spear pinwheeling across the floor.

Moments like this ate away at him: times when he knew he needed to work on a single task, but his heart pulled him to be a wild card among the assailing forces, blasting them to pieces and evading death by the skin of his teeth. He was certain there were people out there dying so he could finish putting all this together, and he vowed to pay off the debt he was incurring *more* than generously.

His eyebrows shot up with excitement and hope as he noticed yet another change; the foundation of the building had solidified while his attention was fractionally divided.

Beams started to sketch themselves into place, a framework, practically a skeleton of the final structure fading into existence as the seconds swiftly *swished* along. Taking slow, deep breaths, Joe centered himself as his ambitious project took shape. "They have to last. At the very least, I need to *trust* that they will. All I can do is my part now, then take responsibility afterward as the person who brought them here."

As if the world had timed itself to intersect new developments with his thoughts and emotions, a deep *braying* sound reverberated through the valley. For a stomach-churning instant, Joe assumed the worst: perhaps a Titan had arrived, or a fresh contingent of monsters had raced up the slopes. Then the sound resolved into *horns*—deep, angry, yet filling him with an immense sense of relief at the realization that reinforcements had arrived.

Flashes of light washed through the room as spellfire rained down on the monsters of Jotunheim. The air heated up, a thick humidity taking hold as penguins began burning and bridges of ice were converted into steam. The sounds of combat raged louder over the next short while, clearly the Sect having to cut their way through a massive backlog of monsters pressing in on the most-likely-wavering wall of defenders still holding out.

Then, almost between one moment and the next, cries of pain and rage shifted to a back-and-forth between squad commanders as the reinforcements arrived alongside the faltering protectors, set up a new defensive line, and gave the others some relief for the first time in nearly twelve hours.

By the fourteenth hour, the previously translucent building achieved full solidity, and any further magical workings in the interior were hidden away from sight. The roof settled into a perfect square, though a set of spikes on each of the four corners continued growing upward; eventually resolving into an antenna stretching up and eventually nearly brushing the top of the stone ceiling before halting its growth.

"Did you build an *antenna* on that thing, Joe?" Devoe called in a flustered voice, his hands shaking with exertion. A glance at the Dwarf revealed blood running freely from his nose down to his beard, now spraying out in a fine mist as he spoke. "Wait, what's *that* thing supposed to be?"

An enormous scoop began to rise from the far side of the structure, a smooth curve that grew almost to the same height as the antenna. It ended its creation without a rooftop growing across the open mouth, revealing itself to be a chute of some kind. Needing his companion to get back on task, Joe quickly snapped out, "It's a *hopper*, Devoe. Come on, I'll give you a tour when this is *over!*"

As the sixteenth hour of channeling power into the ritual

approached, the air thickened with the taste of pennies and petrichor.

The immense turbulence Joe had been fighting against in the ambient area ramped up even further as the mana density rose, actively drawing in the drifting clouds of potency moving through the valley. A single door cut itself into the side of the structure's wall—as nondescript and boring of an entryway as Joe had ever seen. If there'd been any windows, he was certain the vibrant clouds would have found a way to seep through, but as they tried to pass through the singular entrance, the wisps of vapor and energy curled back on themselves, rebuffed by the overpowering presence of the still-forming structure.

"Only a few more minutes!" Joe cried out in excitement, his words punctuated by a thunderous *boom*, along with a pale, light-gray illumination that shifted his vision into photo negative, "No... wait, that was actual thunder?"

His muscles stiffened as a huge burst of mana reached him at that moment, and Joe was caught off guard as it tore through his arms, finding plenty of space to move, but investing too much *punch* into the sigil the Ritualist was imbuing. The entire ritual destabilized in that instant, and only the 'passive precision' trait of Somatic Ritual Casting allowed Joe to correct the forced error, allowing him half a second to undo the slight jolt of his fingers that had sent a cascade of mana outside the limits of the sigil.

Just as he managed to suck in a sharp breath of relief and begin pumping power along the next set of sympathetic links, a flash of *white* light preceded yet another immense thunderclap. Now prepared for what was about to happen, Joe carefully braced himself, aware of the potent energy sinking through the dome of the ritual and targeting its core functionality—which he was acting as the conduit for. Now that he wasn't taken by surprise, what the Ritualist now recognized as Common-rank lightning was simple to account for...

...yet he was *certain* more, and worse, was coming.

He was proven right almost instantly, as a bolt of silver lightning crackled through the clouds entering into the cavern. Joe watched carefully as the energy forked, striking the golden dome and causing it to ripple. Thankfully, it was unable to directly obliterate the light, but the world wasn't done with him yet.

As light-blue lightning zapped toward him through the ritual, the others shrank away from the dangerous source of power. Joe didn't have that option. Instead, he reached out with his left hand, fingers splayed wide as the far-more-condensed bolt entered his palm and followed the carved mana channel through his chest, then out through his right, jamming itself into the core of the ritual.

Somewhat tamed by his intervention, the immense power source joined seamlessly with what had been created, ever so slightly altering the 'flavor' of the ritual but also adding a noticeable tint to the still-overwhelming gold coloration that was suffusing the world within the dome. The next strike was insectoid green, a Special-rank strike which Joe could only assume was a response to the 'Swarm' aspects he'd added to the design of the Ritual of Marching Fishes, as nothing else matched up. That was swiftly followed by indigo, and finally Artifact-orange before Jotunheim gave him a moment to collect himself.

Joe had smoke rising off of him, his hands blistered and charred where the influx of power had passed through him. His sweat had long since evaporated. Strangely enough, his skin was clean and practically *shining* now that everything caked onto him since his most recent shower had been crisped off or rebuffed as his body took on a potent static charge. The Ritualist was barely hanging on, panting for ragged breaths, trembling and shivering as his muscles spasmed uncontrollably. He was nearly delirious as he focused on enduring what he was certain would be at least one more strike.

"You gonna make it, Joe?" Devoe questioned the Ritualist, concern pouring out of him at the state of the man directing the final stages of this all-too-powerful ritual. "We're almost there. You can't fail at the last moment!"

Joe's head lolled from side to side, mouth working up and down before his half-sang words could push through into the open air. "F-fail? Not likely! Devoe, my bearded burrito, I'm shinier than I've been in the last year! I'z gotz thiz. Just gotta taste the last lightning, and crispy Joe gets a free refill!"

"*Hoo*-boy." Devoe reached his hand forward, interlacing his fingers with Joe's as he closed his grip tightly. "I'm here. Let me help take the hit."

"Nahh, what? You'll pop like a hot dog in a microwave." Joe struggled to yank his hand away, but the Dwarf wasn't having it. "Let go! I didn't bring you here to die!"

"Well guess what? I didn't follow *you* here to see *you* die!" The Dwarf reached out to his left, and the person he'd nominated to participate grasped the outstretched hand without hesitation. Then the next did the same.

As though it understood the intentions of the gathered people, the golden dome suddenly collapsed inward, and an unbroken chain of Ritualists soon linked together, followed by the admittedly more-hesitant recent inductees in the outer rings. Still, not one of them refused to grab on in the end.

A golden bolt of Legendary lightning exactly matching the color of the now-far-smaller dome lanced through the outer shell and struck the furthest-out Ritualist. Now that the bolt was here, Joe could only accept their conviction and do his best to finish the ritual in its entirety.

They screamed as one, the entire group crying out in perfect synchronization as the lightning arced from body to body in an unbroken, blazing circuit. Sparks flew into the air at each point of contact, snapping and violent as it sought out the endpoint, the connection to the world-altering ritual. Almost triumphantly, it entered the palm of the final obstacle.

Yet, when the energy hurled itself into Joe's hand, he found that it was…

…manageable.

CHAPTER THIRTY-ONE

Joe was on his knees, staring up at the building in front of him through what felt like a long tunnel until his vision slowly cleared. As he shifted slightly, he felt his hand caught under a rock and glanced down dumbly, only to stare in confusion at the thick sausage-fingers of the Dwarf still clutching him. "Wha-"

The last few minutes came back to him in a rush: the Legendary-rank lightning, hundreds of people holding on for dear life, and the ritual completing in a sudden burst, absorbing the tribulation lightning energy into its makeup before the sphere of golden light imploded into the building in a glorious cascade.

Now, the golden glow which had been ever present in the cavern for the last sixteen straight hours had vanished entirely, leaving behind only a single light source...

...the shimmering coffee emblem now emblazoned across the front of the new building's wall.

On closer inspection, it wasn't exactly the same version which had been floating atop the ritual for the better part of a standard day. The steaming coffee cup was still there, but both the steam and the motion lines drawn behind the cup had been slightly altered. As if it were representing spiky flames instead of a gentle aroma, the soft steam now had sharp edges. Jagged lightning bolts with actual energy crackling through them every few seconds had replaced the mundane motion lines behind the cup. Simply *looking* at the emblem evoked the same sensation as a shot of caffeine directly to the veins, though that faded within moments of looking away.

Pulling himself to his feet, Joe slowly pried the massive fingers off from around his own, wincing as he saw a soft char in the area around where their hands had been touching. At least the Dwarf's palm was still-healthy flesh—his own had already been rather severely burned, weeping cracks and blisters covering every inch. "The building is intact, and from the way everyone is starting to stir, it doesn't appear anyone died in the ritual. All in all, I'd say this was an unmitigated success. We'll get everyone some time in a healing ritual, then-"

Before he could inquire after anyone else's health or make additional plans, the system *chimed* brightly in his ears, making him flinch as it pulled open a message without letting him decide if he wanted to see it.

Congratulations! You have successfully created a Pseudo-Legendary building!

Combined with your prior achievement in upgrading an Artifact-rank building to Legendary status, your title 'Architect of Artifacts' has evolved and been replaced by:

Half-step Legendary Architect. Effect:

1) Any action you take that will result in the construction of a new structure will boost the building's overall statistics and potential boosts by 15%!

2) Echoed Legend (Temporary): Upgrading buildings to a higher tier requires 20% fewer resources. This does not include the 'Core' requirement. This effect will evolve further if you directly create a Legendary or higher-ranked structure.

Rituarchitect trait has succeeded: Rituals used to build structures have a fixed 10% chance to absorb a portion of the mana invested in the ritual, gaining an additional effect. The effect will be random unless you learn how to stabilize the mana drawn from the materials.

Additional effect granted: Senseless Senses. Inanimate objects within 500 feet of the structure have a 80% chance to gain one of the five standard senses and a way to communicate them. The object will lose both once they are outside the range of the effect.

Ritualistic Wisdom has captured this natural effect as a ritual diagram!

Looking over the tooltips of his awaiting notifications, Joe frowned at the fact that, somehow, the creation of this structure didn't fulfill the requirements of the Student Rituarchitect quest. "How is this *not* a facility?"

Pulling open the quest, he glared at it until he got to the part where the quest told him he first needed to create five buildings, *then* combine them. He would've rolled his eyes and slammed the status screen closed, but he blinked in surprise as he saw a red thread appear at the end of the words, twisting around itself and seeming to sink into... something. "Is that-? Are you trying to tell me I completed a quest further down the quest chain?"

The system didn't answer him, but the red thread of Luck faded, and Joe was left with a feeling of satisfaction, which he hoped meant he'd guessed correctly. "Most likely I just need to get access to that one, and I'll automatically be moved on to the next-"

Seemingly unable to wait any longer for his attention, the next message appeared, overlaying his vision with red text that flashed to show how serious of a situation he'd found himself in. It was a dense, jagged font, as though the hastily scrawled out words were being screamed from another room.

Warning! You have triggered a tribulation-

"Been there, done that." Joe tried to wave the message aside with his tribulation-lightning-scarred hands, only for the screen to actively *dodge* his outstretched limb and hover closer to his eyes.

You have created a mechanism by which this world as a whole may be impacted, affected, or altered. Safety measures have been activated to prevent your choice from reaching success, and the World Boss itself will attempt to mitigate the change you may effectuate.

In this case, the Jötunn has been alerted to the exact location of the ritual you have completed. The entity will do its best to destroy your creation before it can mature into a threat to itself. If the World Boss is defeated before your creation is destroyed, the network of teleportation pads you are attempting to create using your amalgamation of rituals will face no further tribulations. It will be considered stable and subject only to the standard threats applicable to anything on Jotunheim.

As you are, only one piece of advice can be offered: run and hide. Leave your creation behind, for there is no safety to be found here.

Joe barked out a laugh that hurt his internal-damage-guaranteed lungs, and the shifting panel of light went completely still, as if utterly shocked and somewhat offended at his reaction. "Thank you for the heads up! All this work and worry thinking about how long it'd take to build a teleportation network large enough to find that thing, and now it's going to be delivered to my little bungalow as if I'd ordered room service. Awesome. That saves me *months* of waiting, at the minimum."

The message slowly vanished, drifting away piece by piece as if the mind behind it had become entirely discombobulated. Still, there were plenty of regular notifications waiting for him. As people began to stir and groan, sitting up and prying their still-sizzling hands apart, Joe went over each message one-by-one.

You have created a Pseudo-Legendary building! Rituarchitect experience gained. Experience gain increased, as this is the first time you have directly created a building of this rarity. Experience gain increased as this is the first currently standing structure of this rarity to be built on Jotunheim. Total experience gained: 10,000.

Level up! Rituarchitect level 14 → 15! Congratulations! For reaching this milestone specialization level, this class has gained the following benefit.

Near-Instant Completion: When using a ritual to construct a building, you may invest additional resources and mana to reduce the amount of time necessary for completing the build. To instantly complete a structure, the mana cost will be doubled. A total of 50% of the highest-rarity aspects invested (rounded up) will also need to be provided.

This process can also destabilize the ritual, but at your level, you should be able to handle it!

Quest update: Dulling the Sword of Damocles. You have made significant progress in slowing the ever-increasing karmic debt between yourself and Occultatum.

2) Take three steps into the light. It has become easy for you to complete projects using the gifts given to you by your faction leader. You must complete at least three major workings under your own recognizance which would be easier to complete by using the resources on hand. Do not invoke or empower him. (1/3)

Pending Rewards:

1) Speak to Queen Cleocatra for an external Karmic remapping of one of your skills.

2) Speak to Queen Cleocatra for a Karmic wedge.

"Kill it!"

"Abyss, now what?" Pausing in his reading and hobbling over the slow-moving lines of ritual helpers, Joe creakily made his way to the mouth of the cave, his joints not bending as easily as they should, his muscles working to force him to slow down and rest. Still, he couldn't pause until he was certain that the existent threat of the swarming monsters had been taken care of.

When he popped his head out suddenly, a twitchy human nearly lopped it right off—likely startled by what looked like another ethereal-pale snow wight. Only the Ritualist's enhanced Dexterity saved him, and a muffled curse at the warrior earned him the chance to slowly reappear and look around at the winding-down battle.

Between his blistered and flaking-off skin, blood seeping from small cracks across his body, Joe couldn't blame him… much. Still, his words came out harder than intended, "Does anyone have some *good* news for me?"

The annoyed glances sent his way vanished as soon as they saw his face beneath the mess, and a man leaning on a spear stumped over, offering a nod in lieu of any other respectful gesture such as a salute, since they were on an active battlefield. "Our lines are intact, First Elder. Got a little dicey there, but when the reinforcements from the Sect showed up, we were able to push back the monsters. Now that the ritual isn't drawing them in actively, they've been routed. Or, at least, they aren't appearing in such great numbers as they were."

"Fantastic. All of you did extremely well. Far better than I deserved, with how little time I gave you to get ready." He narrowed his eyes, trying to think of how best to reward the people here, but had to simply shrug and go with a promise. "I'm going to make sure everyone here gets a hefty chunk of contribution points on top of the other benefits I mentioned. Then... probably wouldn't hurt to set up a well-funded pool for my future quests to be paid out of, now that I think about it."

Everyone in range perked up significantly at the mention of being paid a bonus and let out a companionable laugh as Joe called over the sudden hubbub, "Although I told you not to show up, even *you're* gonna get paid, Gage!"

Returning into the twilight-level darkness of the now fairly full cavern, Joe found Devoe staggering toward him, beard streaked with dried blood and eyes burning with equal parts pride and exhaustion. "Now *tha'* was worth getting hurt for, Joe."

"Oh! Yes, we'd thought you all might get some skill levels; how'd it go for you?" Joe was inquiring only to be polite, but seeing the Dwarven grin growing to an almost uncomfortable width, the bald man started to pay more attention.

"Six of us, Joe." The words were rasped out, full of incredulity. "There were *six* of us who managed to step into the Master rank."

Only blinking for a few moments, as he couldn't formulate a response, Joe finally repeated the Dwarf in a soft, disbelieving tone. "...*Six?*"

"It's a good thing we did this the *way* we did it." Looking down at his hands as if not quite believing his own words,

Devoe explained himself. "It was that last strike of lightning we all linked up to share the burden of. There was a flash of *Enlightenment* that traveled through every last one of us. All of us together shared it, which left just enough for a proper Inspiration. Frankly, I'm not sure if we shouldn't have let you take that alone. It likely would've created an unshakable foundational Enlightenment for you if we had."

Even before his companion finished speaking, Joe was adamantly refusing with a rigorous shaking of his head. "It would've *fried* me, buddy. If you hadn't all come together and taken that hit with me, all of this would have failed, and I'd be sitting in my respawn room grumbling about how unfair this planet is. Fact is, you all saved me and probably a good chunk of the mountain at the same time. If that doesn't deserve something extra special, I don't know what does."

Quietly, so as not to ruin the moment, Joe allowed his eyes to go distant as he checked... and there they were: six additional Mastery Merits waiting for him. A *windfall* that would help him progress further.

Now that most people were back on their feet, though some seemed happier about it than others, a groggy, but inevitable question made its way over to the Ritualist. "After all that, you're going to tell us what this does, right? Is this where we go to teleport? Is that what we all nearly just died for? Looks kinda... boring."

To be fair, Joe had to give it to the whiner. He'd captured the essence of the edifice in a single word. As his gaze swept across the brutalist, boxy design—the little building squatting in the cavern like a rogue DMV—he had to admit that it was an utterly *boring* creation. It looked like a square box made of gray stone, the antenna stabbing upward to the top of the cavern drawing the eye only because it was lit up, and perhaps because it was slowly sucking in the clouds as mana was siphoned out of them.

Lastly, the huge hopper attached to the backside of it looked like the tail of an over-excited terrier. Frankly, the only truly interesting portion of the structure was the emblem carved into the wall that was sparking intermittently.

Joe absolutely loved it.

"It's anything *but* boring! This is the *Joe To Go* headquarters! The future center for all coffee across the world!" As he gestured at the monolithic structure, his over-enthusiasm caused all of theirs to die on the vine. "Once the hopper over there is connected to the main portion of the Sect, everyone will be able to drop in anything they need disposed of, and we'll be able to upcycle all of that material into-"

"Upcycle? Don't tell me we just made a glorified *recycling center* for the Sect?" the same frustrated voice wheezed out. "You're telling me all of us risked our lives to build-"

"It's more than that!" Joe snapped back, then realized this reaction was exactly what he'd been aiming for in the first place, and his smile returned. "This isn't like Earth; it's not just garbage you can put in here. It's trash, sure, but also rubble, monster corpses, broken swords, alchemy goods! No need to sort anything out, because *all* of it becomes fuel for the magic."

"Look, thanks for the skill levels, and this was a fun team-building exercise, but I've got better things to do then stand around and sing Kumbaya instead of getting back to grinding out my skill levels." Shaking his head and muttering darkly, the disciple walked out of the cavern, starting a mass exodus as the vast majority of those who weren't actively seeking to become Ritualists filed out.

Before they had gone too far, Joe stepped out of the cave into sunlight once more to call out instructions. "Anyone who came here as a stone shaper, engineer, or anything that would be useful in designing a way to connect this building to a large open chute into the Sect, I'm going to be paying a hefty sum of contribution points for making that happen. I need it done *today*! Logistics wait for no one. I want it smooth as *glass*, people! Other than that, no bells, no whistles."

Then he went back into the room, a mischievous smile on his face as he regarded the other Ritualists who'd come here to learn under him. "Now that all of that's out of the way, and only the *truly* interested remain... who wants a tour?"

Joe led the group forward, throwing open the door placed almost directly under the coffee logo, and led the exhausted Ritualists into the open concept structure. While he was happy to see that his ambitions for the place met up with his expectations, he didn't feel truly *satisfied* until the Dwarf walking alongside him let out a soft gasp. Only then did the Ritualist feel like he had truly succeeded.

Even Joe himself had to let out a low whistle: it was one thing to design the plan for the building; it was another thing entirely to see it in person.

The hopper outside of the building led into a massive square warehouse of a room, with an intense lattice built into its metal floors, walls, and ceiling: a permanent Ascendant Matrix. While he knew it wouldn't stay this clean and pristine for long, at the moment, it was flawless and crystalline, reflecting a thousand shards of light across the beautifully geometric mirror chamber. Just outside of the barn-door-style entrance was a statuesque plinth that would sink into the floor after it had been slotted with Natural Aspect Jars, ready to harvest every trace of aspects generated within.

"All sorts of refuse will come into that space there, get converted into aspects that are stored here, which will be drawn from to make the actual magic happen." To demonstrate, Joe walked over to the swirling sculpture of a plinth and slotted the jars in, everything from Common to Unique rank. Anything stronger than that was unnecessary for anything Joe wanted to build out of here, so he held onto his more potent containment units.

"Is *that* how you're powering this place? How'd you even figure out how to design a nuclear reactor, and does it even work the same as it does back on Earth?" A shortish lady was looking upward with wide eyes, clear nervousness in her posture as she gestured at what appeared to be an unshielded reaction room that was glowing brighter by the second.

"Good question, and *no!*" After placing the final jar, Joe tapped a rune carved into the top of the metallic sculpture, and the plinth smoothly rotated down until it was flush with the rest of the floor. A rainbow of lines began flowing from the aspect jars along the floor, drawn over to a massive, six-ringed gyroscope set up on the left side of the room.

The antenna, actually a mana collector, was smoothly pouring power into the mana condenser, what had been incorrectly labeled as a reactor. As the aspects reached the gyroscope, the bottom of the condenser lit up, and a ring of glowing crystals began to shine and light up the entirety of the interior of the headquarters. Turbulent mana continued to pour into the condenser, gaining structure as its rapid whorls and shifts were stripped away, becoming *usable.*

Even Joe had to bite back a yelp of surprise as the crystals were suddenly hidden behind beams of pure magic that flowed outward far slower than their laser-like qualities suggested. Purified mana reached for the top of the gyroscope, connecting and pouring into the device in a constant, precise laminar stream. Now that the gyroscope had gained an energy source, the outer ring began to spin, followed by the next, and so on.

Someone started to speak, but Joe gently raised a hand, gesturing for the others to simply watch. "Now you get to see what all of our work actually did. Pay attention, because I'm going to have recurring quests for people to maintain this place on my behalf. Should be fantastic for your skill levels over time."

His words quelled any protests and forestalled any further questions.

With a soft *humm* of displaced air, the gyroscope got up to speed and began draining aspects from the floor, mana from the ceiling, and mixed them together in incredibly precise sequences. Only a few moments after the process began, a marble-sized ritual had formed and was spat out onto a tiny set of rails, rolling down and along the track until it reached the center of the room. It came to a halt on an enormous dais the others had mistaken as simply a feature of the room—what Joe knew to be the grand teleportation pad all future versions would be based on.

When a few dozen of the marbles had rolled into a pile on the carefully constructed stone, Joe leaned forward eagerly, and the others unconsciously mimicked his stance.

"Here comes the *cool* part."

CHAPTER THIRTY-TWO

The gyroscope came to a stop all at once, each of the rings in perfect alignment with each other as they *clicked* into place. Joe chanced a glance over, his brow furrowing slightly as his smile dimmed. "That's supposed to keep running in unison, not starting and stopping... oh."

He had forgotten that the mana condenser was only faintly glowing, and the process of the clouds being drained of turbulent mana had only just begun. There was no power built up and available for use. At the moment, each of the different functions of the structure were taking turns getting power instead of falling into the smooth, continuous flow that was supposed to be happening. "Whoops, made a little mistake there. Might need to turn this all off and let it accumulate power for a while. Or... no, we'll at least see this next part once or twice."

Turning his attention back to the small pile of marble-sized rituals, Joe waited with bated breath as another ritual lit up over the platform.

"Hello? Where am I?" A small voice began shouting from somewhere in the room, and only Joe's exceptional senses allowed him to pinpoint the source—right where he was looking. "What am I looking at? Rock? What's a rock?"

The intensity of the light continued to grow, and a small flame appeared around each of the miniscule ritual-marbles. A moment later, the flames expanded outward into spines, tails, gills, then full-blown fish.

"Ahh! It's dark in here! What's a stomach, and why am I seeing one?" The new voice was now distinctly muffled, and Joe found himself looking forward—with a bit of discomfort—for the moment the inanimate ritual that had just been 'swallowed' left the area of effect of the 'Senseless Senses' the headquarters exuded.

He inspected each fish, relieved to see that none of the koi that had been pulled as the first batch were identical. "Good, we're not going to have any accidents with trying to resummon another fish that is already out in the world. They're all about the same size, though; that's good. Pretty sure creating a sardine around one of those marbles would just break both of 'em."

The school of summoned fish flopped on the dais for only an instant before the summoning ritual faded and another crackled to life. In that heartbeat of activation, the Ritual of Cloudstep washed over each of the summons, and Joe noted with relief that the marble-sized rituals that had been swallowed weren't activated by the mana—as he'd hoped, they were protected by the bodies surrounding them. With that final concern out of the way, the Ritualist was able to fully enjoy the moment that the fish realized they were no longer trapped on a dry surface.

With a swish of their fins, the koi took to the air, bodies flexing in rapidly undulating S-curves as they searched the room for an exit. Eyes going wide, Joe rushed over to the wall and pulled off a tablet, the 'Robert Roswell's Happy Little Notebook' given form as a control device for the building. Taking the attached stylus, he zoomed in on his local area and quickly poked thirty spots in a circle around this initial location.

The fish responded instantly, as though their brains had been replaced with the guidance system of a homing missile.

The swooping ribbons of shimmering clouds they'd been casually trailing across the open space turned into thirty nearly straight lines as each of the koi immediately converged on the Ascendant Matrix room, then blasted up and out of the open-topped hopper. One of the other Ritualists in the room let out a nervous chuckle. "Kind of looks like the stream fighter jets used to leave behind when they were flying super high up. Not my favorite memory. This, just checking, *isn't* a weaponized ritual, right?"

"*Certainly* not!" Joe placed a palm over his chest, trying to cover how quickly it had started beating. "It's a transport system for people and coffee, with the teleportation zones initially delivered by fish. Since we're on that topic, who wants to be on the first shift for directing the summons? It pays…"

Taking a moment to check with the others what a proper and acceptable amount of contribution points would be, Joe added fifty percent on top of their recommendation, then went to the edge of the room and held the tablet up so everyone could see it. "If these dots turn golden, it means the fish reached their destination… and the teleportation pads are active."

"Ooohh-hee-hee-*hee!*" A sonorous, bone-shaking voice shook the entire room. "That felt *stra~ange!*"

"Celestial feces, the building is ticklish. How long does each instance of this effect last?" Joe muttered under his breath as he waited patiently for the black dots to turn gold, ignoring the side-eye he was earning from the coven members by pretending not to hear the voice of the headquarters. The minutes ticked by, and while he was *certain* the fish were on their way, he couldn't help himself from getting nervous as five minutes turned into ten, and the dots still remained dark.

Then, one after another, the targeted locations brightened with a tiny starburst, and the entire group of Ritualists looking on burst into applause and cheering. For his part, Joe simply let out a turbid breath then allowed a satisfied smile to appear. "We've decided on pay, so who wants the first shift of mapping out the next layer of teleport locations? We need them placed so that anywhere within a triangle is reachable within thirty minutes... for coffee delivery!"

"Hey, Joe! This is pretty neat. Looking forward to seeing how this pans out." Devoe stepped forward, reaching for the tablet, then slapping Joe on the back. The bald man instinctively braced against the force of the hand so he wouldn't be flung away, even as Devoe took the tablet and started tapping on it. "Still not sure what the punchline is with all your coffee talk. I mean, here. Why did the queen send the coffee to jail? Because it was *not-tea*! Get it? See how I told you the end of the joke? How about it, Joe?"

The Ritualist couldn't respond, his mind fully engaged with a vast flood of notifications.

Your muscles have been tested in a trio of exceedingly unique ways within the last day! What's this? Strength is evolving! Quick, make your choice with strong conviction, or be forever saddled with a weaker, random version.

Option one: Strength of Arms! One arm lifts little. Many arms, bound as one, move mountains.

Your Strength is no longer yours alone, but is there to share! Any ally in direct contact with you, or someone in contact with them anywhere within an unbroken line with no upper limit, gains a percentage of your Strength Characteristic until they are no longer a part of the chain.

As soon as he read over the first option, Joe's eyes went wide with excitement. This choice had almost certainly been offered to him because of how the entire group performing the ritual had linked together and stayed strong through the Legendary Tribulation lightning bolt. That, combined with how it was a *three*-word descriptor—instead of the two word phrase like 'Dark Charisma' all of his other stats were comprised of—made him wonder if this was of a higher-rank rarity or something to that effect. Even before looking over the other possibilities, he was leaning toward this.

Option two: Core Strength. Trees do not fall because their branches break but because their trunk gives way. Your Strength starts from your center and braces your form. When lifting, carrying, or bracing against impact, your Strength is counted as double.

The Ritualist's eyes flicked to the Dwarf, who was seemingly frozen in place as Joe's mind spun through the options quick as thought. It was because of this bearded fellow that he'd gained this particular option, he was absolutely certain—even now, he hadn't fully reset his stance after pushing back against the oversized hand that had slapped his back. Frankly, this option was off the table without any further consideration.

Option three: Quad Strength. When you need to get somewhere, don't walk. Run. Your legs no longer simply move you from place to place, they accelerate you until arrival. When using any movement-based skills which rely mainly on your legs, your Strength modifier is counted as four times higher.

Seeing option three, the stranglehold the first choice had on his thoughts was broken. Though it was only a 'two-word upgrade', Joe was absolutely certain Omnivault would count as 'a movement skill relying on his legs'. Still, he was also pretty sure that when he managed to push the skill into the Grandmaster rank, he would no longer be quite as bound by gravity. "Does it matter if I can jump really high, if I can *fly*?"

Make your choice! 3... 2...

"Abyss! I wanna jump real good!" Joe yelped out as he slapped option three, not caring one *whit* that everyone in the area had suddenly gone quiet and was looking at him as though Devoe's slap had given him a concussion.

The bald man staggered forward, his legs surging with heat that pooled in his thighs and calves. He sucked in a sharp breath as the muscles bunched and bulged, grabbing the bottom of his loose pants and yanking them up to inspect his legs, just as they began swelling. Veins rose across his skin, and the fabric he had scrunched up *creaked* in protest as his engorged muscles tried to burst through.

"Feces, man, are you allergic to fish or something?" One of

those gathered muttered as Joe's leg became bright red, capillaries bursting and forming bruises as his body molded itself into a slightly new form. "Anyone got an epipen?"

"Abyss, I missed my chance to have the most epic abs ever!" Joe spat as he dropped his pant leg and cut off the clear view. Still, that did nothing to hide how shapely his legs had become, seeing as they had turned his previously loose trousers into what were essentially linen skinny jeans. "Don't worry about that; I'm fine."

"*I'll* say."

Though he couldn't pick out who in the crowd had murmured the words, Joe appreciated the sentiment nonetheless. "Thanks? Ugh... I need something to eat. Devoe, have you mapped out the next-"

"Got it all set!" the Dwarf quickly replied as he finished tapping on the tablet with the stylus. Not a moment too soon. The gyroscope had been spinning on the other side of the structure while they'd been distracted, and a sufficient number of the marble-sized orbs had arrived on the center of the teleportation pad.

Moments later, a school of fish appeared once more, this time oversized butterflyfish... which looked closer to actual butterflies than fish. They even had actual wings, though they were the kind clearly designed for moving through water, rather than air. With a flash of light, they were wrapped in clouds, but before they could begin struggling into the air, they simply vanished.

"It *works*!" Joe slapped his hands together in excitement as he looked at the empty teleportation pad with bright eyes. "As soon as I got that warning, I knew it was going to work exactly how I had it planned out."

"Warning? Hold up, you *weren't* sure it was going to work?" Devoe laughed humorously as Joe quickly backpedaled.

"Well, you know how it is! Any prototype has a chance of failing spectacularly, even if you designed it and built it correctly." The Ritualist glanced around the room, seeing dozens of unimpressed faces looking back. "I gave it at least a seventy-percent chance of success. You know. Better than even odds!"

"Hmm." Devoe noncommittally spoke for the group, only a little distracted by tapping on the tablet to create new teleportation pad points. "Well, I've got this handled for a while. Anna, you good with setting up a rotation for someone to replace me and a maintenance schedule for the rituals in this building? Since the First Elder is sponsoring this program, I'm sure the pay will be generous for all of us, no matter *what* role we take in supporting it."

"Absolutely." Joe didn't flinch away at that clear provocation, knowing that with the success of this transport network, he was likely about to become the single most wealthy person on the planet... *after* it had covered the planet *and* after any donated resources or goods actually started coming to him instead of being fed to the Ascendant Matrix to allow the pads to expand outward further. "Er... actually, I just realized this is going to be pretty expensive to-"

"I'll take second watch!"

"Dibs on third!"

"Put me on the schedule!"

With a soft groan, Joe decided that he'd simply need to start charging people for use of the teleporters at a higher rate than he'd been planning initially. Suddenly, half a year of free use for hundreds of people felt like *way* more of a benefit than he had expected. "Fine! You're all worth it, so that's just *fine*. Now, who wants to skip the walk back up the mountain and just teleport there with me?"

Not a single person spoke up, and he frowned in concern as Devoe started snickering at his expression. "You only gave this a seventy-percent chance of working in the first place, and we don't even know if the fish survived their first teleportation. Maybe *you* want to be the first to give this a test?"

"The teleportation problem bothers me." Joe heard someone murmuring to their neighbor. "Are we still *us* if we teleport away? Is this destroying us and reconstituting us somewhere else, or just creating a new body and putting our minds in it?"

"How many times have you all died in Eternium?" Joe grumbled as he pushed his way through the crowd and hopped up onto the teleportation pad. "If that's the issue holding you back, I think you just haven't been paying attention."

As soon as he was on the stone, a small interface appeared in front of him, showing his location as '0, 0, 0, 0, 0'. "Let's see, this is the point of origin, so that's up, down, left, right, then altitude. If we find high enough mountains, that last one will likely be *real* important. I want to go to my mountain, so that's zero, one, zero, zero, zero. Definitely not looking forward to when this is a bunch of geo-coordinates instead of simple ones and zeros. Or, no, wait. That would mean it's all set up and functioning correctly. So…"

Just before he could accept the transportation, there was an enormous *boom* that almost caused him to dive head-first off the platform and roll for cover. Glancing back at the source, he saw hundreds of pounds of rock and boulders clattering down through the hopper and into the warehouse section of the structure. "Abyss, that got me good! Just the mages and engineers carving a tunnel? Perfection itself; that's *lots* of low-level aspects this place can use."

The only downside was that the teleportation interface vanished as the stored mana instead went to empower the Ascendant Matrix built into the warehouse. Joe didn't mind, as he always loved watching enormous quantities of stuff dissolve into seeming nothingness. As the room became charged with power, the next wave of falling stones turned into rubble, then sand, then nothing even before they could hit the ground.

"After we teleport out, tap the pause button for an hour or two, Devoe," Joe instructed the Dwarf, who sent him an over-acted Legionnaire salute. The Ritualist rolled his eyes in response, then waited patiently until the teleportation interface appeared once more. Not waiting another moment, he accepted the location he'd already chosen-

-appearing the next instant on the outskirts of the mountain peak with his home and training areas.

Drawing in a deep breath of the clean mountain air, Joe leaned back and simply let himself *be*. The constantly coiling ceiling of clouds above churned and shifted through every color spectrum, turbulent Mana generating an endlessly rearranging canvas. Only when a stray gust of wind powerful enough to move these monoliths of mist came through was it possible to view the neighboring peaks. While looking on, Joe felt a smile touch his lips as he saw faint streaks carving through the air to meet the cloud cover—his ritual-lifted fish leaving behind sparkling trails as they sought their final destination.

"Just a few hours before Novusheim is linked." Focusing on the main peak, a massive open area on top of the mountain where the majority of the Sect was meant to be housed, Joe vanished from his current location, only to appear in the center of the city. He grimaced as his mana pool was impacted, the cost no longer subsidized by the Pseudo-Legendary building he had originally teleported away from.

"Oof. I'm gonna have to watch that. Hopefully, once the medium and large teleportation stations are dropped, we won't have to worry about it draining us dry when we move around." The Ritualist noted his location then made his way to the Sect Hall. After a quick explanation of what was happening, dozens of disciples followed him to the teleportation pad and immediately began erecting defenses around it.

For a moment, the Ritualist allowed himself to feel a hint of immense pride. He had finally become so competent and renowned that, with a single conversation, the Sect recognized the strategic resource he'd just put together and moved to defend it as *he* had requested. A wall quickly went up around the pad, weapons aimed inward *and* outward to ensure no one came into the heart of the Sect with bad intentions, nor could a fugitive fleeing justice escape easily—not that either of these should be a serious concern at this point, but it was better to plan for success instead of failing to plan at all.

With these necessary steps out of the way, Joe teleported back to his peak and entered his home.

"At long last, it's time to figure out how to break through this Characteristic bottleneck." Joe's hands were practically shaking with excitement as he looked around and made sure he had the room to himself. "The World Boss is on the way, I'm about to figure out the final chunk I need for the enchantment portion of my ritual, and then…"

Joe shut the door behind him, sinking deeply into his thoughts as he prepared to seek out the next step in his growth, "…then I get to see it all come together."

CHAPTER THIRTY-THREE

Immediately reopening the door, Joe shouted for a messenger. Between the immense volume he could boom his words out, combined with his position as First Elder, one of the many people who was on standby waiting for any such opportunity immediately appeared in front of his house and sketched a quick curtsy.

Joe sucked in a sharp breath, preparing to shout again, but the suddenness with which this lady had appeared nearly caused him to choke on the energy-packed air. Her words were professional and polite. "Do you need a message or package delivered? Something picked up? Trust me, I'm the gal you want for the job."

"Uhm." Shaking off his surprise, or at least trying to, Joe quickly put together a proper letter and handed it over. "Are you part of the Sect or just an opportunist?"

"Trying to decide how to pay me?" She shot him a wink and a knowing smile, "Definitely part of the guild, so I'm happy to accept contribution points as payment. Where am I going?"

Still rather nonplussed, Joe looked over the messenger standing before him. Her clothes were plain, simple traveling gear all of a singular dark gray color. "This needs to get to Grandmaster Fari of the Stormbinder's Tower. She's a Wolf-man, came down from Vanaheim, and was here not terribly long ago. That's really all the information I have; is it enough?"

"Without a clear destination, there's a thirty percent finder's fee added on." She lifted her hood and pulled on a pair of goggles not dissimilar to what Joe had seen in old war videos— thick leather and glass things meant to protect someone's eyes as they traveled through high speed wind. "Shouldn't be a problem, though, First Elder. Ask anyone. I'm not just a courier, I'm *The Courier*. Just need this as an official quest, and I'll be on my way."

Joe raised an eyebrow as a notification popped up, letting out a low whistle when he saw the fee associated with this service. "Lot of people try to back out after the delivery?"

"Jotunheim is a big planet. Not many people realize exactly *how* big." The Courier shook her head in mild disgust. "Or they want something sent back to Midgard, or up to Vanaheim, and expect me to *not* hunt them down if they refuse to pay. 'All you do is walk to them,' they'll tell me. As if getting my walking skill to this level *wasn't* a nightmare until I got my Perception and Intelligence high enough to be able to get to where I actually wanted to go."

She accepted the quest, took a deep breath, then a single step… and abruptly vanished into the distance.

In the same moment, Joe was knocked backward into his house, and the massive sonic boom set all of his papers and loose items to swirling around. Flinging himself to his feet, the Ritualist pushed against the onrushing wind, grabbing his open door and slowly shoving it closed. In a straight line away from him, there was a lady-shaped hole in the cloud, a perfect outline of The Courier with her foot raised to take a second step.

"Guess we've all gotten stronger." The Ritualist let out a low whistle as he remembered that this *wasn't* the first time he'd encountered her. Back then, she was a pitiable existence, someone who'd gotten her skills too high for her Characteristics to keep up. There would be a shrill scream, then someone would slam into a wall, more often than not being sent to respawn. "I would've tried to heal her if I'd been able to keep up with her. Looks like she's refined herself pretty well, so that must've all worked out. Not many people can take a single step and go directly to the horizon."

Reopening the quest, Joe added an overly generous tip, deciding it was better to stay in this person's good graces. Then, with that task complete, he returned to contemplating the threshold that had been bottlenecking him for far too long.

"Every one of my Characteristics has evolved, and now even my stubborn Strength is ready to go." He looked at his Characteristics, each of them a polished jewel that had been pushed to the limits and beyond, stretched in ways they were never meant to go, and as different from their original selves as a fantasy novel was from a pharmaceutical.

Characteristic: Effective Ability Score
Quad Strength: 299 (Capped)
Dialectic Dexterity: 299 (Capped)
Stoic Constitution: 299 (Capped)
Light Intelligence: 299 (Capped)
Ritualistic Wisdom: 299 (Capped)
Dark Charisma: 299 (Capped)
Karmic Perception: 299 (Capped)
Red Luck: 299 (Capped)

"Now the only question is, how do I take this from a scattering of polished jewels and turn it into a crowning achievement?" He sat on a thick mat, meditating deeply on each of his individual Characteristics as he-

Pow.

Joe let out a strangled yelp of pain as his chest ripped open, shards of metal embedding themselves deeply in his flesh and blood immediately gushing out over his pristine white robes.

Your Ritual Orb of Strength has undergone a catastrophic failure! It

was bound to 'Strength', and after continuously searching for that Charac-teristic and being unable to find it, the orb has finally given up and relin-quished its connection. Strength set to 50% of maximum until a connection has been established with a new Ritual Orb.

Quad Strength: 150 (Damaged. Capped)

A stream of curses erupted from his mouth as Joe got to his feet, went to his door, and slammed it open. Stomping the entire way to the nearby forge, Joe manifested aspect hammers in each hand and gripped them hard enough that his hands shook and his knuckles turned white. "Is the world conspiring against me right now?"

There was exactly one open station, and Joe immediately began swinging his hammers rhythmically, beating up on a defenseless collection of aspects as he started chanting a mantra. *"Blow me up on my own deck? Just watch me break this bottleneck!"*

The forging took longer than he wanted, seeing as his mana flowed out like a leaky faucet instead of a steady stream, but even so, he quickly managed to make... a mess.

Just as the Ritual Orb took shape, infernal fire blossomed out of his hammers and consumed the aspects and the forge, melting both to slag before Joe managed to pull far enough away to cut off the flow. As he looked on with a deep sense of falling into a spiral coming over him, the ritualist perked up as the melted slag began to glow while solidifying. Instead of the usual pile of useless bits, the goop turned into a fine powder, shimmering with a slightly creepy radiance that slid between green, violet, and black.

Congratulations! You have created Infernal Residue (Unique) for the first time. This is a highly sought-after component in multiple disciplines, ranging from alchemy to enchanting and most professions in between. Use caution, as it is a banned substance on most worlds with unified governments.

"I'll just have to pretend that was a win of some kind." Joe quickly scooped up the residue then marched out of the smithy without looking back, deciding to just pull one of his spare

Ritual Orbs out of storage instead of making a new version to replenish his stores. "Did I have too many successful things happen in a row, and now I'm being punished for it, or what?"

As he returned to his meditations, this time focusing exclusively on his Quad Strength, the Ritualist quickly managed to figure out the sympathetic links between himself and his Characteristic.

Inscription tool flying across the surface of the orb, he drew out exactly what he needed, the final image of which looked like nothing more than a stick figure up top, with grotesquely muscular and *way*-too-detailed legs below. He set the orb down and stepped away, fully expecting that it would pop like an overfull water balloon sometime in the next few seconds.

"Nothing? You *sure?*" Joe spoke to the world itself but luckily didn't get a reply. Reaching for the orb, it suddenly lit up with a warning flash of gold and red, and he flinched away... only for the Ritual Orb to go back to its normal coloration. He snatched it up and stored it in the bandolier that had already repaired itself, shaking his head at whatever part of the system was messing with him. "Not cool."

A short while later, he had re-bound himself to the new orb and was once more trying to forge a connection between all of his upgraded Characteristics and... and...

Joe opened his eyes, letting out a deep sigh. "I've got no idea what I'm supposed to do here. I have all my Characteristics upgraded, but no one will talk about what I need to do to break through this threshold. Am I missing something? System? A little help here? What do I do?"

Final condition complete: Just ask.

New quest available: Integrating the Foundation.

"Well, there it is." As much as Joe didn't want to admit it, he approved of the cheeky humor the system seemed to have. "I wonder how long it takes most people to figure that out? I'd bet that, the more arrogant you are, the longer you're stuck at that bottleneck, huh?"

The quest began unfolding in front of him, slower than

usual, as though someone were handwriting the script instead of dropping a fully formulated task in front of him.

Before anything else, be aware that all details of this quest, including and especially the final requirement of asking the world for assistance, cannot be shared with someone who has not already completed this quest or is currently going through it themselves. Any intentional attempts to do so will be punished, and any inadvertent explanations such as eavesdropping will be blocked from succeeding.

"Well, that explains a lot about why everyone was so *squiggy* when I was asking them about this." The Ritualist thought back to all of the pauses in conversation, the hesitation in people's voices as they spoke, and the blatant redirections and conversation he'd put up with to this point. "Why so many rules, I wonder?"

You have evolved each of your Characteristics and refined each of them to the maximum of the fifth threshold. Your task, when you choose to accept it, is to integrate each of them into a singular Foundation you will build all future progress upon. In the sixth threshold, Characteristic points matter more than ever before. Training them will be far more difficult, with each point requiring at least double the time and effort generally necessary for a singular increase.

Now, as to the quest itself…

Quest offered: Integrating the Foundation. Upon accepting this quest, you must choose a single title you have earned. This title will become your goal for integration, and upon broaching the seventh threshold, it will give a new shape to each of your Characteristics. At that point, this title will cease to be a title and will instead become an inherent trait.

Warning: do not accept this quest if you lack sufficient achievement. By choosing an insufficiently potent title to base your future on, you only weaken and bottleneck yourself further. Each of your Characteristics may permanently stall at the next threshold.

The only way to know for certain is to try, but failure means resetting to the entry point of the sixth threshold and forfeiting all Characteristic gains previously made.

Many things were becoming clear as he read over the quest, not the least of which was why his mentors, especially Pete, had been so very invested in going over his titles. Between the Pearls of Wisdom to store his weaker titles, to the all-but-direct *demand* for him to start getting fractured titles and clicking those modular pieces into place, to an explanation on how to get more, faster. "All this time, I thought they were basically just casual buffs I could take or discard as needed."

Joe had a light bulb moment. "*Ah*. I get it. That's why we're not allowed to tell anyone about this... to make sure they chase potent titles all on their own without knowing that they *need* them. Abyss, this quest is *insidious*. Even if someone fulfilled all the other requirements, without a powerful enough title, they'd be trapped here for however long it takes them to hunt one down. Or worse, they'd be gambling on pushing through with a title that could never get them across the threshold."

Even he knew that it was easier to get better titles when you were doing something far and away outside of what your skillset should allow. If he wanted to seek out incredibly potent titles *now*, with many of his skills Mastered and his Characteristics maximized for his threshold, he would need to be out doing something utterly ridiculous and almost certainly bad for his health.

Accept quest? Yes / No?

Joe's chin bobbed downward as he stared intently at the prompt and reached for the 'yes' button. Just before he could mentally select it, the words vanished, and another warning popped up.

It looks like you were about to say yes. Once more, if you lack sufficient achievement, you may stall here permanently. However... the more powerful of a title you choose to use as the basis for your integration, the more punishing the trial to integrate it will be.

Rewards will scale accordingly, potentially opening new and interesting paths for advancement.

"Aim high, but prepare to fight the whole time." Joe could only shrug at that thought; he'd never done anything *but* try to punch above his weight class. Even so, he still hesitated to press 'yes' as the words appeared once more. "Hmm... maybe I shouldn't use 'Tatum's Chosen Legend' like I was planning. Guarantee that's the most potent title I have, but… that would tie me closer to Tatum, and I'm actively trying to push off to stand on my own right now."

Feeling his ribs expand as he sucked in a deep breath through his nose, Joe still slammed the button.

Choose a title to use as your Foundational integration goal. Title chosen: Monarch of Mana (Upgradable). Are you sure you would like to use this title? Warning: the tribulation you will undergo will absolutely be upgraded alongside this title if you manage to upgrade it before the seventh threshold.

Yes / No.

As he reached for the button, only for it to vanish once more, Joe let a low growl rumble out of his chest as his fingers swiped through empty air.

Last note, as a favor! It looks like you're about to break through into the sixth threshold of Characteristics! If you have a large stack of deferred Characteristics, they will all be applied at once. Please ensure you are in a safe location, and if possible, have some form of cleansing available. It is highly likely that massive surges in Characteristic growth will be… messy.

"Okay, I can appreciate that one," Joe reluctantly allowed, hopping off his mat and walking over to his bathroom. Stripping out of his robes, he sat on the floor of his shower, turning the water on at full blast before selecting 'yes' once more. "Monarch of Mana fits me perfectly. Mana is used in every ritual, every craft, and is at the heart of every insane thing I've managed to pull off. By the time this is all over, I'm going to have an absolutely *ridiculously* sized pool of mana to draw on, I just know it."

That was the last cognizant thought he had for an unknown amount of time. His blank eyes stared up at a status screen hovering above him without being dismissed, foam boiling out of his mouth as his body locked into a disturbing bridge of writhing muscle.

Quest initiated. Bottleneck breached. Integrating the Foundation begins now. Allocating deferred Characteristic points. Determining tribulation…

Joe couldn't see the system notifications, he could only try to force his lungs to expand as his body attempted to crush him into an ingot of human flesh as every ounce of growth, every last drop of potential that had been waiting, rushed into him all at once.

Fire ants gnawed on his bones, lava surged through his veins, his epidermis cracked and sloughed off as the next layers grew outward to accommodate his suddenly expansive musculature. Each of his nerves was destroyed then rewired, reconnecting to his brain in a surge of sensation just to test that it had been correctly formed.

If the process had happened slowly, the points being applied as Joe earned them, the results wouldn't have been nearly as dramatic. As it was, if an outside observer had been able to see what was happening, they would've only had a moment to look on in horror as Joe formed a bridge with only the top of his head and the tips of his toes touching the ground... then he all but exploded apart in a wave of gore.

Every nook and cranny of the bathroom had blood dripping down its surface, bits of skin were hanging from the lights, and loose fatty tissue slowly seeped across the floor toward the drain in the center as the water from the shower carried it away.

He collapsed, hitting the ground with a wet *splat* that had nothing to do with the water still flowing down on him. For a long few minutes, Joe simply stayed in place as his brain rebooted. As he came around, only one thing made the horrifying sensations worthwhile:

The gains.

Characteristic: Effective Ability Score
Quad Strength: 299 → 400
Dialectic Dexterity: 299 → 400
Stoic Constitution: 299 → 400
Light Intelligence: 299 → 364
Ritualistic Wisdom: 299 → 364
Dark Charisma: 299 → 364

Karmic Perception: 299 → 400
Red Luck: 299 → 367

Tribulation determined: Corrupted Characteristics. At the heart of a monarch lies one true fear that everything they have built will be corrupted and rot away as soon as they delegate power to others. You must deal with this sensation and still push through.

Effect: Each distinct time you use mana, temporarily lose one point in your Characteristics (Chosen randomly). The temporarily lost Characteristics will return upon death or broaching the seventh threshold. If any Characteristic drops below a total of 300, the monarch in you will rebel, and you will instantly self-destruct.

Note: This is total Characteristics, not including being inhibited on lower worlds.

"Cool. Cool. Just gained a hundred points in four of my Characteristics. I can do that again." Joe quickly calculated how long it would take to gain enough Mastery levels to simply force the evolution if he stayed in his room and didn't interact with anyone, but something told him that relying on his Loremaster skill to make this happen all on its own would result in a substandard foundation.

"With that, I think I'm ready to push for my mana channels to be rebuilt. Let's get the last few pieces and…"

Pushing himself up onto his elbows, Joe's upper back came free of the floor with a drawn-out *squelch*. "Before that, maybe I can figure out what I'll need to pay someone to get in here and clean up this… sloppy Joe."

CHAPTER THIRTY-FOUR

Having left the grisly scene behind him, Joe walked across the mountain peak, stretching his arms overhead, farther and farther, expecting his shoulder to pop, but never quite reaching that point. His bones, though feeling exceedingly durable and as if they could casually take a strike from a war hammer without breaking, were surprisingly supple and flexible. "Jaxon, wherever you are, you're going to have to *work* to adjust me the next time we meet."

Quest update: Dulling the Sword of Damocles. Choosing to live as a Monarch, and not as the Legend Tatum has been creating for you has further slowed the ever-increasing karmic debt between yourself and Occultatum.

2) Take three steps into the light. It has become easy for you to complete projects using the gifts given to you by your faction leader. You must complete at least three major workings under your own recognizance which would be easier to complete by using the resources on hand. Do not invoke or empower him. (2/3).

Pending Rewards:

1) Speak to Queen Cleocatra for an external Karmic remapping of one of your skills.

2) Speak to Queen Cleocatra for a Karmic wedge.
3) Speak to Queen Cleocatra for a Karmic upgrade of an item.

As he glanced around the area, Joe realized that something looked... different. It could be just that he was looking at the world through new eyes—possibly literally, assuming they had popped along with the rest of him and regrown—but more likely, it was just how his Characteristics had adjusted to allow him to see as if looking through a new lens. The clouds shifting overhead had distinct edges between the various mana types that they were circulating. The previously monotone coloration of the bedrock his peak was being built out on was now varied gradients and ombres.

Oddly enough, certain areas practically seemed... high-lighted. Not as if they were hiding something special, but as if his body was telling him that he could move through that area with ease.

Every loose rock, ridge, and crevasse around the area was practically inviting him to waltz along them without even the slightest possibility of slipping or falling. "Let's go test this body out. I need to figure out if this is some strange side effect filling me with overconfidence, or if I can really handle it as easily as I *feel* like I can."

With half of his Characteristics increased by a full third compared to earlier in the day, he was certain he'd be able to pass through the training areas he'd set up without much issue. Each step he took sent him bounding across the surface as though he were an astronaut walking across the moon for the first time, and in only a few moments, he was at the initial entry point for the jumping course he'd set up. While there *was* a line, there were a few benefits to being in charge of not only the area, but technically the person who was supposed to be training the others.

"Gather around if you're working on your Jumping skills!" Just before starting, the Ritualist decided there was no reason not to turn this into a teachable moment. He waited until a fairly substantial crowd of thick-calved people had formed into a U-shape around him, then he started a mini-lecture. "Today, I'm going to demonstrate the benefit of working on your Jumping skill in *conjunction* with your Characteristics."

He was about to say more, inadvertently explaining the benefits that would also come with pushing their Strength Characteristic in the direction of something like his own Quad Strength, but he found his tongue swelling up in his mouth. Hacking and coughing as though a fly had just zipped down his throat, Joe turned and faced the course that he had designed to be challenging even to himself, at least in the upper portions.

Crouching slightly, he focused all of his Strength into his legs and used the version of Omnivault which didn't require mana. As he prepared to push off, his vibrating muscles caused a light wind to spring up in a swirling whirl around him, catching dust and lifting tiny rocks off the ground. "Right... I think I'm going to start with something a little higher up the difficulty than the Novice entry point."

Finally releasing the tension he'd built up, Joe pushed off the ground and got to experience for the first time what a four-times multiplier really meant for his Omnivault. The ground below him cracked and bounced into the air as it rebounded off the lower levels of stone, creating a small geyser of rubble that pelted the people who'd been standing around him. From a total standstill, Joe shot up, *up*, passing by the Journeyman portion of the course, sailing above the Expert rank, and easily managing to land on the Master-rank platform a bit over three hundred feet in the air.

Knowing they wouldn't be able to hear him from this far away, Joe allowed himself to express his own shock at the successful, almost *casual* jump. "Abyss... that was *awesome*. Note to self? Make sure I can land safely after jumping so high. It should be fine, but terrain damage is hard to calculate without just tanking it and seeing what happens."

Making sure all eyes were on him, Joe stepped forward and gathered himself, watching as the rings of illusionary light he'd set up wobbled back and forth. At just the right moment, he took two quick steps forward and shoved off—with far too much strength. Headfirst, the Ritualist blasted forward like a rocket with an overly shiny tip, wind tearing at his loose robes as he quickly twisted himself to the side. Reaching down, he managed to grab the ledge at the end of the Master-rank jump pad with one hand—casually and easily arresting his momentum entirely.

He held himself there, creating a forty-five-degree angle with the platform for a few seconds as he contemplated exactly how far he might've gone had he missed the grab. "Omnivault takes my Strength divided by five, multiplies it by three if I'm leaping instead of jumping, then Quad Strength quadruples that. Nine hundred and sixty feet? Celestial feces, I just about chucked myself off the mountain!"

Only then did he flip and spin from platform to platform until he was back on the ground. He landed in a heroic pose and waved at the crowd of Jumping enthusiasts, who stared back with slack jaws. "That's with my Jumping skill at only the peak of the Master rank! Imagine what I'll be able to do as a Grandmaster. Imagine what *you'll* be able to do when you get here with your own variant!"

Skill increase: Teaching (Master 0 → Master I). Sometimes the best way to teach someone to do the impossible on their own is to do it right in front of their eyes. Current amount of time those learning from you may pass on what they learned to others at 50% efficiency of your direct teaching: 15 seconds.

You have gained 5 points in each Characteristic for increasing a Mastery level!

"Don't want to jinx this, but… I think I'll *somehow* manage to fight through this tribulation." In moments, he was able to see the results of his instruction, and the people amazed him. Instead of scattering to tell about what they'd just seen, the group instead—one by one—tried to demonstrate what they'd managed to glean to the others. Dozens of people teaching at fifty percent of his Mastery skill over and over meant *incredibly* rapid gains among the group, even if they only had fifteen seconds to get the most out of it.

"I'm going to have Mastery Merits to *burn* at this rate," the Ritualist murmured to himself as he looked on with a pleased expression. "I'm glad my Teaching skill is so high; this would've been quite the slog otherwise."

Now that the others were distracted once more, and he'd found that the current setup posed no challenge, Joe decided to try a different method of testing out his physicality. With a couple steps to build speed, he leapt in a straight line to cross hundreds of yards in an instant. Seeing so many people look his way, Joe straightened his back and held his hands together behind his back, leaping forward once again as though such movement was a casual thing *anyone* should be able to achieve.

1,000 people have looked at you during the last minute with immense respect in their eyes! You have earned a temporary boon: Charismatic Leader. For the next 24 hours, your words carry additional weight to those who hold you in a position of esteem. Whether you are leading them into a dark place, or on a righteous charge, the effects of your Charisma will be increased by 5%.

Joe turned in midair, putting his feet down and stopping his movement with a single toe before slowly lowering his foot until it was flat on the ground, a perfect single-leg calf extension. A few more steps put him on the center of the teleportation pad, and with a slight *whooshing* sound, he found himself at the base of the mountain in the 'Joe To Go' headquarters. A Ritualist looked up from the tablet she was tapping away on, seemingly startled that he had appeared.

"Oh! First Elder! I was just looking through the settings, and I realized you hadn't turned on any of the pay-to-use functionalities. Did you want to...?"

Blink. Blink.

Joe managed to keep his thoughts on the inside and simply graciously accepted the tablet instead of smacking himself in the head or anything else that would appear less than First Elder-y. "Thank you for catching that so early; it would've been quite the pain if I hadn't thought to check for the next few weeks."

It was simple to set up a few different payment options, with his Sect members being able to pay with contribution points and others needing to leave behind materials—whether fully created goods or raw components—based on the distance they were going to teleport. "Keep an eye on this for me, would you? When the payment is accepted, it should appear on the edge of the platform over there, then fall onto the conveyor belt built into the floor. Goes straight into the recycling room."

"What keeps people here from just grabbing whatever they want off the conveyor?" Her question wasn't filled with greed, but simple curiosity. Even so, her casual insight nearly floored Joe once more.

"I guess... nothing? Part of why it's so important to only allow a few people in here. *Trustworthy* people." His words caused a slight flush of pride to appear in her cheeks, and she sat straighter as Joe handed the tablet back. "Again, a great catch, and I'll make sure to give you a reward for that. Anything else before I go?"

"Just wondering when you're planning on setting up the coffee shop that'll send out orders to people." She met his eyes, though it was clear by her fidgeting that she wanted to get back to placing planned teleportation points on the slowly filling out map. "I have a few friends working as message runners who are looking for a change of pace."

"Soon as I get some free time." Joe had no choice but to brush off the question without a real answer. "The shop itself will be 'Joe To Go', but I'm going to need to work on a design to create specialized coffees and such, once orders are placed by anyone with an order... talisman? I'm thinking I'll call it 'My Morning Ritual', but I need to work out how it'll actually function. I've got a few months, since we need a wider range before really spinning it up."

"Understood, and thank you for letting me know."

Joe looked at the platform, seeing dozens of fish beginning

to appear. He hopped forward, swiping his hand over the teleportation pad just as the Ritual of Cloudstep activated for an instant. Immediately, both of his feet were surrounded with a pair of tiny nimbus clouds. "Then, I'm off."

Going out the singular egress, Joe approached the opening in the mountainside and looked on with great approval at the dozen warriors watching for any monsters while scores of people worked to build terraced defenses around the entrance. Brushing by them, Joe chose against interacting, wanting nothing more than to *move*.

Soon he was at the base of the path which would lead back up to his peak, but instead of getting on the carved surface, he tilted his head back and stared up to where the mountain vanished into the cloud cover far above. "Spot there, go rock to rock. That crag looks like it'll hold if I land on it carefully…"

A simple glance was enough for his Perception to take in the route, his Intelligence to plan the best method of using it, and his Wisdom to rewrite some of what his Intelligence hadn't accounted for. Joe leapt forward, missing his initial target but easily sinking his fingertips into the stone and tearing through the surface to halt his momentum just before he would've begun to fall.

Joe scuttled up the wall, Dexterity allowing his fingers to thread into grooves which shouldn't have been enough to support his weight. Balancing on the tips of his toes at a ninety-one degree angle like a mountain goat, he was able to push off, jumping up hard and sailing to his original first-planned stop of an outcropping. Glancing down and back, he saw the drifting trails of clouds that followed him like a tracer, using them to account for how his body had moved in actuality, versus how he'd planned to get around, lastly weighing how the motion had *felt* as it was completed.

"Hmm. Seems I'm still underestimating my capabilities by about eighteen percent." As soon as the knowledge settled in his mind, Joe shifted slightly on the balls of his feet, changing his planned center of gravity just before pushing off the ground once more. This time, he came to a rest on a stone spire, his toe gently settling *exactly* where he had intended. "There we go. Now we just need to do a bit more fine-tuning…"

Easily able to jump hundreds of feet with each push, Joe quickly scaled the mountain, bouncing back and forth like a pinball someone had landed a perfect hit on. Glittering rainbows of clouds trailed in smooth arcs back and forth, allowing him to see how he'd succeeded and where he'd misjudged his capabilities. By the time he crested the summit, Joe felt that he had perfect control of his body once more, and his grin was brighter than the gleam emanating off his bald head.

Then he saw a Wolfman rushing him, and his smile ran away.

After the initial flash of danger had filtered through his mind, Joe recognized with a sigh of relief that the predator's stare boring into him was one of excitement, not bloodlust. "Grandmaster Fari! You're here sooner than I expected."

There was foam literally dripping from the corners of her mouth, giving the intensely focused Wolfman a rabid cast as she skid to a stop in front of him, bent over with her enormous hands clenching and unclenching, leaving long furrows in the stone where her talons pulled through with a *screech* sharp enough to make Joe wince.

"Where is it? Your message said you know where the World Boss is going to be. *Where*? No, first, *how* did you find it? Did you do as you had hoped and make it replicable? Tell me you can find it *again!*"

"Truly, the pleasure of seeing you again is *mine*, Grandmaster-" Joe's eyes had wandered to the distance, where figures were trudging over the crest of the mountain in a neat formation. They had banners being tossed back and forth by the turbulent wind through the clouds, their armor glinting and sparking as conflicting mana types brushed against them.

"Do not play *games*, bald one!" Fari cut him off with a growl, nose practically poking him in the chest as she leaned in, eyes mere inches from his own. For a moment, Joe was entranced by his own reflection as sweat trickled down his head and collected along the hem of his robes. "Your message promised results, and we have *burned* resources to get here in time."

"Hold on," Joe politely yet firmly demanded, waving ambiguously into the distance. "Let's speak somewhere where we won't be interrupted... or *overheard?*"

Fari seemed to remember herself at that moment and impatiently nodded as she turned to the side to allow Joe to pass. "Can we move quickly? I am greatly enthusiastic about gaining some news."

"Sure." Joe took a step forward, then leaped with all his strength, for the first time ever creating a hint of a sonic boom behind him. A glance over his shoulder at the stunned Grandmaster allowed his smile to cautiously return, and he murmured under his voice as he contemplated the Charisma boost he'd gained. "Sometimes it might be better to allow people to underestimate me, but there are clear benefits to showing what I *can* do. Just got to make sure it doesn't turn into a head swelling with ego. Don't get swept up in your own propaganda, Joe. Don't *do* it! Well... okay, fine, maybe just a *little*."

As he and the Wolfman appeared outside of his house, a half dozen cleaners wielding mops, buckets, and grim expressions filed out, a pungent aroma lifting from a large garbage bin they were hauling. Fari watched them go then glanced at Joe with a curious expression he wasn't able to decipher.

"Did you die in there?"

"Ah! No, not quite. I popped like a soap bubble made of gristle." Joe smacked his leg twice, the sound closer to hitting a boulder than human flesh. "Pushed into the sixth threshold a little while ago; that's actually what I was trying out when you caught up with me. Just balancing out what my body can actually do with what my mind *thinks* it can do. I had a few deferred Characteristics, uh, applied."

To her credit, the Wolfman winced away in sympathy. "Did you ruin a perfectly good outfit? I know when I broke through, they had to burn the entire tent. There was just no saving it with the people we had on hand. Right, I suppose congratulations are in order, but…"

"You're looking for an explanation. Understood." Joe quickly went through his design of the teleportation network, its intended goal, and finally the alert that the system had given him: how the World Boss was on its way. By the time he finished explaining the nuances of how they'd be using this in the future to track the World Boss—essentially watching for teleportation pads being destroyed one after another, the Grandmaster was looking on with dawning understanding.

"This works, I suppose. I can't think of something that would work better, obviously, or I would've done it myself. Excellent ingenuity and use of resources. No idea how you can make that happen, but since you *can*…" She rolled her shoulders, flicking her ears in a way he interpreted as 'whatever works'. "Fantastic. I suppose the question then becomes… no, I'm sure you've thought of that."

"I can almost *guarantee* I haven't," Joe quickly interjected. "Please speak freely."

"You… ah. You have placed your Sect in great danger. I simply had assumed you had made contingencies." The Grandmaster fidgeted slightly, baring her teeth at him for a few heartbeats before leaning back, seemingly resigned to explaining. "Generally, I would leave you to your fate, or at the bare minimum charge you for this information you clearly do not have. Yet I find myself in a predicament, as it is in my best interest to ensure we maintain a good relationship."

Taking a deep breath, she leaned forward. "A World Boss like the Jötunn is not an entity which moves alone. They carry entire ecosystems with them, parasites, predators, scavengers. This world is vast, and only a fraction of the potential monsters across its surface have threatened you here. Generally, with a Kaiju-style monster such as this one-"

"Kaiju in this case just meaning 'big', right? Not a particular monster type?" For an instant, Joe had visions of massive lizards standing on their hind legs and sending beams of energy to destroy city blocks at a time.

"Yes," came the simple answer, "if by 'big' you are vastly understating the fact that the Jötunn is multiple times taller than the mountain we stand on and wider than its entire range at the moment. Also, it is engulfed in flame from head to toe, meaning that, instead of riding along on its body, the ecosystem it generates will instead precede the entity as well as following along in its wake. While I cannot guarantee this, it is highly likely that at least one or even multiple of its main subordinates will accompany it."

"While my expedition is equipped to hunt the World Boss, that is all we will be hunting down. I'm sure you understand." She tilted her head to the side, the equivalent to a human archly raising their eyebrow. "Any other threats are... unrelated to our deal."

CHAPTER THIRTY-FIVE

Doing his best to keep his cool, Joe left his home and strolled over to the messengers. They'd taken to hanging out in a kiosk near his house, technically not an approved build on his mountain, but he wasn't going to kick up a fuss over someone trying to score a few contribution points here and there, especially not when it suited him so well.

"I need someone to get over to the Sect Hall and put out an immediate alert. I'll be there in the next hour to have an emergency meeting with the leadership… or whoever's here." Joe looked each of them in the eye, trying to determine who'd be best suited to this mission. "This is an extremely high-priority alert, with the fate of this entire mountain range in the balance, let alone our foothold on it."

"I can run over there in less than three hours!"

"Two and a half!"

"I've been practicing with your new teleportation system, and I can get there in five minutes."

"You've got the job." Joe pointed and outstretched hand at the last person to speak, his fingers rigid as he waved the man over. "You said five minutes; I'll give you ten. *Actually* do it in five minutes, and I'll add in a bonus."

"I'm already there." The man was shouting over his shoulder as he sprinted into the distance.

"Excellent." Joe hurried away, trying not to show his current level of distress, or at least not as much as he was actually feeling at the moment. "I *knew* things were going too well. Maybe I should've activated my Karmic Shroud when I was… no, better idea. When the fighting starts, *that's* when I'm going to activate it. Three days of the world not tilting to send crazy wandering monsters my way. Maybe even a plan that goes the way it's supposed to go for once. Man, what would *that* be like?"

Glancing over at the war camp taking shape on the outskirts of his mountain peak, Joe decided to explain the situation to the rather concerned Sect members who were gathering and staring at the expedition from Vanaheim. A single jump put him high enough to be seen from any point on the mountain, provided the clouds weren't swirling into his face too badly.

"*Attention!*" His voice carried out, echoing back to him and drawing the eyes of most of the people in the open area before he resumed speaking. "This is First Elder Joe. Effective immediately, the Wanderer's Sect is on high alert. Sometime over the next few weeks, a World Boss will be arriving in this area, specifically targeting our Sect mountain."

He decided to leave off the part where it was actually going after a particular teleportation ritual, hiding within a building, dug into a cave, in the depths of the mountain. "The World Boss will be handled by our friends over there; don't worry about fighting the Mythic monster. Even so, we're to assume that its entourage will include up to multiple Grandmaster-rank threats and an army of monsters large enough to rip the mountain apart stone by stone. All disciples are to begin war preparations, from combat training to armament creation. All Ritualists… come see me."

Hopping off his ledge, Joe quickly found himself surrounded by nearly a hundred Ritualists of various ranks. "I have a plan, and I think you're all going to like it. First of all, don't worry too much about all this World Boss business. At the end of the day, if we're about to be overrun, there's nothing that says we can't just flee the area. We've got teleportation available now!"

His words went a long way toward immediately easing the tension in some of their faces, and Joe capitalized on that moment to push a bit harder. "If there's one blessing we have in all of this mess, it's that we've got the high ground. We've got a few weeks to get some proper defenses set up and make sure that this mountain peak is the most dangerous to attack, to the point where any invading force would rather knock down another mountain entirely rather than have to test our defenses."

"To that end…" Joe held up a copy of the Ritual Combat Manual in one hand and a ritual tile in the other. "We're going to spend the rest of the day setting up towers along the mountain. Anyone here know a good Stone Mage? I'd rather not have to carve out foundations for these towers myself; there's been a bit of a shift in what it costs me going forward."

"I know a few!"

"I can get to Novusheim and hire an entire platoon if we need 'em!"

Hands went up around the group, which got Joe to nod appreciatively at them, but he didn't push for them to run off and gather their friends—or mercenaries—just yet. "What I'm going to do is *direct* all of this, only stepping in once we run out of prepared rituals. When we're done, I want each individual person here to claim one of the towers as their own, to maintain the attack ritual you're going to have on top of it. If there's two things we aren't lacking on Jotunheim, it's plenty of space and vast amounts of free mana just waiting to be used."

He led the group over to the top of the main path leading into the flat peak area. Devoe, as his most-trusted second in command on this world, was given detailed instructions on how to raise the tower, then Joe simply placed a few aspect jars in position and participated in the ritual to ensure they flowed correctly; all without donating any of his mana to the actual efforts. Nor did he channel it, allowing Devoe to run the show. As the tower settled into place, an imposing spike partially hidden by the low hanging clouds, Joe glanced at his Characteristics to see if he'd taken on any 'temporary' losses.

Characteristic: Effective Ability Score
Quad Strength: 400 → 404* (-1)
Dialectic Dexterity: 400 → 405
Stoic Constitution: 400 → 405
Light Intelligence: 364 → 369
Ritualistic Wisdom: 364 → 369
Dark Charisma: 364 → 369
Karmic Perception: 400 → 406
Red Luck: 367 → 372

"Abyss blast it, where'd I slip up?" Joe hissed under his breath as he glanced at the tower, the ritual tile, the aspect jars... which were connected via a minimal Ascendant Matrix. "Gah... didn't even think about the matrix before I set that up. It was such a normal thing to do. Yeesh, this tribulation might be harder than I give it credit for."

Nearly an hour had passed since his first announcement, so Joe excused himself to go and explain the situation to the Sect, tasking the coven with scouting out the best areas for the remaining ritual towers. Everything went incredibly smoothly as he stepped across the mountain peaks, one teleportation pad to another, only to hiss in frustration once more as he saw his Red Luck drop by a point.

While Aten wasn't at the Sect proper, Joe was incredibly relieved to find out that he was on the planet and easily able to return within a week, two at the most. After that, he convinced the others to put out a call to every person in the Sect, generating a quest which would appear to all members in every world.

Mandatory Sect Quest announcement: The Foothold in the Foothills. It has come to the attention of the Wanderer's Sect that the World Boss of Jotunheim is moving to destroy the main Sect mountain. While it's unclear why it has targeted this area specifically, the only thing that matters is ensuring that our home is not swept out from under us. An army of monsters will be arriving well in advance of the World Boss, Journeyman-rank up to potentially multiple Grandmaster-rank threats.

In defense of our core mission, 'to take and rebuild a world worth coming home to after wandering afar', all Sect members are hereby ordered to go to Jotunheim so long as they can survive its pressure <u>and</u> participate in the defense of the Sect at the same time.

Rewards will be based on contribution, with a minimum reward guaranteed to each disciple and elder, so long as they arrive in time for the battle. Failure to make best efforts to arrive in time for the defense will be cause for punitive action, up to removal from the Sect.

"Last part seems a little harsh, doesn't it?" Joe inquired of the elder who had crafted the quest and submitted it to the system.

"Not particularly." She spat to the side, the action startling Joe until she finished her statement. "Some of those bureaucrats down on Midgard are surprisingly powerful, but they'd do *anything* not to have to involve themselves in something like this. Listen. There's a standing secret mission from Aten, and it's essentially that we need to take any opportunity to remove them from their positions—at the *minimum*. We don't need over a dozen people among our highest-ranked Sect members that refuse to step up when things get tough."

"I bet they'd keep doing what they're doing if we guaranteed them the same pay and-"

Even before Joe had finished speaking, she was already shaking her head. "Tried that. All of them have plenty of gold; what they *want* is the ability to have a say in the Sect, even though they fight tooth and nail not to have to leave Midgard for any reason."

"Mmm… might that lower our combat potential a little bit there?" Joe offered politely, surprising even himself by being the voice of reason when it came to people like the bureaucrats on the lower world. "They can have one Characteristic higher than the mortal limit, so long as they never leave, right? "

"That's one of their arguments, yes," she answered while eyeing him critically. "But we're a community. When *one* of us needs help, the rest of us show up. It's what we do. It's our mission... First Elder."

His title was added only begrudgingly, rather clearly due to being somewhat disappointed in his reaction. Joe gently stroked his chin while looking into the distance thoughtfully, then he turned and walked away.

"Not going to change her mind with only one conversation, and... not sure that I'd want to in the first place. Seems like only yesterday I fully agreed with and even pushed that opinion. Hmm. What's changed?" As he strolled over to the teleportation pad, Joe still didn't have a good answer. Yet, as he stepped out onto the First Elder peak and looked at the wartime preparations bustling along in full swing, he had a minor breakthrough.

"Ahh... that's it." He hurried to join the slowly recongregating swarm of black-robed Coven members. "I've gained a new appreciation for delegation and how frustrating it can be to get people working for a singular goal... but also how rewarding it actually is. Feces, I definitely don't want to start *empathizing* with those bureaucrats, but perhaps I can sympathize. Just a tish."

Then Joe remembered how they had tried to escape from Towney McTownface, only for the Crab Bucket Curse to force them to remain on site by threatening severe consequences to their personal power. The wavering ember of warm feelings for them was snuffed out in an instant, and he felt his jaw firm up as he realized the Elder at the Sect Hall had made the correct decision for the *Wanderers*. There were always going to be people who railed against a choice that negatively impacted them personally, but he needed to remind himself that he was meant to be one of the people looking out for the good of the *organization*.

Sometimes, that meant getting rid of people who refused to be a proper part of the community. Sure, it sucked for *them*, but everyone else would be better off in the long run. With his odd introspection having reached a satisfactory conclusion, Joe turned his full attention to putting up ritual towers across the entirety of the mountain.

The second one was up within fifteen minutes, a half dozen within an hour, and by the time the sun rose the following morning, dozens of the defensive emplacements were thrusting up from the mountainside, practically a palisade's worth of mainly stone spears looking *exactly* as threatening as they were meant to become. While Joe was pleased with the outcome, he was rather shaken when he looked at his Characteristics, only to notice that he was ninety-three points down across the board.

As they returned to the mountain peak, and everyone was given instructions on building up their own ritual to place atop their assigned tower, the Reductionist took a moment to think over his tribulation.

"I'm beginning to see what it meant when it told me that the fear of corruption was what ate away at a monarch's ability to function well." He was staring at the ground, his eyes dark and hooded. "Every project I complete means I'm one step closer to self-detonation… and it's made me start holding back way more than I probably should. There's a Mythic monster on the way as I sit here and ruminate. This is when I need to be going full-boar, not half-hog. I can take a few detonations to the face for the team."

Recommitting himself to putting in his full effort, Joe started spending his mana a bit more freely wherever he could. Along with dozens of other members of his coven, he quickly put together a Mana Battery recharge station. He ignored the part of him that said he should set it up in a building of its own, trusting that his coven members and the Sect disciples would at least set up some walls and make sure no one tampered with the device.

Within three days, every tower was tipped with a glowing

ritual circle, and the top of the mountain sported a shiny new antenna that stretched into the clouds and greedily sucked mana out of them. By the time Joe had created a Mana Battery enchantment ritual, the last of the preparations he could make while on Jotunheim, he'd shifted four hundred and fifty-three Characteristic points to 'Temporarily Corrupted'.

Characteristic: Effective Ability Score
Quad Strength: 404 → 343* (-61)
Dialectic Dexterity: 405 → 330* (-75)
Stoic Constitution: 405 → 321* (-84)
Light Intelligence: 369 → 341* (-28)
Ritualistic Wisdom: 369 → 367* (-2)
Dark Charisma: 369 → 314* (-55)
Karmic Perception: 406 → 311* (-95)
Red Luck: 372 → 319* (-53)

"Oof." Joe rumbled as he looked over the massive shift that had occurred over the course of the day. "Even my pants aren't feeling as tight around the calves as they were. Pretty sure I lost about thirty percent of my total body weight in muscles melting away today."

"Yeah, you look pretty dehydrated. When's the last time you had some water?" a nearby Ritualist called out with concern in his voice. Joe almost replied that this was his tribulation, not his somewhat lacking self-care capabilities, only for his mouth to gum up and make him realize he'd nearly spouted off restricted information once again.

"Thath probably it." The bald man slurred slightly as his tongue came unstuck from the roof of his mouth. "I don't know, a week maybe? I've had plenty of coffee, but-"

"Can I get a healer over here?" the too-concerned coven member shouted, much to Joe's dismay. He lifted his hands and tried to wave off the people who were reaching out and trying to get him to sit down, but unless he wanted to actually hurt them, they weren't going to let him escape easily.

It took nearly half an hour for a qualified healer to arrive, and, seeing Joe's frustrated face, he wasted no time in casting a diagnostic healing spell of some kind. When the healer's eyes grew comically round, Joe only rolled his own in annoyed understanding. "Yeah, my Mana Channels are all messed up, but my body is in pristine condition-"

"Yeah, if you were a kangaroo rat!" The healer pulled a skin of water off his own belt, unscrewing the top and jamming it into Joe's mouth even as he yanked open his bag and started pulling out what looked like modern IV equipment. "Why are you looking at me like that? Everyone knows a kangaroo rat is the animal that needs the least amount of water to survive. They're the cactus of animals, and I'm pretty sure you aren't one. *Are* you?"

"I'm... not a kangaroo rat." Joe managed to sputter out, along with half a mouthful of water as the healer squeezed on the bag and forced more down his throat. "Stop it!"

"*No!* The only reason you're still functional in the slightest is because of your Characteristics. If you were a normal human, your kidneys would've shriveled into raisins and fallen out by now." The healer looked Joe dead in the eye and directly threatened him. "I know your mother, and if I need to go get her to stand here and glare at you so I can get you rehydrated, I *swear* that I will."

"You...! Why does everyone know my mother and think she's going to come here and reprimand me?" Joe took a deep breath, just about to tell the man to back off again, only to realize the healer had already *sworn* to go bother his mom. If he didn't follow through, that would make the man an oathbreaker, and Joe wouldn't want to put that on someone else because of his own petulance. "Fine, maybe I've been a *little* careless. Generally, I have a skill that keeps me well-hydrated, but it's been broken for a while."

"A *while?*" The healer caught Joe's glare and coughed into his hand, lowering his voice as his tone shifted to being less gruff. "I see. Well, perhaps going forward, you can make sure to be drinking a cup of water every few hours."

"Days?" Joe tried to bargain, only to get an incredulous stare in return.

"Are you trying to *bargain* with me for *your* health? Just drink *water*, dude." Saline vanished into Joe's arm as if his veins were actively sucking on the straw, and a second bag followed before the healer was satisfied even if Joe's body seemingly wasn't.

"What if I just went to respawn every once in a... no? Okay, I'll try to fit it into my schedule." Now that everyone else had calmed down, Joe refused to sit around any longer. "Devoe! Gather the other Ritualists that reached the Master rank in their Ritual Circles skill. It's time to go put together some super-weapons to deal with the Titanic threat. We're going off-world for this one, so I'll give you a little while to get ready."

The Dwarf was absolutely *beaming* with excitement as he rushed off to tell the others the good news, then toss an overnight bag together.

CHAPTER THIRTY-SIX

Adjusting his bright white Ritual Tower robes, Joe fiddled with the Decury Duelist patch on one shoulder as he tried to think of a way to politely turn down the crowd of nearly two dozen people jostling and shifting as they hoisted duffel bags, backpacks, and other travel gear. "Look, everyone, when I told Devoe to go get ready, I only meant for him to bring along the six people who managed to reach Mastery in Ritual Circles-"

He winced as the Experts of Magical Matrices looked at him with open shock, as though he'd announced it was puppy huntin' season. Those who'd been focusing on Ritualistic Forging, humans and Dwarves who shared the common characteristics of being broad shouldered and calloused, merely crossed their arms and glared as if daring him to order them to leave. The Alchemists scoffed, and the very few focused on the *insanely* expensive art of Enchanted Ritual Circles didn't even deign to respond, lost as they were within their own clique's discussion on a fine point of token placement.

At the forefront stood the six Masters, bags packed and ready to move out. Joe let out a grumble as he looked at their nice, tight, focused setup. "Abyss, I'm just saying that it would be better to bring along a group that's easy to manage… it's not a personal attack, Robin."

"But I've calculated that a larger group has the optimal chances of succeeding in the limited time frame you've got before incurring punishments from the Sect, not to mention being instrumental in the defense of, if not the Sect as a whole, this particular mountain peak-" The Expert of Magical Matrices pulled out a notebook with a flourish, slapping one hand on a chart he'd actually drawn up in advance to help make his argument.

Hearing that they might have to make their case just to be able to go along, the crowd quieted down and stared at Joe with a slightly unhinged stare—the distinct expression he only ever saw on people like himself: those who enjoyed magic perhaps just a *little* too much. Eyelid twitching in agitation, the bald man spread his arms and helplessly responded, "It's not that I want to exclude you, it's just that I wasn't planning on bringing two dozen people to my secret workshop on another world. The more people that know-"

"*Ahum* delegation sounds great *Ha-hum*." Devoe violently coughed into his fist, wiggling his eyebrows in an intense manner. "Hey, boss man! Sure would like to *not* have to do all of the heavy lifting on our own, if you're smelling what I'm stepping in."

Puffing out his cheeks, Joe looked to the sky and let loose a slow exhale. "Masters and Experts only! We need to move fast to get there and return in time."

Not a single person left the group, and he grumbled in acknowledgment. He had no way to ensure each of them was being honest about their capabilities without being terribly intrusive. Instead he swept his gaze over the group, and despite himself, began seeing the sense in bringing all of them along.

He couldn't afford to burn out himself or the other Masters just because he felt the need to have only the 'most helpful possible people' working with him. "Everyone brings something to the table, I *guess*. If you don't, I suppose you can still act as a Mana Battery for the rest of us."

"That's the spirit!" Devoe slapped Joe on the shoulder and started directing the others to get into a two by two column. They started walking without hesitation, Joe leading the two dozen black-robed and cowled coven members toward the teleportation pad, feeling surprisingly... intimidating wasn't *exactly* the correct word, but it fit. As they trailed after him with not-quite military precision, all eyes turned to them. Both the Sect disciples and a few elders in the area were watching, as well as the hard-eyed members of the expedition from Vanaheim.

The latter group tensed as the two dozen people closed in on them, only relaxing as Joe shifted to have all of them arrive and get into position on the teleportation pad. For a moment, the Ritualist was a bit overwhelmed as he looked at the massive array of options for locations to be transported, quickly working through the coordinates in relation to the headquarters to figure out where Novusheim fell in the list. "I need someone else to activate the transport; I... would rather not. Select this option-"

Even before he had finished speaking, the world shifted around them, and Joe looked around in confusion at the empty field, just as a pack of monsters noticed them in return. "Who sent us out here without listening to-"

The world shifted again, and Joe felt his gag reflex kick in until his brain informed him that no, he wasn't poisoned, he was just slightly off-balance from the rapid transport across the planet. This time, they were just outside of the city of Novusheim, with dozens of Dwarves staring down at them, weapons at the ready.

"You couldn't have let the fish inside?" Joe shouted up at them, only to get a grim shake of a bearded head in reply. "How many did you shoot down before you left this one alone?"

"Too many," came an echoing voice. "Every last one of them dropped one of those massive stone blocks; we thought it was some bizarre attack! Smashed em' up real good to be on the safe side."

"Well…!" Joe grasped around for something to say, but he could only shake his head and start leading his group away, through the gatehouse and into the spiraling confines of the walls surrounding the Dwarven city. "I suppose I could've maybe let them know it was coming. We can't be the first ones to teleport here though, right?"

"Not a chance," another person answered from somewhere in the line. "I can't believe how quick and easy it was to get here!"

"I remember having to take a bubble from the edge of the city out to the mines back in the day," a Dwarf reminisced, startling a laugh out of Joe as he recalled his early attempts at figuring out transport across the planet. "Faster than running, but all sorts of freaky when you had monsters jumping up and taking a swipe at you."

The stream of black-robed men and women snaked through the walls, quickly arriving into the city proper with the bright white-robed Joe leading them with his head held high. They quickly made their way to the bifrost, forming into a circle around it as though to activate a ritual, instead simply stepping forward in unison so they would all arrive on Midgard together.

Or, at least, that was the *intention*.

In actuality, twenty-four Ritualists shot up the energetic bridge between worlds together, but the man in white rocketed ahead of them like a cork released from a champagne bottle. Jotunheim quickly blurred into the distance behind him as the almost-offended expressions on his fellows' faces faded in the distance. "Ha! They looked so *betrayed* that I can move so much faster on this than they do. I hope—ah, feces. I was hoping to point out the floating notebook and drum up some rumors about it."

When he arrived on Midgard, inhibitor gear in place, Joe finally started to realize the downside of such rapid movement. "I've got what? Two, maybe three hours to kill while they finish just *getting* here? Bah. Okay, let's see… should I quickly build a shrine? That wouldn't be the worst idea, oh, especially since a bunch of them are probably over the Mortal Limit and likely don't have anything to help them stay under it."

The other option was to simply walk into Ardania, but that would take anywhere from thirty minutes to an hour, depending on the group, especially if they were having trouble controlling themselves. "Not to mention, if we marched in there looking as threatening as we do—however unintentionally—we might accidentally cause a misunderstanding. Might be for the best not to accidentally antagonize the kingdom."

Even on Jotunheim, anyone who didn't know them on sight had been slowly reaching for weapons. With that thought as the linchpin, Joe quickly put together the casual ritual circle the creation of a shrine required, building it just off the beaten path leading to this world's entrypoint of the bifrost. Once it was completed, Joe still had plenty of time, though his Characteristics had taken a couple of hits through the process of starting and stopping his mana. He took a few deep breaths to try and turn his mind from his impending explosion and dropped his hand onto the altar.

"Hope you're doing well up there, big guy. I've said this before, but, no hard feelings on my end. If you're moping around Asgard beating yourself up, I'm going to figure out a way to punch you in the face the next time I see you." His words were spoken lightly, and he hoped the friendly intent would reach his faction leader. "Mmm... now that I think about it, if you get a cold read of what I say, just a message, that might come off as more prickly than intended."

His irises dilated and shone with golden coloration as a sliver of the immense karmic bond tying him to Tatum gently tore off of the column, swirling around the altar, then coming to rest on top and manifesting a small object.

Due to your Extended Family relationship, chosen status with Occulta-tum, and having gone an extended time without requesting any boon large or small, you have been granted an item!

Item gained: Deific Ritual Orb (Bound) (Growth). This exotic weapon is one piece of a set of weapons usable by Ritualists only. While it can be bound to anyone at any level, it is a Sage-rank weapon and therefore the immense strain it produces makes it unusable for anyone without enough mental power to control it. Requirements for use:

1 Sage-rank Ritualist Class skill OR

5 Grandmaster-rank Ritualist Core Skills OR

3 Grandmaster-rank Ritualist Core skills, 1 Master-rank Exotic Weapon skill specific to Ritual Orbs, and 1 Master-rank skill which passively supports the Exotic Weapon skill.

Binding this weapon to yourself early will allow it to grow over time based on your experiences, even if you are unable to actively use it in combat.

"Celestial *feces*, Tatum!" Joe wrapped his hand around the ball, frowning in consternation as he gripped it with both hands and started lifting. It didn't budge. Glancing around, the Ritualist winced as he deactivated his inhibitor gear, straining against the weight of the orb as warning messages began popping up in his vision. Legs shaking, he barely managed to get the orb fractionally off the surface, then stored it in his codpiece—finding just enough room to fit it in alongside the enormous chunk of metal that was the capsule he *probably* should have left in his house.

"Is *this* why you haven't spoken to me in the last year? You were saving up or something? Also… I saw how much energy it took to manifest this; why didn't that scrub away more of the debt between us? I wonder-" The Ritualist interrupted himself by chuckling softly, knowing his next words weren't going to be appreciated by the far-distant deity. "I wonder if I could hand that off to someone and have them break it down to make a template, so I can make a full set in the future."

Immediately he felt a shift in his codpiece, as if something were frantically rolling around and trying to escape, and hastily added, "But I never would! This is way too awesome to ever give up for any reason!"

The sensation came to a swift end, and he heaved a sigh of relief when he realized important objects weren't about to be crushed by the monstrously heavy orb.

A soft crackle of thunder pulled his attention into the distance, where a person had appeared in the air and was slowly drifting to the platform at the base of the bifrost. Dozens more arrived moments later, each of them jogging toward him a bit *too* enthusiastically. The trees in the distance danced back and forth as the wind of their movement struck, and each of them froze in place as they received a message from the system.

Cupping his hands, Joe shouted over, "First time back on Midgard after getting past the Mortal Limit?"

"First time here, ever!" one of the Dwarves boomed back, his deep voice rebounding off the dirt and sending a spray of gravel flying as if he'd launched a cannonball into the at an angle. "I'll try not to break it. Can't make any promises. Abyss, this place is... fragile. No wonder humans are so dainty when they first come up a world or two. It's like walking on a giant ball of cotton candy."

"Right this way, let's try not to cause issues for the locals." Joe directed the large group toward him, and they tiptoed over with exaggerated motions as if playing a game—but all of them knew the consequences for 'losing' were *extremely* real. As each of them stepped up, the white-robed Ritualist quickly taught them how to select the correct destination, and they vanished one after another.

When it was just him, Joe paused for a moment to contemplate the differences between the shrine and his own teleportation pad design. "I should figure out how to let people move individually like this does. Right now, everyone standing on it goes together, but I bet most people would prefer *not* to be chucked around the world if they don't want to go there."

In the next moment, Joe was in the intricate temple connected to the Grand Pathfinder's Hall. A glance around showed that the trees and miniature plant life growing along the stream cutting through the room had become more robust. The flames in the sconces of the wall were brighter, illuminating a greater area even as the remaining shadows deepened—always connecting back to Tatum's altar in the center of the pantheon's setup. The juggernauts standing around the room hadn't moved, but Joe still felt a subtle tension leave the air once he appeared in the midst of the large coven.

"Everyone follow me? You should be fine to move normally while in the building, but slow and steady once we're outside." While he could have taken them through the secret tunnel under the creek, Joe had specific reasoning for making their presence known to the city.

The doors swung open on well-oiled hinges, and any excess movements were carefully curated as the group stepped out into the open after Joe. Each pair moved in lockstep, forming a sinister-appearing procession as they streamed out of the temple and swept around to the entrance of the Grand Pathfinder's Hall. Few of the coven had seen the egg shape of the Pathfinder's Hall previously, and now that it had been upgraded, Joe was *certain* none of the others had laid eyes on this wonder.

The massive archway was filled with the depths of space, the edges swirling with a soft purple light where the stone and magic met. Joe hadn't realized exactly how late it was getting, but the twilight only accentuated the brilliance emanating from the lighthouse positioned at the crest of the arch. The coven stood taller, eyes shining with delight as they realized that *this* Legendary edifice was their actual destination, not simply a marker on their route.

Only one... *small* issue impeded their excitement.

"Groups of six at a time at most! Twenty-five of you creepy cultists? That's gonna be a... a hundred gold each." The disinterested voice of the ticket taker in the small kiosk raised with concern as not a single one of their number slowed in the slightest. "Hey! *Hey*! We're closed! You can't just-"

"Did they not fire you the *last* time I was here?" Joe easily recognized the person lounging in the kiosk, her hand reaching for a button built into the bottom of her desk. "Please step out of the structure. I'm going to demolish it."

The wide-eyed malcontent nearly tripped over her own feet as she got out of the kiosk, just in time to avoid Joe grabbing the velvet rope hanging across the path and swinging it with enough force that it smashed the single-person structure in half. "Listen, if you're going to continue working here, I'd recommend standing while on duty. This is at *least* the third time you've caused problems for me, and now it's just getting embarrassing. First, you tried to keep me out when I am the sole owner of this place. Then you called the guards on Boris, which was terribly embarrassing, and this time? Well, to be fair, this time you're just watching an influencer on your crystal instead of doing your job, but…"

He tossed his hands in the air in frustration, not certain how else he could vocalize his annoyance. "You were planning on charging us a hundred gold each? There's no way that's what the city is charging for access."

"See what *you* know. Look, bub, it's *my* job to earn as much money for the Sect as I can. It's the job of people coming here to pay as little as *they* can. It's not my fault if *I'm* better at my job than they are at theirs!" Joe was flabbergasted at this simplistic view, and he could only wonder if that was the policy of the bureaucrats or this individual's personal style. She was glaring at him, a sneer pulling at her lips as she balled her fists as though getting ready to take a swing at him.

He tried again. "That's not what our Sect is all about. Our core mission is to build-"

Joe felt an odd pressure seeping out of him, filling the air for a fraction of a heartbeat before seemingly seeping into the woman glaring at him. Her eyes dilated slightly, and the unpleasant expression on her face shifted into a proper sneer of disdain. "Yeah, well, I'm an *outer* disciple anyway, so who cares about the 'core mission'? Just because you're someone important, you think you are in charge of *me*?"

"First Elder, if I may…" Devoe spoke in a surprisingly professional tone. "Unless you're about to toss her out of the Sect, I'd prefer if we could just move forward. Some people, well, you just can't reason with some people."

"Find somewhere else to work," Joe finally decided to put

his foot down while moving past the furious staffer. "This is *my* building, and I get to say who gets in or not. Perhaps I'll have to set up some more intense rules going forward that other people can't get around."

"Make it free, see if I care," she hissed at his back, the strange tension between them increasing in intensity. "You won't let me be here? Fine! I'll just set up on the road. Public property. Sure it's free to get in, but it'll still cost to get past *me*. I've already trained everyone to hand their coins over; they won't think twice about it! Find another job? Where else can I earn thousands of gold a day? Uh, for the-"

"Gotcha." Joe rounded on her, his eyes blazing with right-eous anger as he realized his previous impressions of her hadn't been even close to bad enough. "You've been overcharging people and pocketing the difference? Even if you were the *wife* of one of the bureaucrats running this place, they'd toss you out for not giving them their cut. You're out of the Sect, effective immediately. You're banished from all Sect territory, and unless you pay back the total amount of money you've embezzled, you'll be detained or attacked on sight."

A token hanging at her waist popped and fizzled, and a large 'X' appeared in the air, crossing over her shoulders and abdomen like a multipoint seat belt. In the next moment, she was whisked away as her right to be in the area was removed. Joe's eyes widened slightly, as he hadn't ever used that function-ality himself—only having had other people try to use it on *him*.

"Handy." He turned back to the others, a slightly guilty expression crossing his face. "Sorry you all had to be a part of that unpleasantness. I think that went sideways like that because of one of my Characteristics, Dark Charisma. It pushes people to more violent tendencies than they'd otherwise-"

"No need to apologize. Even if you were egging her on intentionally, she just admitted to ripping off our Sect for who knows *how* long. As for people getting tossed out? Meh, that's a daily occurrence on Jotunheim," someone piped up, their dismissive tone helping Joe calm down quickly. "Ever since the core mission was established, people have been dropping out of the Sect like flies."

Unsure how he should respond to that, the Reductionist instead looked around, noticing that, even at this late hour, they'd drawn a crowd. Several of the bystanders began clapping and cheering, but he couldn't be certain if they were applauding his removal of the unpleasant scammer or just enthusiastic about seeing the 'Dread Ritualist' back in town. Taking a deep breath, he attempted to speak with as deep and eerie a voice as possible. "If someone were to inform my coven of my return, I'd be *less* inclined to destroy the city when I leave."

"Do it!"

"Blow me up with it!"

"You should've crushed her skull with your bare hands; I just *know* you can do it!"

"He's so *shiny*!"

Joe turned back to the awaiting portal to hide his impending grin, only to lock eyes with a smirking Devoe. "Don't."

"Abyss, Joe. I didn't know you had *that* kind of reputation down here." The Dwarf's chuckle rolled through the area, low and rumbling. "So *notorious*. Dark and *sultry*."

"Don't." Joe's voice took on a warning tone.

"They should call you 'dark ritual daddy'-" Devoe ignored Joe, speaking *way* too loudly, so the bald man grabbed him by the arm and directly chucked him into the swirling darkness, a massive burst of air pressure sweeping the nearest locals off their feet—much to their delight.

Feeling a blush creeping up his neck, Joe quickly followed after the tumbling Dwarf to escape the frenetic cheers.

CHAPTER THIRTY-SEVEN

As he was swallowed by the archway, Joe's eyes widened with interest as he realized he *felt* the slightest fluctuations of space as he moved a vast distance with a single step. "That was new. Wonder what that'll mean for me down the road."

The interior of the Grand Pathfinder's Hall faded away like an illusion, leaving him in the *truly* powerful portion of the property: the Hidden Grand Ritual Hall. Straightening his robes slightly, Joe struck a strong pose—as though a cape were trailing from his back—and connected with the hall. Moments later, each of the Ritualists appeared in the same instance of the area with him and began examining their surroundings with great interest.

"I'm going to demonstrate how this works to everyone, so please pay attention." Lifting his hands to give them a physical motion to focus on, Joe pulled some of the dark, dust-like ritual design particles into the air, shaping it with a thought and leaving a Novice-rank ritual circle hanging for them to gawk at. "All of this is controllable mentally, so long as you can clearly visualize the portion of the ritual you're attempting to make. If not, you can also have it form more slowly, going over it piece by piece."

He demonstrated as he spoke, a black line following his finger as he moved it around, like iron filings chasing after a powerful magnet. "Take a few moments and get comfortable with this. The goal is to create the outline of a ritual, then fill in the interior with... well, we'll be using aspects, but you'd all need to be using your components or whatever else is necessary. Make these hollow, and you don't need to worry so much about placement as you do simply filling the ritual and creating it *exactly* as it's supposed to be."

"Now, as a warning, while this will allow you to create rituals a rank more powerful than you should be able—since you're essentially using a cast instead of specifically and carefully crafting the design—you won't get the same sort of benefits you would for making the full version. What would otherwise be a Master rank becomes only a Pseudo-Master." Joe focused on the space around him, and eight enormous circles burst into being in the open void behind him, spiraling around impressively but ultimately uselessly.

They didn't have any actual equations or syntax placed within them, only nifty-looking runes and unintelligible but mystical-seeming symbols. "While you'll still get the same effect, the system won't count it as *your* success for skill gain purposes."

"Like pouring molten aluminum into an anthill instead of just making an intricate sculpture." A quiet mumble passed between two onlookers, the speaker nodding sagely as if explaining a long-held theory.

"Not exactly the comparison *I* would make, but... sure." Joe focused, and the wheeling circles were ripped to shreds and sent away as if blasted into the depths of the cosmos showing behind him. "After everyone can work with this stuff, we'll start working on the actual project. Actually, now that I think about it, deciding *which* rituals we should be making and bringing back to the Sect would make sense. Let's do that first."

Lumpy shapes of black particulate began condensing in

front of each of the gathered Ritualists, their expressions focused as they attempted to recreate their most commonly used circles. Happily, as even the *least* among them was ostensibly an Expert, they grasped the concept swiftly and were soon able to make clear edges, the shapes they intended, and even move and rotate the designs on the fly.

Then the arguments began.

"The Ritual of Heaven's Lance!" One of the Experts was repeatedly slapping a page in his Ritual Combat Manual. "Think about it, during the battle for Novusheim, that Cyclops basically dropped a frozen version of this to destroy the Town Hall. If we need to pick out a single target and *guarantee* that it dies, this is what we should be making!"

"How are you proposing to gather enough sunlight to make it *happen?*" the heated reply came. "We're nowhere near the bifrost, so if we wanted to actually make that diagram come to life, we'd need to first punch a hole in the cloud cover!"

"I'm just saying, all we really need to do is make sure we survive long enough for the Sect to clean up the monster army," another man was stating almost bitterly, clearly done with the argument that had been raging for nearly a quarter of an hour. "Better an unbreakable defense than a glass cannon. There's no guarantee we'd be able to take out a Grandmaster-rank threat with only a *Pseudo*-Master ritual, anyway."

"Well, there's no way *defending* will kill one of those things."

"That's not the *point!*"

Another of them jabbed a finger toward a miniature version of the ritual she wanted to design. "What if we went with something half defense, half offense? Look at the Ritual of Torrent... we can use it as a way to trap whatever steps into it, then actively launch it away with a Master-rank amount of pressurized water. If we aimed it right, it could send one of them flying away for miles, then flood the valleys around our mountains. Even if it doesn't wash the creatures away, I can guarantee we're going to be experiencing intense freezing again. We could trap an entire section of the horde in one go!"

"That's not what the Ritual of Torrent is *for*, can't you read the-"

"Ritual of Slaughter is always a good setup for something like this, when we're going to be in a single location-"

"Ritual of Endless Scythes!" The others quieted down as Devoe held his book up with his hands trembling with excitement. "Picture tens of thousands of spectral blades circling our mountain, carving up anything that isn't supposed to be there!"

Joe took a look at the design, greatly intrigued, only to practically fling himself back in horror as he saw the associated cost. "Beyond the initial creation, that has a cost per *second* for upkeep! I'd estimate that, if we put every last bit of free resources we had into that, it'd last, what, maybe half a minute?"

"Oh. We need to plan as if we don't have an unlimited amount of resources?" Devoe grumbled as he flipped to a different page. Joe's eyes narrowed as he heard a mirrored rustling of parchment from at least fifteen of the others.

"*Ye~es...*" he slowly replied, though his previous statement had already made it clear. "Is that why we had so many people flocking to be part of this? They thought we were going to have an unlimited budget for making these?"

"I mean...?"

"Isn't this Sect business?"

"What're we even paying a contribution point tax *for*, if not to handle situations exactly like this?"

Using a single hand to massage his temples, his other arm tucked across his chest as he looked down in frustration, Joe took a deep breath and decided to implement some ground rules. "We aren't protecting the entire Sect, just *our* peak. In order to get the space originally, I had to agree to handle its defense with my own resources. That means, no. We don't have an unlimited budget, and we can't just expense whatever we make. We'll pick *three*."

Holding up a matching number of fingers, Joe flatly stated, "We don't know how long we have, so we'll make them in whatever order we think is the most important. If we can't all agree on three of them to make, so help me, I'll turn this group around and get us back to Jotunheim *today*."

"Okay, *dad*," someone grumbled from the middle of the group, sending forth a wave of titters that quickly died off as they saw Joe scowling.

Finally, instead of the endless bickering, they began quietly *debating*. Factions began forming, people pairing up to convert others to their cause, and Joe decided to just let them go wild. He knew they needed to hash it out, and if he stepped in too early, it would end with him ramming his choices down their throats instead of creating projects they were excited to make.

Eventually the twenty-four individuals were separated into four groups, but after some quick discussion, the smallest was absorbed by the other three. When four dozen eyes turned to stare at him, Joe knew they'd made their decisions. "Let's hear it. Give me your best pitch, and I'll decide who we start with. *You*. Go first."

The spokesperson for the chosen group leaned forward, her fingers steepled and tapping against each other as though she were a mad scientist about to get her way. "We liked the original idea of a beam weapon but couldn't decide on what exactly to work with. After a bit of searching, we found a more adaptive, *vicious* weapon we can use."

This was one of the Masters Joe had intended to bring, but he began shifting uncomfortably as he started getting serious 'Kirby' vibes from her. *Way* too evil overlord for comfort. Eyes glittering, she turned to the others and shifted her tone to cajoling. "The Ritual of Opposing Elements. Take a look, page seven hundred and fifty-six. When it hits its target, the pure mana beam inverts against whatever it strikes. That means, you hit something frozen? The beam turns to a heat ray. It's a contradiction weapon, and that means it'll be useful against anything we need to use it on."

Joe quickly flipped to the page she'd referenced. "Are you sure about this one? While it'll have good usage as an opposing element, its overall attack power is lower than many of the other options at the same rank."

"If we knew exactly what we'd be fighting, I'd pick something else tailored to that enemy. But this? This'll be useful, no matter what." She stepped back into her group, who showed enough solidarity that Joe could only agree and approve of their choice.

The next person stood forward, sweating a bit as he started to make his case, but he was mumbling so much that Joe had to ask him to restart. The Dwarf took a deep breath, fiddling with some of the dark particulate as he spoke. "Ritual of Stoneheart Compression. Page six-fourteen."

"I'm not sure I follow." Joe tried to politely push for more information as he looked at the diagram. "This is a utility ritual. It compresses stone into a higher density, but... I'm not sure why this would be useful in our upcoming war effort. Are you wanting to make ammo for trebuchets or something?"

"Naw, it's..." the Dwarf looked back at the others pleadingly, but they shook their heads and gestured for him to press on. Taking a deep breath, the bearded Ritualist spoke more firmly. "It's all about the *burrowers*. Things that come from below. Back when I was working in the mines, we had to set up all the way out of town, or it would allow for digging monsters to pop up in the settlement. Thing is, if this World Boss really is bringing along an entire ecosystem o' nasty critters, we need to be able to trust the ground under our own feet. This'll purge air pockets, condense the base, and while it might not make our mountain entirely unassailable, I bet they'd go after a... ya know, *softer* target."

"Huh. That *is* a good way to think about it." Joe rubbed his scalp as he thought, caught somewhere between exasperation and reluctant agreement. "I can see how you managed to convince the others. Yeah, that's... what about the compression issue? While this might make digging monsters less able to get at us, if there's enough time for it to function as it's supposed to, the entire mountain will shrink. All of a sudden, congratulations, we're easier for the rest of the monsters to get at."

"Better a *solid* mountain that's well-defended than a tall one that gets hollowed out without us even noticing." The Dwarf held his ground without crumbling, which Joe supposed was the entire point.

"I like it, but I'm going to have to admit it's not first priority." Joe stated after a few moments of ordering his thoughts. The Dwarf nodded in understanding, stepping back into his group as the white-robed Ritualist's attention turned to the third and final group.

"Ritual of the Eternal Turtle." This time it was again a familiar voice speaking, as Devoe took the lead to be spokesman for his group, likely due to his current relationship with Joe. "With enough mana, we can create overlapping layers of force, which will defend from all sides. They'll still allow our attacks to go out, but when strikes are coming back at us, only individual chunks of the shell will break at a time. With enough time, it'll eventually become nearly impossible to break through, as the layers get plentiful enough to distribute incoming force and share the burden of it. Kind of like scale mail, but writ large."

Joe's brow furrowed as he flipped through his Ritual Combat Manual, not finding what the trainer was talking about. "Where'd you find something like that, Devoe? Also, would it work to cover the entire mountain? Now, when you say 'enough' mana-"

"Yeah… I'd need you to set up a mana collector and distributor just for this bad boy." The Dwarf held up a shimmering ritual diagram, an item which had certainly *not* come out of the standard combat manual. "This was my Master-rank achievement reward for Ritual Circles. Only problem with this is the massive time requirements it'd usually take to power up, but I think we can mitigate that somewhat. Mostly, it's slow to get useful because people need to constantly be sitting down and pouring power into it, but I figure we could get around that if we just start siphoning off the clouds, like you're doing with your transport system."

"Mind if I…?" Joe looked over the ritual diagram, a *dizzying* array of defensive runes, one and all. "Abyss. Look at the size of that mana capacity section. This is absolutely ridiculous, and it'll only get worse if the mountain range keeps growing taller. Actually, on that note, it might pair well with the compression ritual, since that'll give us less area to worry about protecting."

Tapping on the document, Joe decided to go full teacher-mode and pointed out a few more issues. "This requires seven permanent mana-targeting stations around the mountain. If four of them break, all of the mana and such that had crystallized will revert back to free energy. Depending on how long this thing has been running, you could lose *years* of work. Not to mention what would happen with all that collected mana being released at once."

"So, we keep those spots extra safe. Too easy." Devoe nonchalantly shrugged off Joe's concerns. "Easier than dealing with attacks coming from all sides. Oh, right, forgot to mention it'll also make a dome of force that'll block out fliers."

"If you're open to sharing your reward with the rest of us, *I'm* sold on it." Joe handed the diagram back, then turned to face the first group which had spoken. "Right then, priorities! I think we need to go with the most immediately useful ritual first. A good offense is the best defense, as the saying goes."

"Pretty sure *this* defense is the best defense." Devoe grumbled as he tapped on his document once again.

"Hey, I let you all decide on the rituals, but I told you ahead of time that I would pick what order we make 'em." There were no further complaints, so Joe pointed at the now widely grinning group in the center. "The attack ritual first, shields second, utility third. We're going to do our best to keep the monsters away from us by popping them at a distance. If they get close, I want a safe fallback zone we can still attack through. Don't look so down over there; I fully understand how important it is to keep the burrowers out of our mountain, but we'll just have to keep some Stone Mages on standby to give us a heads up."

"Besides, that's just the order we're *creating* the rituals. Once these are all ready to go, we should be able to activate all of them within a few days of each other." He looked around, meeting everyone's eyes before letting his final question fly: "Are we all agreed? Should we begin?"

A murmur of ascent went around the room, reaching a crescendo as the Ritualists who got their project approved to go first excitedly joined in.

Then an unexpected voice joined into the conversation.

"Mind if we help with the setup? Don't often get to work on Master-rank designs down here on Midgard." Big_Mo spoke with an easy smile, though Joe could see the tension in his eyes as he looked around at all the unfamiliar faces. Behind the man was the rest of Joe's coven on this world: Taka, Kirby, Hannah, and Robert all awkwardly grouped together. They were wearing fairly normal street clothes, which made them stand out only because they *weren't* the comfortable casting robes everyone else was set up in.

"You made it! Fantastic." Joe swept across the room, throwing an arm around Big_Mo and waving to the rest of the room. "Coven from Jotunheim, meet coven from Midgard. I figure, at some point, you'll all meet up in the future, so it's best to get acquainted!"

Now that the arguments had ended, the others had started forming into their usual cliques, so Joe took a few moments to introduce each of the Midgard coven to their associated higher-world counterparts.

"Big_Mo is all about enchantments, but last time I was here, he'd really delved deeply into blood focuses. Why don't you Enchanted Ritual Circle pals get to know each other? Hannah! Come meet these delightful people; they just became Masters in Ritual Circles. Oh, all of you, feel free to meet the other groups, too, and I'd love to catch up on what you've all been doing for the last year, but-"

Kirby had immediately gravitated to the other slightly maniacal Ritualist who had suggested the beam ritual, and they were already chatting like old friends. Still, at Joe's words, she paused and shot him a mischievous look. "Oh, we've been *busy*, alright. Once we got the rest of the Sect to be cool with us being around, they started dumping resources in our laps. All of us are Experts in at least *three* of the core Ritualist skills now."

There was a collective sharp inhale from the others in the room, who looked at the newcomers with sudden respect in their previously doubting eyes. Even Joe was shocked, as he knew exactly how difficult achieving the Expert rank was. In some ways, being a triple Expert was more impressive than being a Master in just a single core class skill. "Abyss, that's *amazing*! I'm going to have to ramp up my efforts, or you're all going to give me a run for my money when I try to make Class Sage!"

Seeing as no one here was from Vanaheim, his words didn't elicit quite the same reaction of laughter or excitement, so Joe coughed and turned back to the task at hand. "Now that I've done my hostly duties of grouping people together with others that hold common interests, let's get to it!"

Immediately, the work began.

What followed were multiple days of sweat, circles being formed and collapsed after a Master came along to inspect them and found issues, and countless hands touching the project in various ways. Layer by layer, the runes stacked up, syntax threaded through sympathetic bonds, and the circles were designed and smoothed. The entire time, Joe felt an ever-sharpening internal pinch, knowing it would have been done faster if he were just able to take over and create this project in its entirety.

He found himself often repeating the mantra Grandmaster Pete had impressed on him on Vanaheim. "If I want to go fast, I go alone. If I want to go far, we go *together*."

As the final inscription was finally put in place, Joe snapped aspect jars into position, formed an Ascendant Matrix to bind it, and took a position *not* as the main conductor of the ritual.

Devoe looked at him with concern writ large on his face as Joe swapped out and put him in charge. "What if I muck it up? Something like this doesn't flop with a sad little *pop*. It goes *bang*."

"Easy, buddy. Just don't mess it up. Like you said, too easy. You're a Master now. You've got this." Giving the Dwarf a double thumbs up, Joe settled into his spot and watched with great expectancy. "I'm going to insert the aspects, but other than that, I'm not even going to be donating mana to the project. For all other purposes, pretend I'm not here."

"Alrighty." The Dwarf pulled back his hood, ensuring everyone had a clear view of his face as he barked out orders. "Positions! Take a deep breath, and remember this'll only be as difficult as pulling together a peak Expert-rank ritual. First influx of mana going in... *now*."

CHAPTER THIRTY-EIGHT

"Well, that backfired," Joe quietly lamented, feeling the strain in every inch of his body as he stood next to the completed Pseudo-Master ritual.

Dozens of times over the last few hours, Devoe had accidentally drawn mana from him. Joe had assumed that, with his level of control, he'd be able to avoid getting tapped into for power. But, since the Dwarf was the conductor of the ritual, and Joe was a 'willing participant', his mana reacted without needing to be 'asked' when called upon.

Characteristic: Effective Ability Score
Quad Strength: 405 → 314* (-91)
Dialectic Dexterity: 405 → 302* (-103)
Stoic Constitution: 405 → 321* (-84)
Light Intelligence: 369 → 322* (-47)
Ritualistic Wisdom: 369 → 361* (-8)
Dark Charisma: 369 → 301* (-68)
Karmic Perception: 406 → 300* (-106)
Red Luck: 372 → 318* (-54)

"Would've been better just to access my mana *once* and channel it the entire time they were going. Then it would have only been a single activation instead of the starting and stopping I allowed to happen." Even as he was kicking himself for his failed experiment, the others were genuinely basking in the afterglow of their first successful creation of a Master-rank ritual, pseudo or not.

They had every right to be happy. The project had taken days of coordinated effort, hundreds of corrections and alterations, and a desperate need for patience as people asked *endless* questions of each other. But now it was done and ready to be stored away for use on Jotunheim.

As they gave each other excited hugs, high fives, or devolved into conversations, Joe sucked in a slow breath through his teeth. "Yeah... there's not a *chance* that I'll be able to help with the next part. Frankly, I think it's only the random selection factor of the corruption that's kept my Karmic Perception at three hundred. Literally *any* use of my mana has a one in eight chance to make me explode right now."

Turning to the assembled coven, now a bonded unit of people who'd gone through a shared, dangerous experience, the Reductionist forced his lips into a smile and joined them in celebrating for a few moments. But it was as he saw their bright eyes and excitement that he realized he needed to speak right away, for one simple reason.

They were already pushing to start the next one.

A simple clap of his hands sent a reverberation through the literal space around them, and all eyes turned to rest on the white-robed Ritualist. "Great work everyone, and I can tell that you're all ready to begin on the eternal turtle. Now, the only thing I need from you before you do that is-"

"Why do you keep saying 'you'?" Hannah had known Joe a long time and was rather sensitive to his particular phrasing, so it wasn't all that surprising how she was the first to pick up on his subtext.

"Just getting to that." Joe forced this smile to remain in

place. "I'm about to get sent to respawn for reasons I can't disclose, but essentially, I'm a ticking time bomb, and the timer is about to hit zero."

"You're *cursed?*" Instead of the surprise or concern Joe had been expecting, the bespectacled Ritualist who seemed to be the standout leader of the Enchanted Ritual Circles group looked at him with her glasses perfectly positioned to reflect light. The glare off of the lenses added a maniacal cast to her face as a creepy grin slowly bloomed. "We've been looking for someone who can help us figure out how to break curses people have on them. Until now, it's only been rumors or confirmed anecdotes from higher worlds!"

"Not a curse!" Joe swiftly spoke with a rising tone, trying to cut off any further comments or guesses. "As I was saying, I'll be gone for the next day or so, and when I get back, I expect to see the design ready to be filled out! Now, if everyone will exit the building in an orderly manner, give me five minutes, then come back in and get to work... that would be delightful."

"Have a nice break, Joe." Big_Mo clapped Joe on the shoulder, then vanished from the space like a soap bubble popping as he chose to exit. One after another, the others vanished as well, until it was only Hannah and Joe remaining. She cocked her head to the side, observing him for a long moment... but when he couldn't find anything to say, she vanished as well.

Somatic Ritual Casting flared to life as Joe generated Rituals of Glimmering just for fun. As he made them, he pushed forward and sent them flying away like comets soaring through the darkness. One after another, the purple motes of light flew away, zooming on and on without end, or perhaps simply leaving a trail in the air, which hung there after they hit the far edges of the building. With each usage of his power, Joe flinched.

"Seriously, it's the not knowing when I'm going to detonate that's the worst-"

Dialectic Dexterity has fallen to 299!
Tribulation of the Monarch has inflicted backlash!

Your title 'Monarch of Mana' has activated!

Joe's body went stiff as an immense amount of mana flared through him, his body superheating and glowing like the sun before detonating in a supernova sphere.

You have died! Calculating... You have lost 8,400 experience!

You are now a level 29 Ritualist.

Time until respawn: 12 hours.

Don't worry, sweet... sweet Joe... you'll lose less experience upon your next death.

Skill increase: Mental Manipulation Resistance (Journeyman III → Journeyman IV).

Blinking in the light which was suddenly around him—an intense, fluorescent glow—Joe allowed himself a disgusted shiver at the sibilant words he was certain the skill had whispered into his mind as he died. "Welp, thanks, I hate it. Now it's getting to the point where the skill can talk to me? Or maybe it always has, and now I'm just able to hear it because it's reached a high enough level?"

Br~rrink!

In the next moment, the Ritualist was delighted to see something he hadn't in years at this point: a CSV file! When opened, it turned into a full-blown spreadsheet. From the moment of his death, a new line had appeared every few moments, a soft ringing chime signaling the values as they were inserted and concatenated.

"Oh! Sweet file system, how I've missed you! What's this now? Teleportation pad deployed. Teleportation pad designed. Designed... goes on like that for a while. Summoning complete?" Joe's eyes went wide as he remembered having set up Big Brother's Notification Service, and he let out a deep laugh of delight. "Fantastic! I get to let Master Darling know this ritual works as intended. I have no idea if it'd be useful to anyone else... no, I'm sure at least a few of my coven from Midgard would get use out of it. Hopefully not often, but I wasn't planning to use it, either. Ha! I bet that freaked someone out when it suddenly started glowing and activated all on its own."

Just then, Joe realized there was a possible secondary use for this ritual. "Ooh, I suppose I could have someone keep an eye on the ritual, and they could use that to know I died. Probably useful for scouting or even if it's just that someone's looking for me. I just need to make sure only *trusted* people get access to this, otherwise my enemies would know when my important projects are undefended."

For a little while, Joe just watched as the data streamed into the file, neat little printed rows detailing rituals being completed, the timestamps associated with them, as well as the mana and component cost. Far to the right, in a section that was currently untouched, a graph appeared—the first non-magical bit of analytic data Joe had seen in far too long. "Mana in, mana out. Resources in, and out. Wow, not many aspects remain. How is it still functioning?"

Truly, he shouldn't be surprised, as he hadn't given his little headquarters much time to build up assets. While the graph showing mana had slowly ramped up over time, as it endlessly pulled power from the turbulent clouds of mana on Jotunheim, the aspects graph was nearly a perfect inverse. He'd given it full Natural Aspect Jars to work with, and while they automatically refilled slowly over time, there was no way for them to keep up with the demand. "Going to need to get collectin' garbage sooner rather than later. Wonder if Jake has any barrels of toxic sludge he'd like me to get rid of for him?"

It felt fairly absurd that watching paperwork fill itself out could keep his attention so well, but... it had been so long since he'd delved into the mundane that it had truly gained some charm. Even so, there was only so much time he was willing to spend on something like this, and soon Joe turned to the messages that had been piling up and waiting for his attention. "Let's see, spam? ...Why? Why would someone go out of their way to figure out how to send out mass ads in a magical world?"

Finally, he got through the annoyances in his backlog of

messages, having trimmed it down to only the things that were actually important. "Message from Teddy, asking me politely to come and pick up my cheese. Shoot, that was more than six months ago. Follow up message, less polite. This one was from last week, a *demand* letter? Come on, Teddy. How much cheese could you realistically have waiting for me?"

Selecting 'all from Teddy containing the word cheese', Joe deleted the group and moved on to the next from the leader of the Golden Greens Guild.

The follow-ups were various comments about how they were using the land in his duchy, including various production reports, logistics, updates about what they were constructing on the land, and details of the loose alliances with the neighboring communities. She profusely thanked him for sending someone to handle the trade routes and specifically pointed out that they were now producing nearly one one-hundredth of all of the food being consumed by Ardania—an absolutely massive amount, and increasing by the day as they expanded their farmland.

Joe was suitably impressed by the time he moved on to letters from Poppy, who was taking the time to give his own thoughts on the duchy, especially the security concerns, though the Ritualist almost fell off his beanbag when he saw the final letter: an invitation to the Duelist's upcoming wedding. Before doing anything else, the Ritualist accessed his email options and wrote an extensive letter to his mother, requesting that she put together an elaborate gift for the Duelist on his behalf.

As he reached for the 'send' button, he found his hands frozen in position over his keyboard. Going back to the body of the message, he quickly typed out a much more in-depth message, murmuring the last few lines as he finished the extensive letter. "That's everything I can think of that has happened since the last time I saw you. I'll be on Midgard for the next week or so. If you're free and done with your honeymoon—wait, no, that was a year ago. I can't imagine they've been on vacation that whole time. Delete that. Instead… please do stop by the City of Towny McTownface if you have some free time. I'd love to see you, and I promise to visit more often!"

After hitting send, he leaned back on his overstuffed beanbag chair and let out a long, drawn-out sigh of relief. "Well, that's everything. Maybe I'll take a nap?"

By the time the full twelve hours necessary for his respawn had elapsed, Joe had been walking back and forth in the small space like a caged tiger for *way* too long. As soon as a shimmering portal spiraled out of the ground and shimmered into existence in front of him, he was diving through headfirst...

...only to come out on the other side walking along casually as if he didn't have a care in the world. The entrance to this plane of existence vanished behind him, and the Ritualist grumbled, "Someday, I'm going to figure out how that works and *fall* out. No one ever expects someone to land on their face after coming back to life, so maybe they'll just think I figured out a new form of instant travel."

Directly behind him was Tatum's shrine in the Grand Temple attached to the Grand Pathfinder's Hall. More out of curiosity than true greed, he reached over and placed his palm flat on the surprisingly warm stone surface, only getting the barest sense of someone chuckling at him in the distance instead of another divine weapon.

"*Tsk.* Cheap." Joe snorted as he stepped away, only to find himself crashing into the far wall of the temple with a resounding *kaboom*. For a moment, he glared at the distant pantheon setup, thinking he'd taken a smite to the face for his flippancy, only to realize that he was once again working with over four hundred points in most of his body Characteristics while on *Midgard*.

There was none of the massive suppressing energy pushing against him like he would find on Jotunheim, which made his movements feel normal. On this planet, he was figuratively in a frictionless environment with rockets strapped to every last joint in his body.

"Ah, that was my own fault. Right, I took my inhibitor gear

off while I was in the Grand Ritual Hall." He looked at where he'd impacted, seeing a fine lattice of breakpoints in the surface of the stone, but nothing too deep. "Good thing Legendary buildings can take a beating. Still... don't want to put my inhibitor gear on if I'm only going from door to door."

Connecting to the temple, he felt it respond with slightly sullen acceptance as he opened the passageway in the floor. Joe slipped down and walked along the hallway, aiming to get pulled into the Grand Ritual Hall. "Hey, it's not like I meant to hurt you. Don't grumble at me."

One of the steps he was walking down dipped a few inches, causing him to stumble slightly, though the random retry of his Dexterity kicked in, and Joe found himself with his foot hovering above the suddenly lower step—still able to perfectly recall falling on his face. "Wow, that's... trippy."

The tunnel he was in convulsed slightly, as if his words had done more damage to the structure than bodily flying into the wall had.

"Alright, I'm sorry! Didn't mean to smash into you. Friends still?" With a spring in his step, the Ritualist pressed onward, only to find yet another difference between the Artifact and now *Legendary* rank of this building.

Instead of the tunnel opening up into a room, there was simply a smaller version of the deep space portal spinning ever so slightly at the end of the path. He plunged through it without hesitation, popping into existence among his fellow coven members and causing a few of them to leap away, cursing as they spilled their drinks.

"Oh? Celebrating, are we? Well, don't let *me* stop you!" Joe glanced at the dark particulate in the distance, pleased to find it had been shaped into a new full-blown completed ritual diagram. Reaching into his storage ring, he joined the celebration in his own way, pulling out a fistful of cores that he pretended to chomp into as he absorbed them. "*Nom.*"

"You're back!" Devoe rushed over, cheeks flushed with success under his bushy beard. "We did it in a *day*, Joe! Sure we had a system-gifted blueprint to work off of, but the fact that we've been able to get our act together this quick? Nothing less than a showcase of *brilliance* by these fine coven...ers? Covenites?"

"I figure it's best to just stick with 'coven members'." Joe spoke around a mouthful of shining gems, his teeth highlighted by the intense glow blazing between the gaps. "Otherwise everyone's words tend to drift to 'cultists', but that's a totally different thing."

"You know I *know* that you aren't actually biting into those," Devoe grumbled even as he took a cautious step away from the bald man. "They detonate if they aren't cut *precisely*, so crushing them with your teeth would just cause your head to explode."

"Yeah," Joe flipped a Common-rank core in the air, using his immense Dexterity to catch it in his mouth as it fell. "But it's still fun to mess with people."

Glancing at his rings, the Ritualist frowned ever so slightly. "Running out of low-ranked cores, though. Gonna need to go on another hunt soon. Hmm. Kind of regretting not spending more time collecting the last time I was here, but who looks at a bunch of coppers rolling around on the ground and thinks 'I should spend a bunch of time picking those out of the grass to get rich', you know?"

"I have no idea. Either who would do that *or* what you're talking about. However, I do know that there are gathering classes focused on extracting cores and valuable parts from monsters. If you're going to go on a big killin' spree and don't want to clean up, just hire a team to follow along behind you. On to the important stuff." The Dwarf waved for Joe to follow him, escorting his teacher over to the diagram. "Mind taking a look and letting us know if you find any flaws?"

Diagram in hand, Joe swiftly made his way around each of the circles, rotating the immense construct in place as he went over it with a critical eye. Careful inspection required hours, but he was more than willing to invest his time in making sure the ritual was as stable as possible.

When he finally finished, he turned to the anxiously waiting Dwarf and offered a huge grin. "Looks like you aren't a Master of Ritual Circles for nothing! If there's something wrong with this, *I* certainly can't find it. Great work."

Now assured that they could move to the next stage, the Ritualists decided as a group to get back to full effort once again, having taken the time Joe was inspecting their work to rest.

Once again, Joe took a position in the Novice-rank circle, directly adjacent to Devoe, and directed the Dwarf to be the conductor of the design. As the process began, this time he made sure not to repeat his mistake: Joe kept a trickle of power flowing into the ritual from start to finish—a *single*, continuous usage of mana.

"Two down, one to go!"

CHAPTER THIRTY-NINE

People came at all hours of the day to admire the view into the depths of the cosmos that the arch of the Grand Pathfinder's Hall provided. During working hours, there was also a near-constant stream of people coming to find previously charted paths to walk on to advance their class, or, now that the option existed, directly swap over to a new one.

When Joe stepped through the boundary and returned to the surface of Midgard, most people didn't give him a second glance. But as a one, then a handful, then dozens of Ritualists in black robes filed out one after another, the sheer uniformity of their appearance caused rumors to begin spreading through the the City of Towney McTownface like wildfire.

"Let's get out of here before people try to get me to use them as a ritual component or something," Joe murmured just loud enough for the group with him to hear, earning a few appreciative-yet-teasing comments. They began their slow, methodical march around the arch, doing their best not to accidentally generate tornadoes or the like, when the Ritualist heard his name being called.

At first he lifted a hand to cover his face, but found himself frozen in place when he recognized the voice. "*Mom?*"

Turning to look at her, Joe realized why he hadn't been able to pick her out of the crowd. The last time he'd seen her had been at a wedding, but before that, she was a simple merchant in training. In short, the clothes she wore were practical, and she was always prepared to move and hustle as needed.

Now? Now she looked every *inch* a noblewoman. Her hair was pinned up with bejeweled combs; the robes wrapped around her were a shimmering cascade of colors... and, to his eyes, a *dictionary's* worth of stitched sigils and mana-infused metallic threads.

Having been stunned into stupor, Joe couldn't react in time before being swept into a hug, even with his inflated Characteristics. He carefully wrapped his arms around her, deciding against being too enthusiastic and accidentally snapping some of her bones. "What in the world are you *wearing?*"

She playfully smacked him on the chest, then stepped back and looked him over from head to toe. "You're wearing new clothes, too! As in, I can tell you've changed them in the last day or so. Looks like both of us are getting some new fashion habits."

"*Mo~om,*" Joe groaned softly as he let his head fall back so he could stare up at the bright morning sky. "You've clearly been hanging out with Minya for too long. Still, it's good to see you, but-"

"You can take *five* minutes and have a conversation with me." She wrapped her arm around his, and waved a hand to shoo off the rest of the coven members staring at her. "Well? Go on! What are you, little ducklings that can't waddle your way home on your own?"

Ignoring her taunts, the group looked at Joe—who nodded at them solemnly—before turning and leaving. When he looked back at his mother, she was studying him with calculating eyes. "Interesting... it seems you've entered a new phase in your life, if you have such a large group of people hanging on your every word like that. I'm happy for you. I always felt you were taking on too much, and I'm glad to see that you're finally starting to share your burdens with others."

"Coffee?" Joe offered after a few moments of struggling to find a way to respond to her far-too-perceptive comments. "We can sit and chat?"

"As long as you aren't buying it from any of these stalls." Brenda turned and glared at the rickety buildings, thrown-together kiosks, and far-too-corporate setup which rounded out the rest of the downtown area. "It makes my *profession* hurt to be standing here looking at these."

"Pretty sure Mate would go on strike if I tried to buy subpar coffee." Pulling two small but comfortable chairs out of his ring, Joe set them facing each other, along with a short table he quickly had cups placed on. As his Elemental summoned itself, it glanced at Brenda with its tiny bean eyes and let out a happy squeal, as if a tea kettle had just reached the perfect temperature. "She's happy to see you, too, Buddy. What's your best blend?"

A fragrant aroma filled the air as a swirl of coffee with just a *hint* of cream filled the large mugs to the brim. Then Mate poured itself out of its usual home and trickled up Brenda's arm, swirling around her wrist and palm for a few moments. It didn't escape Joe's notice that the elemental had tried to go farther, but was prevented—bringing his attention back to the ridiculously enchanted robe his mother was wearing.

"Want to tell me about your getup? It looks... heavy." Leaning forward, the Ritualist scooped Mate back into his mug, gently patting it on the head before clipping the Ebonsteel container onto his belt. "Unless I miss my guess, you're wearing the magical equivalent of about a foot of tank armor? Even has some massive magic resistance or a barrier of some kind on top of all the rest of it, going by how Mate kept getting pushed back."

"Of course *that's* what caught your eye about the outfit. The magic. Never change, my boy." Brenda laughed as she flicked a sleeve, then matter of factly explained, "This is Profession gear, in the same way you're wearing Class-specific gear. I've decided to go all-in on being a merchant, and as you might imagine, that leaves me rather lacking in the combat department. Luckily, Minya had this laying around."

As she pretended to throw a punch at Joe, Brenda's hand suddenly slowed midair as she strained against a sudden restriction. "As you can see, I couldn't swing a dull butter knife or put together the simplest combat spell, but it's the best possible non-combatant gear available. I'm able to walk anywhere on Midgard confidently, knowing that there's practically nothing that can leave so much as a *bruise* on me."

"That's... *wonderful*." A wave of tension flowed off his shoulders as Joe settled into his seat. "My mother, safe and indestructible. Love hearing that. Have you been doing much traveling, then?"

She bobbed her head, taking a long drink of coffee in lieu of answering. "Oh my, that's *quite* good. If you could get your little buddy there producing this quality of coffee nonstop, you could have quite the lucrative side business."

Before he could get too excited and start telling his mother about his world-spanning coffee delivery plans, she answered his question. "As a matter of fact, I've been doing more walking in the last year than probably my entire life to this point. First, I want to say that one of the main reasons I came here and waited a few days in hopes of catching you was to thank you. I'm not sure if you realize exactly how much you've done for my profession, but being the exclusive merchant for an entire duchy has been rather... whelming."

Joe glanced at her with narrow eyes. "Is that the proper term? Not overwhelming, not underwhelming? Is 'whelming' a word on its own?"

"Mmhmm," she informed him as she finished off her coffee, setting the mug down with a decisive *clink*. "It's been just enough to handle on my own, keeping me *quite* busy, but not overmuch. I'm sure as it grows more, I'll need to start contracting out, but even that will be beneficial. Thus far, the deals have been almost entirely food related, but all sorts of gatherers are on their way to the frontier. I'm certain someone will be finding some rich deposits of ores in the near future, or perhaps gemstones, and I'll make sure it is properly licensed and taxed on your behalf. Which brings me to the main *issue* of my visit…"

She stood and shifted her shoulders, grabbing at something and swinging it around. Only as Brenda **thumped** a massive rucksack onto the ground did it become visible to Joe, and his jaw dropped slightly at the sheer size of it. "How were you…? That's taller than you are! Were you sitting on it?"

"Me first." Her left eyebrow twitched, a tick he hadn't realized he'd gotten from her. "What in the world were you thinking when you requested that all of your personal tax revenue be converted to *cheese*? Do you know what that looks like after a full year of a duchy-sized piece of land producing goods? *Especially* when you don't have a tax burden to pass on to the kingdom yet?"

"I'm guessing… a very large sack of cheese?" Joe raised his own eyebrow questioningly. "Roughly a mother and a half in height?"

"Goat cheese. Cow. Aged rounds. Spiced curds. Smoked blocks. Quarter barrel slices. An experimental blue cheese with a mold I think *might* be slightly self-aware." Brenda's glare intensified even as she ramped up her blinking per second to a concerning level. "You didn't leave them anywhere to forward your cheese. It was starting to spill out and onto the ground before I intervened. An entire warehouse, full to bursting with a year's worth of cheese they produced or traded for. Congratulations, you've single-handedly destabilized the dairy market of Midgard."

New title offered: The Duke of Cheese. Aren't you the cheesy-

"Refuse. I'll let that one be unofficial," Joe muttered without reading over the details; he could feel that it was more of an insult than a benefit. "Then this bag is…?"

"It's a cheese delivery." She took a deep, stabilizing breath. "This is a merchant spatial bag, specialized for raw materials only. It has an absolutely *massive* internal capacity and can only hold goods collected by people with gathering professions. Herbs but not pills, raw ingredients such as cheese but not meals, ores but not ingots. It's also expensive in a way I cannot quite properly explain and essentially indestructible. As a favor to you, I will let you *borrow* my bag. I expect it to come back *shortly*."

Reaching out, Joe opened the rucksack and looked in, jaw dropping slightly at the dense aroma wafting out intensely enough to make his robes flutter. Looking into the canvas folds, he found that the interior space was surprisingly well-lit, and shifting his hand back and forth moved the contents as though it were on a three-dimensional conveyor belt. "That's a lot of-"

"If you make a joke right now... I *swear* I'll-" Brenda cut off suddenly as Joe snapped the bag closed and swept her into a hug. "Oh, get off, it's not that big of a deal."

"You don't know how wrong you are." He let her go, stepping up to the bag and swinging it over his shoulders. Joe grunted with effort as he lifted the sack, limited as he currently was by the restrictions on Midgard, and looked at his mother questioningly.

"My robe handles most of the weight for me." She gestured at the now-invisible bag. "What's with the surprise? You're carrying around a warehouse worth of cheese, and there's only a ten percent weight reduction. The restrictions on it are what allow it to become powerful, just like my robes."

"I guess I should be glad it's not ores, then." Joe shifted back and forth until the bag got comfortable. "Teddy's doing okay? Also, how do I pay you for this? I should've had to go over and pick this up myself-"

"Nonsense." All traces of ire left her face, a slow grin creeping across her lips to replace her previous disgruntlement. "Do you have any idea how profitable a Ducal trade route is? How rare it is for *one* individual to be able to broker every deal?

I don't just mean in coin. Every sale, every agreement, earns me more experience for my class and profession than I could get in a day's work at Minya's shop. There's scores of deals every *hour*, Joe. We're already providing nearly a hundredth of the food needs of the capital city, and I'm fairly certain we can get that to one ninetieth by the end of the year. At this rate, I'll be a Grandmaster with maxed out professions and supporting professions in no time flat."

"I'm… I'm taking over a planet," Joe stammered out, trying to show his own achievements in the face of his mother's overwhelming success.

"Keep your planets, I'm happy with steady customers and healthy margins. For now. Let me know when you want to run the logistics of your world." Brenda and Joe both stared at each other for a long moment, but she was the first to crack, laughing uproariously as she bent over. "You don't have to look *that* shocked! Where do you think you got *your* ambition from?"

"I got it all on my own," Joe shot back with his nose held in the air. "Wasn't like you were gonna share yours!"

"Ahh… it's good to see you. Make sure to come back soon and visit, and not *only* because you're bringing me back my bag. But yes, do that first, *then* visit for fun." She pulled him into one last hug then motioned for him to get on his way. "Better hurry; all of your friends have probably left the planet already."

"No rush. I'll still get there before them." With a confident grin, he activated Beam to Bifrost and allowed the mana to begin channeling into a packet of power around him. "You see, I've got this spell in my back pocket…"

"You're all about the magic, sometimes to your detriment." Brenda shook her head, though there was still a fond smile on her face. "Sometimes you need to look past that, and recognize that a pretty outfit is sometimes *just* a pretty outfit."

"But… *do* I?" Joe's irises focused down, and for a moment, he could make out the individual sigils in the threads of her robe, as mana sparked along them like energy passing through neurons. "There's so *much* to try, to learn, to experience. Magic is... *wonderful*."

"Of course you do! How else am I ever going to get grand-children?" His mother's question caught him off guard, so much so that Joe could only blink in surprise as his mouth worked like a fish yanked on to dry land. Before he could formulate a proper response, his spell completed, and he was whisked away.

"Talk about good timing. Saved by the spell." He let out a slow breath as the world blurred into motion streaks.

As he passed over the world, his Perception allowed him to pick out individual details, though his mind needed a moment to process what he was seeing and categorize it into something to be thought on later or ignored. People fighting monsters, a woman holding up a brightly glowing... *something*... as she shouted to the sky in triumph, absolutely *coated* in the blood of dozens of monsters around her. People taking their first step into caverns, monsters ripping apart a section of forest to build a den of some sort.

Then he was zipping through Ardania proper, the city too small for him to truly make out any individual highlights before reaching the bifrost and launching into orbit. His speed doubled, then doubled again, and for a moment, he was abso-lutely positive that he'd just passed by a large group of black-robed individuals—though happily the bifrost kept them contained within their own energy sphere, and his passing couldn't interfere with theirs.

But what made him pump his fists in excitement was a collection of items just on the other side of the rainbow bridge: fishing nets, bits of fabric, and even a few long spears drifting in pieces through space. Each of them was charred along their edges, tangled up and heavily damaged at the minimum. "No way! People must've started trying to grab the document on their way past!"

As he contemplated the reason for the damaged items, versus his own letter, which appeared perfectly fine at a distance, the Ritualist realized that the difference was likely due to people trying to extend things outside of the beam of energy connecting the worlds. "I just tossed it out; they're trying to hold on and grab it as they move past. No wonder the nets started on fire... *oooh*."

He winced in sympathy as he realized it was possible that people had been yanked out of the bifrost by their actions. "Hope no one got hurt trying to get that. Hey, System, any way I could turn that into an actual... you know, really cool reward if someone manages to snag it? Then I wouldn't feel so bad about my little joke."

Joe didn't receive an answer, which meant he could only assume it was a 'no'. "Ah, well. At least it'll make for a good story if someone does get it. Hey! Maybe they'll come and return it to me, and I can give them something for their efforts. Yeah, that'll make me feel better."

As he landed on Jotunheim, the Ritualist sprang away and rushed at the wall, causing a bit of a stir behind him as he left the Legionnaires patrolling the city wondering if he was an enemy combatant who had just arrived. "No time to explain!"

He hoped that his shout was heard and understood and was certain that at least a few of the people had recognized him. Looking up, Joe swallowed a suddenly dry throat as he realized they'd built the walls quite a bit higher over the last few months. Still... that wasn't about to stop him.

Not with his Quad Strength.

With a grunt of effort, Joe threw himself up and over the wall. In only a moment, he was looking down at the walkway as various Dwarven patrollers tracked him with crossbows and pulled back spears, watching as the pale, robed man pinwheeled through the air above them. Happily, none of them launched their attacks, and Joe started approaching the ground, projectile free. "Now comes the part I was worried about-"

Not only had he managed to clear the first wall, but the second, third, and fourth in a row. He tucked and rolled, getting to his feet and sprinting along the warm surface for a moment, even as he thought about how much this place had changed with the simple accidental ecosystem destruction he'd wrought by releasing the flaming flower seeds so long ago. "If we could just do something about all that cloud cover, I bet we could make spring or even *summer* a permanent feature of this planet."

Once he was certain activating Omnivault wouldn't be yanking mana out of his system, he leaped forward, easily clearing the remaining walls, though the final section had a battlement rising above the rest that nearly caught his ankles as he sailed over it. Then Joe was past it, grinning like a fool, only until he realized the ground was coming at him far too fast.

-88 heath. (Terrain damage.)

Shoving himself out of the shallow pit he'd created, Joe swiped his hands over his robes and kicked up a small dust cloud, then strolled leisurely toward the teleportation pad. With a full Legionnaire salute to the incredulous guards atop the wall, he teleported himself back to his mountain peak.

The Plateau was alive with motion and sound, organized chaos where the vast majority of people were ritualists working on honing their skills. Circles were being formed, pulsing faintly in the air as students faced off while instructors barked corrections at them. A dozen structures were slowly appearing in the distance, most of them being barracks or apartment buildings with direct paths cut to an associated profession workshop. People working on their jumping skills ran through the obstacle courses, struggling to maintain balance and make it through without faltering or dropping to the ground.

People spoke freely, laughter mingling with conversation, rising above the dampened hammer blows Ringing out in the distance. Taking a deep breath of the incredibly fresh air, Joe began a slow meander toward his smithy, contemplating the exact reason why being here felt even better than being in Novusheim. "Everything is more impressive. My peak isn't just a little homestead, it's a nexus for training, experimentation, and purpose. Perhaps there's some benefit to being so close to the cloud cover? Even breathing is... every breath is full of power and *alive*. It's... this place fills something inside me."

Without realizing it, Joe had placed his hands behind his back and was staring into the shifting kaleidoscope of turbulent mana as he moved along, only his dusty visage ruining the sagely aura of a First Elder he was suddenly exuding.

Perhaps it was the satisfaction he had in his current clarity of purpose, maybe it was the adrenaline of the successful creation of each ritual he'd set out to make, possibly it was just how relaxed he felt after finishing everything on Midgard and having a good conversation with his mother. Whatever the reason, he found himself suddenly and overwhelmingly lost deep in thought.

A light trance overtook him as his feet carried him onward, hands moving on their own to begin to create what he'd rushed home to work on.

"What about this place makes it so wonderful? Is it the height? The view? The fact that this is uncontestedly *ours*?" The Ritualist went into the smithy and prepared his aspect hammer, rearing back to begin the process of forging a modified Mana Battery recharge station. Just before his hammer came down, a hint of a frown shifted his entire demeanor.

"But isn't it also true that those who claim ownership also invite loss? Is holding onto a mountain going to become part of our Sect identity? Does a home base that requires so many people to function pull us away from our initial goal of being *wanderers*?" Without realizing it, Joe's words settled into a rhythm, forming an *actual* mantra instead of a repetitive set of words as he distractedly hammered out the first of three pieces needed, the Mana Collector.

It was swiftly completed, and he moved on to the next piece, the Mana Condenser. "Isn't it also true that when someone gathers without holding, they may fill all of their vessels? What buckets do I have that I need filled? My *self* is damaged and needs work. This is my first and currently ever-leaky bucket.

Work? Overflows. Community? That's… slowly filling more often."

The beautiful containment setup was pushed to the side with as much care as if Joe had picked up a stick then had grown tired of it and tossed it away. The mana transfer output soon took shape, even as he allowed his thoughts to rumble along without guidance. "What was it about the mountain that captivated me as soon as I stepped on it? It's giving and keeping nothing from us, yet it grows taller by the day. Its resources are mined, and we live on its surface. Even though we plan to make it better, it's never *required* anything of us."

He hauled all three pieces out of the building, not noticing that the smiths around him had formed into a crowd and were following along as he spoke, their eyes far distant as words continued to roll from his lips. "If I don't claim to own it, but instead simply work to make it better, gather without holding —just enough to fill my vessels, and keep nothing back, allowing any good person to learn from me… what can we accomplish? Can a Wanderer ever truly have a home? Perhaps, if we only grasp it loosely, let go as needed, and be ready to move to the next when it's required of us. Yes… I think that's it."

As he tightened the last bolt, combining all three of the large pieces of equipment into a single one, the Ritualist snapped out of the light trance that had taken over, staring at the slightly modified system he'd put together.

Congratulations! You have created a new item: Mana Transfer Unit. This is a variant of the Mana Battery Recharge Station, formulated during a brush with a dao fragment carried on the wind ahead of an approaching apocalyptic threat. The M.T.U. will work to continuously absorb mana from the surroundings, layering it into a structured form and pushing it outward.

A single unit can be used to power massive enchantments, rituals, or settlements up to the 'Town' size, based on quality of life inscriptions built into the structures. The M.T.U. needs to be manually deactivated once it has been started, as the protective measures of the original design have been stripped away to allow the greatest amount of mana possible to pass through.

Joe was so thrilled with the creation of the new item that he nearly missed a hint embedded in the flavor text.

"Carried on the wind ahead of an... *apocalyptic threat*?" Spinning around, he almost rushed off on his own, only to stumble and lean back as he saw shimmers of gold flickering next to the eyes of dozens of people staring at him. "What's wrong with all of you?"

In the next moment, Devoe was next to him, clamping a hand over Joe's mouth. "Quiet, something you did gave them *Inspiration*. I caught the tail end of that; sounds like you were *almost* quoting some old-school Taoist deep thoughts. Let this play out, and you might have some more Mastery Merits by morning."

Blinking a few times, Joe pulled back and grinned at the Dwarf. "Glad to hear it. Also... nice of you to finally show up. Think we can go ahead and get those rituals set up? Finally? Pretty sure the World Boss army is getting a little too close for comfort, and this peak is still all but undefended."

"Yeah, yeah... you and your speedy bifrost surfin'." Devoe pulled Joe back and away, leaving the Inspired crafters to stare at the Mana Transfer Unit as though it was a relic from a forgotten age. "Some of us still have to *walk* from place to place, ya know?"

"Hey, I've seen a high-level Walking skill that's ten times as fast as my top speed. Just because you have little legs-"

Whack!

The Ritualist laughed through the pain as Devoe chased after him, taking swipes at the taller human whenever he got in range. Joe was hunted until he escaped into the large group of returning coven members, their numbers growing by the minute as word spread that there were a few massive rituals to be set up. The Dwarf finally let up as Joe started talking to the group—though there was a look in his eye that promised they hadn't finished their 'short' conversation.

CHAPTER FORTY

"Option one!" Joe called to the group of Masters on down, the returnees quite tired by their travels going by their weary expressions and rumpled clothes. "We all take a nap, recharge, and get ready for a couple more days of hard work."

Several among the group nodded at that, soft smiles gracing their lips as their eyes fluttered as if they were already halfway into a dream… only for Joe's next words to wake them up better than any shot of espresso could.

"Or… we set up the Ritual of the Eternal Turtle right now and *earn* that nap while our defenses build themselves up over the next few days."

"Yaaa! We can sleep when we're dead!"

"My respawn room has a bed!"

"Can we at least have breakfast so we're fed?"

"Be *quiet*, Ned!"

"I *love* it when people ignore the advice coming from their Constitution characteristic." Joe took a deep breath, even as he started pulling mugs out of his storage ring. "Coffee on me, then we'll turtle up!"

A tired yet determined cheer lifted from the ranks of the

black-robed coven. The most bleary-eyed among them hurried forward with hands outstretched, hands tightening around the grip of their mugs as Mate went from rim to rim, happily caffeinating every last Ritualist who stepped forward.

Joe watched as they all did their best to quickly down their coffee and decided to give them a few minutes to let it kick in. "While you're all getting ready, I'll handle the placement of the ritual plates myself. Actually, they're more like ritual *anchors*, since it's all going to work together to pull the top down and the bottom up. Yeah, I like that. Ritual anchors. We'll meet up over by that thing—it's called a Mana Transfer Unit. Don't worry, you're gonna love it."

Pulling out the central portion of the ritual, Joe handed the slab of specially prepared alloy they'd captured it in and handed it to Devoe. "Careful with that, but perhaps you can work on getting it set up while I drop off the anchors?"

"You're talking *re~eal* fast, Joe. I think ya need to sleep more than the rest of us. Look, I'll give you half an hour, then we're starting without ya." The steely look in the Dwarf's eyes informed Joe that he hadn't been fully forgiven for his jests yet. "I'll just have to assume you're being slow because your *legs* are so *long* that you're always trippin'. Or maybe you fell asleep jumping around the mountain like a jackalope and dropped to your death."

"Short legs, short temper... you're starting to sound like my last girlfriend." Joe laughed as he backflipped over a knife the Dwarf whipped at his chest. "You even throw like she did, so you're not helping your case. *Ah*! Fine, *fine*! Stop throwing knives at me, I'll be right back."

"Oh, I'll stop with the *knives*, alright." A massive hammer appeared in Devoe's hands, and the Dwarf started stalking toward the Ritualist.

Joe 'casually' jogged out of the group, twice as fast as he'd been moving a moment before. He leaned forward the moment he was past them, toes digging into the dirt as he bunched his muscles. "Omnivault."

Though he didn't use any mana, there was still a twinge of pain that echoed through the wrecked channels in his legs. Still, Joe ignored the stinging as he kicked up a cloud of dirt.

Fwooomph.

His ears popped as he breached the sound barrier, reaching the edge of the mountain a second and a half after leaping forward. He touched down, barely able to slow before going directly over the edge, only his laughter echoing back to the group giving them hope that he hadn't just tumbled down the slope. In fact, the only thing that had kept him close enough to the ground to keep from going airborne was a last-minute grab at his Ritual Orb of Strength, the mid-fall shift allowing him to pull his body back enough to slide down the scree *instead* of sailing away until he met the ground with inevitable effect.

"First spot to place this, southwest ridge. It's got good density already, so the compression from the other ritual shouldn't displace this too much. Even if the mountain shrinks, I'm pretty sure this section will remain stable." He quickly approached mediocrity—the proper term for the midpoint of a mountain—and began slowing himself down. "Here we go, neither at the peak nor on the ground, just halfway up and perfectly okay with that."

An Ascendant Matrix sank into the stone, and a moment later, Joe was able to set the ritual anchor over the space, letting go and allowing it to slip into the hole with a perfectly flush movement. The lip was perhaps half a millimeter below the surface of the rock face, leaving it perfectly hidden while also eminently stable. "Uuhgh. That's *satisfying*. On to the next."

The mountain blurred below him as he carefully jumped along its surface, the ground beneath him just streaks of browns, grays, yellows, and other earth tones that mixed together into a muddy stream, thanks to the speed at which he was moving. Each anchor placement went easily, though they cost him a Characteristic point each: a worthy trade, in his opinion. "Five down, two to go."

As he zipped along the mountain, every once in a while

kicking off Ritual Orbs to redirect his momentum or gripping onto boulders to throw himself at a new angle, Joe also inspected the ritual towers that had been set up along the entirety of the mountainside. "Looks like that one is coming along well, but what's that ritual supposed to do? Some kind of... teleportation trap? Even if it sends them away—ooooh, it sends them *up* and away. Relying on terrain damage to take 'em out? Interesting, I wonder how they're planning to power that. Won't have much effect on the Penguins; they can bounce like nobody's business. Maybe they worked out a deal with the neighboring towers or something?"

By the time he placed the seventh ritual anchor in the ground, Joe was really starting to feel the long days of no sleep. Putting his Quad Strength to the test, he pushed himself to scale the mountain in as few jumps as possible, grabbing onto the ledge and pulling himself over with a forward roll that left him sprawled on his back, breathing heavily. "I... *pant*... *love* this world. Might and magic, what more could anyone want?"

Getting to his feet, he trudged over to the group, trying to keep his posture straight and a confident smile on his face. "Ritual anchors are in place! Let's crush this mountain."

His time away had seemed to give Devoe enough space to calm down, but Joe was decidedly surprised to see the Dwarf step aside and let one of the others step into the leading position for the ritual. Glancing at his number two to confirm he knew what he was doing, Joe reluctantly remained quiet as the gathered Ritualists moved to their assigned positions. Soon, power was flowing from hundreds of mana pools, being woven Expertly—*only* Expertly—by the Ritualist directing the entire process. Joe remained in the Novice circle, constantly channeling power to the lady who was standing in his usual spot.

Since the ritual had been formed and created already, and all that was left was to activate it, he'd been expecting this to take, at most, a few minutes. So it was with great annoyance that only two full *hours* later the connection finally broke, and a massive nova of unexpected mana rippled out across the surface of the mountain peak, extending past its edges then dropping sharply as it demarcated the outer edge the barrier would form along as it grew.

"Great work, Nixie." Devoe reached out and shook the hand of the absolutely sweat-drenched Ritualist. She turned to Joe next, an excited gleam in her eye, and he made sure to enthusiastically compliment her Expert handling of the Pseudo-Master ritual.

One of your students has achieved Mastery in Ritual Circles! You have earned a Mastery Merit!

"Congratulations, *Master* Nixie." He shot her a surreptitious wink, keeping his voice down as her cheeks flushed pink with pride.

"Next up, Alchemical Ritual Circles," she proudly declared with a straight face. Joe could only beam at her in excitement—he would love nothing more than to have every last one of the people here join him on Vanaheim and form a massive faction of incredibly talented people under his banner.

"Looking forward to it. Let me know if you'd like some tips, one Master to another." Only then did Joe realize that there was no visible effect from the ritual yet, and he snapped his fingers as he pointed at the antenna-topped machine standing off to the side. "Did you want to start the M.T.U.? I don't mind, but I figured, since you activated the ritual…"

She happily walked over to the machine and threw the only movable object on its surface: a large, double-shafted lever.

Klonk.

Immediately, the clouds corkscrewed at the tip of the antenna, power being drained away as the condenser lit up. After a few long moments of everyone patiently watching, the first beam of energy exited the transfer unit and connected with the oversized plate of alloy that was swirling with a ghostly imprint of the ritual they'd just activated.

"With that, this project is officially complete. Now all that's left is to let it power itself up over the next… forever." Joe looked around for the taciturn Dwarf, who'd initially suggested the Ritual of Stoneheart Compression, jutting his chin upward as their eyes met. "Yours is next. Do you want to run it yourself or pass it off to someone?"

"I'm a Magical Matrices Dwarf myself; let one of the loopy group use it to grind their skills up a bit," came a grumbled reply.

"Loopy group? The Ritualists focused on ritual circles, also known as the *main component* of any ritual?" Joe blinked tiredly as he processed the unexpected offhand remark. "Right... well, I think it's time for us to go take that nap I called out earlier. Yeah, let's do this later."

The crowd broke up, smatters of excited chatter breaking out as the coven split into friend groups that each left to pursue their own interest. Joe watched as at least a quarter of the group left for the edge of the mountain, almost assuredly going down to take a look at the initial stages of the barrier that was forming. After a long moment, he turned toward his house and started making his way there, only to let out a soft groan as he realized he still had work to do before they could activate the next two rituals.

"Both of those are going to need a Mana Transfer Unit, aren't they? Constant power to compress the mountain, and unless I want a conga line of Ritualists to keep the Ritual of Opposing Elements powered up, we'll need one for that as well." With a tired grumble, he made his way over to the smithy, aspect hammer in hand yet held limply at his side.

He pushed the doors of the smithy open and froze in place as his mind struggled to comprehend what he was seeing.

Three new Mana Transfer Units were being constructed inside the smithy, each in a different stage—but the first was all but complete. For some reason, the Dwarf working on it was polishing the underside with a grimy rag, as though he could get its burnished bronze surface to have a higher reflection value. As the bald man closed in, the rag-wielding Dwarf looked up in annoyance, only for his expression to shift to delight in the next moment. "Elder Joe! Surprise!"

"What... *how?*" The bald Ritualist stumbled over his words as he looked around the room in confusion. "Don't get me wrong, I'm happy, but-"

"You *Inspired* us!" The conversation caused most of the work to come to a halt, if the smiths weren't working on a delicate portion of their craft at the moment. Tossing the rag up on his shoulder, the Dwarf stuck out a hand for Joe to shake. "Then you even left the blueprints on the machine for us to use? Do you know how rare it is for someone to freely turn their blueprints open source like that? We just... we wanted to show our appreciation. What you were talking about out there, teaching us at the same time as working on your own project? Gathering without holding, shaping without claiming? It just... it *clicked.*"

"The fact that you then *followed through*, proving those words weren't hollow by leaving the blueprint in our care?" a human spoke up, his head shaking in disbelief. "That really showed us what we should be doing with and for the Sect. When we're here, when we've made the commitment to be a part of this, why would we hold back? *Any* of us?"

"I knew joining was the right choice."

"Learned more in the last year than I did in the last decade under my last Master," another voice chimed in.

"Inspired," Joe repeated with a slow downward incline of his chin. He hadn't meant to be teaching; he'd been swept up in some kind of nearly melancholy trance forced on him by the impending arrival of the World Boss—no doubt due to his overwhelming karma putting him in the right place at the right time. Still, there was no need to bring the mood down.

He had long since learned that, when people were coming to him with emotion, he needed to meet them there and not with facts and reason. That could come later, after the adrenaline had died down some. "Excellent work. You've captured the essence of what I've been teaching. Perfectly. Nailed it."

"*I'm* making nails!" a young voice called from the back of the room, only for an Expert standing nearby to flush with embarrassment and step in front of the Novice wearing the black robes of the First Elder's coven.

"Errr… we're teaching one of the influencers from Midgard how to be someone with useful skills," the Dwarf explained as he rubbed to the back of his neck.

"Fantastic. I'll leave you all to it?" Joe started backing out of the room, only for the grimy rag to be waved at him as the first Dwarf he'd been speaking to looked on with panicked eyes.

"Wait! Do you want this? We weren't sure if you needed more than one, but they're all almost ready."

Joe happily agreed to take all three of the devices, thanking the group profusely as they quickly spun up to full-speed work once more. After giving directions for where they should be delivered, two to the center of the mountainous peak, and the final one to his personal residence, he left the building with a spring in his step that he definitely didn't have when arriving.

"Ooh, you squirrely little nap, you've been avoiding me for days. I'm going to come find you right now. No more escape." The bags under Joe's eyes had bags of their own, and *those* ones were hauling luggage. As soon as the door shut behind him, the Ritualist tipped over onto his bed, dirt and sweat ignored in favor of passing out as quickly as possible.

He was asleep before his body hit the surface of the bed and slept a full, *glorious* two hours.

His body was humming with energy, his mind was sharp, and he bounced out of bed with the energy of someone who forgot they had to work in the morning and was already late. "Let's get the other rituals set up!"

Marching out of his house and toward the central terrace, he felt his bright smile shift into abject horror. "They… they…"

Hundreds of Ritualists were moving in perfect synchronization as mana flowed out of them, over them, and into the central controller of the Ritual of Stoneheart Compression.

Finally, Joe managed to force out, "They started *without me*?"

"Well, good *morning* sunshine!" Devoe called over as he walked along the perimeter of the act of ritual, watching the mana flows with a critical eye. "Figured you needed your beauty sleep but... from what I see, you should probably go back to bed."

"This is your revenge? Couldn't you have just stabbed me in the back instead of keeping me out of the fun?" Joe looked at the Dwarf with sad eyes, only to get a snort of derision in response.

"Stuff it, ya windbag." Devoe snickered evilly, already turned away from his bald mentor. "Can't have you in there sucking up all of the skill experience, not if you want those merits anytime soon. Plus, if you think *this* is bad..."

Joe followed the index finger pointing up, higher and higher, then let out a shocked gasp as he clutched at his chest. "You're activating both of them at the *same time?*"

"Nixie's keeping an eye on that one, but yeah." Devoe turned back with a grin that showed far too many teeth. "Guess there's nothing for you to do now but watch as we get them all powered up and ready to be used."

"How could hundreds of people get together and work on a project without me! Oh, Horatio, this *betrayal!* Now cracks a noble heart. Good night, sweet prince-" Joe dropped to his knees, overacting his distress; though in reality, he felt a surprising amount of happiness at getting the next few hours to work on his own goals.

"Stop that, you're creepin' me out."

"I'll never call you short again, I promise!" Joe swiftly changed tactics. "Just don't keep me out of the circles! I'll... I'll move to the outer ring! I'll-"

"That's enough, I suppose. I'll let it go... this time."

Even before the Dwarf had finished speaking, Joe was on his feet and walking away, waving a hand over his shoulder. "Sounds good!"

His sudden nonchalance caused his fellow Master to grumble, but Joe had already moved on, both physically and mentally.

"I guess... if I've nothing else to do for the next little bit, this might be the perfect time to make a deal with Jake, grab that Ichor, and head to Vanaheim. If I play my cards right, I should be able to come back down and be a part of the upcoming conflict at full power." Mind made up, Joe took a single step toward the teleportation pad in the distance, sun shining bright off his head warmly, as though to affirm his decision.

He took another step, the smile on his face going flat, then one more before it was gone entirely as he realized what was feeling *off*. "The sun... is shining on me? Through *that* cloud cover?"

Turning, he looked into the distance, squinting at the brilliance on the horizon. "What's happening? Why's it rising in the north?"

"That's not the sun," a deep voice growled as Grandmaster Fari came to stand beside him. In the distance, a shape was slowly coming over the curvature of the planet, hundreds and hundreds of miles away, yet still viewable thanks to the *almost* flat surface of the world. "That would be the World Boss. Just like you promised."

She turned to him, her eyes shining with an uncontained glee, even as the hair on Joe's arms slowly stood straight from the domain of *dread* impacting him even from this distance.

"The Jötunn has crested the horizon. I suggest you prepare your Sect for war."

CHAPTER FORTY-ONE

"Is it just me, or is the sky on fire?" Joe tried to speak as nonchalantly as possible, but found himself frustrated by his inability to control the waver invading his voice. "I know that *thing* is covered in flames, but the clouds themselves are burning?"

Grandmaster Fari inclined her head ever so slowly, her eyes on the distant World Boss. "Indeed. The Jötunn is taller than this mountain, and the flames surrounding it are hotter than fragile condensation can bear. They'll quickly fill in after it moves away, so it's an unreliable tracking method. Due to this effect, there's a constant deluge at the outer edges of its immense flaming aura, a thick steam in the inner portion, yet the closest sections are all bone dry. As you may suspect, the heat evaporates even the most stubborn droplets."

The breeze began picking up, a thick, humid air rolling across the world and causing Joe's robes to flap violently. "It's hundreds of miles away, and still having this much of an effect? Are you sure you're going to be able to handle that thing?"

"This is what we came for." Fari's voice was filled with excitement, though there was a strange undercurrent of hunger as she turned to the Ritualist with a flash of her canines. "You are *certain* you'll be able to find this again? I must admit, I hadn't expected results this quickly. Tell me true. *Will* you be *able* to do it *again*?"

As she repeated her question, the words had far more force in them, her eyes blazing with challenge. Instead of trying to make a convincing argument, Joe just allowed his confidence to shine through. "I guarantee it. Of course, it'll be far faster if I'm able to portion off a few chunks of its body for use as materials to build out my network faster…?"

A snarl slipped out of Fari's muzzle, and for a moment, Joe thought he'd pushed her too far. Then he realized she was simply chuckling, her head slowly waving back and forth, still unwilling to take her eyes off the World Boss. "Such audacity. You remind me of a younger version of myself; I was practically feral as a pup. Just like one of my own, you see something to sink your teeth into, so you'll bite down and fight until you are destroyed or tear off enough to fill your belly. Come now, the battle is afoot, and I am ready for the hunt to begin."

"You're ready to go? Right now? Don't you think you're moving a bit quickly?" The Ritualist squinted toward the horizon, then turned to regard the expedition group already marching toward the teleportation pad. "Hmm. Seems they're thinking along the same lines as you."

"You should be relieved." Joe was taken aback by the fervent enunciation in Fari's voice. "The sooner we begin the hunt, the less collateral damage your Sect will need to deal with. I highly recommend staying as far away as you *possibly* can."

The Ritualist considered her words for a few moments, then stood straight and rushed over to the teleportation pad. "Hurry up! Groups of fifty, I want all of you out of here in the next five minutes! I'll be dropping you within a thirty-minute run of the World Boss, so plan to start taking damage immediately. Defenders at the front, get off the pad and push back any monsters in the area; set up a defensive perimeter!"

Fari watched him work, chuckling to herself but not countering his orders. As Joe snapped out coordinates for the group to use, the incredulous group of Masters and Grandmasters stared at him slightly condescendingly, but decided to play along. The first fifty people vanished with a slight *pop* of displaced air, a blue shimmer covering the surface of the tele-portation pad for an instant.

Finally deciding to get involved, the Grandmaster took over to get her people moving faster. "Next group! Move! Your brothers and sisters from the tower are already under attack!"

Joe shot her an appreciative grin. "Hope you're ready for all of this. I can't tell you exactly how hopeful I am that you succeed."

"Yes. I understand. If we chose to walk away at this moment, it is likely your Sect would be destroyed in its entirety," Fari agreed without preamble. She sent him a knowing look, just a hint of threat beneath the surface. "This is why I am so happy we are working together. A long-term trust is building up between us. Correct?"

"Absolutely, Grandmaster," Joe responded with a solemnity that he rarely used in serious situations. "The Wanderer's Sect thanks you for your friendship, and... I hope that, when I return to Vanaheim, you'll have a more positive view of the Tower of Ritualists. As you can see, the utility we provide is beyond compare."

"I wouldn't go that far, but I am certainly impressed." The last few groups were rushing to get onto the platform, and the Grandmaster stepped forward to join them. Just before she got on, she glanced back with a wolfish grin. "Any last words of advice, oh highly-utilized Ritualist?"

Joe hesitated, not certain how much he should admit, but as he folded his arms, the Grandmaster looked at him with slowly deepening concern. "Perhaps. The World Boss is engulfed in flames at the moment, but that is not its own effect. The flames are a production of a type of flower that, erm, *was* released. The plants themselves feed off the cold, growing and repro-ducing faster the colder the environment. If you wanted to rid yourself of that horticultural hazard, you could focus on destroying every plant and seed covering the World Boss. Not sure if you have something capable of doing that, but, even if you do, then you'll have the opposite problem and will have to deal with the cold."

"Hmm. 'Was released'. What an interesting statement you just made." The Grandmaster hesitated for a moment, reaching into a pouch clearly stored just behind the fold of the front of her battle robe. "Happily, I specialize in strange contingencies during battle, and we *did* come originally prepared to deal with the frigid temperatures. I'll take your words under consideration."

She and forty-nine others vanished in the next moment, a slight **pop** and a shimmer of blue light being the only signs of their successful transportation.

Taking a few deep breaths, Joe considered the stone platform, but after a moment of hesitation, turned away from it. "Not my fight. As much as I'd love to see what's going on up there, they have no obligation to keep me alive if I intrude. Gah... sometimes it sucks to be *responsible*."

Seeing as the rest of his coven was busy putting the finishing touches on their rituals, Joe decided that his first step should be going down and inspecting the Ritual of the Eternal Turtle to make sure that its placement had been correct. He murmured to himself as he made his way to the edge of the mountain, "Sure would suck to get down there, only to find a massive gap between the ground and the first layer of protections. While it would be funny to see a few Penguins run into a wall midair, the rest of the monsters would just flood through."

Quickly making his way down the winding path, simply hopping to the bottom of several massive drops instead of dealing with switchbacks, the Ritualist quickly found himself breathing easier. This section of the mountain was partially shielded from the onrushing heated wind, and he hadn't even noticed until just now how thick and moist the air was becoming. "If I didn't know better, I'd say we're about to have a massive storm. Might actually be nice. I don't think I've seen it rain since the bifrost came online… but I think that was more to do with the clouds being messed with."

As he arrived at the valley floor, he could already see the impact the Ritual of the Eternal Turtle was having—from this angle, it was impossible to miss.

Enormous, translucent scales hung suspended in midair, overlapping with each other at their bases in a ring extending as far as Joe could see in either direction. Unless he'd messed up somewhere along the way, the ring should fully wrap around the mountain and connect back to itself. "Looks like it's working… oh! The second layer is already starting to form."

As he got closer, it was clear that a new row of scales was forming, growing by the second to fill the gaps of the first. Upon reaching the correct width, the scales began growing upward in a tapered form, creating a dense, perfect fit behind the first until it looked just like the knotted skin of an aurora-filled sugar apple. Once Joe was certain that the design was being formed correctly, he stepped through the first layer.

While he was slowed down fractionally, there didn't seem to be any major imposition. Not until he turned around.

The first layer of scales extended fifteen feet into the air, and when he reached out to push through, the Ritualist found himself completely blocked. Tapping on the surface released a light *chiming* sound, like a crystal glass having a finger rubbed along its rim. "Interesting, there's just the barest hint of distortion when looking from this side. There were prisms of light shining on the ground on the other side, but that's not coming through at *all*. Did we forget to—ah! The whitelisting! Right, good thing I remembered that now, or else I'd have needed to direct people over to the teleportation station just to get onto the mountain."

It was easy enough for him to leap over the—to him—laughably low barrier, but he was certain other people had already been trapped outside. Now with a clear short-term goal, Joe raced back up the mountain. "Working just like it's supposed to; we probably have another day or so until the monsters are close enough to cause problems. By then, it'll at least keep out most of the standard monsters that are running around. If it got that high already in only a few hours, it should be a proper barrier by this time tomorrow."

Once the Ritual of the Eternal Turtle had fully surrounded and encapsulated the mountain, it would pump additional mana into each individual 'scale', reinforcing them to an absolutely absurd degree, given enough time. Within a year, only a Master-rank attack would be able to punch through, and within a decade, only a group of Grandmasters working together would even have a chance.

Ten minutes later, the pale Ritualist shot up over the edge of the mountain, arms wheeling in place as he kept his knees tucked to his chest. The ground quickly came up, and he slammed his feet down, launching himself forward and across the open area. Within moments, Joe was next to the massive slab of alloy which was the linchpin of the Ritual of the Eternal Turtle, and he carefully reached in to shift a single variable. "Exclude... only monster. Done. Semi-permeable barrier."

Now able to focus on other issues, Joe glanced around and found that he was just in time for the Ritual of Stoneheart Compression to begin its work. The coven of Ritualists were backing away from a gargantuan, inverted spike, practically a mountain in its own right.

He could feel the immense amount of mana humming in the air as the spike began sinking down, notes of magical melody *singing* in his ears, thanks to his Magical Synesthesia. The tip of the spike touched the ground and sank through it without disturbing so much as a pebble, slowly being absorbed into the heart of the mountain until the entirety of the representation had vanished.

Klonk.

Joe's eyes flicked over to where a beaming Ritualist had thrown a lever, and in the next moment, the Mana Transfer Unit began drinking in the low-hanging clouds its antenna was pushing through. Moments later, the ground began to tremble, a subtle but continuous vibration felt in the bones. Glancing around, he saw that while everything on the mountain peak was already being affected by the motion, the buildings *he* had created were having no issues weathering the harmonic damage.

"Can't imagine that even an Uncommon building would be able to handle this for long. Well, not that one of those would last long in Jotunheim's turbulent mana field in the first place, but still."

As the now-ever-present *humming* of the ground being condensed started to fade into background noise, Joe realized there was a secondary effect happening thanks to having two of the Mana Transfer Units running continuously. What had started as a barely noticeable thinning of the cloud cover on the mountain peak quickly sped up into a still-limited, yet far-clearer view of the surroundings. It was only mostly noticeable due to the Jumping skill training area, as more of its design was viewable after a few minutes.

"Look at that… I wouldn't be surprised if we even started to have more than just the occasional glimpse of the surrounding peaks. Good, it's not probably healthy to feel so isolated for so long." There was only one concern, but after staring up at the ever-shifting clouds, Joe slowly allowed his worries to fade. "No chance we run out of power. This isn't the Earth, where the clouds are limited to only about ten miles of troposphere; there's at least fifty, no, I'd go so far as a *hundred* miles of clouds stacked above the surface of Jotunheim."

A brilliant flash in the sky above him grabbed Joe's attention, and as black-robed coven members began descending the Jump skill tower, chatting animatedly, he figured it was probably a good time to go see the results of their efforts. Unlike the others, who took ladders or slid down ramps to quickly descend, Joe jumped to the top of the tower fairly easily, using the skill-based challenge course for its intended purpose.

Unlike the other two rituals, which were having fairly large-scale effects, the power of this ready-to-be-operated ritual had condensed it down into a single form. He strolled across the platform, where only a few remaining people were inspecting their work. "Did you build a throne in the clouds on purpose, or was that just a happy surprise?"

"Happy surprise!" Nixie, a Ritualist Joe was quickly becoming far more comfortable with, motioned him over. "Take a look at this! From the front, it looks like just an oversized chair. A throne, just like you said. Wait for a moment... there. See that bubble hanging over the throne? If you come around to the side, you'll see that this design actually resembles a scorpion more than a throne. The ball up there is a focus for the mana that's going to be channeled up through all of this, and it's going to be controlled by the joysticks on either side of the seating area."

"That's cool..." Joe looked at her with excited eyes and a slowly growing grin. "Have you tested it out yet?"

"No," she replied with a disappointed sigh. "It has a maximum number of activations, but we can keep it going nearly indefinitely once we *do* get started. So... you know, we figured it would be best to wait until we needed to use it. Still, when we *do*, we'll have the coverage to hit almost anything in line of sight. Anywhere on the peak to about halfway down our mountain."

Joe agreed with her silently, until he had a somewhat startling realization. "Didn't you just say anywhere in line of sight? Why would that only cover *our* mountain? Don't you think you can target monsters climbing toward the other peaks?"

"Yeah, we figure if we can handle ours, they can do the same." Her placid permission of their peers' probable peril pressed on the Reductionist more potently he could have predicted.

"Hmm." Joe took a moment to think over how he wanted to phrase his next words and decided to choose them carefully. "Nixie, we're all one Sect living under the same sky. When we're working with the intent to be there for each other, it will help *all* of us prosper. I volunteered to handle the defense of this mountain on my own; it wasn't forced on me. Please make my wishes known that we all go out of our way to help each other."

"Isn't it odd that we haven't been offered *any* help, though?" she grumbled while fiddling with the joysticks of the throne, causing it to jerk back and forth sharply. "Everyone's using the transport network you set up without any issues, but when's the last time someone came here and didn't need anything from us? Got us so much as a cup of water because we were thirsty without asking?"

"Though I agree with you to an extent, I'm going to press this point a little more." Joe reached over and gently grabbed the joystick, keeping her from twisting away. "Please tell me that you'll make sure that the others know, if this weapon works the way we think it will, you'll at least fry monsters if *we're* fine, and they need help."

"Fine, fine! If we have a clear shot and nothing to do, *and* they can see that the monster coming at them is something they can't do anything about, we'll make sure to let them know that we can help them from all the way over here. Even if *they* aren't going to do anything for us." Nixie let out a sigh, shaking her head in agitation even as Joe relaxed. Then she perked up, her eyes peering into the distance as she looked past the First Elder. "Whoa, what's that?"

The awe in her voice had shifted to fear halfway through her question, and Joe spun around in response, Ritual Orbs lifting into the air as he prepared to attack whatever was sneaking up on them. Instead, the orbs nearly dropped out of the air alongside his falling jaw. In the distance, a massive ring of daylight was spreading from where the World Boss had last been seen.

Every cloud for miles around the Jötunn was racing away, being blown outward as a single, colossal ring expanding farther by the moment. The sky above the monster bearing down on them was now utterly cleared of weather, allowing Joe a perfect view of the quintessential combat spell Fari must have decided to open combat with.

The Grandmaster had called down a meteor.

At this distance, it seemed almost to be moving slowly, but then the city-sized flaming rock struck the World Boss.

An immense light blotted out their view. One second, two, and the illumination faded, but still hadn't vanished. As he blinked away spots, Joe saw a mushroom cloud extending from the ground to the sky, rapidly extending out to fill the void left by the clouds that had been shoved away.

"Everyone..." Joe's voice started low, but by his second word, he was shouting with as much force as he could muster, his words echoing off the surrounding mountains back to him.

"...*get to cover!*"

CHAPTER FORTY-TWO

The wind quickly picked up, going from a rough, almost painful breeze to a howling gale in only moments.

"Ground-level!" Joe bellowed over the wind as he sprinted toward his house. "Get inside anything that looks heavier than you are! Don't just stand outside, open the door and go in. It's just my workshop, it's not gonna bite ya—*move your meat!*"

Disciples scattered into the various buildings, most of them pushing their way into whatever structure was most familiar, though a good chunk did the smart thing and rushed into whatever was *nearest.* Joe was proud to see Master-rank people directing Experts and Journeyman with much less care for their own wellbeing, calm and collected in the face of what was almost guaranteed to be a blast that would sweep every last one of them off the mountain if they took the hit unprepared.

By the time he got to his own residence, almost everyone was in shelter of some sort, to the point that there was literally no space for *him* to get in. A quick glance showed that people were stacked on top of each other like cordwood, pressing against the ceiling. Trying not to show any hint of frustration,

Joe pushed the door closed, turning to face the blast wave as it swept over the last few hundred meters.

"Come on then!" he roared into the wind as he bunched his muscles, tightened his core, and prepared to use every last bit of his Stoic Constitution to hold out, no matter what.

Thhhh~woooom!

Pressure pushed down as a heavy wind whipped across the mountain peak... but *just* wind. The Ritualist frowned upward as the clouds above him undulated like a blanket being shaken out; rising and rolling downward with what should've been catastrophic effect. Then a wash of the last dying embers of daylight flowed over him.

For a long, beautiful moment, Jotunheim in all its glory sprawled before him, a world so massive that it appeared to be nothing more than a flat plane of existence, only the incredibly distant World Boss peeking over the horizon showing that there was any curvature to this planet at all. Enormous forests with trees nearly as tall as the mountain range he was standing on currently, lakes that were small only in relation to Jotunheim itself, and a sparkling clarity and freshness was quickly being overwhelmed by the shockwave and dust cloud rushing closer.

Sucking in a breath, Joe realized there was more to the wall of dense air than he'd expected: the blast was carrying *things* tumbling around inside of it. Thousands, tens of thousands of monsters were tumbling, flailing and being rattled around as they were dragged through the air like plastic bags caught in a hurricane. "Why does everything on this planet have so. Much. *Health?*"

Once more bracing himself, this time for the true blast wave, Joe let out a challenging shout as the wave of detritus finally reached his mountain. He didn't flinch as it swept toward him, dropping into a horse stance and pushing both elbows to his side as he prepared to jump forward in an attempt to negate the knockback. Once more a huge gust of wind washed over the mountain, but... but...

"No abyssal *way*." Joe let out a half laugh of disbelief as the air shimmered. The *faintest* trace of energy divided the choking dust from the clean air of his peak. The roiling fallout bent along the barrier, washing overhead and continuing on past the membranous dome extending fully over the mountain. It continued to flare and pulse for the next five minutes as it was battered by stones, trees, even a few monsters that were rendered to paste as they splattered against the unyielding surface.

Finally, the destruction wrought by the meteor strike passed by them, and the flickering dome faded back into transparency. Letting loose a shaky breath as his muscles relaxed, Joe practically sagged in place. "Must be the Eternal Turtle. Was the first stage of the protection creating a full-blown dome for the scales to be placed on? Makes sense that it wouldn't just start all the way down there and leave the rest of this unprotected, but... I'm going to *have* to get a copy of that diagram from Devoe."

Glancing in the opposite direction of the epicenter of the blast, Joe winced slightly as he saw how badly each of the Sect mountains had been hit—the main portion of the massif looked like it had been sandblasted smooth along the entire slope, with easily half of the buildings at the top having taken severe, if not catastrophic damage. "Feces. Hope their defenses haven't been totally demolished. I need a *messenger*!"

Now that the immediate danger had passed, people were flooding out of the buildings and shouting to each other. The Ritualist didn't miss the fact that a good chunk of the conversation was focused on how well they'd taken the brunt of the blow; it put a scowl on his face as he heard them taunting the other peaks for their 'weakness'. Still, there was nothing to be done at scale to change their attitudes, so he simply started barking out a message as various runners came up with excitement in their eyes.

"Get over to the main mountain and get me a status report! You! Get me information on... abyss, what're those two called? I can't see any standing structures remaining on them."

"Dragontalon Peak and Cloud Seven Pavilion Peak, respectively, First Elder." One of the messengers informed him, ready to run at a moment's notice. "First one is focused entirely on close-range combat, second one is a combination of a treasure hall, auction house, merchant district, and luxury resort services."

"Seriously? Resorts?" Now burdened with the knowledge that someone had been trying to set up relaxation vacations in an active combat zone like Jotunheim, the Ritualist could only bite back his frustration. "Well, someone get over there and let me know if they are as destroyed as they look."

He felt slight tugs at the edges of his mind as quests were created and accepted, automatically pulling from the pool of contribution points he had allocated. Happily, they didn't require him to individually go through and approve them, giving Joe the opportunity to focus on other issues. "If they haven't noticed already, there were monsters being pulled along by that blast, so have everyone get into a combat-ready state! That goes for the rest of you as well. Assume we're *actively* being invaded!"

An alarm went out, someone with a cowbell began ringing it wildly to alert everyone to the impending danger. Joe looked on as Ritualists streamed across the mountain, rushing down to their assigned towers to ensure everything was ready for the upcoming battles. "Ugh, I sure hope *only* the World Boss is being attracted to the 'Joe To Go' headquarters; otherwise, that's probably going to get overrun pretty quickly."

A person appeared a dozen feet away from him, afterimages flashing through the air behind her even as she started pulling her goggles off. "Reporting for duty!"

"The Courier!" Joe waved her closer even as he started moving toward the new arrival. "Perfect timing, I need someone who's able to move faster than makes sense."

"Thanks for getting my title correct." She glanced around the scoured mountains in the distance. "I'll waive my typical mid-combat fee, since it looks like we're about to have some problems. What's your needs, bub?"

"Streets aren't what they used to be, kid." Joe joked back in the same old-timey tone she'd ended on, glad they could find some levity in the current situation. "Since I know you don't need to teleport to get between peaks, just hang out for a few minutes until I find out who needs the most support. I wouldn't be surprised if some of the platforms got destroyed already, but if that's the case, we should be seeing some fish fixing them up in the next few minutes, anyway."

"Uhh. Fish. Sure." Glancing around, The Courier eventually shrugged and walked along with Joe as he began strolling along as if he had no cares in the world. "Look, if you're just going to have me hanging around, mind putting me on retainer? Plenty of people trying to get messages to their friends across the way."

"Sure, start your meter."

"Not a cab driver; it's just a flat fee." She allowed herself a low laugh as she matched Joe's languid movements.

"Dragontalon Peak!" A heavily breathing man shouted at Joe as he sprinted up, "Impact wiped out the outer walls and destroyed the first palisade. Repairs are underway, but about five percent of their fighting force got sent to respawn. Or... they can't guarantee that, but a couple hundred people got tossed into the open air over the valley, and they don't expect that they survived the fall."

A response came next from the main mountain. Surprisingly, they had weathered the burst quite well. The messenger hesitated, a low laugh leaving his lips as he delivered the rest of the missive, "They actually *gained* a few combatants. Some of the people yanked off the other mountains landed there and were able to get healed up enough to join the defenders."

"That's lucky for them. Any sign of monsters yet?" Joe's question went unanswered as the messengers simply shook their heads and shrugged. "Any word from Cloud Seven? Anyone?"

Seeing only shaking heads, and knowing that the return

should've been faster than going to the main mountain, Joe inclined his head at The Courier. "Looks like you're up."

"Returning in ten, nine…" The Courier pulled her goggles down over her eyes, and in the next moment, Joe's robes were dancing back and forth as the displaced air of her passing whipped them around. With two seconds to go before her self-imposed time limit ended, a shadow flicked across the bedrock, slowing down to a blurry streak of motion, only to resolve an instant later into The Courier—halted in a perfect crouch as dust swirled around her steaming boots. "Yeah, I wouldn't go over there again. Absolutely obliterated. Sorry to say, I found where the monsters are congregating. The whole mountain is *crawling*. Looks like there's some huge tunnels getting formed as well, but I didn't see what made 'em."

"You heard her!" the Ritualist barked at the other messengers. "Don't just stand there, get back to the other *Sect*-tions and relay this information!"

Over the next few minutes, responses came back, everything from simple acknowledgments to various requests for aid. Unfortunately for the other mountains, Joe had no intention of stepping foot off of his own… but that didn't mean he couldn't help in other ways. Maintaining his seemingly carefree stroll, he watched the World Boss battle in the distance with a sharp gaze that belied his relaxed demeanor.

The clouds were reforming, slowly closing in and hiding the otherwise unobstructed view of the heavens above. While twilight had officially set in, it was obvious that Fari hadn't done anything to quash the rampant growth of flowers coating the Jötunn—colossal flames still raged, as though a Bunsen burner of epic proportions had been lit on the horizon. "Kind of hoped a meteor to the face would've been a bit more effective than that. I guess I don't know what she was trying to do, though? Maybe she managed to shatter its armor and is even now having her people carve mountains of flesh out of that thing."

As he allowed himself to get lost in the daydream of the

World Boss being cut down at a safe distance, thanks to having packaged the expedition and sent them out, Joe had a sudden thought. A *dangerous* thought. A wickedly cunning plan formed from the initial idea, and he slowly turned to The Courier with a nearly malicious grin carving across his face.

"Since you're on retainer, I hope you won't mind me asking you a few questions. First, if I gave you a package, one you absolutely *couldn't* open, no matter what, but it needed to be delivered to a location with a very high chance of you dying... can I trust you to deliver it safely?"

"No questions asked... *after* my fee is paid. Death is just one of those things we have to take into account in Eternium, but I'll do my best to make the delivery before I head back to my respawn room to recover. Plan for thirty percent on top of the usual rate with that kind of-" She reached up for her goggles, but Joe motioned for her to stop.

"Not just yet. Stay close, though; I just had a *great* idea." Just as he finished speaking, a new sound reached his ears, pulling Joe's attention *up*.

Krracckaa.

His brow furrowed as he stared at the brilliant arcs of energy flowing into the Ritual of Opposing Elements, the orb above the chair snapping with contained power scintillating with all colors of the rainbow. The deep hum shifted into a *crackle* as a thick arc of energy cut through the air and out of sight over the edge of the mountain. Light pollution began flooding the sky, the effects across his mountain creating multi-colored reflections off the restored clouds above, as if they were starting the most intense rave of all time.

"Monsters are on the move." Joe took a deep breath and stood straight, moving to the edge of the mountain while managing to maintain his composure, then simply looked over the edge to see what was happening.

To his delight, the systems they'd put in place were working perfectly. The defensive towers arranged in a loose grid pattern across the slopes had bursts of power launching out of them at high angles, their payloads illuminating clustered packs of monsters as they detonated. The beam of light from on high was sweeping across the ground like a searchlight, locking onto larger monsters and engulfing them in constant detonations of whatever element was most effective against their innate protections.

Penguins turned into enormous balls of flame as their blubbery bodies were turned into torches. Leopards were forced to the ground as enormous shards of stone came into existence along bodies, penetrating through and pinning them in place. Floating wights were hit by... some form of *solidity* that had nothing to do with a natural element, their automatic reaction to pain being to shift into intangibility perfectly countered as the beam ripped away their ethereal nature and made them all-too-intact.

The Ritualist watched with a critical eye, for once simply observing instead of running around trying to triage the situation. "Huh. This feels... weird. Not casting some kind of emergency shield, making enormous rolling bubbles of acid, or throwing together a last ditch all-or-nothing ritual. Is this what most Ritualists feel like? Pick a place to build up, then let the automatic defenses take care of aggressors?"

He pondered that for a moment, thinking of the tower on Vanaheim, "I suppose it *is*, isn't it? Neat. I'm actually using my class the way it's designed to be used for once. Everything is just *working*. Weird."

With that thought in mind, Joe reached up and flicked the Bell in the hollow of his throat, activating the first of his three karmic shroud charges. With the beacon putting a spotlight on him now hidden, he noticed an immediate shift in the creatures' directions. The immediate confirmation that His Mountain would have likely been swarmed immediately caused a grimace to cross his face.

With the threat to his peak somewhat mitigated, part of him

wanted to use his idle hands to get onto the other mountains and start fighting on the front lines. But, even with how devastated the defenses of his allies over there might've been, from what he could see, they seemed to be holding their own. "Well, all but Cloud Seven... though I'd guess they'll probably have to rename it Cloud Eight if they manage to rebuild."

Pulling out his Ritual Combat Manual, Joe began flipping through it as he walked along the ridge. Slowly, calmly, because he knew exactly how quickly panic would spread if he dashed off with a wild look in his eyes, especially due to being the leader in charge of this entire area. "What can I do to help out without interfering? This one—no, that's not actually helpful. Maybe if I... but do I *want* to start putting together combat rituals? That's a good way to get my Characteristics dropping like a rock again. What's going to be the most *helpful?*"

"Can I go pick up some other jobs, if you're just going to keep muttering to yourself and-" The Courier quieted as Joe shook his head with an ambiguous mumble at her. "Cool, I'll just hang out here. I guess. Retainer. *Ya~ay.*"

"I need someone nearby who can get a warning out if I find something important." Joe's voice was softer than he intended, as his eyes were focused on drinking in the details of a ritual he had stumbled upon. "This one... yeah. Illusions, that should work."

As he came to a stop at the juncture where he was facing the monster-infested mountain peak, with the main Sect mountain making a triangle on his other side, Joe lifted his right hand and delicately manifested an inscription tool made of shining aspects. With his other hand, he tossed out various stabilizers around his position, guiding them into place with careful application of his extreme Dexterity.

While he was technically a peak Expert at Somatic Ritual Casting, Joe still found sweat beading at his temples as his movements moved far slower than necessary; precise, nearly meditative, as a glowing ritual took shape in the air in front of him. The true challenge was drawing each circle while managing to end on a sympathetic link to the next—an attempt at creating a full-blown Student-rank ritual without lifting his inscription tool and interrupting the flow of mana.

The diagram took shape in the air, a complex weave that he *actually* managed to form in one, single, continuous motion. Finally done, he let out a deep exhale and stepped back, a faint smile on his face as he reached forward and pressed his palm against the activation sequence. "Let's light 'em up, up, *up!*"

Fffsssshew. Pop!

A single beam of violet light lanced into the sky, detonating in the clouds above like an enormous magical firework launched out of a man-sized mortar.

Then the enormous flare dropped out of cloud cover and ever so slowly began to fall. By itself, the incandescent orb cast the landscape in sharp relief, nearly as bright as pure daylight. But the ritual wasn't finished.

With another enormous explosion, the orb turned into dozens of motes of light, which in turn blasted apart, again, and again… until the night sky was shimmering with slowly falling stars.

Then they sped up, turning into streaks that remained visible as they raced down and landed on any object moving through the area. Aggressively violet ribbons connected to thousands of monsters that had been slowly disseminating through the valleys. Now that they'd been marked, the air filled with a cacophony of shrieks and challenging bellows. Instead of moving cautiously and stealthily, the tide of monsters rushed out… and up.

Far worse than the thousands of tiny guide-lines was the *singular* band of light, so dense that it appeared like molten glass slowly spinning in the air as it illuminated… something. Something nearly half as tall as the mountain Joe was standing on.

At first, only a jagged spur of bone was visible, hovering midair. Then, when it became obvious it wouldn't be able to shake off the illumination, more of the monster began appearing. First its head, somewhat reptilian in design, then its humanoid torso twisted and hunched like a grotesque, malformed caricature of a man. Finally, four segmented legs connected to its abdomen as though the creature had half a spider attached to its lower abdomen.

The Legendary-rank monster let out a roar of annoyance that it had been spotted, the force of the bellow striking Joe and causing him to skid back several inches across the smooth surface he stood on. "A *Titan*? How'd it get so close without us noticing? Active camouflage?"

The half-troglodyte, half-arachnid monster began skittering forward, in moments a quarter of the way up the main Sect mountain. Without needing to take care not to be noticed, it began unleashing its abilities. As it crouched slightly, Joe expected to see the Titan leap upward, but instead it belched out a thick miasma below itself. The gasses washed down and out, hitting the ground and roiling outward without concern for its monstrous brethren running alongside it.

"Nasty. Is that thing a boat? Because it gives me the Titan-ick." Joe's nose wrinkled in disgust even as he tried to analyze the dense fog the creature was unleashing. "It's a Grandmaster-rank threat, just like Brisingr, so that's gotta be a frost cloud-"

His assessment cut short as lesser monsters tumbled out of the cloud, not stiff like frozen statues, but instead convulsing as foam bubbled from their slack jaws, fur falling off in thick clumps, and skin rotting away in mere moments. Even with the distance between them, Joe recoiled in horror as the thin barrier of the Ritual of the Eternal Turtle flared to life in front of his eyes, a thin spiderweb of cracks forming for a moment before smoothing out as the damage was fixed.

Even so, a stench made it through the barrier: a thick aroma of ammonia combined with a sweet rot—like a slaughterhouse trying to hide its scent with a fancy candle.

"Courier-"

"*The* Courier." Even as she corrected him, she was putting her goggles in place and preparing to move.

"Inform the Sect. Grandmaster-grade threat on their slope."

Joe hesitated for a heartbeat. "There's nothing we can do to help at this distance, except maybe annoy it a bit. Let them know they're on their own."

"Consider it done." Even as the words reached Joe's ears, The Courier was arriving on the distant mountain peak.

CHAPTER FORTY-THREE

"Focus fire on that Titan! Nothing else matters." Joe bawled the order directly upward, and though he meant it specifically for the person manning the Ritual of Opposing Elements, a good half of the ranged attackers across the mountain swiveled to start launching their attacks in high parabolic arcs.

The sphere above the throne flared, the M.T.U. attached to it draining the energy out of the restored cloud cover so quickly that they became clearly highlighted against the shifting sky. The tightly twined beam swung, carving across the valley floor as it was reoriented. Air turned molten where the beam passed, ground erupting as superheated shards as it carved a shallow chasm along the entire breadth of the valley. Then, finally, the sweeping beam raised to smash into the Titan's back...

Only for the roiling corruption to close around the Titan like a curtain. A low crackle of thunder echoed back to the First Elder's peak, as the energy mingled with the miasma and lit it up like stained glass, soft blue light flaring into gold tinted turquoise then spinning into nothingness as the white cloud burned crimson.

"Pseudo-Master, and it can't even cut through that abyssal *condensation*," Joe spat as he watched the two forces meet.

The beam burst into a roaring Inferno where it touched the miasma, only to die screaming as the putrid poison consumed the flames whole. Though it was perfectly countered by its oppositional element, there was simply too much of the cloud being emitted by the Titan for the beam to tip the balance in the Sect's favor. Nixie's voice floated down from on high: "What's that stuff made of? Entropy given form?"

"Looks like we're destroying the cloud, but only maybe a quarter of what it's outputting!" Joe's head snapped to the side to stare at the person speaking to him—expecting some tactician—coming face-to-face with a pale messenger who was quoting something he'd been told. "First Elder, I have three requests for aid from different peaks. They're warning that they're going to be overrun."

"Not much I can do for them, kid." Joe started to turn away, but he realized that wasn't necessarily true. "Actually, get over there and tell every messenger to tell the other Sect members to evacuate. Either come here or... I guess they can't flee to Novusheim; the Sect order is still in place. Get them moving. I'll have someone here to receive the disciples. Remind them that we've only been building this place for a short while, and we can always rebuild later. We just need to survive today first."

Then he turned back to the Titan, still on the slope and approaching the plateau, its position marked by the shimmering violet line extending into the sky. "Come on, someone hit that walking lung infection while we can still see its head."

Just as the Titan got high enough to step off the slope, it instead veered to the side and began scuttling laterally along the rim of the mountain. Its legs were perfectly situated to allow it to zoom along the outside of the peak without its upper body shifting to face a different direction, leaving its beady troglodyte eyes always positioned perfectly to watch for any threats coming toward it from the Sect.

Every step it made dug a trench, sending boulders and rocks

tumbling down at its monstrous companions. But it was the fresh waves of foul fumes spewing out that were the true danger.

As it had already shown by closing the gases around it as a defense, the Titan had at least some control over its toxins. As it raced around the entire mountain, it left a thick ring of roiling clouds that only went up to a certain height, only ever creeping *inward* toward the central portion of the settlement. Within a minute, the summit had been fully ringed with poison.

"Focus on burning a hole in that! Make sure we have a clear line of sight, and they have a path to escape, if anyone needs to leg it!" Joe shouted upward then turned to face the enormous crowd gathering to watch the distant spectacle. "Anyone with wind-based magics, or anything you can use to generate large gusts of air, I want you on that teleportation pad and with the main Sect right now! Even if we can't blow it away, I'm sure we can buy them time to escape. Go!"

People began moving, but *far* less enthusiastically than when they thought they'd be able to stay in a nice, currently well-protected location. Still, they understood what was at stake. Soon, anyone who had any proficiency in gust spells, creating vacuums, cyclones, *any* form of air manipulation at all was rushing to be a part of the main conflict.

Turning back to watch the fight, Joe watched as the smoke in the distance shifted and bubbled, as if it were being attacked from the inside and flexing back… but it never tore, nor did it fade away. Each time he caught the slightest glimpse of a building through the haze, the Titan was mere moments away from finishing another pass and reinforcing its foul barrier.

At this point, the overbearing mountain looked like nothing more than a volcano halfway through an eruption, the sickly emission having reached cloud level and seamlessly joined with the overcast sky. Now fully hidden by the thickening wall of fog, only the violet beam tracking the threat revealed that the Titan hadn't scurried away and hidden while its potent abilities whittled away at the defenders. Even knowing it was likely everyone inside was going to succumb to the asphyxiating effect, Joe could only clench his fists and reluctantly be impressed at the power.

"I wonder what that spell is called? It's building a death halo around the mountain, and it's resisting practically everything being thrown against it." Joe watched as the miasma rippled outward again, more powerfully this time, likely due to the additional Mages he'd sent into the heart of the danger zone joining into the push against the death cloud. "It's almost like it formed into some kind of elastic instead of just being a vapor like it *should* be."

Part of him was hoping that, if he could analyze it fully, he'd be able to find a way to properly counter the Legendary threat the monster presented. Another, smaller, yet *far* more passionate part of him wondered if he could recreate the attack for his own purposes in the future. "It still hasn't attacked directly... probably. Going by the location of my marking ribbon, at least. Maybe it has extremely limited close-range capabilities? Mmm. That would make sense, but no one's going to be able to charge into melee and last very long. Celestial feces, even those monsters that I always complain about having way too much health and an enormous Constitution died with only a single breath, and it *still* had enough juice to melt them into puddles."

Reluctantly, he tore his gaze away from the distant battle and focused on the ones happening closer to home. Joe peered over the edge of the mountain, focusing on the chaotic battlefield near the base. Monsters were hammering against the layered scales of the Eternal Turtle barrier, claws and teeth releasing a crystalline chime with each strike, even as the natural weapons cracked and failed against the dense magic hanging in the air.

With a hiss of alarm, Joe saw a massive beast he didn't recognize—somewhere between a bear and an elephant coated with tusks and armored plates sharpened into enormous blades —slam into one of the crystals and smash through.

Even before its head had fully pushed through the small opening, a half dozen ritual towers had focused fire on the tanky beast. Various energies slammed into its face, crackling with unspent power only to discharge into the monster. It roared in victory, even as its skull crumpled in. The other monsters behind it, in a startling display of coordination, hooked their claws and teeth into the fallen, massive monster and dragged it out of the way, the sea of beasts trickling through the destroyed section like a tributary attempting to carve a new river bed.

The attacks rained down from the ritual towers, joined by another, which dropped enormous orbs of force that detonated with little destructive power, yet enough force to toss monsters through the air. Dozens of pre-placed rituals powered up, latching onto the monsters and draining them, sending beams of energy in a recognizable pattern.

"Ha! They're using ritual clusters! I *knew* people would love that idea." Joe unconsciously tracked the large group of monsters that had just been scattered through the air, realizing the intent behind the attack. "Now *that's* smart. They can go out of the barrier without being blocked, but then they're still bottlenecked coming back in! Absolutely brilliant use of the effects. I'll have to commend Devoe again; they've been well-trained."

The mass of creatures seemed to realize most of them wouldn't be useful here, and in a very un-monster-like manner, the majority of them turned and ran off as a single pack— moving toward another mountain that wasn't such a tough nut to crack. "Not a soft target, as we intended. Still… not exactly happy that I'm making it harder for everyone else."

Glancing over his shoulder, Joe was relieved to see the tell-tale smattering of blue mana signifying a successful teleportation, as a large group of people appeared where before there'd only been an empty platform. Dozens of panicked figures rushed off the flat surface, Joe's perception allowing him to practically zoom in and pick out the pale-faced crafters, merchants, and other non-combatants who had been staffing the other mountains. Moments later, another group followed, these ones wearing robes which were distinctly different from the first groups.

"Looks like the main mountain isn't the only one being overrun," the Ritualist murmured as he walked along the ridge, tension filling him even as he tried not to show how concerned he was for their allies slowly being choked by poisonous mists across the chasm. "We're not going to fare much better if they fall. How can I plan an evacuation order, if people think they're still going to be kicked from the Sect if I make them run for it? Can I override that mandate?"

Fretting more than he wanted to let on, Joe watched as hundreds of people arrived every handful of seconds, his face going grim when those who appeared were warriors and mages —albeit heavily wounded. "Looks like they're doing a full retreat and evacuation at this point. I wonder how far the perimeter has collapsed around the teleportation points? Note to self, put *grand* teleportation pads on each peak. Still, who would've thought we'd need large-scale deployments for our people this quickly? Bah. I *hate* being reactionary."

Dozens of disciples were swiftly pulling people out of the way, helping the injured over to the large-scale Ritual of Healing, which was always active in the training field. While that would stabilize them, Joe knew it wouldn't be getting them back into the fight soon enough to make a difference. "Hey! Once the fighters are in a good enough condition to fight, get them over to the Ritual of S-*Tea*-mina, the Stamina boost will help them fight longer. Once they're prepped for re-engagement, I want a line of *fighters* replacing the lookie-loos eating popcorn on the ridge!"

"*Hey.*" An affronted voice reached Joe's ears, but by the time he turned to glare in the direction the word had drifted from, whoever had spoken out had realized their mistake and huddled into the crowd.

Just as the Ritualist finally decided he couldn't handle

standing there any longer and needed to find a way to provide some relief to the main Sect, the world *lurched*.

It took him a moment to realize the planet itself hadn't tilted; he had simply staggered, almost dropping to a knee even as everyone in his line of sight collapsed to the ground in slow motion. "What's…"

His first thought was that the poison was far more insidious than he'd expected. As he shifted to glare dizzily into the distance, Joe's expression shifted to one of confusion as the swirling nimbus of death lit up from the inside—an immense golden light leaking through the thick cloud barrier and turning the swirling dome into a cloudy snowglobe of epic proportions.

Quad Strength: 405 → 383… 352…

The Ritualist almost missed the notifications sprinting across his vision, as each of his Characteristics took an absolute *nosedive*. "Whoa! No, no… what's happening? I've been so careful with my mana usage!"

Joe's heart was pounding in his rib cage as not only his Characteristics fell away, but each of his resource pools drained alongside them. His health tumbled downward, his already depleted mana siphoning away, and the loss of Stamina shining through as he struggled to stay upright. Wrapping himself in sheer willpower, and relying heavily on his Stoic Constitution, he pushed to cut off the strange Characteristic-sapping connection between him and-

"Wait, that's not an attack." Reevaluating the sensation, Joe realized he had felt this particular pull before. His eyes honed in on the radiance condensing in the distance. A golden pillar *sliced* up and through the cloud layer, cleanly parting the miasma under the Titan's control. It hung in the air for a long moment, resolving into a colossal blade of purest energy before it shifted forward.

Then the blade *descended*.

The golden light merged with the ribbon of purple, splitting it perfectly down the middle, even as the sword aura extended outward further. The wave of intense sharpness flowed away, passing through the Cloud Seven peak as if it had missed the mountain… but the slow shift of nearly a third of its summit to the side, followed by a massive landslide of hundreds of thousands of tons of stone gave lie to that misconception. An uncountable number of undulating, burrowing monsters poked up from a myriad of holes in the mountain as though the skyscraper-sized sword had cut through a rotten apple and exposed a clew of worms.

"*That's* not gonna be fun to clean out." Joe's incredulous gaze flipped back to the main mountain, where the deadly smog had been blown away by the attack. The Titan was standing perfectly still, staring down at a shining figure that could only be the Sect Leader: Aten.

"Get it, buddy. You've *got* this." Clenching his fists in a combination of disappointment and fury, Joe growled as the Titan began moving again… only to feel his jaw drop as he realized it was moving in *two* directions simultaneously. "Abyss! Wait! It's *falling*. He split it in half!"

Sect announcement!

Rejoice! Sect Leader Aten has accomplished an amazing feat! By slaying a Legendary-rank Titan in a single strike, he has earned recognition of his Sect's position on Jotunheim. The Sect territory claimed by The Wanderer's Sect is doubled, as of this moment, with the original core section gaining an influx of power from the death of the Titan, which will act as a constant warning to any monsters within the area. Only the strongest creatures and their entourage may ignore this and willingly enter the area.

In the next moment, Joe felt his Characteristics surge back into their rightful place. Strength, stability, and clarity of thought flooded through him as he stood straighter. He was breathing easier now that he wasn't having to fend off the draining pull that would've pushed him to the limit and caused him to detonate. "If I'd been a fraction of a second slower… no, it's fine. Aten didn't know he almost killed me, and even if he had, I'd have made that trade in a *heartbeat* if it meant taking that thing down."

Thinking about the incredibly unique skill the Sect Leader

had, Joe wondered what it must feel like to be able to draw in and use the Characteristics of so many people at once. "What did that used to be called? 'Might of the Guild', or something like that? I wonder if it has a new name now that we upgraded. Oof, I can't imagine what letting go of all of that power must feel like. He's probably about as useful as a deflated balloon right now. Actually, I wonder what the backlash of using that skill is. What's the cooldown?"

Absolutely enthusiastic now that the main threat had been put down, Joe allowed his inquisitive side to take over for a long few moments, until his mutterings started drawing a bit too much uncomfortable attention. Then he glanced over the edge of the ridge once more, and his relief deepened as he saw how the bizarrely coordinated monsters were now acting as they normally did: feral and ferocious. None of them were patiently lining up to pour through the gaps in his barrier, and there were no carefully synchronized strikes landing on shimmering scales.

There was just an enormous roiling mass of teeth, claws, and snapping beaks.

"I guess it's just cleaning up the battle at this point." He didn't mind that, not one little bit. Glancing around, he could see that people were still evacuating from the other peaks, but there wasn't the same frenetic energy rolling off of them. There were no more healthy and hale combatants teleporting in, which he hoped was a sign that they were able to push back the loose collection of creatures—instead of the other potential outcome of the other peaks having been totally wiped out.

Over the next few hours, he watched as the disciples pushed back the hordes, coming back from the brink of destruction and shifting from desperate survival and into extermination mode. As the dregs of twilight faded further, the clouds lit only by mana and reflections, enormous groups of fighters were even moving down the slopes and clearing out the last stragglers.

Soon they would be combing through the valleys, and by the first seventy-two hours of darkness of the two standard weeks of night, the Ritualist was certain there wouldn't be a monster to be found for miles in all directions—in no small part due to the discomfort they'd feel from being in the presence of a Titan slayer.

Joe sat down and looked to the far northern horizon, where the massive flame in the distance had faded into embers creating flickering shadows in the sky. "Looks like they won as well."

As if to confirm his words, the system dropped a message in front of his face.

Tribulation defeated! You have earned the right to impact the world as a whole, and your teleportation network can no longer be directly targeted and hunted down… by monsters.

"Stop trying to be ominous; I don't need your foreshadowing," Joe grumbled as he dismissed the notification with a sharp wave of his hand. "I get it, I'll set up some nasty surprises for anyone coming after the source of the teleportation pads. But for now… I'm just going to enjoy the victory and wait for the expedition group to drop that Mythic Core in my lap."

CHAPTER FORTY-FOUR

"You're *sure* it's not going to cause any issues?" Aten questioned the absolutely ecstatic Joe as they stood at the edge of a massive hole in the ground. The battle had ended hours ago, the final cleanup having cleared out every monster within a handful of miles of the central Sect mountain.

Cart after cart was being hauled over, heaps of monster remains splatting to the ground and *squelching* into the hole before falling far enough that no echo of their landing came back. Only a few pops of flesh, bone, or chitin as they bounced off the circular walls of the massive chute that ran straight down through the mountain.

The Ritualist finally managed to tear his eyes off the spectacle, doing his best to control his facial muscles as he switched to a serious expression. "Absolutely, Sect Leader! As I said, anything added here will be broken down and reused more efficiently than any compost heap you've ever imagined."

"It's just..." Aten rubbed the back of his neck with a hand shaking with exhaustion, looking into the distance to where the Cloud Seven peak had a glass-smooth surface where one third of the summit had stood previously. "We *all* wanted to use the

Titan's materials. But every part of it exudes corrupting miasma even after death, and I'm worried that even *you* will run into issues while containing it. Kind of like nuclear waste, isn't it? You can bury it, but it's going to stay dangerous for a very long time?"

"It's never going to have that chance." Joe pulled out a Natural Aspect Jar, flashing it at the powerful warrior alongside a grin. "I'm going to break it down the *moment* it hits the bottom. Even better, pretty much every part of this is going to be used to extend the teleportation network across the planet. Soon, any Wanderer will be able to travel anywhere on Jotunheim with little more than the decision to do so."

Just then, dozens of warriors started marching close, their faces set in grim lines as they leaned as far away from their burden as possible. Mages and healers were on standby, the former constantly creating a shell of air that held the toxins inside a foul bubble, and the latter there to step in if any of the fumes managed to escape and latch onto someone.

Aten looked on curiously as they got closer to the hole. "It's funny, it's almost like they're walking along with a smoke-filled bubble on sticks. If I didn't know what was in there, I might want to pop it and see what the prize is at the center."

"Just death and pain!" Joe cheerfully informed him, eyes never wavering from the Legendary resources waiting to be collected. "Drop it like it's hot, friend!"

A massive chunk of the Titan *splurped* into the hole, the warriors stepping back in relief even as the mages pushed harder, shoving the air downward so it'd all flow to the very bottom of the chute. Not that they had to do all *that* much, as the dense haze was more than happy to settle as low as possible. Once it was out of the reach of the wind, it slowly descended without any more input.

One of the healers walked over and offered a salute to Aten. "We've got its claws, main fangs, and horn set aside under containment. Anything else to watch for?"

"Any word on its core?" The Sect leader intentionally

avoided glancing at Joe, who was shaking his head in disbelief at the man's dangerous greed.

"Didn't come out while we were cutting it into hole-sized pieces. Sorry to say, but we can't pay anyone enough to get in there and dig around." The healer shrugged helplessly. "I mean, technically we *could*, but they just won't last long enough to find anything."

"Aren't you little bit worried about holding onto those monster parts?" Joe did his best to seem only concerned instead of letting his own desire for additional aspects shine through. "You'll have to have multiple people there full-time to keep them from destroying everything else around them-"

"If you find the core, you can keep it." Aten rolled his eyes as Joe immediately stopped speaking then went on to answer the stated concerns. "We're keeping the components for making weapons. Our various professionals want the chance to work with them. We figure we can forge devastating artillery weapons from the horn. The claws and teeth we are going to turn into weapons for the elites of our Rogue and Assassin classes. They'll need specialized training and storage, but if we enchant the handle and sheath correctly, we should have some *exceptional* one-hit-kill blades."

"No kidding they're going to need some training, and I mean *exotic* weapon training. The only people who'll take you up on that are those who don't mind using an airborne poison that'll kill its wielder just as easily as their target." Joe looked askance at the Sect Leader. "You're going to have them going back to respawn a dozen times before they can use the blades effectively."

"But then they'll be deadly anywhere on *this* planet... or any of the others." Aten finished by shifting the dynamic of the conversation slightly. "Just to make sure, I get free access to the teleportation system from now on, right?"

"For the low, low price of a Legendary monster and its core? Here's twenty-five permanent passes." The Ritualist quickly pulled out a small bag of marble-sized metal balls he'd drawn ritual diagrams within. "Give these to whoever you want; just have them smear a drop of blood on them and chuck 'em in their inventory. Permanent free access."

"Are those-" Aten had been around long enough to recognize some of Joe's handiwork. "It only takes a Novice-rank ritual to gain free access?"

"Hah, no, actually." Joe shot him a sly wink. "That's just an overlay I created that only *looks* like a Novice circle. Anyone who tries to recreate that by following that ritual will dye their skin bright pink for a month. Hey, leaving so soon? It was good to see you again; any idea where you're going from here?"

"Deep into Jotunheim." The Sect Leader's tired voice strengthened slightly, a fanatical gleam in his eye. "We found an old map that led us to a sunken vault, and inside of it, we found a reference to a potential class specialization that I'll need a specific profession to gain. If this pans out, I'll have a Legendary body-augmentation class that hasn't been seen in thousands of years."

"Hope you find what you're looking for." Joe clapped his friend on the shoulder. "Stay in touch! Shouldn't be too hard, what with the transport system constantly growing. Even if you get way ahead of it, it'll catch up eventually."

"I'll admit..." Aten took a deep breath and let it out slowly, a grin appearing at the same time. "The possibility of coming back here after a hard day of fighting, getting a shower, hot meal, and comfortable place to rest *might've* factored into how much of the monsters I was willing to dump into this pit."

"I'm all about helping out with the core mission." Joe waggled his eyebrows at his friend as he turned to leave. "Go out and fight. You work on taking the world; I'll focus on getting you back home after wandering afar."

The Ritualist felt a slight pang of melancholy as one of his oldest friends in this world walked off, only to quickly meet up with his adventuring party. Steadying himself with a deep breath, Joe decisively walked over to the teleportation pad, taking one last look around the area before moving out as well.

The surface of the mountain was pitted and damaged as though creatures had been gnawing at it, the results of the corrupting miasma burning through the bedrock itself. Many of the homes and workshops had been fully destroyed, but even as he looked on, repairs were underway. People were fixing up the structures with smiles on their faces, and mages were smoothing out the surface by pulling from enormous wheelbarrows full of gravel their coworkers were hauling around next to them.

"Yeah." The teleportation interface opened in front of him, and Joe quickly set every coordinate to zero. "This is a *great* group to be a part of."

Then he was in the Joe To Go headquarters, watching as the Legendary creation sent an enormous amount of mana into the aspect chamber. "Huh, I've never seen the doors all shut... a safety precaution since there's such dangerous material in there? Oh, *abyss*! There's nowhere for the aspects to go!"

He hurried over to the smooth section of floor that pulled up into an aspect jar container, the sculpture-like installation swiveling and revealing massive charges gathering into a huge clog. Joe quickly stepped forward, inserting his codpiece into an open slot, and let out a long sigh of relief as the golden energy drained out of the containment and into his safe, Legendary storage device.

"A-*hem*." Joe froze in place, eyes fixed on the ceiling as his smile was replaced by a horrified grimace. He slowly turned to look behind him, still working on draining away the onrush of aspects, only to see Nixie looking at him with an incredulous expression. "Should I... leave?"

"No, I think I'm almost finished-" Joe grumbled as she turned away, intentionally misunderstanding him. "Abyss. Just... you know?"

He stayed nearby, keeping an eye on the accumulating aspects and stepping in only as needed—doing his very best to ignore the Ritualist giggling at him from the corner. Finally, he couldn't stand it anymore. "Where do the cores come out?

There should be a hopper that drops them after every scrap has been removed."

"I haven't seen anything like that." Nixie looked up and frowned, then her eyes went wide as saucers. "If *I* haven't seen it, that means either no one knows about it, or someone's keeping it secret. Where *should* they come out?"

"Err... never mind, I forgot-"

"You're going to be gone, like, all the time. You need someone to clean it out every once in a while. I *know* you do." Her glare was filled with just a *hint* of avarice. "Spill it."

Knowing he was defeated, Joe walked over to a section of the aspect chamber wall that didn't seem any different from the rest of it. Pressing his toe into a tile, he simultaneously placed his index finger and thumb on two incredibly subtle marks, and a panel slid open with a *hiss*.

Tink! Clatter, clink! Ping-ping-ping.

The small chamber was stuffed with the tiny gems, to the point that, as the panel swung open, a cascade of crystalline sounds filled the air as they erupted into the open, only to scatter across the floor as though mimicking the stars in the sky. He began scooping them up by the handful, vanishing them into his spatial ring without a second thought.

Then came a heavy *thunk*... and the room was thrown into sharp relief as a Legendary core popped into the compartment and landed on a bed of gems. Nixie lifted her hand in front of her face, twisting away in pain. "Gah! It's like driving straight at a *train* at night!"

Not giving himself any time to dissuade himself from his planned use of the core, Joe plopped himself down and began the process of surrounding it in a shell of mana. The actual act of turning a core into a Natural Aspect Jar wasn't all that difficult, just time, aspect, and mana intensive—especially with something this powerful. After creating a membrane around the brilliantly luminescent gem, he simply needed to hold it in place as he continuously poured twined energy into the thin space around the core.

An hour passed, thousands of mana pouring into the tiny bubble, and a thousand seventy-one Legendary aspects. At three hours, Joe began to get a bit nervous. When the ten-hour mark arrived, he fully calmed down and settled in for the long haul.

Oddly enough, it was at this point that Nixie thought he should be giving up. "Why aren't you struggling like you've been for the last bit? I can see that you're still doing something, but hasn't it already failed if it's taking this long?"

"Nah." He shook his head, sending sharp reflections scattering off his shiny scalp and around the room. "I just realized that if I've devoted... eh, nearly two million mana to this, and it *hasn't* ruptured and blown me to smithereens, so *something* must be happening."

At the fourteen and a half-hour mark, the core in his hands suddenly melted into a liquid form, and Joe nearly screamed in panic as it tried to splatter to the floor, oozing out of the bubble he was using to contain it. Luckily, the sheer density of power held the goo-ified gemstone in place long enough for the Legendary liquified core to recrystallize. A golden shell formed around the bubble he'd been making, condensing downward as it finally formed into a *Legendary* Natural Aspect Jar.

Congratulations! You have paradoxically created a Natural Treasure at the Legendary rank! This is not supposed to be possible. Pending review, your skill 'Natural Magical Material Creation' has been removed. If, after review, the skill is returned to you, sufficient compensation will be granted for the time it has been unavailable. If removed, you will be compensated accordingly.

Item gained: Legendary Natural Aspect Jar. This container, shimmering with the golden coloration of legends, was formed using Legendary aspects and a Legendary core. It will gather nine Legendary aspects per hour, to a maximum of 18,000 aspects.

Before allowing himself to think about the first message, Joe drew out all of the remaining golden particles of power from his codpiece, then placed the jar into the plinth. A large amount of power flooded in, the headquarters itself seeming relieved as he drained away the potency that had been stopping it up.

"Yeah, *that's* the stuff. I was getting *sick* holding that in." Joe stared at the abstract sculpture with a dead fish stare as it spoke to him. The Ritualist grabbed the top of it and shoved the rotating plinth down. "Hey, wait! I like having a nice view, and you owe me dinner after holding me like-"

Any further words were only muffled exclamations coming from below the floor.

"Why? Why the Senseless Senses?" Joe turned to Nixie, who had waved off her replacement, pulling a double just to learn everything she could from what Joe was doing. "We will never speak of this again."

"I mean I knew you *liked* buildings, but this is a new side of you I've never expected-"

"What did I *just* say?" Joe grumbled as he walked over to the teleportation pad, "I'll be back for that in a few... I want to say days, but I just don't know. Goodbye for now."

"I think it's for the best. Even *I* need a drink after all that." She snorted at the *look* he sent her way. "Fine! Have a safe trip. Going back to Vanaheim?"

Joe paused for a moment, eyes going distant. "With just one short detour first."

A thin sheet of blue lightning covered the teleportation pad he was standing on, and Joe found himself staring up at the walls of Novusheim. A single step turned into a jog, then a sprint as he prepared himself to jump over the outer wall.

Pushing off the ground, he slipped the surly bonds of gravity and shot upward, a wild smile on his face as he tumbled through the air *away* from the planet. As the top of the wall zipped by under him, Joe pulled out his Ritual Orb of Strength and held onto the central bar of the dumbbell-shaped weapon, locking it in place with his mind an instant later. Immediately, his momentum was arrested, and he flipped in the air, only to begin dropping at a sharp angle.

As he ran along the inner wall, Joe's eyes were already on his destination: the Pyramid of Panacea. Soon, he was carefully calculating the distance from the ground, once more pulling himself to nearly a stop midair before casually landing with barely bent knees. Despite his over-exuberant entry into the city, no one paid him much mind as he trolled down the streets toward the pyramid looming in the distance.

"Time to make a deal." The Ritualist steeled himself as he prepared his best arguments, but eventually let loose a turbid exhalation. "I can only hope he goes for it."

CHAPTER FORTY-FIVE

"Thanks for meeting me here!" Joe called cheerfully from the center of the bridge of the Pyramid of Panacea, not *quite* on the marble steps leading up to it and not in the alchemy hall proper. He'd deliberately chosen this spot, knowing that it wasn't the smartest idea if he wanted protection, people to guard his back, or an escape route.

No, the Ritualist had set up here *specifically* to show his confidence in himself and those he had chosen to work with.

"*Grr~*eetings, Joe the Ritualist." Grandmaster Fari turned her snarl into an attempt at being pleasant as she stepped up the last step, leaving a selection of people from her expedition behind as she came to stand directly opposite to the bald man. Her throat worked as she swallowed hard, an immense air of aggrieved satisfaction surrounding her. Her triumphant look was heavily tempered with pride, calculation, and... *possession*.

One of her hands slowly reached back, slipping into an open-mouthed bag tied to her hip. The Wolfman slowly pulled out a cube of wood, a *heavily* enchanted box. Though Joe's initial thought was that it would probably have been smarter to inlay the enchantment on a more sturdy material—a cube of high-grade metal, for example—he kept his mouth shut and a pleasant expression on his face. Fari crossed the bridge incredibly slowly, each step taking a few additional seconds as her hesitation ramped up.

"This is the first Mythic Core anyone from Vanaheim has retrieved in well over a century." She lifted the box and presented it to Joe. "Now, after enormous struggles, I'm here to… to give it away."

"No, as payment. You're *not* giving it away." Joe reached out, keeping his motions slow and controlled as he wrapped both of his hands around the surprisingly warm surface. But, as he tried to pull it back, he found it completely immobile—Fari hadn't let it go. The Ritualist waited patiently, but couldn't help himself from speaking as the moment dragged on. "How long do you think it'll take for your arm to get tired?"

"I remember our agreement, Ritualist." The Wolfman took a long, slow breath, her chest expanding as though she were getting ready to try intimidating him. "There's also the fact that this, by itself, would be enough to open the path beyond Vanaheim for my entire world. I find myself wondering if it would be worth allowing myself to be a sacrifice for the cause. It is truly only for a noble reason that I hesitate."

"But then what, Fari?" Joe didn't back down, having been fully aware that this exchange might end up in some form of politicking. "No more access to the teleportation network, no more Sages among your faction, at least not unless you go to whatever world opens next and hunt that World Boss. 'Cause I can *guarantee*, if I can't keep working with your faction, I'll find someone else I *can* trust."

Her yellow eyes narrowed at the implied threat, her grip tightening ever so slightly. "I am uncertain how much of what you've done is due to careful planning and how much is simple dumb luck. Once more… swear to me that you will be able to find the Jötunn and get us there."

"I swear." Joe increased the amount of effort he was putting into pulling the box back, yet it still didn't budge.

"What are you going to use this for?" Fari's voice trembled as she leaned back, dragging Joe a few inches closer to her. "Grandmaster Stompetti of the Tower of Ritualists is famously neutral when it comes to politics. Even so, we've agreed that you'll keep this on Jotunheim. It's in the very wording of the quest. But we never said anything about him sneaking down here or something like that. Are you going to use this to work against us?"

"While technically it's not *any* of your business what I'm going to use this for..." Joe paused only to take a breath, knowing that she was in a volatile state at the moment. "I'll use it right here, in front of you."

"You-?" As she leaned back in surprise, Joe used the motion to leverage the box up and out of her hands. "Hold on! You're not about to become a Sage right now, are you? That would violate the spirit of our agreement!"

"It absolutely would *not*," Joe fiercely rebutted, though as she crouched slightly as if in preparation to spring at him, he gripped the sides of the box and stared her down. "But I am not even a Grandmaster yet, Fari. Take it *e~easy*."

"You're going to use it now? Here? For what purpose?" The words came out rapid fire, but there was no real intent behind them, there was only an overwhelming nervous energy flowing off of the massive Grandmaster. The other members of her expedition, sensing something amiss, started to draw their weapons, talismans being pulled out of carefully constructed storage devices as the air grew even more turbulent with a deep draw on the ambient mana.

"I'm not just a Ritualist, I'm a *Rituarchitect*." Joe spoke in calm tones as he pulled on the box top, the hinge not making even the slightest of squeaks as the container opened. Light burst upward, a ray of silver-speckled black energy that was instantly washed away with what was nearly divine illumination. The light formed into a beacon reaching up to the clouds that could be seen for miles, a pillar of light dense enough that a part of Joe wanted to test if he could hop in it and float upward.

Entirely awestruck by the sight, everyone halted and stared at the light as long as they could bear it, eventually glancing away and blinking rapidly... only to be involuntarily drawn back to the source like moths to a flame. Joe's hands dipped into the box, and he felt around until his fingers clenched around the core. For a long moment he simply held it, wondering if he was feeling his own heartbeat through his digits, or if the pulsing sensation was actually coming from the gem. It certainly felt alive, and he wouldn't be surprised if it had already started forming a will of its own.

"I've been waiting to do this for a long time," Joe stated solemnly, picking the core up and holding it in a cupped palm.

Quest update: World (Boss) Sa-Fari.

Main objective: Create a permanent method of pinpointing the location of the Jötunn.

Reward gained: You have been given the first Mythic Core to be harvested from the World Boss.

Reward gained (being calculated): 1/50th of all Mythic-grade materials (by weight) harvested from the World Boss.

Clause 1 *has come into effect. The first Mythic Core has been delivered successfully. The tracking and transport system must be maintained and operational until a second Mythic Core is successfully harvested by Fari or her subordinate. Upon successful harvesting, either party can terminate the quest upon final delivery of rewards with no further obligations.*

Clause 2 *has been activated. The first Mythic Core delivered to Joe must be used within 48 hours of delivery, and cannot be given, traded, or sold to any individual or organization with political power on Vanaheim.*

*Failure to adhere to **Clause 2** will result in targeted, specific reparations, beginning with your class, professions, and all skill levels being stripped.*

"Yeesh." For a moment, the warning the system was showing him almost made Joe want to toss the core back in the box and hand it back to the wolfman. After all, he already had almost everything he had wanted to gain from this. Transportation network, a good relationship with another faction on Vana-heim… the Ritualist shook off the fear-based thoughts and gripped the core more tightly, lifting it higher.

His bones were highlighted through his skin by the immense incandescence contained in his palm. The Grandmaster leaned in, absolutely enraptured by the view, captivated by the desire to see what the Ritualist was going to use this rarest of materials for.

Nom.

His hand came up, and Joe chomped down on the core.

Fari made a sound somewhere between a strangled scream of fear and a growl of fury as she lunged forward, catching herself just before slapping the bald man silly—the Mythic Core had already vanished. "What are you *doing*? I will cut it out of your stomach, you foolish-"

She stopped as she felt power moving all around them.

The core's outrushing energies didn't dissipate into the air, but instead folded down and seeped into the bridge they were standing on. Each individual ice crystal on the bridge darkened as though it were beginning to rot, the darkness swiftly racing outward. In moments, it was covering the entirety of the pyramid, the obelisks around it, and the chains connecting the two before sinking deeply into the structure.

"Like I was saying," Joe gently pressed on, trying not to stare at the sharp talons only inches from his eyeballs, "I'm a *Rituarchitect*. This building is one of my creations, and by using the Mythic Core, I'm able to forcibly evolve it to the next rank. There's a good reason for me to do this and many amazing opportunities that are going to become possible, thanks to this core being used here."

"It's… it's already gone." Fari's composure cracked as she failed to contain her grief, and it washed across her face. "You fed it to a building, so that mere alchemists could work a percentage more *efficiently*. Couldn't you have taken the time to realize what gifting this to us would have changed? For so many people?"

"Fari." The Wolfman leaned back as Joe's voice shifted to a far more intense tone. "All I did was accept your payment. We have a deal, and it is *intact*. The next cores are yours. Now that this one has been used, the Jötunn will be able to respawn over the next little while. Don't try to guilt trip me for simply following through on what we agreed on, together. I got the core; you'll get tracking information and transportation to continue your hunt indefinitely. Everybody's happy."

"Happy." She echoed bitterly, her words coming out disbelievingly. "Yet you are the only one who has benefited from this agreement so far. We saved you from a tribulation-"

"The result of doing what needed to be done for *you* to get what you want. Think of it as expediting your first takedown. Probably knocked three months off of getting that first Mythic Core out of the way," the Ritualist agreed, refusing to let her build up steam. "I have people on standby monitoring the network at all times, ready to get you a message as soon as the first hint of the World Boss returns. You've a mountain range worth of materials ranging from Mythic on down to work with."

He waited for The Grandmaster to say something, but when she remained silent, Joe pushed just a touch harder. "Not only are your future hunts going to be far faster because of the weapons you'll be able to make using those, but you won't have to run around this planet blindly like your competitors are doing. Now, also, *I* have no choice but to fulfill my end of the bargain going forward. As you said, I've already been paid. How much worse will it be for me if I try to get out of it? I'll literally lose everything I've ever worked for in Eternium, as a *starting* point."

She stood still for a few moments, then ever so slowly flicked her ears at him. "I know what you are saying is correct. It still does not make it any easier, knowing that all of our aspirations were in my hand, and now they are months if not years away once more. Yet, now there's nothing that can be done about it."

She gave him a solemn salute, a fist pressed to her heart.

"My behavior was… uncharacteristic. Let me know if there's anything I can do to-"

"Actually, yeah. If you really don't mind-"

Fari bared her teeth. "Are you truly so *shameless*? What could you *possibly* want at this moment?"

"Just a note!" Joe explained quickly, holding his hands out to the side and crouching to make himself appear smaller, placating her instinctual reaction slightly. "I'm planning to return to Vanaheim, and the last time I went there, the blockade nearly tore me apart just to check if I had a Mythic Core in my possession. Could you write a letter to your people and let them know that we're on good terms and that I used it in your presence, under your supervision?"

She eyed him up and down, lips twitching as she considered his words. "You plan to leave soon? Today, by the look of you? Then this request is wholly unnecessary. Anyone with a shred of insight will be able to feel the remnant dissipating energy of a Mythic Core. It will cling to you for *days*, and it is unmistakable."

"That's cool and all, but I don't know if they'll take the time to carefully examine my energy signatures." Joe ruefully smiled. "Beyond simply making it off the bifrost, I was hoping to perhaps hire an escort to handle the Tower of Blood Rites. I foolishly made an enemy of them the first time we met, and they've set up a second blockade specifically for my class tower. I was thinking that a few words from you might save me quite a bit of trouble…?"

"Perhaps a few quick deaths would help you learn tact and proper manners." She grumbled at him, sending his pulse racing, even as she conjured a small roll of parchment and quill. "For the sake of our good relationship going forward, I will write you an introduction to my faction. Though I can't guarantee they'll help you with any of your personal issues, I can at least convince them to not actively work against you."

Joe waited patiently as she quickly wrote out a letter, signing it, then drawing a complicated seal on the paper which sparked faintly for a moment, then practically radiated her personal mana signature—something all but impossible to forge. She handed it over with a warning. "Show that to anyone who questions you in my faction, and they will allow you to move along. But if you find a way to misuse this, I will lead an expedition specifically to hunt *you* down, goodwill notwithstanding."

"I'd never dream of it." Joe tucked the letter away into his ring, then formally bowed to the Grandmaster, holding the position for a few long seconds. "Thank you for your assistance, and I look forward to nothing more than following through on my agreement with you, to the *letter*."

She grumbled, somewhat mollified by his sincerity, and by the time Joe straightened up, she and the rest of her expedition were loping into the distance, no doubt on their way to replenish their stock of doomsday-device talismans using the immense resources they'd gained during their battle with the World Boss.

Once the Wolfman was out of sight, Joe leaned forward once again, gasping for air as he allowed the massive surge of adrenaline that had been thrumming through his veins to dissipate. "Abyss... that could've gone *so* wrong."

When he was finally able to stand straight once more, Joe opened his hand, and an intricately engraved and enchanted wooden box popped into existence. "Can't believe she didn't notice me store that away. I know *I* would've asked for it back."

Instead of heading for the bifrost right away, Joe turned around and strolled across the shifting energy matrix of the bridge, lifting his hand and pounding on the immense door barring him entry. As his fist came down, waves of energy cascaded away with each strike, the building practically overflowing with power from the Mythic Core it had absorbed. "Jake!"

There was no answer, just as he *knew* would happen. He slammed his fist down again, harder this time, and kept going until finally there was a *thunking* sound from the other side. In the next instant, the door swung open just a crack, barely enough for Joe's glare to meet the placid gaze of the Alchemist on the other side. He held up the wooden box, and reluctantly, the door opened slightly wider so Joe could fit it through.

Jake's breathing ratcheted up, the Alchemist's pupils dilating as his mouth shifted incongruently, as though his skin were melting and reforming to better show the muscles bubbling to the surface.

"You going to be able to hold yourself together, Jake?" As soon as he let go of the box, Joe snatched his hand back, barely dodging the door slamming shut without a reply. Seconds began ticking by, then long minutes. Just as his patience was about to run out, the door once again began to open.

Jake stepped half out of the building, handing the box over with a trembling hand. In the other he extended a small, yet deeply important item—a large bottle of bright orange fluid churning all by itself.

Accepting the items, Joe lifted his hand and winced, "Ahem... the, uh, ten Legendary cores as well?"

"*I'll kill you.* No. No, I won't." Jake's guttural words were bit back as the Alchemist's eyes turned from black to crimson. When he spoke again, his voice came as a soft whisper. "A deal is a deal... even if it is not ideal."

The slightly incongruous eyes, one of which seemed to have slid about an inch lower on his face, tracked Joe's movements as he stored away the box, Legendary cores, and the bottle. Then the Alchemist took a step back, gaze locked with Joe's as he slowly closed the door between them.

"Celestial feces, why's he so freaky?" Joe gulped as he quickly backpedaled, then turned and actively *ran* from the pyramid. He knew, deep in his heart, that it was taking every-thing the Alchemist had *not* to attack him on the spot and loot what he was carrying on his person.

The Ritualist didn't stop running until he was standing at the base of the bifrost. Even then, he was trembling from an excess of adrenaline, impatiently bouncing on his feet as he waited.

"I'm early... I guess panic will do that to a man." Joe had only one last task he absolutely *had* to complete before jumping between worlds, and it was done after a quick exchange only three minutes and four seconds later.

Then he was stepping into the immense beam of energy and racing toward Vanaheim.

CHAPTER FORTY-SIX

Joe had barely stepped off the bifrost when the uproar began.

The residents of Vanaheim greeted him like a powder keg welcoming a spark—a tsunami of detection spells washing over him and lighting up with warning lights, screeches, and various effects meant to immobilize him. The Ritualist stood stock-still, holding the letter from Grandmaster Fari above his head—not that he *could* move, having been wrapped in so many restriction debuffs that he could see at least six inches of air warped around him.

"Abyssal remnant Mythic Core energy," he managed to spit out through his lips, which were parted just enough for him to speak, but certainly not loudly or clearly. Now he could even see the energy clinging to him like static, a shimmer of silver-speckled darkness tingling up and down his body.

"What faction do you hail from?"

"Who're you working with?"

"I recognize him! How'd he get past the blockade again? He should've been stuck on Vanaheim for the last-"

The sky began to boil, the ground started trembling, and auras began sparking off the people who were huddled too close together, their defensive magics springing into place as they prepared to escalate into a full-blown war at the base of the bifrost.

"Don't you have anything better to do than hitting a bald guy who can't fight back?" Joe shouted with as much force as he could muster with his petrified jaw. "I have documentation!"

"I don't recognize him." An enormous man stood coated in armor that was shimmering through dozens of colors, prepared to tank any blow coming his way. "Not as a faction member, that is."

"Nor I," his opposing counterpart spoke up, a woman dressed in deceivingly simple robes covered in tens of thousands of what looked like pieces of confetti, yet Joe could recognize as individual talismans placed with meticulous intent. "Tell us, Ritualist, which faction has your tower decided to support? Stormbinders? If so, we will protect you with everything-"

"You can't protect anything without *us*." The armored man stared at Joe with a sunken gaze. "Tell me you haven't done something foolish and permanent. No, there's still time for it to be undone. Swear for us-"

"Can't. Move." Joe's words seemed to finally get through to them, and both Grandmasters glanced at each other. They seemed to come to a silent agreement that either of them could handle a simple Master on their own, and over the next few seconds, the restrictive spells coating Joe were peeled back layer by layer. Soon he was free, yet still rather unhappy. "Really? None of you are going to give anyone coming here a chance to explain themselves?"

"The scanners work," the representative of the Stormbinder's Tower told him simply. "While it'll take some time to reset, it's certainly not necessary anymore, now *is* it?"

"If any of you would've given me a chance to *explain!*" Joe lifted the paper, smacking it with his other hand to call their attention to the document, "Or looked at me with your own senses instead of relying on detection spells, you would've seen that I'm covered in *remnant* Mythic Core energy. I have a signed letter from Grandmaster Fari herself, stating that I did have one, and I *used* it."

"So you're one of *them*," the armored man stated with a deep, threatening growl to his voice that caused Joe's own chest to vibrate in resonance. "Hand it over, or-"

"He said he used it." The lady from the Stormbinder's Tower stepped forward and plucked the document out of Joe's hand, reading over it with a cheerful look on her face that slowly darkened into a scowl. "Ah. Abyss. You *actually* used it."

"She saw me use it; I was upgrading an Alchemy Hall on Jotunheim," Joe carefully explained as he saw the lady reach the part where she explained how Joe was helping them find and hunt down the Jötunn. "Again, if you scan me, you'll see that I'm covered in what I was told was an 'unmistakable residue of a Mythic Core being *used*'."

The leaders hesitated, taking careful steps closer as they kept an eye on each other, and Joe, to ensure there were no under-handed tricks. Squinting at him up and down, both leaders let out a sound that was half relief, half intense disappointment. The armored man spoke first, "As he says... discharged Mythic energy. I'd recognize it anywhere, after seeing so many of the people *I* protected bind themselves to Mythic Cores and ascend to the Sage rank in front of me, leaving me ever-trapped in the Grandmaster rank."

"You used it?" the sharp-eyed woman coated in talismans pressed, "You'll swear to it?"

Fully understanding that paranoia was justified, Joe placed a hand over his heart and swore that he used the Mythic Core. The crowd around them murmured as the leaders relaxed, practically slumping in place as they shifted being on the blade's edge of brawling to biting their nails at the immense amount of power they had just wasted.

"Could Fari not have told you there'd be scanners in place for this?" The lady let out a deep sigh, anxiously clutching her hands together. "Resources are ever-scarce on Vanaheim, and mishaps like this have potentially ruinous consequences."

"Stand down," the armored Grandmaster called in a terribly disappointed voice, halfheartedly waving his faction off. "False positive. *You.* Stop leaving the planet. If you have some method of going out and coming back, just know that, the next time I see your face, I'm going to smash it in and search the left-over paste to see if there's a core that clatters to the ground."

"Graphic." The Ritualist still nodded in acknowledgment and began taking slow, careful steps through the crowd of people at or *far* above his own level of combat ability. Before he went too far, he paused and turned back to glance at the faction lead of the Stormbinder's Tower. "Hey... I've been having problems with the Tower of Blood Rites. They're targeting my tower pretty hard; could you point me toward some people who might be willing to let me hire them to keep the bloodsuckers off my back?"

"I have better things to do than solve your problems. Perhaps if your tower would choose a side in this... debate... I'd be more inclined to offer you assistance." She turned back to the bifrost, carefully examining it for a moment before stepping away and deeper into the crowd.

"There's always large groups of people milling about the area out there." The armored man spoke with a touch of angst in his voice, but he was still unable to completely ignore a request for protection. "Provided you've enough in the way of payment, I'm certain you could convince some of them to join you for a short walk instead of sitting around and betting on the outcome of our expeditions. Some things should be held *sacro-sanct*, and the actual fate of this world should be *one* of them."

Joe inclined his head at the man, genuinely surprised that he would offer any advice after he had all but declared his favoritism toward the Stormbinder's Tower. "Thank you, kind sir."

There was no answer, simply a flinty stare that motivated Joe to get moving. The Ritualist took the hint and passed through the remainder of the group, not failing to notice how twitchy they were, how a lingering stare would have them reaching for a weapon, and how a hint of a smile on his face practically sent them into a fury.

Controlling his expression as carefully as possible, Joe tried to channel his inner stoic as he stared at the ground until he was past the blockade in its entirety and looking at a sea of faces that were much more uninterested.

He had plans to change that. "Looking for an escort!"

A few interested parties looked over, and soon someone was walking toward him. "What's on your mind, *big boy*?"

"Let me try that again..." Joe shivered and cleared his throat, then stepped to the side and changed his request as the bell on his neck chimed loudly. "I'm looking to hire a protection detail to bring me over to the Tower of Ritualists! You've got spare time, I've got spare cheese!"

"Why would some big, strapping man like yourself need help just walking over there?" a man called out with a jeering tone. "I can see from here you're *shredded*!"

"Ah, yes, cheese jokes." Joe put on his best customer support smile. "Thank you for that. As I was saying, just need some combat capable people to walk me around! Keep unsavory elements off my back."

"I'll get you there for ten wedges," someone called out from the milling mob of gamblers and bystanders. "Cheddar, sharp."

"Ten wedges just to *walk* with him? That's practically daylight robbery. I'll do it for eight." Soon a large group of bright-eyed, interested people were casually forming around the smiling Ritualist, each of them arguing with each other over what was the appropriate payment.

"That should be fine; I'll do ten wedges each. Anyone who wants to participate." Joe's words caused the murmuring to grind to a halt, and all eyes turned to him.

"Anyone?"

"Any Master rank or above-" Joe paused as he saw disappointment flash through a good chunk of the crowd, so he slightly shifted what he was about to say, "-will get fifteen. Experts get ten."

He felt a pull at his mind as the system shifted his request into an actual quest, confirming he had the resources on hand to make the payment he was promising. It seemed satisfied, though it resolved into a different number than he'd been expecting. "That is... looks like I can take up to forty-six Masters and two hundred Experts."

"If he has that much of the gouda stuff on him, what else do you think-" a quiet, yet obviously greedy voice slithered through the crowd before it was cut off sharply, as though someone had elbowed the person speaking.

"What? You gonna just attack him for his cheese and get your entire tower sanctioned?" someone called out loudly, though it was obvious they didn't know who'd spoken originally.

A few people stepped closer to Joe, obviously acting protective in an effort to earn a higher profit. "Don't worry, we'll get you there safe and sound! You don't need all of those-"

"No, no. I want *anyone* who wants to help." Joe cut off the overly friendly speaker, leaning away from the 'friendly' arm the man tried to drape across his shoulders. "Just so you all know, if anyone fights, I'll pay you to step in on my behalf."

A few people winced at that, backing away slightly. "Look, that's not a cheddar level problem. If you've got any asiago, maybe we can talk, otherwise you'll a-see-*me*-go."

"It won't be a problem," Joe firmly informed the people around him. "If you're willing to fight, I'm willing to pay. I've got all sorts of cheese I'm willing to spread, so long as I get there *instead* of dead."

To punctuate his words, he pulled out a small round of goat cheese, and as the faint whiff of aging cheese wafted through the air, people began to look at him with dark expressions. "What in the world are we supposed to do with *that*? That's not cheese! That's some kind of abomination."

"I guarantee it's viable." Joe was definitely starting to lose them, and a few shook their heads and turned to walk away.

"Oh! Is that the goat stuff?" The boisterous cry came from a familiar voice, as the gaudily dressed Mak rolled up, his enormous cheese wagon clattering loudly across the cobblestone road as he rushed over. "I'll take it! As much as you've got, I'll take it!"

"Whoa, hold on now..." one of the previously reluctant men interjected, stepping between Mak and Joe. "That's a quest reward you're talking about; he can't just hand it over. But, you know, since it's a quest reward I'm going to get in just a few minutes, what're you willing to trade for it?"

"Ahh..." Mak grimaced as he realized his mistake, letting out a defeated grunt as he was forced to set the market price publicly. "I'd take one of those small rounds for a large wheel of cheddar, a wedge of asiago, or a thin slice of ten-year Parmesan."

"You're kiddin' me." The group immediately turned back to Joe, suddenly all smiles and shining eyes. "Say... how about you point us in whichever way we should be walkin' to run into your least favorite people?"

Ignoring them for the moment, Joe walked over to the cheese wagon, and in a show of wealth, started stacking small rounds of goat cheese on the counter. Mak was in his wagon in a flash, and as the Ritualist pulled out a seemingly endless supply of the white delight, the Kraftsman's face flushed with genuine excitement.

"Hold on, let me grab my scale..." After a few swift calculations, Mak swept the goat cheese into the depths of his conveyance, then rolled a multi-hundred-pound wheel of Parmesan over and hoisted it onto the counter with a grunt. "That's enough for a yearling Parm. That work for you, or would you prefer a quarter round of five year or a triple wedge of ten?"

Joe considered his options for a moment, but decided to accept the large wheel, seeing as the conversion amounts made absolutely zero sense to him. "Thanks, Mak, but I think I'll take this as my first real investment opportunity on the planet. You'll see it again in ten years or so, I bet."

"What a keen eye for business you have, young Ritualist!"

the Kraftsman practically sang as he leaned forward. "Go on, what else have you brought for me today?"

"That should do it for now, otherwise…" Joe trailed off as he glanced back at the glaring crowd he'd just hired, "uhhm, I might accidentally start a riot?"

"Come see me soon! Just remember, I'll take anything you've got!" Mak hopped out and cheerfully returned to his position at the front of the wagon, rolling it out of the road and to the edge of the large crowd before starting to shout and call attention to the people waiting around, offering snacks, cheese exchanges, beverages, and even comfy chairs they could use while waiting around for one of the expedition groups to come back. As he mentioned this new service, Mak turned and sent a broad wink at Jce, who only shook his head in admiration of the hustling merchant.

As per usual, a line of rolling cart kiosks followed after the enormous cheese wagon, and Joe smiled as he saw a familiar orange-haired Nyanderthal hauling her goods. "Beth! So good to see you! How have you been? Weather been pleasant for you? Got any new products to show off?"

As per usual, Joe tried to bait her into conversation, but she deflected him with her usual words. "Welcome back to my little shop, customer. I have flowers, chocolate, and coffee. Feel free to browse. If you need something, I guess I'll be here."

"Nothing… um. Nothing new, huh? Same stuff, different day? Not my favorite motto." Joe felt his smile slip slightly. "Look, is it me? Am I just so unpleasant to talk with that you try to put me off like this all the time? I'd really like to be friends."

"Welcome back to my little shop-"

"Come on," Joe interrupted her, shooting a pleading glance at the Nyanderthal. "Everyone has nice things to say about you, and I've seen people buying from your kiosk fairly regularly. Do you have a different sales pitch you use on them? It's… I don't *need* you to like me. At the same time, I kind of feel like, you know, maybe I do? Being the only person who doesn't get along with you just seems wrong."

She didn't respond beyond tilting her head to the side and staring at him with the same bored expression she always wore in his presence. After a few moments where he didn't speak, nor peruse her wares, she grasped the handles to her cart and rolled off to her normal position behind Mak.

"Huh." The too-friendly gambler nudged Joe with a strange look in his eye. "Never seen Beth so animated. She must *really* not like you if she's gonna be acting *that* mad."

"You're joking." Joe glanced at the man but realized he was dead serious. "That was her being *animated*?"

"You see how her ears were twitchin'? Tail shiftin' back and forth? I thought she was about to pounce and gut you like a fish." Tilting his chin down, the man gently punched Joe's shoulder. "You might want to keep your distance from that one."

"Started out with me just trying... *haah*. I guess maybe you're right. Just more proof that you can't trust anyone who doesn't like puns. That motto has served me well 'til now." Trying to put the awkward interaction behind him, Joe smacked his cheeks and stood straight, then started walking down the street, taking the most direct path to the Tower of Ritualists as he possibly could.

Nearly a hundred people joined him for his afternoon stroll, the sight inflicting a dark grin on his lips. "Ah, well. At least now I get to have the fun part."

The procession wound its way along the clean streets that were *exactly* the same. No art, no ornamentation, simply the same almost organic-looking stone lining the streets that the towers were made of. Joe would've called the locals out on it, if he hadn't had this explained by Mak on their first meeting— anything left out was absorbed by the world itself, sinking through the surface for reasons and purposes unknown.

Within minutes, they'd drawn an immense amount of attention. The people out and about scouting for the Tower of Blood Rites ran up on him, only to freeze and turn tail with their challenges to duel dying on their lips as they saw the enormous group surrounding Joe. Scowling, they ran off with frustration etched in their faces, but the Ritualist knew the relative peace wouldn't last forever.

The closer they got to the open field surrounding the Tower of Rituals, the more they saw the black-and-red-robed blood magic users running ahead of them, packs of ten converging yet never stopping to confront the group escorting Joe back to the only place he could call home on this world.

Finally, as they passed the final tower leading to the clearing, the Ritualist felt his heart sink as he saw at least two hundred members of the opposing tower in formation, blocking their path forward. Though they were simply *standing*, aggression rolled off them in waves. A tall, broad-shouldered man stepped forward, eyes filled with fury and practically trembling with a bloodlust to the point that even his fastidious pompadour was quivering.

"Joe the Ritualist!" Surge shouted above the annoyed grumbling of the group pressing in around the bald man. "You would never go this far unless you have something to hide! Step forward and fall to my magic in an honorable duel. I officially challenge you, before everyone present!"

"Master Surge," Joe grumbled as he scratched the back of his neck in consternation. "My least favorite person on the planet. Let me ask, when I show up alone, you accuse me of trying to sneak past you because I 'must have something to hide', right? Why is it that, when I hire people to walk me in because you've been harassing my tower, that *also* means I have something to hide? Could you tell me the appropriate number of people to bring with me? What amount shows I'm just trying to get home and take a shower?"

His words caused a ripple of mocking laughter from the group around him, though everyone facing them didn't even twitch.

"I'm on to your tricks, Joe the Ritualist." Master Surge stepped forward, both hands in the air and ready to begin casting at a moment's notice. "You will neither be able to run away, nor will I stand close and let you take me down with you when you are slain. I specialize in mid-range combat, and I shall use this to my advantage."

"I don't *want* to fight you-"

"Then *I* challenge you to an honorable duel!" the next person in line behind Master Surge called out, stepping forward immediately. "Each of us is prepared to stand here and drain the Honor of your tower until you either admit to what you're carrying and hand it over, or your tower falls to ours."

"Hold *on*, will ya?" Joe growled at the man who'd interrupted him, who could've been Master Surge's brother, seeing as each of them wore the same hairstyle, robes, and even took the same stance. To be fair, that was every last one of the members, so the resemblance could've been a coincidence. "As I was saying, I don't *want* to fight you, but I'm more than willing to pay whatever it takes-"

"You think you can buy Honor with *cheese*, Ritualist?" Surge practically spat as he stepped forward threateningly, "You think you can bribe your way past us, when honor demands *blood*?"

"Seriously, can I *finish*? No manners between the whole group," Joe grumbled as he pulled out the massive wheel of Parmesan he'd just traded for. On top of that another was set, then three more, each in different years of aging, having been purchased on his behalf using the tax revenue of his Duchy.

Cheddars, havarti, specialized craft versions… soon there was a tower of cheese stacked above Joe's head, and he stared down at the opposing Master as the crowd he had hired looked on with their pupils dilating, greed showing on every face.

"You say I should be afraid of you, that you're going to show me all of your spells and special attacks?" Joe slowly shook his head as his Dark Charisma worked on every person among the literal Honor guard around him. "No, Surge. I'm going to pay whatever it takes to make sure you don't get to send so much as a *teaspoon* of blood at me."

CHAPTER FORTY-SEVEN

"You mean to tell me… you're going to literally attempt to *cheese* your way past us?" Surge's voice was awash with disbelief, as if he were seeing his society fall apart in front of his eyes.

"I'm not going to *attempt* anything." Joe lifted his arm, pulling back his robe to expose his muscular arm and shoulder. "I'm the unofficial Duke of Cheese, and I'm here to spread joy to my subjects."

"Love that can-do attitude!"

"What? With that much melty goodness, he can afford to have a *fon*-due attitude!"

"I'll fight Surge myself for a wheelbarrow of that goat stuff!"

"Let me do it, I'll give you a wheel-y good deal!"

"I can't *brie*-lieve this is actually happening. I'm rich!"

"What a munster of a wallet he's packin'!"

"His pockets must be deeper than an entire *cavern* of swiss!"

"Please stop," Joe called out weakly. "I understand that cheese is your currency, and you've had your entire lives to think up jokes like this, but you can go ahead and save a few of them. Keep them on the inside, you know?"

"Sorry if our words are grating." Someone slipped one final jab, just as the situation started to rapidly devolve.

"I challenge you to an honorable duel!" one of Joe's protectors called out, pointing at a seemingly random person in the battalion of the Blood Rites.

"I refuse," came the instant answer, cool to the point of frosty. "We're here for one purpose and one purpose only."

"Then I challenge you!" another called out immediately, mimicking the antagonistic words the Blood Rites members had harassed Joe with. A stricken expression flashed across the challenged man's face, and he looked to his leader for guidance. "You think *you* can all gang up on one guy like this? Taking on a tower is one thing, but he's just trying to walk down the street, you know?"

"Thanks for the free Honor, sucker!" The first person laughed as he pointed at another pompadour-coiffed person, once again seeming to choose on a whim. "I challenge *you*, now!"

More duels were refused at first, but the crowd was absolutely relentless. When one person refused, another two stepped forward, simultaneously challenging and mocking their potential opponent for cowardice. A hundred duels were declared in the next five seconds, and the opposing force went even paler than usual as they clenched their teeth, unsure how to react.

Finally, Master Surge lifted his hand, and the noise quieted. "Accept them all. Tear them apart, and I'll make sure to hunt that Ritualist myself. I did promise him that any allies he brought with him would be cut down, and I am nothing if not a man of my word."

Joe flinched as one of the people with him smacked him on the back, then plucked a small round of cheese off the tower and pocketed it. "Looks like it's nacho fight anymore, brother."

Within minutes, the Blood Rites Tower had squared off with their opponents, hoping to start reclaiming the Honor they'd been hemorrhaging. Soon Joe was surrounded by only a handful of people, who were badgering Master Surge—though the steely-eyed man only had Joe in his sights. "I declared a duel before any of you, and so far, I have not yet received an answer. What say you, Ritualist?"

"I think…" Joe looked at the tower in the distance, then back to Surge with a mocking smile on his lips. "Pretty sure I can turn down one little duel today. I've got places to be, you know?"

"So be it." Surge spoke in a low voice, barely louder than a whisper, and Joe had just enough time to dive to the ground as a sheet of multicolored blood swiped above him. The people alongside him weren't as lucky, three of them having been cleanly beheaded, and another two having their outstretched arms removed. "I tried to remain honorable, and you twisted the rules… playing the merchant instead of the combatant. If you won't be honorable, then *I* refuse to be so constrained."

"Master Surge! What are you *doing*?" The words, surprisingly enough, came from another of the black-robed pompadour-styled combatants, who was staring at Surge with an expression of betrayal so absolute that even Joe realized the Master had just broken an ironclad taboo. "You? Dishonorable? *You*? The sanctions… what have you *done*?"

"Enough!" Master Surge was slowly being coated in a swirling wave of rapidly hardening blood, armor forming over his limbs, torso, and head. "Once I prove it, once I kill you, and the Mythic Core clatters to the ground, the only thing the Sage's Council will do is *reward* us! Our tower will remain strong, and I—*get back here!*"

Joe had taken the chance during the monologue to step forward, leaping across the ground and clearing the scores of individual battles happening below. In an instant he was nearly a thousand feet away from his starting point, and the blood-curdling roar behind him only encouraged the Ritualist to start running as hard as he could.

Pouring on the speed, he counted down the seconds until he could activate Omnivault without mana once more, only to feel a shiver race down his spine as a soft song of death and blood echoed in his ears. He dove to the side, narrowly avoiding a line of hardened blood that shot out of the ground like earthen spikes, only to melt away into a liquid form as they passed him by.

"Thank you, Magical Synesthesia." Joe knew better than to look back, and as the air *hummed* with threat, and the music reached a crescendo in his ear once more, his cooldown ended, and the Ritualist leaped forward, now just over halfway across the field to the sweet succor of the tower. "Come on, I'm not going to last much longer without some help!"

Whether it was his words or simply the standing defenses in the field around the Tower of Ritualists, Joe's fervent prayer was answered as circles sprang to life around the rampaging Master chasing him down. Explosions erupted as though the black-cloaked man were stomping intentionally through a minefield. Deadly effects arced over Joe's head as it actively avoided striking him, likely thanks to his robes demarcating him as a member of the tower. Ambiguous energies rippled around, distorting his senses, even without him being the target of their effects.

From what he could hear, Master Surge was having a far worse time of it. The man's screams of rage and fury had a third component added to them: immense pain.

Even that wasn't enough to dissuade him from this course of action. Crimson lances tore through the air, clipping the Ritualist even with his best efforts at dodging. Crossbow-bolt-sized shards of sanguine sliced sickeningly through his shoulder, and just as Joe jumped for the third time, he cried out in pain as a coil of blood whipped up from the ground, severing his achilles and *nearly* removing his foot entirely before he was out of range.

"You've got nothing, Joe! No defenses, prepared or other-wise! No attacks! Now, I've even crippled your ability to escape. Accept your death and-"

Joe landed, practically within striking distance of the tower's doors, and began rapidly hopping along on his left foot, still refusing to glance back and see how close his enemy was to being able to sink his mana-formed blood-talons into his back. "Almost... there. Open the door, open the *door!*"

The gates were flung wide open, revealing dozens of Ritualists standing and holding grimoires aloft as they worked together to complete a series of rituals. The glow of magic fading from their hands indicated a ritual in the final stages of activation.

A burst of green faded to reveal Grandmaster Pete himself storming onto the field, power wrapping around him with enough force to warp the world. Joe's heart leapt with hope as the strongest member of the tower made his appearance.

"*Abyss* yeah-" The last thing that went through Joe's head was a massive lance made of fizzing and popping blood.

You have died! Calculating... you were dishonorably murdered by a member of the Tower of Blood Rites. Honor +5000. Sanctions have been levied against the offending attacker's tower.

"I was *this* close." Joe let out a heavy sigh where he respawned inside the tower. He turned and made his way out of the tower, where various Masters were wandering about, uncertain what they should be doing, now that the threat to one of their own had ended.

Though he nodded at a few familiar faces, the Ritualist didn't stop to speak to anyone until he stepped out of the gate, looking over to where Grandmaster Pete was hovering slightly above the ground, glaring at a smear of blood coating the field. "Hey there! I appreciate the effort, but it wasn't-"

"Why was he after you, Joe? I received a notification of a dishonorable attack on one of my own and came as fast as I could, but..." the Grandmaster looked over with a deeply pained expression. "You didn't have one, did you? He didn't manage to snag a Mythic Core you were bringing for me? Abyss, what have I done? I've upset the balance of power with my own greed. I put my people at risk-"

"Pete-"

"No, Joe... please, I've realized the error of my ways, and I'll see if I can do anything with the system to allow you to be free of the quest I've given you. I see now that it's too much." The Grandmaster sagged in place, a heartbeat away from openly weeping. "Even if it's not too much for you to take, my own actions may have just plunged Vanaheim into war."

"He didn't get *anything* from me!" the Ritualist was finally forced to shout over the Grandmaster, who closed his mouth with a **click** and stared at him with absolute shock. "I told them when I got here that I didn't have a Mythic Core on me. If the guardians at the entry to the bifrost believed me, I just don't get why *he* wouldn't."

Joe gestured helplessly at the smear on the ground. "Seriously, the guy didn't even give me a chance to explain. *This* is why you don't interrupt people when they're trying to be reasonable. I'm surprised at you, Pete. Even if he *had* gotten one, wouldn't he have dropped the Mythic Core if he had managed to grab it from me after being splattered like that?"

"You... you *didn't* have one?" Immense relief washed over Pete's face in that moment, and he clutched his chest while closing his eyes and breathing deeply. "Celestial feces, you scared me there."

"I just got the last parts of my ritual setup, and I was hoping to get Master Darling to finish the tokens. From there, I was hoping you might be willing to conduct it still?" Joe offered by way of explanation, and the far-more-composed Grandmaster finally stopped hovering and came to walk next to Joe like a normal person. "If that's on the table, even without paying you up front with a Mythic Core?"

Now all smiles, the Grandmaster clapped Joe on the back and fell in step beside him. "As I promised at the outset of all of this, I will do my utmost to help your progression. Why don't you show me what we'll be working with, and I'll start the preparations while Master Darling finishes up?"

"Sounds good to-"

Fwumph.

Robes wildly flapping in the wind, Joe and Pete both stared at the new arrival with vastly different expressions on their faces. The Grandmaster moved first, his Characteristics allowing him a momentary edge over the mere Master he was beside. "Who are you, and-"

"Delivery for Joe the Ritualist?" The Courier lifted her goggles and blinked as she confirmed she was standing in front of the right person. "Ah, there you are, First Elder. I have to admit, I'm not used to someone being faster than me. When we got on the bifrost at the same time, I was originally annoyed that you were having me deliver this to you as soon as possible."

She passed over an ornately enchanted wooden box, and Joe felt a heavy pull at the edges of his mind as his quest Automatically allocated contribution points to The Courier for payment. As it turned out, interplanetary deliveries into a zone where death was extremely likely was *rather* expensive.

"Any issues getting here?" Joe looked for any signs of damage or wounds on her, but The Courier firmly shook her head.

"It was a rather straightforward interaction, as people are arriving on this planet each day. I arrived, as per usual, and there were a few people who asked me questions, but the majority of them were working on resetting some sort of spellwork in the area? They told me I would be stuck on the planet but..." The Courier shrugged, seemingly unconcerned, "They've never been able to stop me before. Anyway, the delivery is complete. Is there anything else you need, or are you satisfied with your experience? Should I stay on retainer, or...?"

"All set for now, thanks so much!" Joe chipperly informed her, handing the box over to Pete without even glancing at the man. "That's for you. As for you, The Courier, safe travels home. I look forward to working with you in the future."

"Before I go... I hear you're starting a coffee delivery service? I know a few people if you're hiring. Us speedsters tend to hang out." She winked at the bald man while putting her goggles back in place, then turned and vanished into the streets of Vanaheim with a shockwave of displaced air.

"All set there, Grandmaster?" Joe smiled over at the Ritualistic Alchemist, who was looking at him with an utterly flabbergasted expression. "Or, should I say, *Sage* Pete?"

"You... it's a Mythic Core?" Pete glanced down at the box, his hand freezing in place as he stopped himself from popping it open and releasing a beacon of light that would alert everyone on the world that it was present. "You put a Mythic Core *in the mail?* Are you out of your *mind?*"

"It worked, didn't it?" Joe laughed and laughed as the gates to the tower closed behind them, guaranteeing their security. "Now, about that ritual..."

Quest updated: The Makings of a Sage.

Complete: You have completed Grandmaster Pete's request of giving him a Mythic Core.

Pending: Support him as he ascends to the Skill Sage of Alchemical Rituals.

Reward: He will provide:

1) Sponsorship in the Tower of Rituals.

2) Training as able. No less than one hour per month.

3) Dedicated support when attempting to break through a bottleneck in your core skills, until each of your core skills enter the Grandmaster ranks.

4) Support should you ever be in competition for the position of Class Sage of Ritualists.

5) Direct mentorship under Class Sage Mirascible.

6) Should you ever be in competition for the position of Class Sage, he will support your bid.

7) Maximized reputation with Pete.

Failure: no longer possible.

Things moved extremely quickly after they were secure within the Tower.

First, and most importantly, within the hour, Joe was sitting across from Master Darling as she slowly carved esoteric representations of his Characteristics into place on one of her enchanted tokens. When she'd finished with that, she took the other and stared deeply into his eyes, hands flashing back and forth as she wrote out whatever it was she was looking at.

"Done." She passed over the final product with a flourish. "Take a look, but I can all but promise you won't know what you're seeing. I'm looking forward to conducting this portion of your ritual... the skill levels and experience are certain to be *exceedingly* generous. In fact, every single slot has been signed up for, which is quite the feat."

"Is it?" Joe laughed as he tried to shake off the warm feeling that had risen in his chest as she stared into his eyes. "I've filled every ritual slot a *bunch* of times."

"Oh, *really*?" She smirked at him gleefully, and Joe bit his tongue as he realized that he'd just stepped into her verbal trap. "I'd *love* to hear how you managed to create something like this *before* now. You're looking at roughly four hundred people per section. The main ritual requires its own conducting, a deft hand such as my own is required to empower the enchanted ritual circles, yet another Master is needed for the operation of the forged equipment... and so on. Five distinct sections working in conjunction means you need at least two thousand people-"

"It seems I misspoke." Joe broke in as she dragged out her words, returning her grin until her smile slowly faded. "What's the matter?"

"You... as I said, the skill levels and experience are sure to be fantastic." The Enchanter turned Master of Enchanted Ritual Circles bit her lip and turned away slightly, "Yet, this process has a high chance of failure, even with so many people putting in their best efforts. Something like this has never been done before, hasn't even been *attempted* before. If you weren't simply repairing and augmenting what had been there at one point, this method would be guaranteed to permanently destroy someone's Akashic Record."

"Don't try to take someone off the street and fill them with Artifact-rank materials; they'll pop. Got it." His attempt at levity went over like a lead balloon, and so he allowed himself to show a bit of his true feelings. "Master Darling-"

"Just... Hilda, please."

"Hilda, then." He tried again, far more serious this time. "As far as I'm aware, I'm in a situation *no one* has been in. My attempts to let it heal on its own aren't working. Everything else I've done has reached the point of such immense diminishing returns that I may as well be sitting there and hoping it fixes itself. This world rewards effort above all else, and I love that about it. So, this is my effort."

"I'll make sure nothing goes wrong..." Hilda swallowed her concerns as she turned to face him. "...with the portion I'm controlling."

"I made sure to choose only the very best to work with." Joe stood and offered a hand, pulling her to her feet. "Now, if you don't mind, I'd like to get this started before someone talks me out of it."

Together, they walked out of her office, then down the winding set of stairs toward the enormous coven gathered on the ground floor. He could feel the excitement in the air, a tangible presence that ratcheted up ever higher as people looked at him and recognized the subject of the enormous undertaking they were about to perform.

Reaching the main level, Joe realized that the room wasn't just packed... it was *overflowing* with people.

A glance up showed that the second-level balconies were also standing room only. Pushing his way through toward the center of the room, Joe felt his stomach clench in nervousness as the enormous pod slid open like the mechanical lotus it was designed to resemble, petals of silver, brass, and argent alloys folding outward to expose the chaise lounge design waiting specifically for *him* to settle into.

There was a new addition as well, an enormous glass cylinder standing next to the pod, filled with a huge amount of swirling, neon-orange Ichor.

"Abyss, where'd that all come from? No, worse, where do

they think all of that is going to *go*? That tank is bigger than I am!" Joe grumbled as he was guided forward by Hilda's hand on the small of his back, though he was slightly resisting now that he was actually about to be put inside an enclosed chamber.

"We had to dilute it!" came a cheery response as the chosen Alchemist fiddled with hoses and injector pumps. "It was too potent to use in its original state, but don't worry-"

Joe waited a long moment, but the Alchemist turned away and went silent. "Kind of was hoping there was more to that statement, like... a reason *why* I shouldn't worry? No? Maybe?"

The air began swirling, pulling Joe's attention to the cavernous space above the enormous forged pod. His eyes alighted on the ritual he had designed and created, awestruck to see that it was already fully empowered and ready to be activated at a moment's notice.

Grandmaster Pete stepped forward, reaching out and shaking Joe's hand enthusiastically. "On behalf of the Tower of Ritualists, I can only thank you for this opportunity. For so many of us to work together on a never-before-seen ritual, it's a historical first. Literally! Never in the history of the tower. This is a true first, for *all* of us."

The murmuring crowd went silent as he started to speak, then began wildly cheering and enthusiastically clapping as he finished. Joe's assistant, Jenny, stepped forward with an encouraging thumbs up, alongside another man approximately her own age. Together, they gripped the edge of his robes and gently pulled as he slipped out, then removed his shoes one after another, until Joe was standing in the room wearing only a pair of shorts and the belled collar around his throat.

"In you go." Grandmaster Pete—having decided to put off his advancement until this ritual was complete—quietly spoke into Joe's ear so he could be heard over the ecstatic crowd.

He helped the bald Ritualist into place, waiting patiently as Joe reached up and activated his Karmic Shroud to keep 'fate' from interfering, then gently patted the younger man's hand as he noticed how it was trembling. The Grandmaster stepped back as the lotus began closing around him. "Don't worry, my boy. By the end of this there won't be one nook, one cranny, not one single cell in your body that remains…"

"…*Unmapped*."

EPILOGUE

The gravel road into the land worked by the Golden Greens Guild was fairly minimal, yet even that was quite the upgrade from marching through untamed wilderness—at least for the small group of people appearing on the edge of Joe's duchy.

"Goodness *me*, what a scorcher today, am I right?" A lady coated in a thin sheen of sweat pulled off her oversized farmer's defense sun hat—the floppy, wide-brimmed hat's back having a long stretch of fabric to protect her neck—and waved it at herself to try and cool down just a bit. "Sure hope this is the right place, eh?"

"Ooh, yah. Looks just like what we were told to expect," one of her traveling companions answered without taking his eyes off the view. "Look at that, what a bea-oo-ty."

Patches of emerald barley, golden-flecked wheat, and open pastures were surrounded by casual fencing which contained all sorts of domesticated animals. There were cows, a few horses, and even at this distance, they were able to catch the sound of chickens *bawking* at each other. But the vast majority of the cattle meandering about were goats.

So many goats.

Unlike the rest of the creatures, the goats seemed to be left to wander free wherever they wanted to go, creating a pleasant clunking with their large cowbells as they moved along. The small group of proudly Wisconsinites picked up speed now that they didn't have to cut their way through underbrush. Soon they were walking alongside the worked fields, pausing to let clouds of honey bees pass by three times before they finally made it over to the farm houses.

It was clear these structures had been mainly tossed together, reaching Common rank at best. Yet the stubbornly existing domiciles, whitewashed and creaking in the wind, were clearly designed only to be a place for someone to rest their head at night. They shouldered up to the enormous red barns, which had obviously been the focal point of the efforts for whoever had helped build this area up. Enormous doors hung on the walls, large enough to let a row of cows ten wide enter the cathedral-sized barn at the same time.

"Ope, *sore-ry* there, buddy!" The group had been staring up at the rooster wind vane swinging atop the building, each of them marveling at the sheer scale of this farmstead, and the short, straw-haired lady in the lead had stumbled directly into one of the locals. The farmer had stumbled back after bouncing off the surprisingly solid woman, and she lunged forward with the reflexes of a woman who'd spent her life around critters with hooves, cleanly snagging the pail of milk he was fumbling. "I gotcha. Here ya go."

"'Preciate it. Can I help you find something? I don't think you're part of the Golden Greens, so you're not really supposed to be wandering around on your own." The farmer relaxed slightly at their casual attitude and easy smiles, and the woman brightened up immediately. "I'm Ed. Pretty new around here myself."

"Oh, fer *su-ure*. Nice ta meetcha, Ed. Call me Becky; I'm looking fer whoever's in charge of gathering up all the cheese in the kingdom. Hey, just to be doubly sure, this is the duchy owned by the Dread Ritualist Joe, yah?" After a short detour for the farmer to drop off his pail, Ed led the chatty group across the enormous Guild campus, pointing out various attractions as they went along the main road, now hard-packed dirt instead of gravel.

"Absolutely! Also, don't believe the rumors too much, he's a great guy. Saved me from a terrible fate that I'd... rather not get into right now. Anyway, see that building?" Ed pointed at a warehouse-style structure sitting next to a slaughterhouse, and even now, people were bringing in large slabs of meat. Surprisingly, there was also a stream of folk hauling in baskets filled with vegetables, and even some early season apples. "He set up something in there that allows us to turn all of our fresh foods into preserved meats, herbs, fruits, and the like. Ritual of Benign Desiccation, I think it's called."

"Meats? Sounds kinda dangerous. Any issues with people popping in and getting all mummified?" Becky smirked at the man as she pushed for some juicy tidbits, but to her quasi-disappointment, he pursed his lips and shook his head, surprised she'd even asked.

"Definitely not! He's a real master of his craft, put in all sorts of safety features. Even if someone tried to put another person in there intentionally, it actually backlashes against *that* guy. Luckily we haven't had any problems with that. We're here to farm and turn seeds into products, not sneak around and stuff people into magic rings." The newly minted farmer waved at a few people walking the other way, and then they were past the barns and walking toward a large cattle house in the distance.

"Mind if I take a picture of this?" Becky lifted her crystal, an expensive design generally used by people with the Influencer profession. "We've been going around documenting the best farms in the kingdom and putting together an app people can use to find the best restaurants, creameries, and the like."

"Don't forget to tell him the requirement!" one of the others piped up. "They've got to have some proper food there. We're talking cheese curds, poutine, fried mozzarella sticks... ya know,

Ed. Anything to warm the heart as they wait for their main meal."

"If the curds don't *squeak*, I don't think it should count," another spoke out in a low rumble, shaking his head at his friend's antics. "How else are you supposed to know it's actually fresh?"

"That's why it's important to fry them after that! Get another week of use out of them." Becky joined in on what was apparently a familiar argument, seeing as they both had their points memorized and responded to the other nigh-instantaneously as a counterpoint was introduced.

Finally, the farmer stopped and pointed up the hill, where a man was sitting in a rocking chair and observing them. "That's Kenny. He's our main cheese producer and figures out the best place to store it all. If you need someone else, I'm sure he can direct you. Hope you have a lovely day; I've got to get back to work."

"Oh, thank ya *so* much, Ed!" Becky wrapped the man in a quick tight hug, then let go and started moving along the road in the next moment, leaving the flustered farmer behind. "Well, hey there, Kenny! I like your goats!"

Kenny McGruff didn't move from his rocking chair, simply watching them come closer, one boot pushing on the ground as he chewed on a long piece of alfalfa clamped between his teeth. "Yawp. Goo' goats. Choo' want?"

"I'm Becky, and we're walking around the kingdom finding the best place to—'scuse me, hiya kid." A goat lumbered right up to her, gently head-butting the woman before pushing off the ground and putting its hooves on her leg.

She gently put a hand on its shoulder and redirected it to the ground. "Yer a *climber*, aren't cha? Anywhoo, Kenny, like I said, we've been doing a loop around, and we've been hearing tell that this place is buying up all the cheese being produced. We made our way out here because we just don't know why that would be. Far as I can tell, you've got a pretty good production going on, so why are you needing to buy it all up?"

"Not so much a problem as it is a concern," a friendly companion of hers chimed in. "The price of a good grilled cheese *alone* has doubled in the last couple months."

"We thought we could help out!" Becky offered, lifting an arm and slapping a surprisingly well-defined bicep. "We've got our own dairy going, but it's pretty far to the south there. Got our hands on some Holsteins mostly, couple of Brown Swiss, and were chatting with some Guild trying to get our hands on some Jerseys-"

"Yawp. We'll buy't." Kenny slowly bobbed his head in time with the rocking chair. "Duke wan' cheese. S'all I know."

Becky beamed at the man. "Thanks so much! Who do we talk to so we can formalize all that?"

"He momma." Kenny gestured with extreme reluctance at a squat building in the distance that had smoke lazily lifting out of its chimney. "She be back 'roun dinner. Ya ca' hang at te' feed hou'."

"Ooh! A restaurant? The Feed House, you say?"

"Yawp." Kenny replied, voice going rough, as though he'd used up all his words for the day. "Good 'un, too."

"Becky! You know what this means, right?"

"I sure do!" She turned her crystal toward the small building and pressed it a few times, images of the feed house swirling into the crystal and staying there. "How'd we miss that one? We'll take a little peaky-peek."

She sent a wink at Kenny, who merely observed her with a tired stare. "I'm telling ya, sweetheart, if it's any good, I *promise* it's gonna go right 'un ma' app, eh?"

ABOUT DAKOTA KROUT

Good. Clean. Fun.

Dakota Krout is a celebrated author known for infusing fantasy novels with fun, punny, and clean humor. With multiple best-selling series—including "Divine Dungeon", "Completionist Chronicles", "Cooking With Disaster", and "Full Murderhobo"—he brings joy and laughter to readers. Dakota's work, renowned for its wit and creativity, earned a place as one of Audible's top 5 fantasy picks in 2017, a top 5 bestseller rank featured on the New York Times, and was chosen by Audible as among "the top 100 fantasy books of all time" in 2024.

Dakota's journey in publishing has been filled with gratefulness, and a deep desire to continue bringing smiles and laughter to the readers. "*I hope you Read Every Book With A Smile!*"

Connect with Dakota:
MountaindalePress.com
Patreon.com/DakotaKrout
Facebook.com/DakotaKrout
Instagram.com/DakotaKrout
Twitter.com/DakotaKrout
discord.gg/MountaindalePress

ABOUT MOUNTAINDALE PRESS

Dakota and Danielle Krout, a husband and wife team, strive to create as well as publish excellent fantasy and science fiction novels. Self-publishing *The Divine Dungeon: Dungeon Born* in 2016 transformed their careers from Dakota's military and programming background and Danielle's Ph.D. in pharmacology to President and CEO, respectively, of a small press. Their goal is to share their success with other authors and provide captivating fiction to readers with the purpose of solidifying Mountaindale Press as the place 'Where Fantasy Transforms Reality.'

Connect with Mountaindale Press:
MountaindalePress.com
Facebook.com/MountaindalePress
Twitter.com/_Mountaindale
Instagram.com/MountaindalePress

MOUNTAINDALE PRESS TITLES
GameLit and LitRPG

The Completionist Chronicles,
Cooking with Disaster,
Damsels of Distress,
The Divine Dungeon, and
Full Murderhobo by Dakota Krout

Metier Apocalypse by Frank G. Albelo

Ether Collapse and
Ether Flows by Ryan DeBruyn

The Lone Wanderer by K. Georgiades

Unbound by Nicoli Gonnella

Lion's Lineage by Rohan Hublikar and Dakota Krout

Wolfman Warlock by James Hunter and Dakota Krout

Axe Druid,
Mephisto's Magic Online, and
High Table Hijinks by Christopher Johns

Tower of Jack by Sean Loomer

Dragon Core Chronicles by Lars Machmüller

Pixel Dust and
Necrotic Apocalypse by D. Petrie

Viceroy's Pride and
Tower of Somnus by Cale Plamann

Henchman by Carl Stubblefield

Incursion by Dennis Vanderkerken

Artorian's Archives by Dennis Vanderkerken and Dakota Krout

The Undying Immortal System by Greg Tolley